To Sara
I hop[...] !

CW01429100

Secrets *at* Sunset

Vanessa Woolley

VANESSA WOOLLEY

KINGSLEY
PUBLISHERS

First published in South Africa
by Kingsley Publishers, 2025
Copyright © Vanessa Woolley, 2025

The right of Vanessa Woolley to be identified as author of this work has been asserted.

Kingsley Publishers
Pretoria,
South Africa

www.kingsleypublishers.com

A catalogue copy of this book will be available from the National Library of South Africa

Paperback ISBN: 978-0-6398420-5-9
eBook ISBN: 978-0-6398420-4-2

To all the people who risk their lives to protect
the amazing wildlife of Africa.
You are true heroes.

Chapter One

Elephant Sands Concession,
Southern Kruger National Park

The thin pink line of dawn appeared on the horizon and there was an eerie silence, that still window of time before the sun comes up and the world comes to life. Ryan stared out into the shadows of the bush as he and Rio drove along the rutted track, the two-way radio popping and fizzing.

They had been searching for over two hours, ever since they'd received the news that poachers had triggered a camera near the eastern border of the game reserve. When Ryan saw the infrared images coming through to the computer in the ops room, of three men walking on the track, one a rifle in his hand, and the others with machetes and sacks, he knew they were on borrowed time.

And he was right. At the top of a small hill, the jeep's headlights bounced off the macabre outline of a dead rhino. His heart plummeted and he jumped from the jeep, squatting down beside the rhino, flinching at the devastating facial disfigurement where the horn had been brutally cut out, dried blood congealing on its head.

He pulled off his night-vision goggles and rubbed his

brow, anger bubbling up to the surface. He'd been working at Elephant Sands for over four years now and this was the first poaching incident on his watch.

"I don't understand how quickly they got to the rhino," he said, his eyes scanning the scrub. "Either they work really fast or they got in somewhere else undetected and were on their way out of the reserve when the camera picked them up." He let out a frustrated puff. "We should have taken that left fork a few clicks back. It's obvious now that they were heading in the opposite direction, having already killed the rhino."

The anger on Rio's face matched Ryan's own. "Yeah, you're right." Rio threw his hands up in the air. "What I don't understand is how they got in. Their tracks are all over the place."

Ever since their call-out earlier, they'd followed the poachers' tracks, the full moon lighting their way, a spotlight in the sky. After a kilometre or so, the road had split in two directions and the tracks had done the same. A clever guise by the poachers to confuse their trackers.

Working on intel from another patrol team from the neighbouring reserve, they'd taken the right fork. This part of the road was less travelled, with shrubs growing close to the edge, and they'd had to yank their shoulders in to avoid the sharp ends of the mopane trees. Sadly, it had been a bad call. The tracks ended and the poachers were gone. All that was left was the poor dead rhino.

They checked over the animal, shining their strong flashlights over its body. The rhino's face now resembled an empty hole, dug crudely with an axe. Ryan winced at the angry slashes that pierced the animal's body. She'd died a horrible death. Udders protruded from her lower body.

"It's a nursing cow, which means…"

"There's a calf somewhere." Rio gestured towards some shrubs behind them. "Let me take a look around."

Ryan knelt down by the rhino and examined it more closely. "I think I know this rhino. She appeared the other day, quite near this part of the reserve. Zach was out on an early game drive with some guests and she trotted across the track in front of them with her calf. Zach reckons it was only a couple of months old."

He left the dead rhino to search the surrounding area, shining his torch beneath shrubs and behind boulders. A faint squeak emanated from behind a large anthill and he found the calf lying on its side, breathing but extremely weak.

He called out to Rio. "I've found it."

The calf tried to lift its head when he approached, its tiny body twitching in fear, blood oozing from its chest and head. Ryan squatted down beside it, running a hand over its shaking body. "Steady, little one. It's all right."

Rio grabbed some blankets from the jeep and Ryan placed one over the calf, all the while gently rubbing its head, trying to calm the fear that resonated through it.

"At least it's alive," Rio said.

"For now," Ryan muttered. "We need to get the vet team out here quickly."

Rio looked ill in the dim morning light. It was his first experience with poaching and Ryan felt for him. "You okay?"

Rio's eyes flicked back to the calf. "Not really, but I'll be all right. I'll call the ops room now."

Ryan placed his hand gently on the calf's flanks, noting deep, penetrating gashes. The poachers must have attacked it too. A needless piece of cruelty. The calf was tiny, maybe only a month or two old with no visible horn.

Bile pushed its way into his throat. "I'm so sorry, little buddy."

As an ex British soldier who'd done two tours in Afghanistan, he'd seen dead bodies, soldiers and civilians blown to pieces by landmines and mortar bombs. A horrific and unforgettable sight. But the vision of a butchered rhino and her calf half alive in the early dawn was not one he'd be likely to forget either.

His cell phone sprang to life. It was Andy Carter, head of operations from Marula Heights, the neighbouring reserve Ryan had called out to help.

He answered after only one ring. "We've found a dead rhino cow. Her calf is still alive, but he's been attacked too. We lost the poachers' tracks somewhere up near Brewster's Ridge. They did a pretty good job of foiling us with their track directions. Have you spotted anything?"

"Yeah," Andy replied. "There's a bloody great hole in the fence near the waterhole on your western perimeter. That's where they must have come in."

Ryan cursed, anger filling him. The western edge of their concession bordered the main part of the Kruger and the fence was under their protection. The sensors had broken on part of the fence a week ago and were on order.

"The sensors were down in a small section," he informed Andy. "But how the hell did the poachers know about it?"

Andy's voice was grim. "I think I can answer that too, I'm afraid."

Ryan closed his eyes to calm his anxiety. "What is it?"

"We found an Elephant Sands employee cap hanging off a bush close to where our western track meets your gate." His voice softened. "I'm sorry, mate, I know you don't want to hear this, but with the fact the poachers knew about the broken sensors and this cap hanging by the gate, it's all pointing to an informer. Someone in your team is giving out information to poachers. Odds on, whoever it is has managed to lose their cap in the midst of it all."

Chapter Two

Kate stared out of the window of the Cessna Caravan, its shadow a large shape on the dry riverbed below. Spread out before her was a vast expanse of bush criss-crossed with tracks like a giant spider's web.

The noise of the engine changed as the plane descended. Through the window on Kate's side, the ground came closer, a line of trees flanking a river and the thatched buildings of a lodge. Her stomach rolled. She was not fond of small planes, and when Sara had messaged her to say she couldn't meet her at the main Kruger airport because of an emergency at the lodge, Kate had been forced to go on one of the small private charter flights that landed nearer to the lodge instead.

For some this would be exciting. A great way to see the African bush from above. But for Kate it was her idea of hell. Claustrophobic at the best of times, she'd clung to the arm rests at takeoff, closing her eyes until the plane reached altitude and levelled out. When she opened her eyes, a cloudless cerulean sky greeted her, with fat rays of sunshine spearing the small windows.

The plane cleared a cluster of thorn trees and landed swiftly on the sandy airstrip. It juddered slowly to the end of the runway and turned towards a low shack. On the side, baboons raced off, their tails bouncing along behind them. Kate grabbed her bag and headed for the small door at the back of the plane, desperate to be out of the stifling space, but the air that greeted her outside was like stepping into a burning furnace. A far cry from the dank autumn evening she'd left behind in London.

She placed a hand over her brow, blotting out the bright sun, and searched for Sara, excited to see her old school friend again. She'd last seen her five years before at a farewell party in London. Sara had married Gavin, her South African boyfriend, and they'd moved to live in South Africa to work at Elephant Sands, a private reserve in the Kruger National Park. Kate missed her terribly, and when, in the weekly editorial meeting, a last-minute writing assignment about poaching aroused her interest, Kate thought of Sara immediately. She was quite literally in the thick of it.

A couple of porters greeted the passengers, their faces beaming in welcome as they helped the guests into the waiting jeeps gathered by the runway. Kate couldn't see Sara or anyone from Elephant Sands and moved under a solitary tree, the canopy of its branches providing the bare minimum of shade. When everyone had been loaded into jeeps, their cameras already out as they tasted their first moment of the African bush, the pilot gave Kate a rueful grin.

"Have you been forgotten?"

Kate frowned, fishing out her cell phone. Sara's last message before Kate's plane left Johannesburg clearly said she would be there to greet her.

Her shoulders sagged. "I hope not. I don't have much of

a cell-phone signal either." She waved her phone at him. "Do you think you might…?"

But before she could finish, a rumble erupted in the sky as a blue and silver helicopter appeared over a large hill, rocking back and forth as it slowed down to land on a flat area of grass.

"It's a rescue helicopter," the pilot shouted over the noise. "I wonder what's up."

As the helicopter landed, a flat-bed truck with Elephant Sands Concession emblazoned on the side headed towards the runway, dust flying out behind it.

"My friend who was meant to be meeting me did say they'd had an emergency overnight," Kate offered. "Perhaps this is what she meant."

"Possibly," the pilot said. "It's an injured animal, so it must be pretty bad if they're evacuating it."

She caught a glimpse of a small mound on the back of the truck, a blue blanket draped over it. Three people sat on the back of the truck, one of them holding a long, thin plastic tube, like an IV-line. A sliver of a memory hit her – of her father's face snowy white against the hospital pillows, the veins in his arms bulging under the strain of the cannulas, machines beeping in the background as the medical staff tried to keep him alive.

"It's a rhino calf," the pilot said. "Its mother has probably been killed by poachers."

Kate gasped. "I'm here to write about poaching, for an article in the *Daily Tribune* in the UK. I'm staying at Elephant Sands. They're going to hook me up with their anti-poaching unit."

"I think you've found them," the pilot said dryly.

Kate held her breath as the team lifted the calf in a

stretcher, moving in a coordinated shuffle towards the helicopter. She wanted to get nearer to the action. This was the front line of protecting wildlife. It was what some reporters would call a scoop. She'd had a few in her career as an investigative journalist, but nothing quite as dramatic as this.

She edged closer to the truck, standing back so as not to get in the way, and was about to take some photos when the roar of an engine signalled the arrival of Sara and Gavin. They pulled their jeep up behind the truck. Relief flooded through her as she made her way towards them.

Gavin jumped out of the truck and ran towards the helicopter, giving Kate a wave as he went. Sara stepped forward, neat as a pin in her Elephant Sands shirt and shorts, her pretty freckled face a mixture of joy and sadness as she embraced Kate. "Fancy meeting you here, Katie Harper."

Tears filled Kate's eyes and she leant against her oldest and dearest friend, feeling the comfort she'd so longed for after the death of her parents in a car accident six months earlier. It was like a dose of medicine, soothing some of the pain.

They'd met aged eleven in the stuffy dorm room of their boarding school on the first day and an instant bond was formed. Over twenty-five years later it was still there. They scanned each other, taking in the changes.

Sara broke the silence. "How was your flight?"

"It was okay. Long and boring," She squeezed Sara's shoulder. "I'm so glad to be here, although…" she jerked her head towards the helicopter "…not such a good start to the visit."

Sara shook her head. "Everyone is in shock. We haven't

had a poaching incident here for a long time."

Kate stared back at the buzz of activity around the rhino calf. "You hear about orphaned rhino calves all the time, but to actually see one…"

Sara's soft brown eyes filled with tears. "I am so sorry about your mum and dad, Kate. I couldn't bear it when I heard. I loved your parents so much. I wanted to come back and be with you but…" she swallowed thickly "…I'd lost the baby and I didn't know if I was coming or going."

Kate glanced at Sara's anxious face, desperate to soothe her. The same week Kate's parents had been killed, Sara suffered a second miscarriage at five months pregnant. Kate couldn't even begin to imagine how traumatic that must have been for her.

She gently touched Sara's shoulder. "Don't worry, Sara. I completely understand. Your health had to come first. The main thing is you are okay now."

Sara pulled a face. "I'm better, and Gav and I are not going to try again for a while. It's all too stressful. Anyway, more importantly, how are you holding up?"

Kate's throat caught and she watched a colourful bird flit across a nearby thorny bush. Was she ever going to get used to this? To the endless sympathy and compassion in people's faces? "It's been tough…"

Sara nudged her shoulder. "I'm glad you finally made it out here. We did wonder if you were ever going to come."

Kate laughed, grateful for the change of subject. "I know. I've been caught up with work." She observed the team who were securing the rhino in a safety harness. "Talking of which, I know time is of the essence, but any chance I can get a quick photo or two? A picture tells a thousand stories."

"Let me find out," Sara said, hurrying over to confer with the vet.

Kate trailed behind her. Standing by the vet was a tall man in army fatigues and a grey T-shirt, his hand placed on the rhino's flank. He looked up at her approach, watching her through dark wraparound sunglasses. Like a bodyguard with his charge.

Sara waved Kate over and in three long strides she was face to face with the calf, so fragile under the blanket and tubes. His eyes were covered in a blindfold and he was motionless, presumably sedated for the journey.

Sara introduced them. "This is Phil Smits. He's a wildlife vet working with the South African National Parks."

Kate forced down the lump that was lodged in her throat. "Is he going to be all right?"

The vet rubbed his hand between the calf's ears, which were both plugged with cloth. "Let's hope so. He's got some nasty wounds on his back and is extremely traumatised, but luckily Ryan—" he gestured to the man in the army fatigues "—found him quickly before anything further happened to him."

Kate studied the man standing next to them. There was something about the way he was connected to the calf that raised her journalist's antenna. His hand was still tenderly placed on the calf as if he couldn't let go.

Her words caught in her throat. "It must have been horrible, finding him like this."

Ryan nodded but didn't speak, his eyes unreadable behind the sunglasses. When Phil reached over to tweak a cannula, Ryan finally removed his hand. Kate sensed his reluctance to let go, like a parent not wanting to hand their

15

child over to a doctor in the emergency room.

"Can I take some photos now?" Kate asked the vet. "I won't publish anything without asking permission first, but we need to show the world exactly what happens when a rhino is poached, and about what's left behind."

"It's okay with me," Phil responded. "What about you, Ryan?"

Ryan shrugged. "I guess so, but we have to careful what we reveal, especially as it is a criminal investigation."

"Of course," Kate agreed, pulling out her phone, taking a few photos from different angles, her hands shaking at the bright red blood staining the crepe bandages on the calf's flank. Only yesterday this little animal was getting on with his life, happily playing beside his mother. And now he was orphaned, left to grieve by his dead mother's body.

Ever since she was little she'd felt a strange pull to rhinos. There was something about the way they lumbered around in their armour-like skin, their huge horns proudly displayed in front of them. A modern-day unicorn. She'd only ever seen a rhino in a zoo and had always wanted to see one in the wild, but this was not how she imagined it to be.

She put her phone back into her bag. "Where is the calf being taken to?"

"To a nearby rhino orphanage," Sara replied. "It's sad these places exist, but we need them."

Kate watched the helicopter as it lifted off, clouds of dust swirling in its wake. Within seconds it was up in the sky, a silver whirl of blades as it gained speed and headed away, taking the calf to safety. She willed the calf to survive, to live.

Noticing Ryan watching the helicopter, his hands clenched either side of him, his shoulders shaking, she took a step towards him. "Are you okay?"

He lifted his sunglasses, revealing brown eyes so molten they were almost black. There was a flicker of sorrow in his eyes that drew her in, and for a moment they stared at each other, the noise and light from all around them disappearing. Then he blinked, and the moment was gone. He walked off without replying.

Kate grabbed Sara's arm and pointed at Ryan. "Who's that?"

"That's Ryan Brown. He's the head of our anti-poaching unit and he's going to be your guide whilst you're here, to help with the article. Of course, we hadn't planned on this poaching happening. It certainly throws the plans off course."

"Not really," Kate said. "It makes them all the more relevant."

"True," Sara agreed. "Sorry he was a bit abrupt; he's under a lot of pressure."

"That's okay. He's got a lot on his plate."

Sara grimaced. "You're not wrong. And now it appears we've got an informer in the team, he's not going to rest until he finds out who it is."

Kate's eyes widened. "Are informers common?"

"Sometimes, but less so in a small, private reserve. We're like one big family. Ryan's pretty cut up about it. He's taking it personally."

Kate glanced over at Ryan, imagining what it must be like to find a dead animal, butchered in your own backyard. She shuddered at the memory of her mother's body lying on the slab in the mortuary, her body twisted and bloody from the impact of the crash. The vision of the calf, with the slashes on its little body and the bloodstained bandages, brought it all back to her. The trauma of death.

A tap on her shoulder returned her to the present as Sara's husband Gavin engulfed her in a big bear hug. "Welcome, Red."

She swatted his arm at the use of the nickname he'd given her when they'd first met. Like the character in her favourite childhood book, *Anne of Green Gables*, Kate had detested her red hair as a child, but over the years she'd come to accept the untamed red curls she'd been born with.

He pointed towards Ryan, who was throwing things around in the back of his truck. "I see you've met Sara's secret crush."

Sara rolled her eyes at his comment. "Ignore him." She tilted her head towards Ryan. "Come over and meet him properly now and then I'll take you back to the lodge."

"Ryan," Sara called out, "this is my friend, Kate Harper, the one I mentioned to you last week who's here to write an article about poaching and you kindly agreed to be her guide."

Ryan's face was red, sweat staining his T-shirt, his close-cropped hair plastered to his head. He gave Kate the ghost of a smile and stretched his hand out towards her. "Welcome to Elephant Sands. You've had a baptism of fire."

"That's for sure," she agreed, taking his hand, an unexpected tingle making its way up her arm. "I really appreciate any help you can give me for the article. I know you've got a lot to contend with now, but I'll try not to get in your way."

His eyes met hers directly. "Fair enough."

He was tall but didn't tower over her, stocky with wide shoulders and chest. His face was rugged with dark stubble and a square jaw. There was an edge to him that made him not quite handsome but attractive nonetheless.

Kate gestured towards the empty space where the helicopter had been. "I hope the calf survives."

Ryan shuddered as if imagining the scene all over again. "Me too. We found him quickly, which means he wasn't necessarily on his own for too long, but he's extremely traumatised."

A lump rose in Kate's throat as she thought of the calf fighting for its life. "Thank you for agreeing to speak to me. There's so much to tell—" she waved towards the surrounding bush "—and we clearly need to get the message out."

Ryan kicked the dusty ground with his boot. "You're not wrong there." He jerked his head back to his jeep. "If you will excuse me, I need to head back to the poaching site."

He made to leave when Kate had an idea. "Can I come with you to the poaching site? I am here to write about poaching and you've got an actual crime scene going on. It would be good to see the forensics team do their stuff and I can learn first-hand what's involved in a poaching investigation."

Ryan frowned. "I don't know. We could be out there for ages."

"I'll take her back to the lodge later if you're not finished at the site," Gavin said. "I think it's a good idea, Ryan. After all, how often do we get a chance to show journos what really happens on the ground?"

"I suppose so," Ryan conceded, "but I am giving you fair warning, it's pretty gruesome. The dead rhino is still at the scene. Are you really sure you are up to it?"

Kate tried not to think of her parents lying in the mortuary, their faces almost beyond recognition. "Of course. As Gavin said, how often do people outside conservation see what goes on in the field? Or as you might call it, on the battlefront."

Ryan's eyes were wary. "Okay, then let's get going. It's nearly midday and we've only got about six hours of daylight left."

"That's settled then," Sara said. "You go with Ryan, Kate, and I'll take your bags back to the lodge and get some food prepared for the people at the site. Gavin can bring you over later." She threw her baseball cap across to Kate. "Take this. It's pretty hot out there and I'll find you some water to keep you going."

Kate pushed away travel fatigue and smiled at her ever-practical friend. "Thanks, Sara. I'm sure I'll be fine."

Sara handed her a bottle of water and a tube of sun cream. "Are you sure you'll be okay?"

If Kate was honest, she was exhausted and hot, and the cropped cargo pants and T-shirt she'd changed into at the airport in Johannesburg were sticking to her body, but when there was a story to chase she certainly wasn't going to miss out.

She climbed into the passenger seat of the jeep. "I'll be fine, Sara. I am more robust than you think, and this is what I do. I investigate and research and write the stories that need to be told, no matter how uncomfortable the surroundings may be."

Sara placed a gentle hand on Kate's shoulder. "I know

that, but I also know what you've been through over the last few months—" she hesitated "—what you've had to deal with."

Kate's heart squeezed at Sara's words but she flicked the emotion away. The chance to be immersed in work was just the distraction she needed. Especially after her world had been turned on its axis. It was fate really, giving her an excuse to go to South Africa. Some would call it serendipity.

Chapter Three

The sun was ferocious, the heat oppressive as Kate watched Ryan's hands skilfully steer the jeep up a steep slope. The track seemed impossible to drive on and she gripped the handles by the door as the vehicle rocked back and forth up the ramp. Ryan pulled and twisted the many gears that sat in between the front seats, his face set in concentration. Neither of them had spoken since she'd climbed up onto the old leather passenger seat, the sharp end of a spring pushing up through its cracked surface.

Silence sat like a vast awkward chasm between them and she let him concentrate for a bit, trying to control the queasiness in her stomach, suddenly tongue-tied. There were so many questions floating around her head, some she'd prepared in advance on the long flight from London and some that came to her now as she boiled under the hot African sun.

Questions about the orphaned calf, about its odds of survival, about why people would kill an animal for its horn, which was made of keratin and had no medicinal benefit whatsoever. The brutality of the attack on the calf brought back the horror of her parents' death. Once again she failed to understand how someone could drink the best part of a bottle of vodka in the middle of the day and get in a car and kill two innocent pensioners as they drove home from the supermarket. She closed her eyes and composed herself. She was still raw; she knew that. It had only been six months after all. A tremor ran through her. What would this trip bring her? Would she find what she was searching for?

They reached the brow of the hill and Ryan's cell phone buzzed. He pulled the jeep over, parking on the side of the track, and checked the screen.

"It's the vet," he informed her as he pressed the answer button. "Hi, Phil. How is he?"

The vet's voice was deep and loud as he updated them. "We've got him into the intensive care container and the carers are settling him in. I've taken off his ear defenders and eye coverings and we're getting some fluids into him now. When he's calmer, we'll take some bloods and give him a thorough check-up, but for now he's doing all right. I'll keep you posted."

Ryan ended the call and stared out over the valley in front of them, his shoulders sloped, jaw tense.

"I'm glad he's doing well," Kate said. "It was lucky you found him so quickly." She shuddered. "I'd hate to think what would have happened to him if you hadn't."

Ryan's lips flattened as he started the engine again and they rolled down the hill towards the open plains.

"It's the first time I've encountered a poaching incident under my watch," he said. "It was every bit as grotesque as you'd expect. I know it happens all the time across this country, the neighbouring concession, Marula Heights, had two rhinos poached recently, but..." he shook his head "...until you experience it up close nothing can prepare you for it."

"I'd really like to visit the calf at the orphanage, if that's possible?" Kate said. "It would be good to see how they rehabilitate rhino orphans, the survivors, so to speak."

A ghost of a smile flitted across Ryan's face. "I'm sure Sara can organise that for you. I wouldn't mind going myself. The last time I was there was when I was doing my training. I spent a couple of days with the orphanage's patrol team and also helped out with the orphans on night milk feeds."

The jeep joined the main track at the bottom of the hill. Up ahead, several vehicles were clustered together, a hub of activity as people scoured the ground, busy with forensic equipment and cameras.

Ryan pulled in behind a truck and they both climbed out. He grabbed a kit bag and eyed her soberly. "The rhino's face has been hacked to pieces. I hope you're not squeamish."

The tension emanating from him was palpable. When she'd been reading up about wildlife poaching and protection, she'd watched a lot of YouTube videos and it had been obvious how dedicated the rangers were. It was not a nine-to-five job. It was a calling, like being a doctor or a nurse or even a soldier.

Kate gave him a wry smile. "Thanks for the heads-up. I'll be okay."

Grabbing her notebook and camera, a trusty old digital her parents had bought her many years ago, she followed Ryan towards the tent, slipping quietly under the other side of the white plastic barrier and coming face to face with the dead rhino.

She gasped. Ryan was right. The image was unbelievably

grotesque; a huge gaping hole was all that remained of the rhino's face. Dark blood congealed around the nose and eyes. It was virtually unrecognisable as a rhino, the horn gone. Flies hovered over the flesh. Kate shivered despite the early afternoon heat.

"Would she have been alive when they hacked off the horn?"

Ryan's face was grim. "More than likely. She was shot first, probably with a hunting rifle. They would have then hacked her horn off with an axe or a machete, or pangas as they are known in Africa. The police have extracted quite a few bullets, so we will see what comes of that."

"And what about the calf? Was he shot too?"

"Luckily, no. He sustained quite a few blows from the machetes though, but preliminary examination shows the gashes aren't too deep. The biggest problem for the calf will be the trauma of what's happened to it. We think it's probably only a couple of months old at the most, so still heavily reliant on its mother. Far too young to be orphaned."

He touched her shoulder. "Are you okay? Once you've seen what poachers do to a rhino's face, it's hard to forget it."

Kate stared back down at the dead rhino, a mixture of sorrow and anger bubbling to the surface. "I can't bear to think about what she went through. The people who did this are evil."

She walked around the carcass, staring down at the waterhole and the fence beyond, trying to gain some sort of equilibrium. She pointed towards the fence. "The poachers came through over there?"

"Yep," Ryan confirmed. "The sensors were broken in

that section. We were waiting for parts to repair them and unfortunately the poachers took advantage of that. It meant they could cut a hole through and not trigger the infrared camera."

Kate's eyes widened. "Which is why you think someone tipped them off?"

Ryan kicked at the dusty ground. "It's one theory we are working on."

Kate stared back at the fence. "Is that Mozambique on the other side of the fence?"

"No, that's the border with another private game reserve. The actual border between the Kruger and Mozambique is about ten kilometres further east. They would have made their way on foot from there."

"They walked all that way in the dark?"

"Poachers will often travel for days searching for animals. They carry sleeping bags and are prepared to wait days for a good result."

She got out her notebook and squinted at the pages. "Can you tell me what you know about the poachers?"

"We found three sets of human tracks, although it is hard to tell; some of the tracks were contaminated by other markings. Poachers do that as a way of throwing us off their trail." He tipped his head towards the group of police officers. "I'm really sorry. I need to talk to the team from Hawks, get an update before they head off. Perhaps we can talk more later, back at the lodge."

"Of course," Kate said. "I'll have a look around and take some photos, if that's okay?"

Ryan frowned. "As long as you don't share them anywhere. Security is highly important."

Kate watched him stride off towards the police officers.

In her research for the trip, she'd read about Hawks, the illegal wildlife trade sector of South Africa's anti-organised crime unit. What she hadn't expected was to come across them on her first day in the country. It would be good to talk to them, but she figured now was not a good time to ask. Ryan needed to get on with the job.

Careful not to stand on any evidence, Kate circled the site, watching the activity on the outskirts. She switched on her camera, her hands shaking as she pressed the shutters, all the while thinking about the little calf that was now lying in intensive care in a rhino orphanage.

She wondered again at the wisdom of her decision to come here, to South Africa. Ostensibly, she had come to write an article for the paper she worked for. As one of their main feature writers, Kate often had her pick of the best stories, but the poaching crisis in South Africa was not her usual type of article. More recently she'd been writing about refugees in Syria and Europe. But when her editor, Greg, had asked if anyone wanted to take over from the Southern African correspondent, who'd been taken ill, Kate had jumped at the chance.

Greg had raised an eyebrow. "This isn't your usual type of gig, Kate."

He was right, of course, but something about the story had pulled her in. She'd paced Greg's office, wearing out the carpet trying to convince him she was the right one for the job.

"I already have a contact. My friend, Sara, is married to an ex South African soldier and they have their own anti-poaching unit on their reserve."

The whole time she'd waited for Greg to make his decision, she'd fingered the necklace around her neck. It was a silver Tiffany heart her parents had given her for her twenty-first. Next to it she had slotted a small rhino pendant she'd bought in a flea market in London. She had to take the job. She needed to go to South Africa.

He'd held up his hands in surrender and laughed. "Okay. You've got the story."

Kate had been heading for the door when Greg called her back, his voice softening.

"I am so sorry about your parents, Kate. I read their obituaries. They both had impressive careers. It must have been quite a shock."

Kate had blinked back tears. "It was."

"Didn't your father teach in Africa at some point? He was a specialist in African economics, wasn't he?"

"Yes. He taught at Cape Town University for a few years, but most of his career was at the LSE."

Greg's brow had furrowed. "Are you sure you're up to it?"

She'd waved his concerns away. "I'll be fine, Greg. I need something to take my mind off things."

"Fair enough," he'd replied. "Why don't you take some time after you've written the article? Stay out there and have a holiday. Spend time with your friend."

And now here she was, on South African soil, a major scoop landing right at her feet. But instead of the usual thrill of a good story, Kate felt only sorrow and fear. Not just because of the horrific slaughter of an innocent animal, but because of the unknown shadows of her past, which lingered somewhere in this hot and dry country.

Chapter Four

It was quiet as Ryan and Kate made their way back to the lodge; the sun dipped low in the sky, sending long shadows across the track. Under the golden haze of late afternoon there was so much to admire in the surroundings. To Kate, the natural world was a place of peace and beauty, but she now understood it was hard to keep the darkness of the outside world from breaching the fragile walls around it.

Seeing the dead rhino triggered a memory, of visiting the crash site where her parents were killed. At first, she hadn't wanted to go there, unable to face the flowers and notes from the kind-hearted people of the small Sussex town who had known Geoffrey and Ginny. It was only later when she'd accidentally taken the wrong way towards town that she realised where she was. The flowers in their cellophane bags were brown and rotten and the thoughtful words on the notes smudged from rain. Seeing it all had hit her like a sharp knife piercing her heart.

She inhaled deeply and let the air slowly trickle out, pushing the memory away. She was normally a rational person, able to separate her professional and private feelings. But ever since her parents' deaths, it was as if she'd been cast adrift. She had no compass any more.

Somehow this rhino cow that had fought so valiantly for its calf struck a chord with her – that a mother's love could be so fierce. But it was all in vain; the calf was orphaned anyway.

At the top of a rocky hill, Ryan pulled the jeep over under a thorn tree and switched it off. The engine ticked over in the stillness. Above, in the tree, two birds with large yellow beaks squawked and frolicked on the branches, before swooping down to the ground and inspecting them with beady eyes.

For the first time since they'd left the poaching site, Ryan looked in Kate's direction, his brown eyes a deep hickory.

"Come and look at the view," he told her as he climbed out. "It will give you an idea of the size and shape of the concession."

She jumped down from the jeep, her legs landing on soft sand, and followed Ryan to a promontory overlooking a vast basin area. The sun was visible to the west, its yellow ball slowly dropping to the horizon. Kate cupped her hand over her eyes and squinted towards the view.

"The border with Mozambique is that way," Ryan explained. "It's about seventy kilometres directly east from here." He then pointed across a wide plain. "That's south towards the N4 motorway and the Malelane Gate. Elephant Sands ends about ten kilometres from here and—" he swung around to the opposite direction "—this takes us north, going up towards the Paul Kruger Gate."

Kate took in the view, mentally trying to picture the map of the Kruger she'd studied before she came. "Elephant Sands is a concession within the Kruger National Park, isn't it?"

"Yes," Ryan replied, "it's about sixty square kilometres and Marula next door is about the same size."

Kate frowned. "What does that mean in terms of conservation and anti-poaching?"

"It means we are fully responsible for its upkeep and protection, but obviously we work closely with the Kruger rangers."

She pulled out her camera and took a few shots of the large sun-splashed granite boulders in the distance. "Those rocks are incredible."

Ryan's lips curved upwards and Kate's breath hitched. Despite the fatigue in his face, the smile illuminated a change in him, a dimple appearing in his left cheek, his brown eyes crinkling towards the sun.

"Those are kopjes, Afrikaans for small hill—" he indicated towards the jeep "—let's head back. I desperately need a beer."

They were soon bumping along on the track again, but this time the atmosphere between them was lighter. A soft breeze fluttered through her hair, pulling at the stray pieces curling around her face. She'd plaited it into a ponytail after her shower at Johannesburg airport, hoping to keep the frizz at bay, but with the heat that was an impossible task.

They headed across a wide, open plain of undulating grassland. Ryan was content to play tour guide, pointing out various animals to her. The area was teeming with grazing animals despite the shortness of the grass. It was nearing the end of the dry season, the South African winter, and the grass was sparse.

Ryan's radio receiver jolted into life and Kate jumped at the sudden voice that came through. She listened as the operator relayed back details of a sighting of a pride of lions. Ryan replaced the receiver. "Want to see some lions?"

Kate's eyes widened. "Yes, please."

He grinned. "Hold on tight. I'm going to have to put my foot down to get there before the lions leave."

He turned the jeep back up the track they'd just travelled down, bouncing and rocking over the ridged track, their arms occasionally being grabbed by low thorny branches, heading towards the area where the lions had been spotted. Kate's spine was groaning in protest when at last they arrived at a clearing and Ryan manoeuvred the jeep between two trucks.

The hairs on Kate's arms prickled with both fear and excitement. Ahead of her, lying in the shade of a small tree, was a huge lion, his golden mane flecked with brown, his tail flicking up occasionally to sweep away flies. Beside him lay the remnants of the kill, the bloodied corpse of a zebra, pieces of ragged striped hair still visible. Nearby, under another tree, were two lionesses and a younger male, his mane much less pronounced. Kate's breath hitched; she'd never been this close to a lion before. At least not without bars between them.

"They're resting after their kill," Ryan whispered. "They probably caught it this morning. There's not much of the carcass left." He handed her a set of binoculars. "Look behind the two females. There are cubs too."

Kate adjusted the lens and zoomed in. The little head of a cub popped up behind the young male followed by another furry ball of fluff.

Her heart burst with joy. "They're playing. They are jumping on the other lion."

"He's probably an older sibling from a previous litter, or from another lioness," Ryan explained. "Males usually leave the pride at around age three or four, so he'll be a bit younger than that."

Another female stalked across the track followed by two more cubs, and they joined the other females flopping down in the shade. They were not at all perturbed by the jeeps sitting nearby, the whirr and click of cameras ever present.

Ryan and Kate watched the pride a little longer, and a gentle breeze rustled through Kate's hair. She thought about her friends and colleagues back in London, the cold autumn air chilling their bones. It was surreal that this time last week she was squashed in between people on the Tube as she made her way home from work.

Ryan interrupted her daydream. "Ready to head off? It will be dark soon and I promised Sara I'd get you back for sunset."

Kate leant back in the seat as Ryan steered the vehicle back towards the lodge. She closed her eyes briefly, a sense of peace washing over her. After seeing the dead rhino and the trauma of watching the tiny calf on its way to the orphanage, coming across the lions had lifted her spirits a little.

The jeep clunked over a huge rocky track and the lodge came into view, backlit by the soft golden hues of late afternoon. She had to admit she was rather looking forward to a shower and some food and she was spurred on by the thrill of the story she was here to write. She peeked briefly at Ryan as he steered the jeep over the cattle grid towards a group of thatched buildings. He looked exhausted, his face drawn, his chin dark with stubble.

She'd only met him that morning and yet she was drawn to him. Perhaps it was because when she'd first met him, he was with the calf, his hand firmly placed on the animal's flank, protecting it right up until he handed it over. He was an ex-soldier and a protector and he intrigued her. The article might be about the poaching crisis in South Africa, but Kate wrote about people and Ryan was very much at the heart of the story.

Chapter Five

Ryan parked under the shade of a cluster of trees near the reception. Kate climbed out of the jeep and stretched her limbs, her T-shirt sticking to her back. Despite the late afternoon hour, it was still incredibly hot and she longed for a cool shower.

Ryan collected his walkie-talkie and handed her bag over from the back. "How are you feeling?"

She fanned her face with her cap. "I'm surviving! I can honestly say that when I got on the plane at Heathrow last night, I was not expecting to see an orphaned rhino rescue and a pride of lions all on the first day."

Ryan tapped the side of the jeep. "It's been a day of two halves, that's for sure." He gestured towards Sara, who was hovering by the reception. "I think someone's keen to see you."

Kate waved to Sara but stayed where she was, waiting patiently as Ryan retrieved the last bag from the jeep. She pointed to her notebook. "I have some more questions…"

He pulled off his cap and ran a hand through his hair. "There's not much more I can tell you about the poaching for now. We'll just have to wait for the forensic reports."

She bit her lip. "I know. I actually wanted to find out a bit more about you."

"Me? Why?"

"For background, really. I…"

Ryan's jaw clenched. "I don't think that will be necessary. Let's focus on your brief, which from what Sara told me is to write about poaching in the Kruger National Park."

Kate shoved her notebook into her handbag. "Sorry. Yes, of course. I'll see you in the bar later."

He shoved his cap back onto his head and strode off, dismissing her with barely a goodbye.

She watched him go and pushed away her irritation. The poor man was exhausted and she should be more empathetic, but she was caught up in the story and keen to learn more about how he went from being a soldier to a ranger, about what made him tick.

Sara bounded down the stone steps to greet her, followed by a smiling lady carrying scented flannel towels on a tray. Sara placed her arm around Kate's shoulders and grinned at the other lady.

"Constance, meet my best friend Kate. She's visiting from England."

Constance shyly handed Kate one of the cool, damp flannels to wipe away the sweat and dust. Kate placed the cold cloth across her face, inhaling the pleasant lemongrass scent.

"Thank you," she said gratefully.

The shady reception area was buzzing with colour, from the bright beaded lampshades to the vibrant cloths framed on the walls and the cushion covers sitting on a large leather sofa.

Sara spread her arms out wide. "Welcome to Elephant Sands!"

Kate contemplated the beautiful surroundings. "I can see why you never want to come back to England. It's stunning."

Sara gave her a wide grin. "It is, isn't it? Why would anyone want to live anywhere else?"

Constance appeared by Kate's side again, this time with a fruit drink balanced on a small tray. Kate drank it down in one gulp, placing it back on the tray. "That was so refreshing."

Once Kate had completed the guest booking form, they walked towards the main area of the lodge, their arms interlinked like they used to do when they were at school.

"How were things at the poaching site?" Sara asked.

Kate once again pictured the dead rhino's face. "Awful…grim…" She gulped. "I can't believe people can do that to an innocent animal. I really hope they catch the poachers."

Sara slowed her steps. "I hope so too. It's been a horrible twelve hours or so." She gave Kate a tight smile. "Come on, let me show you the restaurant and bar area. You are in one of the spare huts in the staff quarters. I would have put you in a guest room, but we're pretty much full for the coming days."

"Don't worry," Kate assured her. "As long as there is a decent bed and good Wi-Fi, I'm not fussy."

Sara laughed. "You are such a townie, Kate Harper. You do realise you are in the bush, don't you? It's not known for great internet or cell-phone access."

Kate's eyes widened in horror at Sara's words, but her friend slapped her on the back. "Don't worry, only joking.

I'll give you the staff access code, and in the main lodge, you can connect to the guest one."

They walked along a path made of wooden stumps dug into the ground. A small gecko scurried across in front of them, its little legs whirling madly. At the main building, which housed the bar and restaurant, there was a huge veranda leading down to a swimming pool and viewing point looking out on a waterhole, a dry riverbed and the scrub beyond. All that separated them from the wild was the river and the waterhole.

She'd heard so much about the reserve from Sara over the years and had drooled over her Instagram posts, but none of it had prepared her for how beautiful and peaceful the place really was. She nudged Sara. "I'm definitely not in London any more."

Sara laughed. "No, you most certainly are not."

A woman in a white chef uniform gestured across the restaurant.

"Wait here for a minute," Sara told Kate. "I need a quick word with the chef."

She scurried off in the direction of the kitchens. Kate wandered onto the deck and leant against the wooden railing, the sun warm on her head. She inhaled the scent of the bush, a heady mixture of animals and earth and the citronella candles surrounding the lodge.

She took in the beautiful thatched huts located either side of the main building, set on stilts and surrounded by low bushes, facing out towards the river. It was peaceful and so far away from her life in London. She rubbed the silver rhino pendant. What would this trip bring her? Would she find what she was searching for?

"All done." Sara's cheery voice broke her reverie. "Let

me take you to your room now. You can have a wash and a rest and we can meet for drinks and dinner at sunset. You must be exhausted." As if on cue, Kate yawned and Sara laughed.

They headed back along the path before taking a right fork to the staff quarters. Kate had expected her room to be less luxurious than the guest rooms but was pleasantly surprised to find Sara lead her to a thatched hut, similar in style, if not a little dated.

"These were the original guest rooms before the last refurbishment," Sara explained.

As they climbed the wooden steps to the deck of the hut, a brown and white monkey jumped down from a low tree branch and ran along the wooden railings.

Kate laughed at the monkey staring at her as it preened itself. "What a cutie."

"They may look cute and cuddly," Sara warned Kate, "but trust me, they'll steal anything you leave lying around outside, and if the door is open, they'll be in before you can stop them. They are the worst thieves out."

The interior of the hut was as beautiful as outside. Dark furniture was decked with colourful covers and cushions, and a snowy white mosquito net hung over the canopy bed.

Kate took in the décor. 'What a lovely room. I feel like I'm on holiday instead of working."

"After what you've been through, you need a holiday," Sara said. "I'll leave you to rest." She made to leave but suddenly turned back, nudging Kate with her elbow. "By the way, what did you think of Ryan? He is rather attractive, in a tall, dark and brooding way. A sort of Mr Rochester in khaki."

Kate had always been obsessed with Mr Rochester. They'd both been *Jane Eyre* fans in their early boarding-school days, scouring Kate's well-worn copy for any scenes of passion between Jane Eyre and Edward Rochester.

"He seems quite intense, but I guess he's under a lot of pressure at the moment," Kate replied diplomatically. She had the feeling her friend was on a matchmaking mission. She was incorrigible.

After Sara left, Kate showered, luxuriating in the cool water and citrus-scented shampoo. She was towelling her hair when her cell phone beeped with a text. She frowned at the unknown South African number, her heart thudding in her chest as she read the message.

Her stomach clenched. She collapsed down on the bed, her head spinning and all feelings of relaxation after her shower now gone. Talk about quick. She'd only sent out tentative queries a few days ago, wanting to test the water a little.

Hands shaking, she tried to call the number, but despite Sara's assurances that the cell-phone coverage was good, she was unable to connect. She quickly typed out a message, suggesting that emails would be the best form of communication going forwards.

Her eyes drifted back to the beautiful scenery beyond. Facing west, the riverbed was backlit by the yellow tones of late afternoon. The sun was melting into the horizon, washing the rocks with pinks and reds. She pushed her feet into a pair of ballet pumps and picked up her room key. The sunset finale would no doubt be spectacular. She needed to hurry, otherwise she would miss it.

But as she walked towards the main lodge, anxiety

clouded her thoughts. She'd made it to South Africa. But what now? Her life had changed so much since her parents' deaths, and even more after their funerals when her godfather, Patrick, had revealed the truth to her. From that day on, everything had begun to unspool, the threads loosening on a tightly drawn reel. But she was here now and it was far too late to back out.

Chapter Six

Ryan pushed his reading glasses up his nose for the third time. Despite the air conditioner humming in the background, his office was stuffy and perspiration trickled down his face. The words on the screen blurred and he buried his face in his hands.

He was trying to write the patrol report from the previous night, but the words were merging together on the screen like the blobs of sweat he could feel on his back. Every single muscle in his body ached, weariness seeping into his bones. What he needed now was a long shower and a beer, a chance to collect his thoughts and regain some control. It would be dark soon, another night with the moon full and bright in the sky.

It reminded him of the many times in Afghanistan when they'd come back from spending hours walking tracks and dodging landmines, each step fraught with danger. He still missed the camaraderie of his army mates, the jostling and joking in the mess after they'd cleaned up, trying hard to forget what they'd seen. He was now building that same relationship with his fellow rangers here in the bush.

The phone on the desk jangled and made him jump. It was Rio.

"I got a call from my mate Ollie at Marula Heights," he boomed down the receiver. "He's been on leave for a few days and stopped at Hazyview to visit family. Apparently, he overheard a guy talking in a bar about a poaching job down near Malelane."

Ryan sat up straighter, his interest aroused. "What exactly did he overhear?"

"The guy was boasting about his new job in a private game reserve down near the Malelane Gate, claimed he was making a packet giving tip-offs to poachers. He told his mates it was easy money."

Ryan cursed. "Do you think he's one of our guys?"

Rio clicked down the phone line. "I'm not sure. Most of our guys are loyal – they have been with us for ages. I really don't think they would suddenly switch sides."

Ryan thought for a moment. "Except for Leonard Nkosi. He only started about six weeks ago."

"I forgot about him. He's pretty quiet, isn't he? Gets on with the job, from what I've noticed."

"Yeah, but he's a bit sullen. Doesn't engage eye contact when you talk to him."

"He's probably shy," Rio said. "You can be quite scary."

Ryan snorted. "No, he's not shy. I don't know what it is, but given the fact that he's the newest member of the team, we really ought to find out a bit more about him."

"Okay. I'll see what I can dig up."

When he'd hung up, Ryan saved the file on the computer and pushed the chair away from the desk. It was time to dive into a long, cold shower. On the way back he spotted Sara carrying a box of files towards the reception office. He hurried on to catch up with her. The box looked heavy.

"Let me get that," he said, grabbing the box out of her

arms. "What's in here? Gold blocks?"

Sara pulled a face. "Sadly, no. It's reams of printer paper and some accounting files. We've got Cassie coming from head office later in the week to do an audit and run through some new software." She grinned lasciviously at him. "I'm sure she'll be keen to see you."

Ryan rolled his eyes. He'd met Cassie when she'd come to visit after taking over the job. They'd got on well and enjoyed chatting over a meal at Sara and Gavin's cottage. Sara, as usual, had been convinced she'd be a good match for Ryan. Despite the fact she lived permanently in Johannesburg.

He was about to hurl back a sarcastic retort when Sara touched his arm gently. "What do you think of Kate? I am so excited to finally have her here."

Ryan thought back to the way Kate's hazel-green eyes had flashed in excitement after seeing the pride of lions, her red hair burnished with the late afternoon sunlight. Her enthusiasm was contagious and had generated a warmth throughout his body which, for a moment or two, took away all thoughts of poachers. Although he'd lived in the bush for over five years and had seen many lions with their cubs, it was as if he were seeing them for the first time too.

He shoved the box onto the desk in the office, avoiding Sara's quizzical eyes, and gave a non-committal reply. The last thing he needed was for Sara to get the wrong idea.

"She seems very professional."

Sara folded her arms. "Professional? Is that all you can say?"

"I've only just met her, and to be honest, I've got a lot

of other things on my mind at the moment."

Sara's face fell. "Sorry, Ryan. You're right, but at least Kate will get a real first-hand insight into poaching. Ryan..." her eyebrows knitted together "...you will be nice to her, won't you? She may exude a professional, hard shell, but she's been through a lot recently."

Ryan gave an exasperated sigh. "Of course I'll be nice to her. You don't need to worry."

He left Sara to her files and headed to his room, thoughts of Kate at the poaching site filling his head. He wondered again about her backstory, trying to remember what Sara had told him.

"She's an investigative journalist," Sara had said, following Ryan around the ops room a few days earlier, "and her paper, the *Daily Tribune*, wants to do a spread in their weekend magazine about conservation and poaching in the Kruger. She immediately thought of Elephant Sands. After all, I've told her so much about it."

Ryan hadn't been fully listening at the time; his mind was rammed with unfinished patrol updates and animal surveillance reports. Besides, the word 'journalist' always sent a shiver down his spine and he'd shoved it away, anxious to get on with his work.

And now here Kate was, thrust upon him on what was probably the worst day of his career as a ranger. He had to hand it to her though; she was stronger than she looked, and she stayed out of the way of the investigators. All in all, a better outcome than he'd expected when she had forced her way to the poaching site. With her cropped linen trousers and stylish shirt, he'd been expecting a townie type, but she hadn't been bothered by the flies or the heat or the gore.

Guilt flickered through him when he remembered how curt he'd been to her on their arrival back at the lodge earlier. It was her question about wanting to know more about him that irritated him. He didn't like speaking about himself and he certainly didn't want a journalist nosing around in his private life. But had he been too harsh? She'd certainly scurried off quickly after that. He'd have to try to find a way to work with her. To trust her. She *was* Sara's best friend.

If he was perfectly honest, he was only helping Kate because Sara asked him to. He didn't like the press and tried to keep away from them as much as he could. But he really liked Sara, the lovely and gentle wife of his best friend, Gavin. He would do anything for both of them. After all, they had saved him.

When he'd come to South Africa for an extended holiday five years earlier, it was Gavin and Sara who had taken him under their wing. They were newly married and still living with Gavin's family in the Drakensberg Mountains. The three of them had headed off in Gavin's beat-up old Land Rover for a six-week tour of South Africa and Botswana.

Somewhere in a campsite in the middle of the Okavango Delta, Ryan had finally admitted he was not okay, that he needed help. Life after the army had not gone as he had imagined, and although he bore no physical scars from his time in Afghanistan, the mental damage was layers thick, built up over time like limescale.

It was Sara who had suggested Ryan become a ranger. Gavin had just finished the training and they were on their way to run a small private concession within the Kruger National Park. A few months after that starlit revelation in Botswana, Ryan was back in South Africa attending a training course and beginning his life in the bush. He'd loved every minute of it, right up until the early hours of this morning when he'd found the dead rhino and her orphaned calf.

Half an hour later he was showered and dressed, sitting on his deck, a bottle of beer in his hand, gazing out towards the view below. The air was still oppressive despite the sun's descent towards the horizon. On the other side of the river, he spotted a group of elephants making their way across a ridge, trunk to tail, their ears flapping in the heat. The vivid colours of a lilac-breasted roller caught his eye and he watched the small bird flit from branch to branch of a marula tree growing near his hut. For him these were everyday occurrences but ones he would never take for granted.

But the beauty of the bush at sunset couldn't remove the memory of the dead rhino and injured calf. They were like a stain etched into his mind and he was determined to get justice for them.

He remembered Rio's call earlier about the guy who was overheard speaking in a bar in Hazyview. It was looking more and more like there was an informer in the reserve, or at least someone associated with a group of poachers. Could it be their new guard, Leonard? There was definitely something about him that Ryan didn't trust. Whenever he spoke to him, his response was always the same. He was monosyllabic, his eyes were always slipping away, and he didn't engage in any kind of conversation beyond a few words. As Rio had suggested, Leonard might just be shy, but in Ryan's experience as a soldier, it could also mean something else: that he had something to hide.

Come to think of it, Ryan had seen him in an Elephant Sands cap. It wasn't part of the guards' uniform, but he'd definitely been wearing it a couple of weeks earlier when Ryan had passed through.

Chapter Seven

Kate was the first to arrive in the bar and found a seat out on the veranda with a gin and tonic and a bowl of nuts. A classic tourist image. The waterhole below was crammed with elephants, busy greeting each other and splashing in the water. She watched, transfixed, her mind far away from all the problems she'd left behind in London and the ones awaiting her here.

"Kate!" Sara's ebullient voice echoed across the deck.

Kate hugged Sara, feeling the pull of her cheerful demeanour. "The sunset is beautiful. You are so lucky having this every evening."

Sara leant against the railing to gaze out at the sky. "It is special, but sometimes cloud cover ruins it—" she gave Kate a wink "—but I can't complain."

Gavin arrived bearing more drinks and the three of them sat on the deck, a glorious golden and red sky above them.

"How are you feeling, Kate?" Gavin asked, grabbing some nuts from the bowl. "You must be exhausted after the overnight flight and day in the field."

Kate flashed a tight smile. "I definitely won't be staying up late tonight, but a long hot shower went a long way to reviving me."

"We're so glad to finally have you here," Sara said. "I've missed you so much."

Kate smiled fondly. "I've missed you too, and I am sorry. I know I should have come way earlier than this. I did quite a lot of travelling over the last couple of years for work, but none of the destinations were anywhere near South Africa."

"Sara told me all about your press award. For your report on sweatshops in Indonesia." Gavin elbowed his wife. "She's quite proud of you. She reads all your articles religiously."

"I *am* proud of Kate." Sara beamed. "But then she was really good at English at school. She always said she wanted to be an award-winning journalist."

Kate snorted. "I'm not sure I said, 'award winning'."

"You did," Sara retorted. "You were quite precocious."

Kate laughed. "At least I didn't spend all my time dissecting frogs in my free lessons, like someone else around the table."

Sara raised an eyebrow in mock protest. "Practice makes perfect."

Gavin chuckled in amusement. "My lovely wife does have a thing for the small uglies."

Kate frowned. "Small uglies?"

"Frogs, toads, amphibians of any sort," Gavin offered. "You name it, she knows about them."

"They did form an important part of my dissertation at university," Sara countered. "I feel they are undervalued, that's all. And some of them are critically endangered, especially with their habitats being encroached upon. It's not only about the famous endangered mammals, you know. All wildlife is under threat."

Sara had always been an animal and nature lover. She'd won the biology award in sixth form and had studied Natural Sciences at university. Where Kate was obsessed with literature, Sara preferred studying the depths of a riverbed. Kate was not surprised when Sara told her she was going to work in the bush in South Africa.

She patted Sara's hand. "You're right. I guess we all have something to learn about the small creatures, insects too. And I couldn't think of a better champion for them than you."

Sara blushed. "That's why I love working here. Every day is different and we have so many interesting research projects on the go. You wait until you meet Clemmie, one of our rangers; she's currently undertaking a wild dog project. It's really interesting."

"That does sound good," Kate replied. "I've watched documentaries about wild dogs—" she pushed her chair out and stood "—but for now, that sunset is stunning, I am going to behave like a tourist and take some photos."

The sky was magnificent. Oranges, reds and pinks blended together to form a perfect backdrop for the silhouetted trees and scrub in the foreground. The sky seemed bigger than normal, a canvas of gold and fiery reds. It reminded Kate of her mother, Ginny. She had been a keen amateur watercolour artist, often painting beautiful sunset scenes of the South Downs. Over the years she'd amassed many versions of the same scene. Sunsets in winter with snow or frost, and sunsets in summer, vivid and bright, much like this one tonight. With the house sold, the paintings now sat in a box in storage. Another task for Kate to sort out when she returned to England. Tears pricked at her eyes and she blinked them away, snapping a couple more photos to compose herself.

In the background, Gavin and Sara were chatting to a guest nearby and Kate sensed a presence next to her. It was Ryan, freshly shaven, his hair damp from a shower, the scent of citrus and bergamot in the air.

She faced him, suddenly tongue-tied, not sure what to say, only managing to croak out hello. Up close like this, his hair backlit by the golden sky, he was even more handsome, his jaw square, a dimple visible in one cheek, a lock of brown hair falling over his forehead. It had been a while since she'd felt such an immediate attraction to someone. She hoped it wouldn't get in the way of the story she was here to write.

He sipped his beer, his eyes meeting hers over the bottle. "How are you feeling now? Refreshed?"

She was grateful he had resorted to small talk. That she could do. "Yes, it's amazing what a hot shower and a cup of tea can do to revive you." She tilted her head on one side. "You're a little less dusty too."

Ryan grinned. "Thank you. Getting dusty is an occupational hazard."

They joined Gavin and Sara back at the table. The four of them watched the last few moments of the sunset, swatting mosquitoes and catching up on news.

Ryan eyed Gavin across the table. "We've got some intel from the police."

"Anything of interest?" Gavin asked.

Ryan chewed his bottom lip. "Not sure yet. Apparently, a witness contacted the local police to report suspicious behaviour in a village over the border. It's only about twenty kilometres from the poaching site. The park police flagged it up with the Hawks' team, so they're investigating it." He pinched the bridge of his nose. "We'll have to wait and see what the local police make of it."

Gavin grimaced. "Hopefully, we will get something on the bullets quite promptly."

Ryan leant forward. "Also, Rio called me earlier. Ollie, a mate of his who works up in Sabie, was in Hazyview on leave and overheard a guy in a bar boasting about a poaching job down south. Ollie had heard about our poaching on the grapevine."

Gavin frowned. "So, whoever the guy was in the bar might have been involved with our poaching?"

"I don't think so," Ryan replied. "The timing doesn't fit. But whoever it was certainly knew something or someone. And if it was someone from Elephant Sands, then we have to find out who it was pretty damn quickly."

"Do you know who was on leave from the guard team?" Sara asked. "That might be one way of tracking them down."

"Yes, Rio's following that up now," Ryan replied. "Hopefully, we'll find out tomorrow. I am going to speak to Albert first thing in the morning. I want to get his impression of Leonard."

"Is Leonard the new guy?" Sara asked. "I thought he was okay. He's always friendly and has told me about his life growing up near Timbavati."

Ryan took a long slug of his beer before replying. "He's the newest in the team, and I've always thought he's quite surly. I've tried on several occasions to talk to him about stuff, but he doesn't engage. It's like his mind is somewhere else all the time."

Sara pushed her chair back. "Well, let's hope we get some news back from the investigating team soon. Shall we go and eat? I'm starving."

On cue, Kate's stomach rumbled loudly and they all laughed, the serious tone from earlier lifted.

With only a thin vermillion line left on the horizon and the buzz of insects loud in the background, the four of them ate by lantern light on the veranda. Kate enjoyed the delicious beef stew, peppered with pumpkin and spices, mopping up the last of the gravy with a piece of bread and sipping a glass of mellow South African red wine.

Ryan was sitting opposite her, his quietness at odds with the constant banter of Sara and Gavin. They'd both been teasing Kate about how many sunset photos she had already taken, and despite Ryan's attempts to join in, Kate noticed he was distracted.

Kate herself was silent, weariness from travelling beginning to catch up with her. When Gavin and Sara left the table briefly to welcome some new guests to dinner, an awkwardness fell across the table. Kate was about to ask Ryan a question, anything to break the uncomfortable silence when he leant forward to speak to her, the soft light from the lantern throwing golden flecks on his brown hair.

"How long are you here for?"

She noticed the way his eyes crinkled up at the corners, the dark brown richness at odds with his cool demeanour.

She bit her lip. "It depends on how long it takes to write the article. Both my parents died a few months ago and I was meant to be on compassionate leave, when this opportunity came up. I thought coming here to visit Sara and to write about poaching might help."

Ryan's eyes met hers. "I'm sorry to hear that. It must have been a really terrible time."

"It's not been easy," she admitted. "They were killed in

a car accident, which was a huge shock, and I am an only child, so there has been a lot to deal with on my own."

"I guess you're glad you have your work. I always find it a great distraction from things."

"It is." Kate drained her wine glass. "What about your family? I presume they are all back in England."

"My mum and dad live in a small village near Buxton. They were both Derbyshire born and bred and after a brief stint living elsewhere in England and abroad, they retired back to their roots."

"What do your parents do?"

"My dad was a soldier. He served in the Falklands and in peacekeeping in the Balkans later." Ryan gave her a wry grin. "I was an army brat."

"Is that why you became a soldier?"

Ryan snorted. "Who knows? I haven't really thought about why I chose the same route as him. I like to think it was my own decision."

"And what about your mother? What did she do before she retired?"

"Mum was a primary school teacher. She loved it and wasn't keen on retiring, but she got to her late sixties and the village school closed and she didn't fancy a longer drive to work. She keeps herself busy though – Nordic walking, the WI and all sorts of clubs and things." The corners of his eyes crinkled. "My dad, however, hates retirement. He doesn't know what to do with himself. The army was all he ever knew, really. He plays bowls and drinks regularly at the local, playing in a local darts league, but I think he'd rather still be hanging out in the mess in some barracks somewhere."

"Do you see them often?"

Ryan's eyes were wary. "Not often enough for their liking."

Kate sensed a sensitive family issue. "Any brothers or sisters?"

He grinned, his face coming to life again. "A sister. Emma. She's two years younger but acts like she's older. She has two sons." His brow furrowed. "I think they're around ten and eight, but I lose track."

"I know what you mean," Kate said. "I lose track of my friends' children's birthdays. It's hard to keep up, especially for all the godchildren I have. I have to keep all their birth dates and ages written down in a diary, otherwise I'd get it completely wrong." She caught amusement in his eyes, but then his phone bleeped and the moment was gone.

Ryan reached across for his phone, his head jerking back as he read the message. He clutched his phone, his face pale as he pushed his chair out abruptly and came to his feet, staring out into the dark bush beyond.

Kate's stomach tightened. "Is everything all right?" she asked, her eyes flicking to his phone, which he held tightly in his hand. "Was it more news about the poaching?"

He didn't reply at first and she thought perhaps he hadn't heard her. But then his eyes blinked and with a trembling hand he pushed his phone into the pocket of his trousers.

"It's nothing. I need to go…"

Kate watched him dart across the room. *What on earth was in that message?* Whatever it was, it had certainly spooked him, but clearly he didn't want to talk about it. Fair enough. She was pretty good at keeping her thoughts to herself too. Especially at the moment.

She reached for her phone and was scrolling through

some messages when he appeared at her side again, his eyes downcast and shoulders slumped.

He gripped the side of the table. "Sorry, we should make plans for tomorrow morning. Let's meet at reception at quarter to five. I need to interview the security guards on the gate. You may as well come along for the ride."

"Okay, thank you." She lowered her voice. "Are you sure you're okay?"

He bit his lip and for a moment she thought he was going to speak, but he jerked his head side to side and left the restaurant. Up ahead, she saw him pause to speak to Gavin in the bar, their heads tucked together in privacy. Gavin touched Ryan on the shoulder and as Ryan walked out into the dark compound, Kate could see that Gavin seemed upset too, his own face resembling that of Ryan a few minutes before.

Gavin returned to the table, his normal cheerful disposition gone. "Sara will be back in a minute. She's sorting out a problem with a guest." He gave her a tired smile. "I'm impressed with your stamina, Kate. You seem to be holding up well."

Kate gave a small smile. "I am definitely fading now. I think I should go to bed."

"Probably a good idea," he said, jerking his head towards the exit. "Shall we go? We can find Sara on the way."

They weaved around the tables in the restaurant, now empty of guests. The barman was wiping down the dark wooden bar, humming softly to the music in the background.

Gavin came to an abrupt stop. "Michael, can you give me one of the bottles of Johnny Walker Red Label? Ryan's had some bad news and I'm going to take it over to his room. I'll sort it with the inventory tomorrow."

Kate grabbed Gavin's arm. "What's going on?"

Gavin sighed. "Ryan's had some bad news about an old army friend who's died. It's quite a shock and I am pretty sure he's going to need a drink and a chat. Ex-soldier to ex-soldier."

A flutter of sorrow pulsed in Kate's chest. She was glad Ryan had such a good friend as Gavin. She was still raw from her parents' death, and Ryan's grief over his friend resonated with her.

Unaware of the situation, Sara bounded back to the table, her enthusiasm making Kate smile. "Want to come back to our cottage for a nightcap? We can have a proper catch-up."

An enormous yawn took Kate by surprise and Sara laughed. "Maybe not. I think we need to tuck you up."

"Sorry," Kate apologised, "it has been a really long day—" she eyed Gavin "—and besides, Ryan's had some upsetting news."

Sara's eyes widened. "Oh no, what is it, Gav?"

Gavin rubbed his jaw. "One of his army friends has died. I don't know all the details yet." He held up the bottle. "I'm going to go and have a chat with him. I'll try not to be too late. We're all exhausted after such a long day."

"Poor Ryan," Sara said. "To have this on top of the poaching."

Gavin kissed his wife gently on her head and nodded to Kate. "Sleep well and I'll see you tomorrow."

Kate and Sara walked back together to the staff compound, the stone path lit with small solar lamps. At her room, Kate grabbed Sara's arm. "Are you sure Ryan will be okay to help me with this article? Especially now that he's had this bad news."

"I am sure it will be fine. Finding the poachers is a top priority, and Ryan is more than capable of dealing with it. You've arrived at a difficult time, that's all." She hugged Kate. "I am so glad you are here. I know it's been an incredibly tough time for you."

Kate leant into the solid beat of her friend's heart, tears pricking her eyes. She longed to let it all out, to tell Sara the truth, but she wasn't sure she knew exactly what the truth was, so how could she even begin to explain it to anyone else? Instead she held back, watching her best friend, the person who had known her and her parents for over twenty years, walk back along the path and into the darkness beyond the solar lamps.

A moth fluttered around the lantern on the deck, scattering dust from its wings as it darted around the light. Up above, the sky was littered with stars, a vast twinkling ceiling. Kate's heart ached as she thought of her mum and dad, of the empty hollow their absence had created and of all she'd discovered. She blinked back tears and went into her room, shutting out the night and the memories behind her.

Chapter Eight

Back in his room, Ryan's hands trembled as he fired up the computer, digging out his reading glasses from amongst the mess in the desk drawer, the words of the text he'd received earlier seared into his brain:

Ryan, I hate to be the bearer of sad news. Jim's passed away. I'm heading up to see Heather and the family now so will be on the road. I've sent you an email telling you what I know. Call me when you can. Neil.

Neil was a close friend from his old regiment. They'd both joined at the same time and were inseparable throughout training and when deployed overseas. They even shared the same birthday, having both turned forty earlier in the year. Whilst Neil had celebrated his with a big knees-up in England, Ryan had spent his in the bush on patrol. He hadn't even bothered to tell anyone, but when he'd come back to the lodge, he discovered Gavin and Sara had organised a surprise party for him.

Neil stayed on in the army long after Ryan headed to work in security in Iraq. Now a high-ranking officer, Neil was one of the only ones Ryan kept in touch with. They'd shared too many experiences in Afghanistan to lose contact. Jim had been another member of the team, a good friend too. An incredible man and soldier who'd been invalided out at the same time Ryan had left the army. And now he was dead and Ryan couldn't believe it.

He opened the email from Neil:

Hi. I hope you're well. I've got some bad news. Jim passed away this morning. It was weird really. I'd been thinking of heading up to visit him soon. It's hard for me to tell you this, mate, but Jim hanged himself. Poor old Heather came back from the school run and found him. He had apparently been struggling with depression for quite some time. As you know, he's never really recovered fully from the incident nor from all the shit that was thrown around after the investigation. He's always blamed himself for what happened. But the last time I saw him, he told me he was finally having treatment, talking to someone about it. I was really pleased for him, which is why I am so shocked by his death. But I guess he couldn't carry on any longer.

Sorry to send such bad news. When I know more about the funeral arrangements, I'll send details. I'm heading up tomorrow to see if I can help with things so give me a call.

How's the bush? Keep in touch. N

Ryan's throat constricted and the words on the screen blurred. He hadn't thought about Jim for a long time – had pushed him and everyone else in their team as far away from his mind as possible. Had tried to forget the pain and anger that had stirred within him for months after the incident.

He leant back in his chair and gazed out of the small window by the desk. The sky was inky black, aglow with a canopy of glittering stars. It reminded him of another sky, on a different continent, twelve years earlier. A place where the heat shimmered over rocky outcrops and red desert, much like it did in the South African bush and where the night skies were vast, lit with stars. A place where he'd spent months patrolling outlying villages and towns wondering what the hell he was doing there, where one day two members of his patrol joked and jostled at breakfast and never returned to camp.

Jim barely made it back alive, his leg splattered amongst the thorny trees, and although he'd lived to watch his baby daughter grow up, he was never the same again. Ryan had walked away without a single scratch, but the memory of that day was still etched in his mind as if it were yesterday. Panic pushed up into his chest and he leant forward, a wave of dizziness overtaking him. He'd had no idea that Jim had felt responsible all these years. Ryan had always blamed himself, had come to accept his part in the mission that went wrong. But Jim? In Ryan's eyes, he was completely blameless.

He bunched his hands and stared at the email, reading through the words again, imagining Jim's wife walking through the front door, finding her husband swinging from a rope. It was incomprehensible. He reached for the keyboard of his computer, his hands hovering over the letters, not quite sure of how to comfort a woman whose world had been taken from under her.

There was a soft knock on the door and Gavin's head popped through.

"You okay, mate?" Gavin waved a bottle of whisky in

front of him. "I thought you might feel like a drink and a chat."

Ryan pulled off his glasses and rubbed his eyes, suddenly aware of the moisture in them. Had he been crying? He hadn't even noticed.

"Sounds good. It's been a hell of day and now this news about Jim…"

Gavin found two glasses from the small kitchen and poured a decent measure into each. He handed a glass to Ryan. "I'm really sorry about your friend. What happened? Was he still commissioned?"

"No, he was medically discharged in 2007. He lost a leg to a landmine."

Gavin whistled. "How did he die?"

Ryan stared back at the computer screen. "He hanged himself. His wife found him." He rubbed the bridge of his nose, a headache prodding at his brow.

Gavin's eyes widened. "Oh God, how awful."

Ryan's hand shook as he took a sip of the whisky. "I can't get my head round it. Apparently, he'd been suffering with depression for quite some time, but I don't think anyone realised how bad it was. I certainly didn't." He wiped his hand across his eyes. "I should have made more of an effort to keep in touch with him."

"It's hard when you are so far away from people and you don't know how things really are," Gavin said. "I suppose he's at peace now."

Ryan hoped so. It was tough for those left behind – Jim's wife, Heather, and their two children. They were the ones who needed the support now.

"Do you think you'll go to the funeral?" Gavin asked, interrupting his thoughts.

He hadn't really thought that far ahead. If he was completely honest with himself, he didn't want to go. There would be a guard of honour and most of their regiment would be there, a sad trip down memory lane.

"I don't know. There's too much going on here at the moment. We're short of rangers for the patrol and..." He didn't continue. He didn't want Gavin to think him uncaring.

"There are many ways of honouring someone," Gavin said reassuringly.

They sat sipping the whisky and talking about army life. Ryan was grateful for Gavin's quiet presence. Gavin was ex South African army, and if anyone understood, it was him. He'd lost mates in Angola.

Much later, when they'd each drunk another glass and Ryan's eyes were drifting towards sleep, Gavin left him. Ryan settled into bed and stared up at the ceiling, suddenly wide awake again despite almost falling asleep in the chair earlier.

He hadn't replied to Neil yet, hadn't even tried to call him. Although there was only a two-hour time difference between South Africa and England, it was the early hours of the morning for both of them now. Not the time to be talking about Jim. That was for tomorrow when Ryan could at least think straight.

His last full thought before falling into a deep sleep was that it had only been twenty-four hours since he'd been called out of bed to search for the poachers. And then he'd found the dead rhino and her frail orphaned calf. A long day beginning and ending with loss and sorrow. Ryan wasn't into all that psychic stuff, but the full moon had a lot to answer for.

Chapter Nine

Despite thinking she would fall straight to sleep, Kate tossed and turned in the comfortable bed, the curtain of mosquito net soft around her. Sometime around midnight she gave up trying to sleep and clicked on the table lamp, thoughts buzzing around her like the insects zooming around the lantern outside.

She grabbed her phone and opened the mailbox. She'd downloaded some emails whilst she was over in the bar, the internet speed being quicker there, but hadn't had a chance to read them. Settling against the soft pillows, she scrolled down, her thumb stopping on a message sent only an hour before. It was the one she'd been waiting for. A possible answer to the real reason she was in South Africa.

It all went back to a few weeks earlier. Kate had been down at her parents' house in Sussex trying to get it in to some kind of order. Much as she loved the home she'd grown up in, she'd already decided to sell the property. It was a beautiful, spacious family home, but the rooms were haunted with such happy memories that Kate knew she had to sell it. It needed a new family now, who could make their own memories.

It had been raining all day, teeming down, sending

rivulets of water across the cracked path in the front garden. Taking a break from clearing cupboards, she'd been slumped at the kitchen table and nursing a mug of tea, running her hand over the tabletop. She loved feeling the grooves of the wood, the scratches and marks of a lifetime, imagining her mother, Ginny, standing by the Aga, tasting and tweaking a casserole, all the while helping a younger Kate with her homework. Or steering her through the agony of broken friendships and boyfriend problems.

The front doorbell had rung. She'd brushed dust off the front of her jeans and checked her face in the mirror in the hallway. Puffy skin protruded beneath her eyes and her hair was stringy and dull. She took a deep breath, straightened her shoulders and opened the door to find her godfather standing on the damp porch.

"Katie," Uncle Patrick had boomed. He embraced her in a big hug, the smell of cigars and rain emanating from him. Familiar and comforting.

Her heart had squeezed in her chest at his use of the name her father had always called her. Uncle Patrick was a kind, gregarious man who had known her father since they were both schoolboys, and had been a constant in her life for as long as she could remember.

He'd gazed at her, his brown eyes searching. "How are you?"

Her eyes had slid away to the thick envelope he held under his right arm. She pulled a face. "I've only cleared about a quarter of the house so far."

He'd followed her down the hall to the kitchen. She'd picked up a bottle of wine and waved it at him.

"Yes, please," he'd responded with gusto, plonking his

large body onto a chair.

He'd eyed her as she poured the wine, his face thoughtful. "You know you don't have to do this all now. There's really no rush. It's only been a few weeks. You need to give yourself time."

She'd taken a big swig of the wine, enjoying the warm trickle down her throat as it hit her bloodstream quickly, relaxing her. "I know, but it's best to get on with things."

He'd reached across to pat her hand. "But still…it's a lot to do when everything is so…" he searched for the right word "…raw."

She'd straightened a pile of papers. "I'm okay, Uncle Patrick. You know me, I can't sit around doing nothing all day."

He'd smiled sadly. "Just like your mother."

Kate had pointed to the envelope he'd placed on the table. "What's in there?"

Uncle Patrick had been silent at first, watching her over the lip of his glass. He'd been a great help ever since the dreaded phone call, supporting her through the police investigation, the funerals and all that followed. She didn't know what she'd do without him.

He'd taken off his glasses and wiped them on a handkerchief, his hands shaking a little. "Your father gave it to me after you all came back from South Africa, and asked me to hold on to it. I didn't ask any questions at the time and I'd forgotten about it until…what with being an executor of the wills, I thought I should open it."

"And?" Kate had asked, her curiosity aroused.

He'd pushed it towards her. "And I think you should take a look."

She'd frowned. Why so cryptic? "Am I going to like

what's in it?"

He'd shaken his head sadly. "You need to decide that for yourself."

Apprehension had kicked in then, trickling down her spine as she unwound the binding at the back and dug her hand in, finding a stack of envelopes tied in faded red string.

She'd untied the string and flicked through the stack, noting the South African stamps on the envelopes, and the names of people she'd never heard of. Her parents had lived in South Africa for a few years, both teaching at Cape Town university. They'd moved back to England when she was a toddler, but she had virtually no memory of the country she was born in.

She'd searched his face for clues. Was she meant to read the letters?

"Keep looking, Katie." Uncle Patrick's brow had furrowed. Something in there had him rattled.

She'd found another piece of paper, its edges curled up and yellowing. Placing it on the table, she'd smoothed it flat, her eyes blinking as she focused on the words in front of her, her name and date of birth jumping out at her in faded black ink. How odd; her birth certificate was in a drawer in her flat in London, along with all her other important documents.

The certificate looked the same, but when she looked more closely, her second name, Virginia, was not there. And even more alarming was the name printed in the Mother's section. What on earth was this?

"I don't understand," she'd said, scanning the words a second and a third time. "This isn't my birth certificate. I have mine at home. This can't be right..." She pushed back from the chair, sending it clattering to the ground. "What does it mean?"

"It means exactly what it says, Katie," Uncle Patrick had replied softly.

She'd stared at him in disbelief. How could he be so calm? The burning sensation of vomit pushed up into her throat and she ran to the kitchen sink, throwing up the red wine, her heart thundering in her ears. How many more shocks would she have to endure? How could her life have been turned so upside down in such a short space of time?

It had darkened outside and she'd caught a glimpse of her reflection in the kitchen window, not recognising the pale face staring back at her, an imposter in her own home. Uncle Patrick's voice had been shaky as he followed her to the sink, gently rubbing her shoulder with his hand.

"I knew nothing about this, I promise you," he'd informed her. "I agonised for ages about showing it to you, but you deserve to know the truth and now you have to decide what you want to do about it."

Tears had pricked in Kate's eyes, but she brushed them away angrily. All she'd wanted to do was to throw the documents on a bonfire and burn them all.

After Uncle Patrick had left, she'd dismissed the birth certificate, had assumed it was some kind of fake. After all, she'd had possession of her own one in a drawer in London. The other one had to be a mistake, a clerical error.

But when she'd gone home to London and had retrieved her birth certificate to compare with the other, she'd received a shock. Her certificate, the one she'd used all her life, was a certified copy, dated nearly three years after her birth and processed in Cape Town. It showed her father, Geoffrey Roland Harper, and her mother, Virginia Anne Harper, like she'd always remembered. The other certificate, the one from the envelope, was dated immediately after her birth and stamped in Johannesburg, and whilst her father's name was on that one too, across the section designated for mother, etched in faded black ink, was the name Alison Katherine Voester, and Kate had absolutely no idea who she was.

Why had her parents kept this birth certificate a secret, hidden all these years with Uncle Patrick? She wondered what would have happened if they hadn't died. What if they'd gone on to live for much longer, died of natural causes, two elderly parents in their dotage? Would Uncle Patrick have given her the envelope then? Chances are he too may have passed away, and then the secret would have stayed locked up safe and sound; a hidden lie, never found out.

For weeks after the discovery, Kate tried to ignore its ramifications, disbelief and shock pushing it to the back of her mind. But when the chance to write about poaching in South Africa had come up, it seemed to her like it was meant to be. She could go to South Africa, write the article and search for her real mother. It became an obsession, a desire to chase down the woman who now haunted her every thought.

As an investigative journalist, she had occasionally used private investigators for her research. But never in a million years had she imagined she would need to employ one on a personal quest. And it *was* personal. Kate had not only had to deal with the death of her parents and the trial of the drunk driver, but also the revelation of the truth behind her birth, about who she really was. And it had shocked her to the core.

And so she'd found Allan Prescott from South African-based Albion Investigations online, getting only as far as A in the alphabetical index listing. It was a pretty amateur attempt at finding an agency, but she'd been reeling from her discovery at the time. The agency's references had checked out, and she'd no problem contacting them.

But now that she was actually here, in South Africa, there was an element of trepidation. What exactly would she find? She rubbed her eyes and opened the email from Allan Prescott, blood rushing to her head as she scanned the words:

> *Dear Miss Harper,*
>
> *Thank you for your voice message. I have been unable to find any trace of Alison Voester in any official records since 1989. However, I may have found a relative, a brother, but am waiting for some information from the South African Revenue Bureau, which I should have tomorrow. I will email you as soon as I have more detailed information. Kind regards,*
> *Allan Prescott*

She closed her laptop, thinking about Alison Voester, this unknown woman who was supposedly her real mother. Despite the initial shock and anger, she'd begun to accept the truth, that Geoffrey had fathered a child with another woman and that her parents had concealed the truth from her. And now she was going to find her and try to patch together the truth behind it all.

Chapter Ten

Kate stepped out onto the deck of her hut and inhaled the sweet, cool air of the arriving day. It was still dark, but behind the hut, towards the east, a glow of pink was surfacing. She zipped up her fleece jacket and took another deep breath of air, rolling her shoulders and neck, stiff from the night's sleep. Or lack of.

On the small table of her deck someone had placed a flask of tea and a plate of shortbread biscuits covered in a soft lace cloth. She poured the steaming hot tea into a mug and bit into a biscuit. It was divine, freshly baked, and she wolfed it down. She remembered Sara telling her she would have breakfast later, after they'd been out on patrol.

"It wouldn't do you any good to bounce about in the jeep on a full English breakfast," she'd told her.

Kate sipped the fragrant tea and scanned through the notes she'd made the day before. She still used old-style reporters' notepads to jot down information and a voice recorder on her phone to capture anything she'd missed. When she was training to be a reporter for a local newspaper up near Manchester, she'd worked with an experienced journalist who still used an old-fashioned handheld Dictaphone.

Over the years she'd developed her own form of shorthand, a mixture of the traditional method with her own abbreviations. It had served her well, especially when she was a rookie reporter working for provincial newspapers.

She scribbled down some more questions she would ask Ryan. He'd promised to show her the anti-poaching unit control room after the trip to speak to the guards. She hoped he would open up a bit more about what led him to do this job. As ever, she was keen to go for the 'human' angle.

Then she remembered his face last night when he'd received the text about his army friend, and guilt flickered through her. Perhaps she shouldn't go with him today. He might need time on his own to process what had happened. But she was awake now and ready. Besides, at dinner last night, he'd echoed her belief that working was the best way to take your mind off problems. She'd certainly found it to be a panacea over the last few months.

A sliver of light appeared in the horizon, like a tiny crack under a door letting in light to a dark room. She walked the short distance to reception, her senses taking in the cool air and sweet smell of early morning. The birds on a nearby tree chattered loudly above her head as they readied themselves for the day.

Ryan was waiting in the jeep wrapped up in an Elephant Sands fleece jacket.

"Morning," she croaked.

He gave her a tired smile, his face pale. "Did you sleep well?"

"Kind of. I went off quickly, but I did wake up a few

73

times. Unfamiliar sounds, I suppose."

Ryan threw a bag into the back of the jeep. "It takes a while to get used to the sounds of the bush at night. People think it's quiet when you are in the middle of nowhere, but it's actually quite noisy." He gestured to the front passenger seat. "Hop in. I thought we'd head out to the guards' office at the gate and then we'll come back and you can meet the team in the ops room."

Kate climbed in and buckled up her seat belt. "I'm keen to meet them. Any further news on the investigation since last night? You mentioned something at dinner about a witness?"

Ryan turned the ignition and the jeep rumbled to life. "Not at the moment. We have finished all the forensic investigations at the site. The police are currently trying to track the owner of the gun. It's a waiting game for now."

They pulled out of the lodge, bumping over the cattle grid into the reserve. But within minutes, Ryan stopped the vehicle and craned his neck, staring towards a tall tree in the dim morning light.

"What is it?" Kate asked.

"It's a pack of wild dogs," Ryan whispered. "One of our team, Clemmie, told me she'd seen them last night when she came back from patrol. They're still here."

He pointed to the right of the jeep and Kate saw four or five mounds of fur lying under the tree. If Ryan hadn't pointed them out, she would never have noticed them.

"Clemmie is involved with a research project on this pack," Ryan explained. "A couple of them are collared, so she knows them quite well."

Kate stretched higher to see them. "Their coats are amazing. I guess that's why they're called painted dogs."

Ryan pointed at the mound of sleeping dogs. "The alpha female is at the back. She's the one with a bit more white on her back. She's the head honcho of the pack. Wild dogs don't kick the younger males out like most mammal groups. It's the younger females who disperse. They go off and find other packs where they eventually try to evict some of the resident females related to the other pack members. It's nature's way of preventing inbreeding."

As if she knew they were talking about them, the alpha female popped her head up and glared at them.

Kate laughed. "She's keeping an eye on us, making sure we don't go near her pups."

Ryan restarted the jeep and they moved on, heading out onto the open plain. The air was soft and Kate's shoulders began to feel lighter as she took in the peaceful early morning scene.

She took a peek at Ryan, trying to gauge his mood. "Gavin told me last night about your friend. I'm so sorry. It must have been quite a shock."

Ryan's jaw tightened. "It was a hell of a shock. I am still trying to process it." His brow furrowed. "I feel so bloody useless. I have no idea what I am going to say to his wife."

Kate was silent, wondering whether to offer him the chance to go back to the lodge or whether to give him an opportunity to talk to her about it. She opted for the latter.

"How did he die?"

Ryan pulled at the collar of his fleece jacket. "He killed himself."

Kate blanched. "What? Oh my God. How awful."

"Yep," Ryan replied. "He lost a leg in a landmine in Afghanistan and was medically discharged in 2010. It was a huge rehabilitation process – operations, physiotherapy and different prosthetic legs – but he finally made it home to his family." He tapped a hand on the steering wheel. "We all thought he was doing okay. He'd even had some help with PTSD, but I don't know, it's just come so out of the blue."

Kate reached a hand across and touched Ryan's arm. "We don't have to do this today. You've had a real shock and I am sure you must be exhausted after the last twenty-four hours or so. Let's head back to the lodge."

"No, it's okay. I'd rather get on with things. I have to catch up with some of the guys from my regiment, but everyone's spread all over the place at the moment."

"Okay, but please feel free to cut things short if you need to," Kate said

Ryan didn't reply, instead guiding the jeep down into a gully and up the other side. Spread out below lay a vast expanse of savannah laden with grazing animals. In the distance was a fence line with a few buildings surrounding an entrance gate. Up ahead, a herd of zebras pulled at the grass, their tails swishing back and forth in the early morning sun. As they drove the last few kilometres to the guards' office, Ryan explained a little about how they patrolled the reserve.

Kate's interest flared. "Do you have cameras across the whole reserve?"

"No, the area is too large. We tend to have the cameras mounted near certain junctions along the fence line. And some carefully hidden in natural features like rocks. It's hard to monitor every inch of the reserve."

Kate understood what he meant. Staring out at the waterhole and rocks beyond gave her an idea of the scale of the place. "But you do daily patrols around the entire reserve?"

"Yes, twice a day, in fact. We work in teams and we also do night patrols."

"Do you do any on foot?"

"We do combinations. We might travel along the main perimeter fence that links us with the Kruger and Mozambique beyond, and we will stop and patrol on foot, usually searching for signs of incursion."

At the entrance gate, Ryan pulled the jeep under a shaded area and a man in a guard's uniform came out of the office to speak to them, a wide smile across his face. Ryan introduced Albert to Kate and she listened as Ryan questioned him about the new guard, Leonard.

Albert's friendly face creased up in worry. "I can't honestly tell you exactly what it is about him. It's just a feeling. I've been here for a long time and I have yet to meet someone as disinterested in his job as him. He takes long smoking breaks and we often find him sleeping in front of the security television. And yet the minute he heard about the rhino cow and her new calf, he suddenly showed an interest."

Ryan frowned. "What do you mean?"

Albert's brow furrowed in concentration. "Like, how old we thought the calf was and whether it was likely to stay nearby for a while. I asked him why he wanted to know that and he said it was so he could take a photo on his phone to send to his sister's children. I told him that we shouldn't send any photos of the wildlife to anyone outside the reserve without permission."

Ryan's face was grave. "And what did he say to that?"

"He didn't really say anything. He went back to his sulky

self. I wish I'd told someone about that now. Maybe the rhino would still be alive and her little one not orphaned."

Ryan patted Albert on the shoulder. "Don't worry, you're not the only one caught by surprise." He suddenly remembered the cap found near the fence line. "Albert, does Leonard wear an Elephant Sands cap? You know, the red cap the rangers and lodge staff sometimes wear."

Albert scratched his head. "I haven't noticed him wearing one, but I'll ask around."

"That would be great," Ryan said, "and can you keep an eye on him for me, watch out for anything suspicious that he might do or say?"

Albert's eyes narrowed. "I'll definitely keep a close eye on him. You can count on that."

Ryan and Kate climbed into the jeep and headed back towards the lodge. The sun was higher now, heat already beginning to shimmer across the plains.

Ryan turned off the main track, dipping down into a gully before steering the jeep onto a dry riverbed. The jeep moved smoothly over the sandy floor with Ryan occasionally staring down at the ground.

Kate was curious. "What are you looking for?"

"I thought I saw some fresh rhino tracks earlier."

Kate's pulse quickened. "It would be great to see a rhino, especially after yesterday…"

"You mean one that's alive," Ryan offered sardonically.

Kate showed Ryan her rhino necklace. "I have a thing about rhinos, have done since I was a little girl. And apart from yesterday, I've never seen a rhino in the wild."

The jeep travelled along the sandy track for a few kilometres with Ryan constantly checking the tracks on the ground. They swung up to the left and towards the open plains. Kate's head swivelled back and forth as she spotted animals on either side of the road. It was a wildlife smorgasbord.

Ryan stopped the jeep abruptly. "There's your rhino."

Kate's heart soared as she watched three rhinos grazing peacefully on the short grass.

"They're southern whites," Ryan explained. "We've got quite a few in the reserve."

They watched the rhinos graze for a while, both content to sit in silence in the fresh morning air. The two-way radio spluttered to life and brought them back to earth. It was Rio, asking when Ryan would be back. One of the investigating officers from Hawks wanted to speak to him.

As they drove back to the lodge, Kate leant back in the seat, feeling the warm morning sun on her face.

"Do you really think Leonard is the informer?" she asked.

Ryan blew out a frustrated puff of air. "I hope not, because then it will be our fault for not running proper checks on him."

Kate sensed his despondency. "I guess there will always be the odd person who will fall between the cracks. No security check is infallible."

A slash of red formed across Ryan's face. "It shouldn't be the case though. Our role is to keep the animals safe, no matter what, and we've failed that rhino and her calf."

Kate decided to drop the subject. "Have you always liked animals?"

"To be honest, I never really thought much about them until I came here. I grew up in the countryside and I did a bit of hiking and rock climbing. I suppose I like being outdoors."

"Why did you leave the army?"

Ryan's shoulders went rigid and his lips pulled into a tight line. He continued to drive in silence, his hands clenched on the steering wheel as they made their way up a steep ramp and over a small hill that opened up to a track. The thatched roofs of the lodge's buildings soon came into view and before long they were pulling up in front of the reception.

Kate leant over and touched Ryan's arm, conscious of the tension between them since she'd asked her last question. Had she said something wrong? Was he thinking about his friend who had died?

"I'm sorry, Ryan. I appreciate it's a difficult time for you, and I've overstepped the line. I shoot my mouth off sometimes."

Ryan's broad shoulders sagged and she watched him swallow, his Adam's apple bobbing in his throat. He glanced at her, his brown eyes a brief window of sorrow. And then he blinked and rearranged his features.

"Don't worry." He pulled his sunglasses back down over his eyes and climbed out of the jeep, his voice gruff. "Go and grab some breakfast and I'll meet you in the ops room later."

She watched him go, wondering if she'd offended him somehow. She realised he never did answer the question as to why he'd left the army.

Chapter Eleven

Ryan headed towards the office, dodging the sprinkler that was watering the sparse Kikuyu grass that grew around the lodge's buildings. He honestly didn't know why Gavin bothered. It grew like a weed and wasn't any better for the water. They were coming to the end of the dry season and Gavin was obviously trying to bring the lawn back to life.

He thought of the green pastures of the Peak District, of the rocky hills and valleys, and of his parents' back garden, the lawn so faithfully tended by his father. The smell of a late summer evening when the sun had gone down and the air was sweet and soft, the lawn springy beneath your bare feet. It was all so different from here.

His office was hot and sticky and he switched on the air conditioning. At his desk he leant back on his chair momentarily to consider what to do first. A gecko ran up the wall next to him and he smiled, watching it make its way across a framed picture and up into the open beamed ceiling.

The photos that lined the walls of his office proudly displayed every ranger and guard team he'd trained over the last five years. He was proud of them all. It hadn't been easy. They were often inexperienced and very young when they arrived, coming from outlying villages to do their ranger qualifications. Many of them had gone on to work in other areas and to train rangers themselves, keen to protect the iconic wildlife of their country. He gulped. It was hard to imagine any of them turning informer.

His phone rang as he was making a coffee. It was Ed Webster, the investigating officer from the illegal wildlife trade sector of Hawks who'd been assigned to the case.

"Hi, mate," Ed said. "Can you talk now? I hear you were up at the security guards' station earlier. Anything to report?"

"I've just got back," Ryan replied. "I spoke to the head guard, Albert, about one of our new guys and whether he has any suspicions about him."

"I presume you do, otherwise you wouldn't be checking?"

"I don't have any direct proof, only…" Ryan searched for the right word "…a feeling. Plus, I did see him wearing an Elephant Sands baseball cap recently, and as you know, the Marula guys found one hanging on a bush near the western perimeter. Any news at your end?"

"We've traced the bullets from the poaching to a previous incursion in one of the game reserves about one hundred kilometres north of you. A southern white rhino bull was killed up there about a month ago."

Ryan juggled his phone from one ear to the other as he turned up the air conditioning. "I think I remember hearing about that. It was up near Lower Sabie, wasn't it?"

"Yeah, not far from there. I'll send you the details now. Anyway, it was similar modus operandi – the poachers cut a hole where cameras were down and came in and out quickly, undetected."

Ryan cursed. "Do you think there's a cell operating in the area?"

"It's more than likely. Same bullets, same method. And no doubt using inside help on both occasions."

Ryan took another sip of his coffee. "That's all we need. I'll speak to Rob and other private game reserves in the surrounding community. I guess we need to be on full alert."

Ed gave a rueful laugh. "That's for sure. I'll keep you posted."

Ryan hung up and slumped down on the chair, thinking about the ramifications of what Ed had told him. It was all pointing to an inside job, an informer, and whilst they had found a lodge baseball cap near the scene, it would be incredibly difficult to identify the owner. The caps were worn by members of staff, but visitors often bought them as souvenirs. All they really had at the moment was the connection of the gun used at both incidents.

He rubbed his eyes and switched on his computer. He'd read the forensics report Ed had sent through about the bullets, and when Rio came in, they'd have a quick debrief. He was still convinced there was an informer. How else would the poachers have known to cut the fence at the exact spot where the sensors were down? Not to mention their appearance on the concession two days after the arrival of the rhino cow and her calf. Coincidences never came in pairs.

A messaged pinged on his phone. It was Neil.

Hi. Got your messages. Are you around now to chat?

Ryan checked the time. Kate was due over soon to take a look at the ops room, but he didn't want to keep exchanging messages with Neil. He could always ask Rio or Clemmie to show Kate the ropes. He really wanted to speak to Neil.

He messaged Neil back. *Give me ten minutes and I'll call you.*

He pocketed his phone and headed into the ops room where he found Rio sitting in front of a computer, leaning close to the monitor, his eyes darting back and forth across the screen as he read. It made Ryan smile.

"You really need to get your eyes tested, mate," he told him.

Rio rubbed his eyes. "You're probably right, or it could be that my eyes are allergic to roster tables."

They grinned at each other and Ryan relaxed into a seat opposite. Rio was calm and clear-headed. A good friend and great colleague. Someone he could trust implicitly.

"How did you sleep?" Rio asked. "I slept a full twelve hours."

"Not the best," Ryan admitted. "I was so exhausted I thought I would drop off the minute I hit the pillow, but unfortunately I had some bad news before I went to bed, so it kind of threw things."

Rio sat up straight in the chair, his face creased in concern. "Oh no. Was it about the poaching?"

Ryan stared out of the small window next to his desk. He swallowed thickly. "No. I had some news, from England. One of my army mates died yesterday."

Rio's face fell and he wheeled his chair across the office closer to Ryan. "What happened?"

Ryan explained about Jim, glad of Rio's quiet and gentle presence. After Gavin and Sara, Rio was the closest friend he had now.

Rio listened quietly, his eyes gentle and kind. "I'm so sorry. Are you okay?"

"Thanks, Rio, I'm all right, but shocked and sad. He was a good guy." He gestured towards Rio's computer. "I've got some updates from Ed Webster about the bullets. I'll forward you the report and you can take a look. Also, we've got Sara's journalist friend, Kate, coming to the office shortly. She arrived yesterday morning. I took her up to the poaching site yesterday morning. I don't think you had a chance to meet her."

Rio shook his head. "What's she like?"

"She's okay. She was naturally upset at seeing the dead rhino but she rallied. I don't think she'll get in the way too much." He stretched his arms above his head. "To be honest, we could really do without a journalist following us around."

Rio arched an eyebrow. "I would have thought it's the best time to have someone here. She is here to write about poaching, isn't she?"

"True…but I have enough on my plate at the moment without having to deal with babysitting a journo."

The office door opened, bringing with it a blast of heat and patrol officer Clemmie. She stared at the two men leaning back in their chairs and quipped, "Busy at work, guys?"

Ryan laughed, feeling the tension in his shoulders ease a little. He told Clemmie about spotting the wild dogs that morning.

She was pleased. "I thought they might stick around for a while."

An idea struck Ryan. As a female ranger, Clemmie would be an ideal person for Kate to meet. "Clemmie, I'm so snowed under with paperwork—" he waved a hand at his computer "—that I need you to do me a favour."

She folded her arms in front of her. "I'm not doing any photocopying. Besides, it's broken again."

"No, don't panic," Ryan said. "I thought you might want to help out with the journalist who's staying here at the moment. Maybe give her a female perspective on being a ranger."

Clemmie laughed. "You mean take her off your hands?"

Ryan blushed. "No, not at all. I was out on patrol with her this morning and I took her up to the poaching site yesterday. She's here to write about poaching for a UK paper, but I think she might like to have a more holistic view of conservation than just guns and dead rhinos." He shuffled some papers on his desk and glanced up at Clemmie. "I would really appreciate your help. She's over having breakfast at the moment. Would you mind popping over to get her and we can give her a tour of the ops room? I need to make a call in a minute, and it would be great if the two of you could start off the tour."

"Sure," Clemmie replied, giving Ryan a cheeky grin, "and on the way here, I can fill her in on you two, and your annoying habits."

Rio aimed a screwed-up piece of paper at her as she left, but it only made it halfway across the floor. Their banter lightened the mood, but as he headed back to his office to call Neil, the sorrow of Jim's death came flooding back. He was dreading the conversation. But the call went straight to voicemail. Ryan couldn't decide if it was a good thing or not. As much as he didn't want to hear all about Jim and what had happened, he did need to speak to Neil. To connect.

Chapter Twelve

The dining area was quiet when Kate arrived for breakfast. Most of the guests were still out on a game drive and she sat out on the deck by a tree with wide, sweeping branches that offered some relief from the heat. She sipped her coffee and enjoyed a plate of colourful tropical fruits. The enticing aroma of bacon was too much to resist and she helped herself to some eggs and toast as well. She never normally ate this much for breakfast. It must be all that fresh air.

In the tree next to her, a bird was making a loud, nasal whoop. Kate twisted her neck and stared up at it. It was pale grey with a long tail and a crest of feathers above its head. It glared back at her, repeating its loud call twice. Its cry was familiar.

"It's a go-away bird," a voice interrupted.

It was a slender young woman dressed smartly in a ranger uniform. Her face, pretty with high cheekbones and full lips, stretched into a wide smile.

Kate returned her smile. "A what?"

"It's a grey lourie bird but is usually known as the go-away bird, because that is what it sounds like it is saying when it calls out."

Kate inspected the bird again. Two others had joined it, and they babbled away at each other. She listened carefully as they made their call, picking out the 'go away' phrase.

She laughed. "I see what you mean."

"I'm Clemmie," the young woman told her. "Ryan asked me to find you." She gestured towards her empty plate. "If you are ready, I can take you to the ops room."

Kate wiped her mouth on a napkin and collected her notebook and bag. "Yes, thank you." She held out her hand to Clemmie. "It's nice to meet you. Ryan showed me the pack of wild dogs you've been researching, yesterday."

Clemmie beamed. "Yes, I've been monitoring them for quite a few months now. It was great you saw them. They are often way over the other side of the reserve."

They left the cool shade of the veranda, heading towards a group of buildings behind a large wooden fence. Clemmie gestured to a long building with several doors and a narrow porch running the entire length. "This is the staff living quarters."

Kate smiled. "I'm quartered here, too, in the Mopane hut. Do most of the staff live here the whole time?"

"They tend to work six weeks on then two weeks off, but it depends on their job and how far away they live."

"That must be hard for people with families."

"It is," Clemmie agreed, "but at least they can provide well for them."

At the other side of the compound stood a large wooden building with several satellite dishes on the roof. Next to it were two big kennels and a fenced-off area with concrete and grass. The head of a dog was lying half in and half out of the shade of the kennel, a long tongue protruding from its mouth.

"Are they guard dogs?"

"They are our anti-poaching K9 unit. Elvis and Elton are highly trained tracking dogs."

At the sound of their names, both dogs came running and sniffed at Clemmie's hands through the metal fence.

Kate took a step back. "They're huge. What breed are they?"

"Elvis is a Bloodhound – he's our tracker dog – and Elton is a Belgian Malinois, a prime attack dog. I'm one of their handlers. They are really hard-working and skilled at tracking down suspicious or unwanted people on the reserve." She crouched and crooned at one of them. "They're big softies really."

Kate wasn't so sure. She wasn't a fan of big dogs. "They don't look soft to me."

"They're not meant to be pets," Ryan cut in. He appeared at the door of the ops room, a coffee mug in his hand. "They're trained to track and attack if necessary to help us apprehend poachers and criminals."

Clemmie gave a rueful grin. "He's right." She winked at Kate. "But they do have a soft side."

Inside, the air was pleasantly cool and her eyes adjusted to the darkness of the room. Several computers and monitors were placed along one wall, each one showing a different picture. Kate peered closely at one of them, recognising the main entrance to the game reserve, with the date and time detailed below. Another screen showed part of a perimeter fence, which ran along a track.

A tall young man strolled across the office towards them.

Ryan gestured to Kate. "Rio, this is Kate Harper."

Kate held out her hand to shake Rio's. "Nice to meet you, Rio."

Rio's grin was wide and friendly. "You too, Kate. Welcome to Elephant Sands."

Ryan gave her a tour of the office, explaining all the various security locations to her and showed her a large monitor on which the digital location of each patrol member was indicated by green or red marker points.

"This shows the exact locations of various patrol members when they are on checks. It helps us gauge where everyone is when we need to respond urgently."

Kate was fascinated by the security measures. It was amazing that it took all of this to keep a sixty-square-kilometre reserve safe.

Ryan's phone rang and he excused himself to take the call. Kate toured the room, chatting to Clemmie and Rio and asking questions. In the adjacent room, Ryan was visible through a small glass panel. His face was serious as he spoke, his shoulders slumped and his face downcast. He looked up and caught her staring. Embarrassed, she moved away and headed towards the other wall with the monitors.

Pulling out her camera, she snapped a few shots, thinking of a line she might use to describe the control room. She was imagining something like 'in the high-tech world of anti-poaching' when suddenly a hand grabbed her camera and Ryan's angry face was in front of her, his lips curled into a snarl.

"What the hell are you doing? You can't take photos in here. There's lots of highly sensitive equipment and information on view."

She gasped in shock, surprised at his sudden change of mood. He was holding her camera firmly in his hand, a vein throbbing in his neck. Clemmie watched them both over the top of her monitor, her eyes darting between them.

Kate's eyes blinked. "I'm sorry! Only you let me take photos at the poaching site yesterday, so I assumed this would be okay."

Rio glared at Ryan and prised the camera from his grip. "I am sure she meant no harm."

Ryan stared mutinously at the floor, his cheeks flushed red. Rio handed the camera back to Kate. "Security is highly important. There's always a potential threat of information leaking out to the wrong hands. It's important to maintain that level of security. Some poaching syndicates are quite sophisticated."

"Fair enough," Kate said, switching on her camera, finding the photos she'd taken and deleting them. She understood that everyone was nervous at the moment, especially if it was possible they had an informer in the team, but Ryan didn't need to be so rude. It was a complete turnaround. Was he annoyed with her for probing about his army past earlier?

She gazed defiantly at Ryan. "All deleted. From now on, I'll ask beforehand." She placed the camera back in her bag. "I usually take photos alongside notes and taped interviews as an aide-memoire. I rarely use any of my own photos in the actual article."

A pulse throbbed in Ryan's neck. "Nevertheless, I would prefer no photos of any sensitive information."

They stood awkwardly in the middle of the room. Kate was about to change the subject when the tinny sound of her cell phone rang from the depths of her backpack. It was Allan Prescott. She groaned inwardly. Talk about bad timing, but she really wanted to speak to him. She gestured towards her phone and exited the building to take the call, feeling Ryan's eyes on her as she left.

Allan's voice was excited. "I'm so glad to finally speak to you, Miss Harper. I have some good news. Have you read my emails about finding Alison's brother?"

"Yes," Kate gasped. "Have you found out more?"

Allan's accent was thick and he spoke quickly. Kate had to concentrate to keep up. "I've managed to get hold of a phone number for Jacques Voester in Pretoria. I can send it to you now and I've also emailed across a scanned photo of Alison's student card when she was at university. It's the only image we can find. As I said, there's very little information about her at all since the late 1980s."

Kate's heart thudded in her ears. With Ginny and Geoffrey both being only children, Kate had never had any relatives other than her grandparents. On her mother's side, her grandparents had been in her life until her early twenties. She'd loved her Scottish gran and grandpa and had spent many summers in their holiday home on the Fife coast, enjoying the beautiful beaches and walks. Her father's parents had lived in Spain, an eccentric pair who doted on their only grandchild. But all four were long dead and with her parents' deaths, she had assumed she was all alone now. But now she had unearthed an uncle.

"That would be great. Hopefully, he will be able to tell us more about Alison, or maybe even where she is."

'If she is still alive," Allan pointed out. "Sorry to be blunt, but given the lack of information about her in the public domain, it is possible she is deceased."

Kate didn't want to believe that. Not now that she'd come all this way. "Surely you would have found a death notification in your searches. I'll call Jacques Voester today. He's got to know more."

"Who's got to know more?"

She whirled around and found Ryan standing directly behind her, his eyes cold.

Her face grew hot. "I've got to go," she whispered into the phone. "Please email me the photo and the contact details and keep me informed of any further information you dig up."

When she'd hung up, she saw Ryan was still standing by the office door frowning at her. "Who were you talking to?"

Kate was incredulous. "It's nothing to do with the article," she retorted. It *was* none of Ryan's business. He'd been rude to shout at her about taking photos earlier and even ruder now for interrupting a personal call. What had got into him?

He stared at her, his eyes unreadable, before eventually shrugging and heading back towards the office. She sagged with relief. It was scorching now, even though it was only eleven o'clock in the morning. The sun was like a white-hot laser, its powerful beams piercing her skin. She was flustered and desperately wanted to get away from Ryan's prying eyes – to regroup.

She called out to him. "Actually, Ryan—" he popped his head back through the open door "—I'm going to call it a day. I'm still tired from the long day yesterday and would like to freshen up and go through my notes from today. Can we talk this evening if you're free? Perhaps make a plan for tomorrow and I'll run some questions by you."

Ryan leant against the door jamb, his voice flat. "It's boma night, so we'll have to work around that."

Kate remembered Sara mentioning the guest braai evening. It was a weekly special event where guests and staff ate together under the stars in a makeshift boma, or kraal.

"Okay. Listen, I'm sorry about the camera thing earlier. I…" But he'd already shut the door firmly in her face.

She poked her tongue out at the closed door and headed across the compound towards the lodge, eager to call Jacques Voester. Despite what the PI had suggested, she had to believe that Alison was still alive.

At reception, she found Sara, fresh as a daisy after her morning off, greeting guests arriving from airport pickups. Kate watched as her friend deftly helped an elderly couple into the building, making sure they were given cool drinks and flannels to rinse away the sweat of travel.

Sara's eyes lit up. "How was your morning? Did Ryan show you around?"

Kate told her all about the pack of wild dogs they'd seen in the morning.

"Clemmie told me they were back. They have a vast territory, stretching further north towards Sabie Sands. Have you met Clemmie yet?"

"Yes, this morning. She took me over to the ops room. She's lovely and so brave handling those big anti-poaching dogs every day."

"She's great and is one of our most knowledgeable members of the ranger team. Sadly, we're going to lose her soon. She's off to university in Johannesburg to study ecology."

"That's brilliant. And how exciting for her."

"I know." Sara groaned. "But we will miss her. She got a full scholarship too. She's one bright cookie."

"Well, she definitely knows a lot about animals and plants." She nudged Sara's arm. "As do you."

Sara's eyes twinkled. "I know, I'm amazing, but I do have help." She gave a wink. "I am married to a rather gorgeous ranger. Talking of rangers, how are you getting on with Ryan?"

Kate pulled a face. "O-k-a-y. I thought things were going well. This morning we visited the patrol gate and he spoke with Albert about Leonard. He didn't get much information, but I think he feels Leonard might be involved. We came back here and I had breakfast then joined him at the ops room with Clemmie and Rio—" she frowned "—and then he practically bit my head off about taking photos. I wasn't going to publish them or anything."

Sara's lower lip stuck out. "I thought you two would hit it off."

Kate pointed her finger at Sara. "Don't go matchmaking, Sara. I am here to write a story and nothing else. Okay?"

Sara rolled her eyes. "Yes, boss, but you know, it's been a while since you've dated anyone. How long has it been? Two years or more? There was that Richard guy, who I thought sounded great, by the way, and then no one since."

Kate huffed. "I haven't really been in the mood for dating recently, Sara. In case you didn't notice, I've just lost both my parents."

"I know, and I didn't mean it like that. But unless you've been hiding a secret lover, I get the feeling you've been on your own for a while."

Kate stared at the ground, pushing her foot across the coir matting of the reception floor. "I'm fine, Sara. I decided to have a break from dating after Richard and I broke up. It's all so tiring and tedious and then I was busy with work and then with my parents…"

Sara hugged her. "I'm sorry. I shouldn't have pushed you. And as for Ryan, he shouldn't have shouted at you." She jerked her head towards the ops room. "I'll have a word with him."

Kate shook her head furiously. "Please don't, Sara. I don't want to cause any problems and he's busy trying to solve this poaching case, plus he's no doubt upset about his friend's death." She pointed to the reception office. "Any chance I could use the office to make a call? I need somewhere with a good cell-phone signal."

"Of course, but come to our quarters. We have our own booster. And it will be quieter."

Kate followed Sara down a path towards the back of the main building, dodging sprinklers as she went. A go-away bird flew up to a branch and gave its distinctive call. A frangipani flower fluttered to the floor in front of her and she picked it up, taking in the heavy scent of the waxy petals. The fragrance triggered a memory, flickering across her mind like an old cine film.

In her mind's eye she saw a picnic blanket under a blue sky, the go-away bird echoing in the background, and a woman, tall and slender, barefoot with a silver charm anklet, dancing to George Michael's 'Faith'. The images slammed into her, causing a wave of dizziness, and she leant against a tree trunk, watching the retreating back of Sara as she walked up the path.

She'd seen that scene before, had dreamt it, and when George Michael died, she'd heard the song played on the radio, feeling an unusual pull towards it. Who was that woman? Could it be her real mother? Or was it just her mind playing tricks on her?

Chapter Thirteen

Kate waited for Sara to return to reception before dialling her uncle's number. They'd chatted for a while over a coffee, but Kate's thoughts kept slipping back to her uncle and what she would say to him. She felt guilty for not filling Sara in about the search for her real mother. She would no doubt be a great support. But what if Allan was right and it turned out to be all for nothing and Alison was dead?

The phone rang a few times before a man's voice sounded down the line. "*Wie is dit?*"

He was speaking Afrikaans. It hadn't occurred to her he might not speak English. She hesitated. "Hello…do you speak English? Is that Jacques Voester?"

His voice was deep and melodic. "Yes, who is this?"

"My name is Kate Harper. I don't know how to say this… but I am your niece. I have just discovered that Alison, your sister, is my real mother and I…"

His voice was raised. "I'm sorry, what did you say?"

Kate repeated her statement. "I'm your niece. I asked a private investigator to search for my biological mother, Alison Voester. There's virtually no information about her since the late 1980s, but the PI found you. The only information we have is that she was born in 1960 in the Bot River district of the Western Cape. We also know she studied at Cape Town university from 1979–1982 and then after that it all gets a bit patchy. No tax or health records, nothing."

His voice dropped a notch. "You are really Alison's daughter?"

"Yes, I only found out a few months ago, and as I was coming to South Africa for work, I thought I would try to find her."

He was silent for a while and Kate heard him breathing softly down the phone line. She carried on, gabbling into the silence.

"After my parents, Ginny and Geoffrey Harper, were killed in a car accident six months ago, I discovered a hidden birth certificate, my original one, which recorded Geoffrey as my father but Alison Voester as my mother. The birth certificate I have had all my life was a certified copy dated three years after my birth." She paused, emotion rising in her chest. "I grew up completely unaware that Ginny wasn't my real mother. All I can assume is that my father had an affair with Alison and I was the result." She gave a wry laugh. "Of course, I can't corroborate that as they're no longer with us."

Jacques whistled through his teeth. "I am sorry to hear about your parents' deaths. It must have been a shock for you, finding out the truth like that. I *do* have a sister called Alison, and she *did* have a child. I think the baby was born around 1984. I haven't had any contact with her since then." He sighed. "We were once close but we drifted apart. She was studying at Cape Town university in the early eighties, and I met up with her occasionally before I moved to Pretoria. She'd fallen out with our parents and was trying to pay her way through a master's degree." His voice became thick with emotion. "Alison was very bright, much brighter than the rest of the family. I had no idea she'd had a baby until one day she contacted me out of the blue to tell me she had a two-year-old daughter. That was around 1986, I think, as my wife Anneka and I had already moved to Pretoria. As you can imagine, the news was a surprise. Anyway, I travelled to Cape Town to see her. Anneka had just had our first child and I wanted to see Alison again and try to patch things up. I'd missed her."

Kate's heart fluttered in her chest. "Was I there? When you met her?"

"Yes. The little girl, you, was a sweet thing, the spitting image of Alison, a riot of red curls and hazel eyes. You sat quietly at the table colouring in and chatting away to yourself."

Kate's heart almost stopped. "What happened, at that meeting?"

"There was something not quite right about Alison. She'd always been highly strung, but she behaved strangely; she was nervous and wouldn't make eye contact. She wouldn't tell me who the father was or what had happened. She said she was broke and needed money, urgently. I have to say I was shocked. I was expecting a happy family reunion not a demand for money."

"Did you give her any money?"

"Yes, although not very much. I'd only just got married and had a child and I wasn't earning a lot. I gave her what few savings we had. I remember Anneka was furious with me at the time. She'd never met Alison so she didn't understand the bond we'd once had."

"What happened to break that bond? You said you drifted apart…"

Jacques's voice grew defensive. "I loved my sister, don't get me wrong. There were four children in our family and she was the only girl and the youngest. We grew up on a sheep farm and our father was strict. He spent his days working the land and his nights praying. Alison was different; she had a passion for nature and for animals. She refused to conform and when she was a teenager it turned into rebellion, which needless to say didn't go down well with our father. She managed to get a full scholarship to university to study biology and she never really went home after that."

"What happened after you gave her the money?" Kate asked.

Jacques's voice sounded sad. "I didn't hear from her for months after and then our mother died and I contacted her on the only telephone number I had. It rang and rang and a woman eventually answered. She didn't know where Alison was, but I left a message in case. I rang a couple of other friends who knew her, and I wasn't sure if she'd received the messages until she arrived unannounced at the funeral. She came late and sat at the back of the church. By the time the coffin was being lowered into the ground she'd disappeared again and I didn't get a chance to speak to her. When someone doesn't want to be found…"

"How long ago was that?" Kate asked.

His voice trembled softly down the line. "Must be at least thirty-two years."

Kate pondered his words, doodling the dates on her notepad. "I left South Africa with my parents when I was three. That was thirty-two years ago now. So, she'd probably given me up by then…"

She tried to imagine this invisible woman, her real mother, attending the funeral of an estranged parent so soon after she'd given up her own child. She wondered what it must have been like for her.

Kate hesitated before asking the next question. "Do you think she is dead?"

Jacques's voice was gruff. "I honestly don't know. I'm sorry, I know you want answers, but the telephone is not really the best place to talk about these things."

Kate's heart squeezed in her chest. "You're right. I'm sorry, I've rather bombarded you with questions. Can we meet? I am currently staying in the Kruger, but I could get to Johannesburg. I understand you live near there?"

"Yes, in Pretoria. It's only an hour's drive down to Johannesburg."

Kate thought quickly; she really wanted to meet Jacques, to find out more about her mother. But how would she manage to do that without revealing to Sara what she was doing? She stared up at a wedding photo on the wall of Sara and Gavin, their smiling, happy faces beaming out at her. She would have to think of some way of doing this without arousing Sara's interest too much. Kate would present it all to Sara when she knew more, when she could tell her the facts. At the moment it was still a mystery waiting to be solved.

"I really appreciate you talking to me. It's been a stressful time for me, especially coming on top of my parents' deaths. Let me work out my schedule over the next few days and I'll call you back. If that's okay?"

"Yes, of course," Jacques agreed. "It is indeed a

shock, but a nice one, nonetheless. I must admit, I did wonder about you from time to time. I have two sons and a grandchild now. There have been many times when I thought of Alison and wished I could share my family with her." His voice was wistful. "Have you had a good life with your parents?"

A lump formed in Kate's throat. Despite her parents' lies, she'd been loved. "Yes. My parents were wonderful and I was extremely happy. It's just…" she didn't know how to voice it properly "…when I found out the truth, I was hurt. I thought my parents had a happy marriage. I am struggling to accept that my father got Alison pregnant when he was married to Ginny, my mother, and that Alison was somehow forced to give me up."

Jacques's voice was gentle. "That may not be the case. She may not have been forced. Adults make difficult decisions for the sake of their children. It may have been the best thing for you and for Alison at the time."

Kate bit her lip. "I suppose you are right. The frustrating thing is I will never know the truth. Not unless I can find Alison and ask her."

Kate thought about this later as she was walking back to the main lodge from Sara's cottage, the conversation with her uncle swirling around in her head. It was late afternoon and the sun was dipping low in the sky, another beautiful sunset on its way. Back at her room, she stared down at the waterhole, her mind furiously trying to make sense of it all – of why she'd begged Greg to give her this assignment, of why she wanted to search for a woman who had given her away so easily.

She thought of Uncle Patrick the last time she'd seen him, before she'd left for South Africa. He'd expressed concern about Kate rushing off in search of Alison.

"I can understand you wanting to know more," he'd said, "but I think you should take some time to plan it a bit more, not go rushing off in an emotional state. Let the PI do some digging. Your mother and father loved you so much, and I know you're angry with them, but knowing your parents, knowing who they were, I am sure there was a good reason for all of this."

Tears had filled Kate's eyes and she'd dashed them away. He was right. She was angry and she felt betrayed. But she was determined to find out the truth. It was all she had now.

She had given Uncle Patrick a steely glare. "That may be, but it's my decision. Put yourself in my place. Everything I ever knew about my life has been turned upside down. I have absolutely no idea who I am."

Uncle Patrick's brown eyes had been sorrowful. "You are still the same Katie Harper you always were. You are the clever and strong young woman your parents raised. Ginny may not be your biological mother, but you are every bit her daughter. You have her intelligence and her strength. Sometimes it's about nurture rather than nature."

Chapter Fourteen

Ryan drove out of the lodge, the late afternoon sun fierce on the back of his neck. He didn't really know where he was going, only that he needed to get away from it all, from the office, the lodge, the memories.

After Rio and Clemmie had left for lunch and other duties, he'd chewed his way around a sandwich, not really tasting it, his eyes scanning forensic reports from the police and images from the cameras' footage. Apart from the bullet match, there was nothing much else to go on. No clues, nothing. The Elephant Sands cap found near the boundary with the neighbouring reserve yielded only partial fingerprints. He hoped they'd get a breakthrough soon.

More than anything, Ryan needed to clear his head about Jim. His conversation with Neil earlier had been as grim as he'd imagined. Neil had been at Jim's house with Heather at the time and had taken the call outside.

Ryan heard the despair in Neil's voice as he filled him in. "It was a big shock," he'd said. "Heather really thought he was doing okay. He'd been seeing a counsellor for a while and had recently changed jobs. She said he was happy. They had even been planning a trip to Disneyland

Paris in the next school holidays."

They'd spoken for a while before Neil's phone was interrupted with another call. After he'd hung up, Ryan stared down at the desk, trying to imagine what Heather and the kids must be going through, about the life ahead of them without Jim in it. He knew lots of soldiers suffered from PTSD. When you'd spent time in a war zone, it was hard to unravel what you faced on a daily basis. The scars weren't just those on the surface, the physical ones.

Out on the reserve, the air was still. Clouds drifted in slow motion, white puff-balls in the sky. A headache prodded at his brow, and when he reached the top of a small hill, he pulled the jeep over and climbed out. This was one of his favourite views and it was quiet, just him and the bush spread out below, a few granite boulders punctuating the valley. He grabbed his water bottle and took a seat on a large boulder, the top of which had flattened out over the passage of time, making a perfect place to sit and think.

He couldn't believe Jim had killed himself after all this time, that despite everything, a wife and family, he'd really never recovered from that day. Lord knows Ryan had tried hard to forget, had trained himself not to let those thoughts come back. But every now and then they did. The flash of an explosion as an IED flipped the armoured vehicle in front of his. The horror of watching two of his team manning the truck being blown to tiny pieces in front of him.

And it should have been him. He was meant to be driving the first truck, the one that checked for mines, but he'd hurt his shoulder the day before, playing football in the compound, and didn't feel up to driving. He'd swapped at the last minute, sending Jim instead. Jim had rolled his eyes and called Ryan a sissy. Only a few hours later Jim lay in a field hospital with half his body blown away. The two other soldiers, scouser Jamie and posh boy Matt lay scattered on the ground, their blood seeping into the red dust.

At first, after the incident, he'd been angry and had wanted answers, to ensure that what happened to the two men in the patrol would never happen again. They'd been sent in with no warning, no plan. But the army was not interested in retrospection and he'd been unable to find his way back. Leaving the army had been the most painful, and the best, thing he'd ever done. Painful because he didn't know what to do outside of it, and best because he couldn't carry on pretending he cared.

He stared down into the valley, trying to find the peace it usually gave him. This place had got under his skin; its fragile beauty was embedded in his soul. But now that too had been violated, with the brutal poaching of the rhino.

Below, a giraffe and her calf, majestic in the golden sunlight, ambled out of the scrub and into view. Ryan watched them browse on the nearby shrubs, the mother's mouth moving from side to side as she masticated pieces of thorn from the bushes. Ryan's heart lifted as the calf frolicked along, curious and adventurous, pushing his patient mother's boundaries.

Two zebras trotted across the road, their tails swishing away flies. An oxpecker bird landed on the zebra's back, busy feeding from the microscopic insects that lived there. A common view out here in the bush. It grounded him somehow. It was hard to remember there was a whole world out there, beyond the boundaries of the reserve.

He reluctantly made his way back to the jeep, his

movement sending the skittish giraffe and her calf back into the thicket. Over to the east was the poaching site, a place that would now forever be associated with death. Frustration and anger bubbled inside him. It was impossible to cover every inch of the reserve, but he'd thought they did a pretty good job of protecting it. Occasionally, they would find tracks and snares and evidence of poacher encampments, but the killing of the rhino had spooked him. It was like an omen somehow, a portent of something much worse. One he couldn't shake off no matter how much he tried.

He moved the jeep on, bumping over the large rocks and rough track heading towards the lodge. Much as he loved spending hours watching the natural world unfold in front of him, he had a job to do and it was time to get back to business.

As he reversed the jeep under the shade near the office, he caught a glimpse of Kate walking across the compound, her head down, shoulders rounded as if she was upset. Guilt flickered through him. He'd been unnecessarily rude to her earlier, overreacting to her taking photos in the ops room. He didn't really know why he'd behaved like that. He didn't like losing control of things, and now with Jim's death as well as the poaching, it was as if all control was slipping through his fingers like water through a sieve.

But it was more than that. Kate's behaviour in the ops room and the mysterious way she took the phone call afterwards had triggered a memory in Ryan, one which, alongside the last twenty-four hours, had left him feeling more than a little unnerved.

Chapter Fifteen

The aromas from the cooking hit Kate the minute she stepped down from the lodge's dining room onto the path leading towards the outdoor area where the evening meal was to be served. Inside the boma, she found a space at the end of a long wooden table adorned with lanterns.

The man on her right, an American called Dave, introduced himself and his two teenage daughters, Megan and Beth. They were on a ten-day holiday of South Africa, their first time in the country and his first time with the kids as a single dad. Within minutes of her taking the seat next to him, he'd told her his entire history, from marriage to his college sweetheart and his job as a company executive for an oil firm, to the birth of his daughters and more recently, the bitter divorce. Kate listened patiently and responded in the right places. She was happy to sit and let a complete stranger take the lead. Anything to take her mind off the conversation with her uncle.

Dave was an attractive man, tall and blonde with a charming personality. He was good company, asking her about herself without being too pushy or nosy. The girls were sweet, a little shy at first, the eldest, Megan, behaving like a classic teenager, with the occasional pout when her father told her to put her phone away. Kate began to relax. Sara and Gavin were busy hosting separate tables and she would occasionally catch Sara's eyes and share a smile.

Ryan arrived shortly after they'd sat down to eat, taking a seat opposite and placing his bottle of beer on the table. They hadn't spoken since their disagreement in the ops room and she was surprised when he leant forward and greeted her.

"Kate, I'm sorry I was rude to you this morning. I know you didn't realise about using the camera, and I shouldn't have reacted the way I did." He ran his fingers through his hair. "I know it's no excuse, but I guess I am a little out of sorts after the news of my friend Jim's death."

Kate met his eyes. He was genuinely remorseful and she clinked her wine glass against his beer bottle. "Thanks, Ryan. I can only imagine what you must be going through, and with the investigation on top of it, you're bound to be stressed. I'll try not to take it personally."

Ryan grimaced. "Please don't. I can be a bit of grumpy old git at times."

Kate laughed, the tension between them easing. "That's what Sara said."

Ryan folded his arms in mock anger. "Did she now?"

As if they'd conjured her up, Sara appeared by the table, smiling down at them. "Have you two made up? I hope you have apologised, Ryan."

"All done, ma'am." Ryan saluted her.

"Good, otherwise I'd have to bang your heads together."

Kate laughed and all tension dissipated. She introduced Ryan to Dave and his daughters, smiling inwardly at the teenage girls' immediate interest in Ryan as they bombarded him with questions about his work and the game reserve. Throughout the meal, which was a self-service buffet of delicious local dishes served on a table by the barbecue, Ryan chatted with the two girls, their faces flushed in the lantern light.

Sitting under the soft light of the lanterns with the delicious red wine flowing through her veins, Kate had to admit Ryan was incredibly attractive. He was charming, patiently looking at the photos the girls proudly showed him on their cameras, his eyes crinkling up at the edges as he chatted. And his wide shoulders and muscular physique only added to his appeal.

At one point, Ryan caught her staring at him. She flushed, grateful for the dim light around the table. He was watching her and Dave, leaning forward to join in their conversation.

"Is this your first time to South Africa?" Dave asked her.

"I was actually born in South Africa. My parents were lecturers at Cape Town university at the time and we moved back to England when I was three."

Dave topped up Kate's wine glass. "How much do you remember about your time in Cape Town?"

"Very little," Kate replied. "I do remember seeing elephants somewhere and also watching a cheetah catch an antelope, but it's all a bit of a blur." She laughed. "Funnily enough, one of my earliest memories as a young child was watching the changing of the guards at Buckingham Palace. I took my Nelly the toy elephant with me. I still have her somewhere."

"Is this the first time you've been back to South Africa since then?" Ryan asked.

Her eyes met his across the table. "Yes."

"And what do your parents think about you finally coming back to your birth country?" Dave asked.

Kate plastered a smile on her face. "My parents both passed away recently, in a car accident. I hadn't really planned on coming until an opportunity arose at work to write an article about poaching. I've been wanting to visit Sara—" she waved towards her "—ever since she moved to work here, so I jumped at the chance. When I am finished the article, I am hoping to spend a bit more time with her and maybe even do some volunteer work." She spread out her arms. "The world is my oyster, and to be honest, I do need a break, or rather, a change."

Dave's face creased up in concern. "I am so sorry about your parents." He reached across and gently touched her arm, keeping his hand on it for a few seconds. Ryan stared at Dave's hand on her arm and she shifted in her seat, changing the subject and asking Megan and Beth about their school and friends.

Later, whilst staff members entertained them with a traditional song and dance, she found her eyes straying back to Ryan's side profile as he watched the performance. Stubble grazed his cheeks and square jaw, and she wondered what it would feel like against her skin. Heat rushed through her and she sipped her wine, trying to focus on the performers. Drooling like a schoolgirl over an attractive man was not her usual style.

The entertainment finished with rapturous applause, and guests drifted away from the table, returning to their rooms, or retiring to the bar. Kate wondered whether to go to her room or join Sara and Gavin. Ryan had disappeared and she was disappointed at not having the chance to speak to him again to find out the plans for the next day.

She went in search of Sara, finding her with a group of guests, explaining their departure plans for the following day. Kate hovered in the background, flicking through the huge visitors' book, its pages filled with names and messages from tourists from all over the world. Outside, the sky was indigo, fringed by the fierce orange glow of the fire pit. She made out the shapes of guests as they took their seats around the fire, sparks jumping up into the air like fireflies.

Sara made her way over and linked her arm through Kate's. "I am sorry I haven't spent much time with you today, Kate. It's our main guest interaction evening and so it's manic."

"Don't worry. Can you spare some time now? Let's grab a drink and talk about tomorrow's plans."

Sara's face fell. "I can't right now. The guests I was speaking to have had their flight to Johannesburg tomorrow cancelled and I need to go to the office and try to sort something else out for them. Otherwise, they will miss their connecting flight to the States."

"Don't worry, it's fine. I'll probably head off to bed soon anyway. Send me a message about the morning." She groaned. "I'll assume I am getting the usual early wake-up call and make sure I am ready."

"Why don't you check out the fire pit first?" Sara suggested. "It's lovely sitting there under the stars and Michael will be telling some local folk tales. They're always worth a listen." She tilted her head towards the fire. "And I think a certain handsome American tourist is keen to continue his chat with you. I spy a holiday romance."

Kate spotted Dave hovering by the steps, two glasses of wine held aloft in his hands as he nodded towards the fire.

She snorted. "Ha ha. He's on holiday with his two teenage daughters; he's hardly going to sweep me off my feet. Besides, I am not interested in any kind of relationship at the moment. I have enough to do dealing with my own problems, let alone involving anyone else."

Sara frowned. "What problems?"

Kate flinched. "Oh, nothing, you know, Mum and Dad's estate and sorting out all of that."

Sara wrinkled her nose. "Okay, well, if you're sure you don't mind my neglecting you tonight. I promise to make it up to you. I've been thinking that maybe when you have finished the article we could head to the beach for a few days. It's not far to Maputo in Mozambique or we could fly to one of the islands off Vilanculos."

"I'm definitely up for that!" Kate declared.

She gave Sara a brief hug before heading off towards the fire pit, ignoring her parting words about holiday romances. She plonked herself into one of the soft chairs by the fire, joining several others as they listened to African folk tales about the constellations.

The embers from the fire pit glowed brightly, the heat rising up, giving their faces an orange and yellow sheen. Kate watched the sparks fly up into the air and disintegrate back down into the fire. The sky above was bright with the glow of the waning moon and the stars twinkling like a thousand fairy lights. She sat back, resting her head on the soft pillow of the chair, and gazed up into the sky, the buzz of conversation flowing around her.

Dave took the seat next to her and handed her a glass of red wine. "The stars are incredible, aren't they?"

"They are amazing," Kate agreed. "Where are the girls?"

"I took them back to our room. They're talking to their mom. It's early morning back in Connecticut." He stretched his arms up and stared up at the sky. "Man, that sky is beautiful."

Kate had to agree and she sipped her wine and closed her eyes, trying to shut out the ever-present thoughts whirring around in her mind. She knew she would never know why her parents lied about her birth mother, but she was still struggling to accept her father's infidelity. She'd always held her father in the highest regard. He was a world-renowned professor of economics, regularly interviewed on television and author of several books. Her mother, too, was an intelligent woman with a successful career in sociology and criminology, having even worked for the Metropolitan Police Service.

What had happened? And why did they keep it from her? Sorrow lanced through her, visceral and real. She missed them like hell but their deception clouded everything.

Her sigh must have been audible, as Dave stirred from his own musing. "Care to share it? I'm a good listener, or so I've been told."

She shook her head. "Thanks, Dave. I'm just thinking through a few things. You know how it is."

They chatted companionably for a while, talking about their jobs and their travels. It was nice to converse and Kate relaxed, relishing the mellow wine and the atmosphere. A short cough sounded beside her and she found Ryan standing over her, his eyes hidden by the dark shadows that obscured his face. She stood to speak to him, wobbling slightly on the uneven surface of the ground beneath her.

Ryan grabbed her arm. "Steady."

Kate was conscious of a buzzing through her veins at his warm touch. "I think I have had too much of that delicious South African wine."

Ryan's eyes crinkled at the corners. "It can be lethal."

They stared at each other for a minute, Kate's heart galloping at a hundred miles an hour. She inhaled his cologne and it almost went to her head like the wine had.

Ryan broke the silence. "I thought I would let you know the plans for tomorrow. I spoke to the orphanage this afternoon and they're happy for us to visit, if you're interested? You can see how our orphan is getting along."

"I'd love to see the calf. You might have to pry me away when it's time to leave though."

Ryan laughed. "I'll bring some pliers."

"Good idea," Kate said, her pulse galloping like a racehorse. Ryan's closeness was a major distraction.

He carried on, oblivious to the torment going on inside her. "We'll be out most of the day. You'll need to bring all the usual – sun cream, hat and warm clothes for the early morning."

"Okay, thanks." She reached out and touched his arm again, heat sizzling up from his skin through to her hand like an electric shock. He stared down at her hand and she quickly pulled it away.

"See you at five o'clock," he said.

She watched him go, disappearing into the shadows, her fingers still tingling from where she touched him. He was an attractive and complex man, a puzzle, but she pushed away the arousal. Now was definitely not the time to get involved with someone. No matter how sexy he was.

Dave suddenly appeared at her side, waking her from her reverie and waving their empty wine glasses at her.

"One more glass?"
   She shrugged. "Why not?"

Chapter Sixteen

Ryan drove the jeep up a track and over a large rocky kopje. The pastel pink of dawn was brushed across the sky and the air was soft and sweet. He glanced at Kate sitting next to him, smiling as he watched her try to contain the escaped curls of her windswept hair.

He thought back to what he'd read on an online search of her background last night. After he'd left her by the fire pit, he'd headed back to his room, a strange sense of unease filling him. He wasn't sure if it was seeing her laughing with the American guy over dinner and sitting in the moonlight sipping wine with him, or the way he'd seen her yesterday afternoon walking across the compound, her face pensive and teary.

That she was a close friend of Sara's meant Ryan should trust her; his search certainly showed that she had great journalist credentials, but he had been alarmed to read that amongst one of her many acclaimed articles was an investigative piece for a weekend newspaper on bullying in the army.

Published about six years ago, it was well written and articulate. She clearly knew what she was doing. In his opinion, however, she had played the 'sensation' card, the classic view of an army officer shouting at cadets and driving them to suicide. It did happen from time to time, but her double-page spread made out like it was a regular thing.

Ryan was incredibly wary of journalists, having been burnt in the past by an American reporter called Gwen. He'd met her in Dubai where she was working as a foreign correspondent for a European newspaper. She'd sidled up to him in the hotel bar and her warm sense of humour and dazzling blue eyes had distracted him. He was on leave to attend an interview with a security company based in the emirate state, hoping to line up a job for when he left the army the following year.

He was angry that evening, having found out he hadn't got the job and that the investigation into the death of two of his patrol members had been thrown out. Gwen's appearance at the bar had been perfect timing. He'd been sinking a lot of beers and she'd led him to the restaurant where she'd ordered food and sat and listened to his story, her kind words soothing his depressed mind.

They'd spent the next two days together, parting with promises to keep in touch. Ryan was committed to making their relationship work, even if it meant travelling halfway around the world to be with her. She'd mesmerised him with her beauty and intelligence, and when she'd suggested that she write a piece about Afghanistan, he'd agreed, thinking it would be a more general article.

It was only a few weeks later that Ryan discovered her treachery. She'd sold his story to a newspaper in England. His name and those of his regiment had been kept out of the story but it was his tale, nonetheless. When he'd tried to contact her about it, she'd ignored all his calls and emails. He never heard from her again.

His superior officer had queried him about it, but by that stage, he was on his way out of the army. He'd made a stupid mistake in pouring out his heart to her and he'd learnt his lesson. She was a virtual stranger to him, but he'd been taken in by her beautiful face and body. He should've known better. As a man, his pride had been hurt. For the first time in his life, he'd thought he'd met someone who he could spend the rest of his life with. After the fallout from the publication, he'd steered well away from female journalists, when he could, especially attractive ones.

But his attraction to Kate was proving tricky. Every time he glimpsed her hazel eyes flecked with green, and long auburn curls, he slipped further under her spell. There was a vulnerability to her that was constantly at war with the tough, independent persona she presented. No doubt a legacy of recently losing her parents. And he was also wary of her, of what her real agenda was. For starters, he would love to know who kept calling her on her cell phone and why she seemed cagey when she took the calls.

The jeep rattled down a steep and bumpy slope and they crossed a small river. It was the end of the dry season and the water only just dampened the bottom of the tyres. On the other side of the river stretched a wide, open plain and Ryan pulled the jeep under the shade of a tree.

Kate, who'd barely spoken since she'd got in the jeep, faced him, her eyes squinted in puzzlement. "Why have we stopped?"

"Coffee time," Ryan replied. He reached down for his cell phone to check its signal. "We're waiting for Rio and Clemmie to join us. They are busy doing some snare sweeping nearby and we agreed to meet here."

Kate groaned. "God, do I need a coffee."

Ryan grinned at her. "Have a hangover, do we?"

She scowled at him. "Shut up!"

He climbed out of the jeep, going around to the back to get a flask of coffee and some biscuits out of a box on the tail of the jeep. Kate's eyes followed him as he took the provisions to the bonnet and poured out some strong, hot coffee.

He held a steaming mug of coffee up towards her. "Want some?"

She pushed her cap firmly onto her head and climbed out of the jeep, taking the coffee. "Thanks."

They sipped their coffees in companionable silence, gazing out towards the open savannah where, in the distance, several kudu and zebras were grazing. The sky was brighter now, the pinks giving way to light blue with large candy-floss clouds gliding across the sky. Ryan munched on one of the delicious oat and raisin biscuits and watched Kate unfurl as she slowly relaxed. The African bush was working its magic.

A sheen of dust blew up in the distance and the growl of a jeep broke the quiet of the early morning. Rio and Clemmie drew up alongside them, Clemmie smiling widely behind the steering wheel.

"Morning," she said, jumping out and snatching up a biscuit from the plastic box on the bonnet. "Are these Prudence's biscuits?"

She took a bite before Ryan could even answer. "Yes. Would you like one?" Ryan replied sarcastically.

He poured them both some coffee and eyed Kate again. Apart from saying hello to them both, she had still not properly spoken. Must be one hell of a hangover. Unless, he thought, something else was wrong. She'd checked her phone at least three times since they left the lodge, which was pointless given the complete lack of signal.

He closed his eyes behind his sunglasses, remembering the night before when she'd stood to speak to him. She'd wobbled on her feet and he'd found his hands automatically reaching to steady her. His senses reacted to her immediately, sending his pulse racing with the scent of her, a mixture of perfume and woman.

He was about to speak to her, to try to draw her out when Clemmie did it for him.

"So, how are you settling in, Kate?" she asked, grabbing a second biscuit.

Kate moaned. "I think I drank too much of your great South African red wine. My head was a bit sore this morning when the alarm went off."

Clemmie couldn't keep the amusement out of her voice. "I guess that's what happens when you are up late chatting up handsome guys under the stars."

Kate's lips pulled together prudishly. "I wasn't chatting anyone up."

"Sorry, only joking." Clemmie patted her arm gently. "I have some painkillers in the jeep if you need them."

"Thanks, but I've already taken some. They just need to kick in." She gave a small grimace. "Sara was telling me that you are heading off to study ecology at university."

Clemmie gave a wide grin. "Yes, in Johannesburg. I am really looking forward to it."

Ryan gave Clemmie a mock glare. "I am personally quite upset about Clemmie's departure. She's the only one who knows what's going on most of the time."

Clemmie nudged him in the ribs. "That's true. You guys will be lost without me, but I will miss Elephant Sands. I grew up living near the bush, and apart from four years living away at high school, I've always lived here. Johannesburg is a big city."

"Why did you have to live away to go to high school?" Kate asked.

"I come from a small community up in the north. It was too far to travel to the high school, over thirty kilometres, and there was no public transport, and even if there had been, we couldn't have afforded it."

Kate frowned. "Where did you live?"

"With my uncle and his wife and three children, and in return for my board, I would help my auntie around the house."

Ryan watched Kate, in full journalist mode, grill Rio and Clemmie about their lives. She certainly had a knack for making them feel more at ease. When they'd drunk their coffee and the kit was stowed away, Clemmie and Rio headed off to continue with the snare sweep.

He closed the lid of the cool box and nodded towards Kate. "Are you ready to go and see our orphan?"

Kate's soft, full lips lit up into a smile for the first time that morning. "I can't wait."

Ryan's pulse skittered. He busied himself by tidying up rubbish in the jeep. Each time he was with her the attraction grew stronger. It was a nuisance, like a fly buzzing around him. He had to keep a cool head, get through the next few days whilst she was here. There was no way he was going to make the same mistake again.

Chapter Seventeen

The jeep accelerated up a slope, rocking side to side over the deep ruts like a funfair ride. They'd been driving for over an hour now and Kate was slowly getting used to the dip and fall of the vehicle as it broached the sandy tracks. A hot, dry breeze licked at her hair, lifting the loose strands and caressing her cheek. She held her face up to the morning sky and inhaled, her hangover slowly dissipating.

She had staggered to bed shortly after the second glass of wine at the fire pit. Dave had been courteous and polite and she instinctively knew he was reaching out to her, not in any salacious way, but as someone whose life had been abruptly changed by an errant wife. He was lonely and perhaps he'd sensed that in her too. Her loneliness was driven not by hurt from a relationship, but by a feeling of being adrift, lost at sea in her own life.

She'd collapsed onto the soft bed in her room, the air conditioning chilly. The room had spun and she spent the rest of the night nauseous and fretting about her situation. Did she really want to know more about this woman who was her mother? A woman who, by the sounds of it, had run away from her family and given up a child?

She was enjoying the commission though. It was interesting to hear Ryan and the team's account of how they tracked poachers and what they were up against in their fight to protect endangered animals.

As they drove towards the orphanage, Ryan explained about snares and why they had to check regularly for them. "Snares are the cheap tools of a bush meat poacher. They are easy to make, usually a winch cable from a truck, and very effective."

"Do you find a lot of snares?" Kate asked.

"No, thank goodness. We are in the middle of the Kruger, so there's less chance. But we still do regular patrols, especially along the boundary fences. We are a bit spooked after the poaching incident and a wild dog was caught in a snare further north from here about three weeks ago. Unfortunately, it was found too late and had died, no doubt in incredible pain, unable to free itself."

They headed out of the reserve onto the main road that dissected the Kruger National Park. The sealed road shimmered in the heat and the air was slumberous. Kate fought to keep her eyes open, the late night and early morning catching up with her.

Just as her eyes began to droop, they arrived at the Malelane Gate, the Kruger's most southerly gate. A line of cars snaked out from the checkpoint and Ryan pulled up behind the last car in the queue and grimaced.

"Traffic jam in the bush," he said. "It shouldn't take too long, and then we've got about an hour's drive before we turn off the main road towards the orphanage. At least it won't be as bumpy as the tracks in the reserve."

Kate took the opportunity to use the rest rooms and to check her cell phone whilst they waited. There was a message from Greg with the name of a potential photographer who might be available to take the photos for the article. He was in South Africa at the moment and Kate had worked with him before. Kate sent a quick reply to Greg whilst she had a small sliver of signal and told him she'd be emailing later about an idea for a second article. She was thinking of calling it Wildlife Warriors of the Kruger and had already drafted a pitch to send to him.

She was opening the recording app on her phone when Ryan returned from using the facilities. He eyed her cautiously as she held up her phone, grinning.

"I thought I might take advantage of our time in the car. Would you mind if I asked you a few questions?"

Ryan raised an eyebrow. "About what?"

"About you and why you chose wildlife protection as a career path after the army."

Ryan's eyes narrowed. "Do we really need to go into this? I don't see how it's relevant to an article about poaching."

Kate lifted her chin. "I think the people element of conservation is important too."

He eyed her warily. "I don't really need to feature in the article, do I?"

She mentally crossed her fingers. "Not exactly. It's background really. The article is about poaching and about the rhino and her calf, but ultimately, it's also about the people who protect wildlife. People like you and Rio and Clemmie."

They cleared the gate check and juddered over the cattle grid and onto the highway that ran south of the Kruger. Ryan's jaw tightened as he drove and Kate took the opportunity to continue.

"So, the army…tell me about it."

Ryan pulled a face. "There's not much to tell. I joined straight from school then I did two tours of Afghanistan. I left the service altogether about five years after that. And then I became a security consultant in Iraq. That's where I met Gavin."

It was a brief sketch of his army career and Kate suspected he was avoiding giving her any detail.

"Why did you leave the army? It sounds to me like you had an impressive career."

Ryan snorted. "I wouldn't say impressive. I was no different from any other soldier. It involves sheer determination to stay alive. And the ability to operate without fear."

"So," Kate persisted, "why leave?"

A tic appeared in Ryan's cheek. "Because I'd had enough. At the end of the day, too many people had died on all sides and for what? The people in those countries are still not really free. Anyway—" he glared at her "—I still can't see how this links to an article about poaching."

Kate blanched. "Sorry, I thought it would be good to get an insight into what drives you to do this job."

Ryan huffed in resignation. "I was displaced after I left the army. The security work was okay, the money was good and I was using my skills, but it was boring. And I certainly wasn't ready to go into normal civilian life. When I came out to visit Gavin and Sara after they'd moved to South Africa, I had an epiphany. We were out in deep bush in Botswana and came across a team of rangers and vets helping a snared elephant. The poor thing had a wire snare, much like the ones Rio and Clemmie are checking for today, wrapped around one of its front feet.

The animal had struggled so much, the snare had cut through to the bone." He shook his head. "It was a bloody mess. Then when Gavin told me about the ranger training course he'd done, I thought, why the hell not? Protecting animals was the equivalent of helping people and it was something I had the skills for."

Kate tried to imagine an elephant trapped in one of those snares. "I can see why that would have inspired you and I'm guessing a desk job wasn't quite up your street either."

Ryan gave a dry laugh. "Exactly."

Kate was about to ask another question when Ryan took an exit off the highway and headed south past farms and towns. Gradually, the landscape changed again, with more scrub and bush visible. They'd been travelling around an hour when Ryan turned onto an unsealed road and pulled the jeep over to the side of the road.

Ryan's face became serious. "This is where I need to blindfold you."

"Blindfold me?" Kate was confused.

Ryan's face was deadpan. "Don't worry, it's only for a few kilometres."

"I don't understand. Why do you need to blindfold me?"

Ryan winked. "Only joking. The orphanage's location is meant to be kept a secret for security reasons, so we do tend to ask people who visit to agree not to share the details with anyone."

"Do you want me to sign a non-disclosure form?" Kate said.

Ryan started the engine again and laughed. "That won't be necessary."

Chapter Eighteen

Ryan pulled back onto the dirt track and the jeep bumped and bounced along the pothole- ridden road until they came to a large metal gate and fence in the middle of a remote area surrounded by dense scrub. Kate spotted security cameras mounted on two large posts either side of the gate. Ryan pressed a call button and it wasn't long before the forbidding gate slid open.

Once inside, a security officer noted their names and details on a clipboard. His friendly face gave away nothing and his uniform bore no markings or indications as to whom he worked for. "You're all signed in." he said. "The main bomas are about four kilometres up the road. Jerry will escort you up."

Another security guard, younger and again with a wide smile, popped out of the small kiosk and got into a jeep that was parked in the shade beyond.

Kate leant forward to Ryan and whispered, "It's a bit cloak and dagger."

A dimple appeared in Ryan's stubbled cheek. "It is, but it's all for a good reason."

The jeeps moved on and after quarter an hour of bumping along the road, which was fringed with deep bush, they pulled up by a cluster of wooden buildings and fences. The main building had a tin roof and large covered veranda, which ran along the front. A dog lay prone on the stoop, its pink tongue hanging out as it slept. With the sound of the engines its head jolted up and it immediately jumped into action in a flurry of barking. Kate followed Ryan out of the car, her legs stiff from sitting for so long, and eyed the dog warily.

A woman, tall and striking in shorts and a polo shirt, came bustling out of the front door, her feet clad in leather work boots and a long salt and pepper plait flung over her shoulder. Kate gauged her to be in her late fifties or older. She was skinny but with a dark leathery tan and lean muscles that you'd expect with someone who worked outdoors. She quietened the dog with a commanding hand on his head and greeted them warmly, kissing Ryan on each cheek before focusing her dark blue eyes on Kate.

She reached out a hand to Kate's. "I'm Marta. I understand you arrived as the calf was being evacuated."

"Yes," Kate replied. "It was quite a shock to get off a plane and only a few minutes later see a rhino calf being flown off in a helicopter."

Marta gave a brief nod. "And you're in South Africa to write an article for an English paper?"

"That's right, the *Daily Tribune*," she said. "I've certainly been getting the full picture from Ryan and his team, and now I'd like to learn more about the work you do here."

Ryan's phone rang and he excused himself, heading back to the jeep to take the call. Marta bustled Kate into the building where she poured thick black coffee and gave her a general rundown on the orphanage.

"We have to keep our location as secret as we possibly can, hence all the security. There have been cases of rhino orphanages being subject to attacks from poachers. They'll do anything to get their hands on rhino horn. It's all about greed."

Kate had read about previous incursions at rhino orphanages, particularly the violent attack at Thula Thula several years earlier. She sensed a bitterness in Marta's voice, which was different from Sara or Clemmie's positive attitude to their work. Marta was more resigned, like Ryan.

She sipped her coffee, the bitter liquid hitting her veins and waking her up again. "How many rhino orphans do you have?"

Marta pointed up to a cork noticeboard onto which had been pinned photos of individual rhinos. "We currently have eleven, of which seven are in the nursery or younger group. They are located here and will go out during the day in the bomas ringed around these buildings. Three older calves have been released back into the nature reserve, which you drove through to get here, and then there's the new calf, the one from Elephant Sands. He's still in the ICU container, although we are hoping to get him outside today."

Kate studied the photos on the noticeboard, smiling at the images of the orphans with their names and details below. On the other side of the office a series of framed photos of rhinos hung on the wall. A gallery of past occupants, their faces staring out at Kate. All orphaned, their mothers lost to them forever. She gulped.

It was hot and stuffy in the office despite the air conditioning. "Can I meet some of the orphans?" she asked, keen for some fresh air.

"Of course." Marta grinned at her. "It's feeding time anyway and first up is your orphan."

Kate's heart fluttered at Marta's words. She did feel an infinity with the calf, especially after meeting him during his journey to safety. She followed Marta out of the main office and across the compound to a building that housed the kitchen and food storage rooms.

Inside the kitchen, a large room with clean, stainless-steel benches, there was a buzz of activity, as two young women and a man were busy mixing powdered milk into large bottles each labelled with a rhino's name. A radio played softly in the background and a tabby cat wound its way around the legs of one of the young women. Kate became aware of three sets of curious eyes on her.

Marta waved her hand across the room. "This is where we prepare their milk and medicines." She addressed the group. "This is Kate Harper from the UK. She's writing an article about the impact of poaching and she was lucky enough to meet our newest arrival as he was being evacuated. Kate, meet our three carers, Scott, Anna and Mel."

Kate greeted them and walked around the square kitchen, taking in the whiteboard listing names and times for feeding. One of the women, Anna, shook a large, full bottle of milk. "I'm off to feed the little one now. Do you want to join me?" she asked, in a European accent Kate couldn't quite place.

"That would be great."

Kate followed Anna out of the kitchen and across the compound again. "How long have you been here?"

Anna pulled open the bottom half of a stable door and

gestured for Kate to enter. "Around eighteen months. I was meant to be going back to Germany last Christmas but I'm still here."

"You must really love it."

Anna gave a wide grin. "Yeah, but I am going to university next year and I need to get a proper paid job to fund my living before I start." She pulled a face. "I really don't want to leave."

It was dim inside the container. On the far side in a pile of blankets and hay lay a tiny little lump. At the sound of their approach, a head popped up, its ears flapping.

Kate's mouth automatically twitched into a smile.

Anna made a clicking sound not dissimilar to the one you'd make to a horse out in a field. "Come on, little one, dinner time."

The calf came to his feet, still a little wobbly, but as Anna knelt in the soft floor beside him, he immediately latched onto the teat and began to suck. Kate watched the calf take his bottle and drink with gusto. Anna beckoned her forward and she found herself next to him. He smelt of hay and milk. The bandages that were across his flank when she first saw him had been removed, the wounds beneath now covered in a paste.

She heard the click of the stable door and Ryan appeared. She wondered again about the phone call he'd received and if it was news about the poaching. He reached out his hand to gently rub between the calf's ears.

Anna waved the bottle near Kate. "Do you want to have a go?"

Kate took the bottle from Anna and felt the vigorous pull of the calf on the teat. "He's strong—" she laughed softly in surprise "—and he hasn't even noticed that I have taken over."

"Nothing can get between a rhino calf and their milk," Anna said.

The calf continued to drink and the three of them watched in silence as the liquid slowly emptied from the bottle. When it was all gone, Kate gently pulled the teat out, surprised to see the calf try to snatch it back.

Anna laughed and scratched its ears. "You're all done, little one." She smiled at Kate. "It's good news that he took to milk so quickly. We reckon he's about a month or so old and sometimes we can have problems with the younger ones, but he's settled well."

Kate loved rubbing the calf's neck and he was happy for them to sit near him as Anna checked him over.

Ryan watched Anna check inside the calf's ears. "He clearly trusts you," he said. "I did a stint here about six years ago. I remember the first time I came across a really young orphaned calf. He was only a couple of days old and was weak and traumatised. It was touch and go for a long time. We'd just got him to take milk when he got an infection and it went on and on for weeks. By the time I left he was about six weeks old. I kept in touch with Marta about him. I think he was rewilded about three years ago."

"What was his name?" Anna asked.

"Sid. He was named after a local ranger in the reserve."

Anna's head tilted. "That was before my time, but his photo is on the wall of fame."

Kate reached out again to stroke the calf, who had already begun to droop, replete after the milk. "It's so good to see him like this," she said. "Does he have a name yet?"

Anna scratched the calf between his ears. "Not yet. We

usually give them a nickname before they are formally named, but at the moment we've been focusing on getting him sorted."

Ryan tipped his head to one side. "Perhaps you should name him, Kate."

Kate was astonished. "Me? I wouldn't know what to choose, and besides, you're the one who found him."

Ryan's brow wrinkled. "I was thinking of the name Themba. It's a Zulu name which means Hope. I spoke to Marta earlier and she's got no objections."

Kate gazed down at the calf, now relaxed with a full stomach and back scratch. "Themba," she whispered. "It's perfect."

Anna's grin was wide. "Good choice. This place is all about hope."

They gave Themba a final pat and followed Anna out of the barn and into a large fenced area. The sun's heat was intense as they made their way across the boma to where Scott, Mel and Marta were busy feeding the other calves. Anna placed the empty bottle on a ledge and pulled a full one from a crate on the ground.

She gave a whistle. "Wait for it," she warned Kate before calling out in a high singsong voice, "Willow!"

Before Kate even had time to think, there was a thundering of footsteps as a rhino calf, much larger than Themba, barrelled towards them, its snout and ears twitching as it sought out the bottle.

Anna scratched the rhino calf's ears. "This is Willow. She's ten months old now. She is the first orphan I have cared for from day one." Willow latched onto the bottle and guzzled as if she hadn't eaten for days. "I am really going to miss her when I go."

Kate drew closer. "What happened to her?"

Anna's face fell. "Her mother was killed, somewhere up north, and the rangers found Willow wandering around in the bush by herself. They suspect she'd been so spooked she'd run off. She was quite young at the time, only around four months, so it's amazing she survived being alone in the bush. Rhino calves often get attacked by lions or hyenas. She was dehydrated but otherwise unscathed."

Kate and Ryan spent the next half an hour watching the calves finish their bottles. Kate was delighted by the calves' cream-covered lips and laughed as they tried to lick the milk off. When Ryan hinted that it was time to go, she reluctantly left the boma and followed him and Marta across the compound.

She smiled at Marta. "Thank you so much for letting me visit. You do amazing work here and it was so special to see Themba again. He's certainly stronger than he was two days ago."

Marta chuckled. "I am glad he's got a name now. We couldn't go on calling him Boy forever, and yes, he is making good progress. Hopefully, that will continue, but it's early days yet. Luckily, we do have success stories," Marta said as they walked along a dusty track towards the large day boma where the older orphans hung out. "We have released six older rhinos back into the reserve over the last two years."

"That must be tough," Kate observed, "letting them out into the wild again."

"It is," Marta conceded, "but our goal is always to rehabilitate them and then send them back out. A rhino belongs in the wild."

Marta reached out to the large calf who had ambled

over to sniff them. Kate watched in disbelief as this no-nonsense woman bent down to kiss the rhino on his head.

"This is Rollo. He's three and a half years old and is the next one scheduled to be released. He's such a character."

Kate scratched Rollo's back. "You clearly know them all well."

Marta stared fondly at Rollo. "Yeah, each and every one of them has their own personality and quirks. It can be quite entertaining. And they need lots of exercise. We take them on long walks and make sure they get plenty of time wallowing in the mud baths."

Kate reflected on Marta and the three young carers, their faces alight with the sheer joy of their jobs, and felt a flutter in her chest. She'd never been that passionate about her work. Whilst she had seen some pretty horrific things in her job, people living and working in squalid conditions and being mistreated or misplaced, she'd always been able to remain removed from it all. It had served her well; she'd been able to write concise and non-biased accounts that showed the facts without embellishment. Now she was beginning to wonder whether she would be able to do that with this assignment. Something was shifting within her.

She thought back to Clemmie's account of her daily five-kilometre walk to school every day and of how most of the children who lived out in the bush struggled to get to a high school. This assignment was no different from many of her other ones, highlighting suffering and poverty, but it seemed more personal. She imagined the young female wild dog driven out of the pack by her mother, alone and adrift. Rather like Kate felt right now.

It was nearly four o'clock by the time Kate and Ryan

climbed back into the jeep. Back on the highway the sun was slipping slowly over the horizon. For Kate it had been a truly magical day. She'd not thought about the search for her real mother at all, nor the discovery of an uncle.

They'd just cleared security at the Malelane Gate when Kate met the dark brown eyes of Ryan, adrenaline still fizzing through her veins. "That was incredible. Thank you for taking me."

The dimple in Ryan's cheek made an appearance again and Kate's heart thudded in her chest.

"You're welcome. I'm glad he's settled. Let's hope it stays that way. Marta and her staff are extremely good at what they do."

"How are they funded?"

"Pretty much through donations, which is why they rely heavily on young volunteers like Anna who are keen to care for rhinos for free food and board."

Ryan stopped at a crossroads and faced Kate. "Gavin called me when we were at the orphanage and suggested we meet at a viewing platform near the lodge for sunset. There's a wooden deck built near the top. It gives a great view of the valley, different from the lodge's but beautiful, nonetheless. He and Sara will bring drinks and nibbles. Are you up for that or would you prefer me to take you back to the lodge?"

Kate was suddenly aware of Ryan's physical presence, the molten depths of his eyes, and her breath hitched. "Sounds perfect. I don't need to go back, unless you do?

He stared into her eyes, tension crackling between them, then with a nod he pulled his sunglasses over his eyes and they headed off, chasing the sun as it slipped lower in the sky.

Chapter Nineteen

They drove the rest of the journey in relative silence. Kate's heart was beating frantically and she took a peek at Ryan from time to time. When they climbed a high bank and he changed to the second set of 4 x 4 gears, his left hand brushed her thigh. It was only a tiny flicker of a touch, but it sent seismic tremors throughout her body.

She wondered if he'd noticed her shiver, and when she peeked at him, his cheeks were stained red and she knew he'd felt it too. She pulled her cap down further over her head, trying to calm her racing pulse.

Up ahead, a herd of antelope was crossing the track, their coats a pale grey-brown with vertical white stripes. In amongst them was a male, with wide spiralling horns.

Kate pointed towards them. "What are they called? They're magnificent."

Ryan's eyes were warm. "Greater kudu. They're my favourite antelope."

They waited for the herd to scamper across the road, then carried on driving, the sun low and golden in the sky in front of them. At the top of another high bank, a large wooden structure jutted out over the edge of an impressive rocky kopje. A blush of pink stained the rocks at the top of the kopje and Kate leant forward in the leather seat of the jeep, her shirt sticking to her back.

"This is beautiful."

Ryan stopped the jeep. "Yes, it's a great spot. Looks like we're the first ones here. Wait here and I'll check for predators."

He jumped out of the vehicle and Kate leant back in the seat again, gazing out over the view. It was blissfully quiet. A grey heron splashed in the small waterhole nearby before it took flight and headed up into the sky. She watched its ascent.

When Ryan gave the all clear, she climbed out and gazed across the saltpan, spotting the large, unmistakable shape of elephants. A solitary giraffe was kneeling to drink, its nose stretched out to lap the water. It was so ungainly for such an incredibly graceful animal and its long scissored legs made Kate smile.

She watched Ryan as he leant against the truck, his eyes closed, the whisper of a smile on his lips and she took a moment to study him unguarded. His face was held up towards the sky, like a flower soaking up the sun. His arms were crossed in front of him, biceps bulging out from beneath his dark green T-shirt. Once again desire pulsed through her and she turned away, focusing instead on the sound of the surrounding animals – the stamping and snorting of the zebras behind them, the shrieking of birds in the sky above and the ever-present buzz of crickets. But her eyes were soon pulled back as if by a magnetic force to the man beside her.

He opened his eyes at that moment as if he knew she was watching him. Her cheeks flushed and she swallowed slowly. His brown eyes held hers, a question flickering in them. She licked her bottom lip almost without realising she was doing it, and he watched her tongue make its journey. The air was thick and her heart thudded in her chest. One of them had to break the stare soon, but her eyes were stuck in this position, unable to move.

Ryan took a step forward and her heartbeat notched up a level. She stood frozen, waiting to see what he would do, wanting something to happen. She was drawn to him, to the strength of him and to the vulnerability she'd glimpsed. He reached her in a few steps and stared down at her, his eyes on her lips. His head blocked the sun as he bent to kiss her, his lips whispering on hers. She closed her eyes, ready to taste him. His touch was gentle at first, his hand cupping her cheek as his lips touched hers.

"So beautiful," he murmured, brushing his thumb across her trembling lips, his head descending.

Kate's senses went into overdrive. Her hands rested on his chest as he pulled her closer, his hands on her hips, pressing her gently against him. She wound her arms around his neck, loving the closeness of their chests together. Ryan angled his face to deepen the kiss, but the approaching roar of a diesel engine halted his progress and he stepped away, shoving his sunglasses down over his eyes as Sara and Gavin pulled up in a cloud of dust beside them.

Kate was still in a trance when Ryan moved away to greet them, the tingle of his touch on her lips. He helped Gavin unload the cool boxes and table and chairs to take up the stone steps to the deck. She was in such a daze that she hadn't even noticed Sara standing by her until her friend's hand waved in front of her.

"Earth to Kate."

Kate blinked and returned to the present, her face flaming at the prospect of being caught kissing Ryan. She could only imagine what Sara would have to say about that.

Sara waggled her eyebrows. "You two were nice and cosy as we drove up. Getting on better now, are we?"

Kate rolled her eyes inwardly. "We were just chatting whilst we waited for you to arrive, that's all. Don't go getting any ideas, Sara. He's not my type, and besides, he doesn't like me."

Sara snorted. "It didn't look like that to me."

Kate dug her in the ribs. "Shut up. You're seeing things that don't exist. Now, can we please change the subject? Let me tell you all about the orphanage visit. The calf's name is Themba, which means hope in Zulu."

Sara laughed. "Okay, but for two people who supposedly don't like each other, you are both doing a bad job of convincing me."

As the four of them watched yet another glorious sunset, Kate surreptitiously examined Ryan. He hadn't once glanced in her direction since Gavin and Sara arrived and she was beginning to wonder if she'd imagined the kiss. But her lips were still tingling and the desire that had fizzed through her was there under her skin.

When they were packing up the cool boxes and folding down the chairs, Sara slapped her forehead. "Ryan, I nearly forgot! Cassie arrived today. I thought it was meant to be tomorrow afternoon. Remember I mentioned it yesterday? She's here to sort through the new accounts software."

Ryan rubbed his chin. "Okay. Do I need to know about the software?"

"No," Sara replied. "But I think she wants to catch up with you. She was adamant about that. I explained about the poaching incident and that you were busy, but I suspect she'll grab you the minute we arrive back at the lodge."

"Thanks for the heads-up. I can't think why Cassie would specifically want to catch up with me. I don't have anything to do with the business side."

Sara gave a gleeful laugh. "I got the feeling it was entirely a social meeting she was interested in."

Kate had no idea who they were talking about and busied herself by checking her phone for any messages. Remarkably, she hadn't checked it since they were at the checkpoint; the day had been so busy and distracting. However, the signal was virtually non-existent and she half listened to Sara tease Ryan about the Cassie woman and noticed that he was embarrassed. Was it an old flame? She was itching to know but didn't want to ask Sara. It would only give her the wrong idea. Besides, Kate was still fuming about Ryan's sudden withdrawal. He was acting as if the kiss hadn't mattered.

When it was time to travel back to the lodge, she attempted to climb into the back of Sara and Gavin's jeep, anything to avoid Ryan. But Gavin had plonked all the boxes and kit into the back seats, so Kate reluctantly made her way over to join Ryan in his vehicle.

They drove in silence, the headlights beaming out against the now dark landscape. The air between them was thick, not with heat, as the early evening air was cool and soft, but with the stifling wall of unfulfilled desire.

When they arrived back at the lodge, Kate tried to exit the jeep as quickly as possible, but Ryan grabbed her arm, the heat from him burning like a flame through her skin.

"Wait," he said, his face serious under the dim light of the large lanterns in the drive. "I'm sorry."

She stared at his lips and her own quivered at the memory of his touch. "Sorry for what?"

"For what happened earlier. I shouldn't have…"

"Kissed me?"

Kate watched his Adam's apple bob. "It was unprofessional."

Unprofessional? She lifted her chin. "Don't worry about it. Have a good evening."

Puffing angrily, she stomped up the steps into the reception, almost knocking over Sara, who was waiting for her.

Fine. It was just a kiss, and it meant nothing. She should be grateful he was so dismissive about it – lord knows she didn't need the distractions, but did he have to be so goddam rude?

"Kate." Sara's shrewd eyes took in her flushed face and shaking hands. "Are you okay?"

"I'm absolutely dandy, thank you, Sara," Kate snapped. "Fine and dandy."

Sara laughed. "Okay, Miss Fine and Dandy, shall we go and have some dinner?"

Kate was conscious of Ryan hovering in the background. "Sounds good."

They were heading through reception when an attractive blonde woman hurried over to Ryan, almost knocking Kate over in the process. That had to be Cassie, and Kate bristled as she watched the woman fawn all over Ryan. He seemed keen to see her, hugging her close and allowing her to touch his arm as they spoke.

Kate knew that despite the fact she didn't want Sara to

think she was keen on Ryan, she wouldn't be able to hold back from asking her about Cassie. However, they'd been in the dining room for only a few minutes when Cassie and Ryan walked in, her braceleted arm firmly wound through his. As they headed towards them, Kate panicked. She was dusty and sweaty, a day in the bush did that to you, and it was more than okay for her to sit with Sara and Gavin like that, but Cassie was cool and glamorous.

Kate blew out a frustrated puff at the frizzy curls that ringed her face. "Sara, do you mind if I quickly freshen up? I think I'll have a shower and change my clothes." *And give myself a full makeover.*

Sara eyed her suspiciously. "Of course not. I'll sort a table and order some wine. Gavin is on duty now so he'll eat in the office. But maybe Cassie and Ryan could join us."

Kate looked over at the bar, where the two of them were perched on stools, Cassie laughing at something Ryan had said, her hands once again touching him.

Kate was conscious of Sara's eyes on her. "Let's keep it just the two of us. I haven't really had a chance to catch up with you on your own since I arrived."

Sara headed over to find a table, leaving Kate to scurry past the bar and across the compound to her room as fast as her dusty trainers would take her.

Chapter Twenty

Ryan flipped over the pillow and punched it for the umpteenth time. It was the bewitching time when late evening tipped over into the dead of night, when thoughts ran rampant through your mind. The moon, now waning in strength, glowed softly through the window, sending ripples of silver light across the floor. He never slept with the blinds down. There was something about total darkness he didn't like. It stemmed from his time in Afghanistan when they would spend night after night patrolling the bush, the sky a black velvet expanse, and the fear of standing on a concealed mine forever in their minds, searching for a silent enemy who knew the hills and valleys better than they did.

His mind wandered back to Kate and the kiss they'd shared by the waterhole. Her lips had been soft and enticing, the scent of her wrapping itself around his senses, a hint of rose and fresh rain. It reminded him of his mother's rose garden after a gentle summer shower, where the petals were moistened with beads of rain trickling down and onto the soil beneath.

He'd forgotten about his mother's pride and joy, her twenty tree roses and the old- style climbing roses that wound their way up the trellises his father had made. His mother called it her sanctuary and that was how he felt with Kate. She made him feel safe, which was ridiculous, because he didn't need any sanctuary. He was perfectly fine where he was, completely happy and in control.

He had simply responded to a physical attraction to her. A chemical reaction, one that had been building since she'd arrived. It didn't mean anything. Gavin had ribbed him as they unloaded the cool boxes from the jeep.

"Glad you're getting on better with Kate." He'd laughed. "I can't say I blame you. She's almost as good-looking as my wife."

Ryan hadn't replied but knew by the burning of his face that he was blushing beneath his stubble. He had to admit a grudging admiration for Kate though. She'd been incredible this morning, despite admitting to a hangover. She had enchanted him with the way she reacted at the orphanage, her face glowing with joy as she tenderly fed the calf.

But he shouldn't have kissed her. It was merely a physical manifestation of their day together, their connection with Themba, nothing more. He gave the pillow another thump. Who was he kidding? The kiss had rocked him and he wondered what would have happened had Sara and Gavin not arrived when they did.

It was unkind, telling her it meant nothing, that it was unprofessional, and the minute he saw her face after he'd said it, he'd wanted to take back the words. But she'd raced out of the jeep before he could apologise and then Cassie had ambushed him in reception, sweeping him up with her enthusiasm and whirlwind charm.

Cassie was the daughter of the lodge's owner, Glen

Carruthers, and Ryan had met her when he first arrived to work at the game reserve. A qualified accountant, she'd been helping set up the accounts and was a cheerful and fun-loving woman. He'd been careful to avoid any flirtations with her whenever she was at the lodge, and when he'd visited Johannesburg a year earlier, he'd agreed to have a drink with her. She seemed keen on him, and there were times when he was definitely tempted. But he'd held back, not because she was the boss's daughter, but because his life in the bush was simple and straightforward. A woman like Cassie would always want more. And she deserved it.

It had been good fun tonight though. She'd regaled him with tales of her new boyfriend, a quiet German man who'd moved to work in Johannesburg. Across the room vibes of disapproval emanated from Kate. Cassie might be smitten with someone else but she was a touchy-feely sort of person and Ryan knew Kate had observed Cassie's constant touches.

As Kate left to retire to her room, she'd walked directly past their table, her face angled away, not wanting to make eye contact. But Sara had stopped to talk to them, introducing Kate to Cassie. Sara and Cassie had chatted, oblivious to Kate and Ryan's discomfort. Being close to her again, it was hard not to think of the taste of her lips, of the feel of her soft body melding against hers. He'd caught her eye briefly, noticing the blush across her cheeks and he knew she was thinking the same thing.

Half an hour after Kate had gone to her room, he'd left Cassie talking to her boyfriend on the phone and made his way back to his room, a headache pushing at his temples. He'd stopped outside Kate's room and lifted his hand to knock but had pulled away, doubting he'd be welcome and not sure what he would say anyway.

Back in his room, he'd washed down painkillers with two glasses of water and enjoyed a cool shower. He'd been stretching out on his bed thinking about sleep when his phone buzzed on the nightstand, Ed Webster's name appearing on the screen.

"Hi, mate. What's up?"

Ed was all businesslike. "Have you seen my recent email?"

Ryan hadn't opened or checked any messages since he'd returned to the lodge. Unlike Kate, who'd once again been glued to her phone during the evening, even when Sara had been chatting to her. He'd never known anyone so attached to their phone. Except for teenagers maybe.

"No, sorry," he'd told Ed. "I've been at the rhino orphanage checking on the calf."

"How's he doing?" Ed asked.

Ryan took a sip of water. "Good. He's drinking milk and has had some vitamin boosters. I think he'll be introduced to the other younger orphans in the next day or so."

"That's a relief," Ed said. "Listen, I have sent you through the forensic report on the bullets. It's definitely the same gun used in Sabie—" he paused "—but the *really* interesting fact is that the gun was once registered to an owner in Johannesburg who happens to be a director of a hunting safari business. His name is Quinton Cronje. It's pretty idiotic to use a registered gun for poaching, but it may have been stolen from him."

Ryan's interest was piqued. He found the relevant email and opened it, scanning the information. "Okay, I'll have a read and call you tomorrow."

"Also," Ed added, "there's a shell company we believe

may be linked to a poaching syndicate operating out of Johannesburg. It's registered in the Cayman Islands. As expected, any information about the company is scarce; the only name listed is probably a dummy, paid a stipend to provide their name and address. We believe this is a short-term holding bay for laundering money made through poaching and possibly trophy hunting that is not within legal boundaries."

"Do you mean like the case of the Groenewald brothers last year?" Ryan asked, thinking of a hunting safari company and its involvement with fraud and poaching.

"Possibly. Although this is a much smaller outfit. There has been some movement of money between it and various legitimate companies in Mozambique and South Africa. It might be a tax thing, but I am not sure as yet. We're requesting more information."

Ryan finished the call and checked through the email. The bullet report was fairly straightforward. It was quite possible the gun had been stolen from its registered owner but they hadn't reported it.

He rolled over to his back and inhaled deeply, trying to calm his thoughts and allow his body to relax, closing his eyes and hoping sleep would come. But all that he saw were the green-flecked irises of Kate's eyes, her pupils widening as he kissed her. His heart pumped solidly in his chest again, and he put his hand over it to calm it. Outside was silent save for the sounds of nocturnal creatures putting their stamp on the night. He would not allow Kate to get under his skin. Not like Gwen. He would not be taken in again by a pair of beautiful eyes.

Chapter Twenty-One

For the fourth time, Kate deleted the sentence she'd been typing. She'd been trying to write the first draft of her article for over two hours and hadn't got very far. She picked up the cup next to her and drained the coffee, grimacing. It had gone cold. Pushing herself up from the chair, she wandered out to the veranda, the hot air blasting her face as she left the air-conditioned environment of her room.

The sky was dull, with low clouds threatening rain in a humid haze. She felt wrung out and limp like a rag doll. She hadn't slept well the night before, images of Ryan running through her head. Even now she could feel the bunch of his muscles under her touch and the warmth of his lips on hers. But he'd called their kiss 'unprofessional' and had ignored her for the rest of the evening, choosing instead to spend time with Cassie.

Kate was not normally the jealous type, but seeing him so animated with Cassie had brought out the green-eyed monster. Why had he kissed her if it had meant nothing to him? And why was she letting it bother her? She was here to write an article and find her real mother, not to find a boyfriend.

She'd woken that morning with a determination to carry on. No more making gooey eyes at Ryan. Today she was going to be back to her normal self, cool and businesslike. She'd decided to spend the morning in her room working on the article. Sara was busy with guests and they'd agreed to meet up later by the lodge's pool for a swim and chat.

After lunch she would swallow her pride and track Ryan down to get the last pieces of information she needed for the article. He was, after all, the star of the story, alongside Themba. She'd made a list of questions, and with a bit of luck, she'd be able to finish the article in the next day or so. And then she'd go to Johannesburg to meet her uncle.

Her stomach rumbled and she realised it was after midday. A buffet lunch would be set up in the dining room for those guests who wanted it. The thought of Prudence's delicious soup and salads made her mouth water. She'd grab a plate and bring it back to the room.

As she made her way across the compound, she spotted Cassie lingering by reception, encased in white linen trousers and a turquoise top, her blonde hair twisted up into a chignon. She was chic and elegant, unlike Kate, who was currently wearing faded harem pants with an elephant print and a washed-out white T-shirt. Her hair was tied back in its usual plait with curls springing out all around, frizzy with the humidity.

She was approaching the steps to reception when Ryan bounded up behind Cassie. She stepped back behind the large frangipani tree and hid, not wanting to walk past them. They chatted quietly until a jeep pulled up and Cassie threw her arms around Ryan, kissing him on both cheeks before climbing in and heading out with the driver towards the airfield.

Ryan watched Cassie go, his eyes following the jeep until it was gone. Kate stood as still as a statue, the bark of the tree rough under her hand. He seemed lost in thought, his brow furrowed in concentration. His phone rang and he pulled it out of the top pocket of his polo shirt and strode off, talking to the caller as he went.

When she was sure he was gone, she scurried into the dining room and collected some food. She was behaving like a teenager with her first crush, hiding away from a boy who'd dumped her. She was a grown woman, for goodness' sake.

She was reaching for a slice of cold ham when a hand touched her shoulder, making her drop the ham into the potato salad. It was Sara.

"You gave me a shock."

Sara laughed. "I did speak to you, but you were miles away."

Kate continued to fill her plate. "Sorry. I was thinking about things."

"Would one of those things happen to be Ryan?"

Kate huffed. "I do wish you would stop, Sara. I've told you, there's nothing between us and you have to stop trying to match us up." She grabbed a knife and fork. "And besides, he's clearly got a girlfriend."

Sara frowned. "A girlfriend?"

"Cassie, the woman who was here last night. She was all over him and he seemed to be enjoying it."

Sara shook her head. "Cassie's not Ryan's girlfriend. They are friends, for sure, but not involved. She's one of the accountants from the company that owns the lodge. She pops in from time to time and was the accounts manager here when Ryan first arrived. I think she definitely fancied him at one time—" she creased up her face "—but as far as I am aware, nothing happened between them."

"Didn't look that way to me," Kate muttered.

"Do I detect a little bit of jealousy?"

Kate was indignant. "Why would I be jealous? I hardly know Ryan."

"Methinks the lady doth protest too much," Sara joked, "and don't think I don't know what's going on between the two of you."

Kate glared at Sara. "There's nothing going on between us."

"Yet," Sara quipped, "but it's as plain as the nose on your face that you two fancy each other."

Kate picked up her tray of food and walked away. "Funny…I'll leave you to your imaginings. Some of us have got work to do."

Back at her room, as she tucked into her lunch, she turned her thoughts to the search for her mother and the conversation two days earlier with her uncle. She'd been trying to think of an excuse to go to Johannesburg to meet him, without arousing Sara's interest. She knew she had to tell Sara the truth sometime, but she wanted to wait a bit longer, test the waters with her uncle and see if there was even a chance her mother was still alive.

Her computer beeped with a message. Sara had found another booster for Kate to use and the Wi-Fi had improved dramatically. She had two new messages. One was from Greg, suggesting she contact Eliot Vince, a photographer the paper had used before. Apparently, Eliot was in Johannesburg on another commission and Greg thought it would be good for Kate to connect with Eliot and ask him to take the photos for the article whilst he was in the country. Kate was pleased. She'd met Eliot a few times and liked his easy-going nature.

The other email was from her uncle, asking when she would be in Johannesburg. Judging by his words, he seemed keen to meet her. Her heart thudded in her chest. The two emails coming together at the same time were definitely a sign. She could use the meeting with Eliot as an excuse to go to Johannesburg and see her uncle as well whilst she was there.

Chapter Twenty-Two

Ryan was still tussling with the monthly budget figures when there was a soft tap on the office door. He was way behind on all the regular administration and was overdosing on coffee, his conversation with Ed last night and the puzzle of the rhino poaching still working its way around in his head.

"Come in," he called out, pushing back his chair and standing to stretch.

Kate entered the office. She was fresh and pretty, her hair tamed in a long plait that hung over her right shoulder. He was surprised to see her, given the glares she'd been sending him the night before in the bar. Not that he could blame her after the way he'd behaved.

He plastered a smile on his face. "Kate, what can I do for you?"

She was carrying a platter of sandwiches with two apples balanced on the top. "I come bearing food. Prudence mentioned you'd skipped lunch."

Ryan rubbed his forehead. "I lose track of time some days."

"I know what you mean. When I am in the thick of writing something, I often don't even realise it's night-time until I suddenly notice the dark sky outside."

There was an awkward silence as they eyed each other. Kate broke the stare. "I thought I would join you, if that's okay? I've had lunch and the sandwiches are delicious. It can be a working lunch. I still have loads of questions."

He eyed her warily. "Okay."

She pulled up a chair beside him, her ever-present notebook and pen at the ready. "Shall we begin? I am sure you are busy and I need to get a draft off to my editor as soon as...plus I have to go to Johannesburg."

His ears pricked up. "What are you doing in Johannesburg?"

She rubbed the back of her neck. "Nothing much. I thought I would check out the bureau we work with. The guy who was meant to be doing the article is ill and I said I might pop in and meet the team."

When she fidgeted with the drawstring of her trousers Ryan knew she was lying. He was good at reading people. He was about to ask her more when she flipped open her notebook to a blank page.

"What's the latest on the forensic report from the bullets?"

Her businesslike tone riled him. She was certainly determined to ignore what happened the day before. But then that was what he wanted, wasn't it?

He cleared his throat. "They matched the bullets with a previous rhino-poaching case up in Sabie. It was the same rifle."

She grabbed a sandwich and bit into it. Ryan watched her lips as she ate, and groaned inwardly, trying not to think about kissing her.

"Hmm...these are so good. You really should have some."

Ryan reached for a sandwich. "Yes, before you eat them all. Are you always this efficient?"

"You forget I went to the same school as Sara – Miss Organised. It was one of the main things they taught us, alongside Maths and English."

She gave a deep, husky laugh that sent a shiver down his spine. He gave his errant libido a mental kick.

"Have they traced the owner of the gun?"

"Yep," Ryan replied, and in between finishing off the sandwiches, he filled her in on the latest news from the police.

"Have you searched this Quinton Cronje online?" she asked when Ryan mentioned him.

"No, I was just about to when you came in."

She pointed towards the computer. "Let's have a look then."

He put the man's name into the search line. The image of a handsome blonde man appeared on the LinkedIn page for Quinton Cronje. He was the founding owner and director of Sterling Hunting Safaris. Kate peered over his shoulder, her long plait falling across his arm and momentarily distracting him. He inhaled the soft rose scent of her and tensed.

"He is also the owner of a fabric export business in Mozambique and a joint director of a leisure boat company. Both based in Maputo," Kate noted.

Ryan read through the rest of the information and clicked back to the hunting safari company page. It was registered to an address in Johannesburg. Ryan vaguely knew the area, a high-end residential part of the city.

"It's all fairly innocuous."

Kate tapped the desk with her pen. "How do you think

one of his guns ended up being involved in poaching?"

"Perhaps it was stolen. Or he may have been unaware one of his employees was using it. You would have to be stupid to use a registered gun to kill something illegally. It's going to lead right back to you, after all."

Kate's brow furrowed. "Didn't you say the shell company they've traced has links to companies in South Africa and Mozambique?"

"Yeah, they are still doing some digging on it, but they have found some movement between the different companies."

"Who is listed for the shell company? They usually have a front person, someone who is given a nominal director or business manager role. They have nothing to do with the actual company, of course, and are merely paid for the use of their name and address."

Ryan raised an eyebrow. "How do you know that?"

Kate rolled her eyes. "I am an investigative journalist. I've not worked on many fraud cases, but I do know a bit about how money is moved around. It goes on all the time."

"True," Ryan said. "I'll give Ed a call now and find out what else he knows about the shell company."

Rio came into the room, returning three walkie-talkies to the console. He gave Kate a friendly smile. "How are you, Kate?"

"I'm good, Rio. You?"

Ryan watched Kate as she chatted with Rio, her hazel-green eyes shining as she recounted the visit to the orphanage. Desire sparked in him. She was so beautiful, all fire and blazing eyes, and he was in danger of falling for her. He had to keep a clear head.

He was suddenly aware that Kate had asked him something. "Sorry. I was miles away."

"I was asking if you would mind if I interviewed Rio and Clemmie – for the article?"

Ryan leant back in his chair. "I don't mind, but it's up to them, and as long as it doesn't interfere with their work."

"Of course not," Kate replied.

"I'm happy to be interviewed," Rio broke in, "and to be in any photos. With a bit of luck, I might be discovered by a talent scout—" he raised a bulging bicep and winked "—to be South Africa's next great male model."

"In your dreams, mate," Ryan muttered.

Kate collected up the empty plates from their lunch. "I'll take this back to the kitchen and come back in a minute, then we can find out more about the mysterious Quinton."

Once she'd gone, Rio threw a screwed-up piece of paper at Ryan. "What's up with you, mate? Your face is all red. Do you fancy her or something?"

Ryan glared at him. "No, of course not. She's Sara's friend and she's here to write an article. Nothing else."

"You do fancy her! You never blush!"

Ryan swore under his breath. "Get lost, Rio, before I throw the stapler at you,"

Rio gave a thumbs up. "You're the boss. I'm off now. Catch you tomorrow."

Ryan watched his friend go, his long legs loping up the path. He messaged Ed about the shell company and was scrolling through some other emails when Kate's phone rang loudly on the desk where she'd left it. He checked out of the window but couldn't see her coming back. It rang again twice, the name Allan Prescott flashing up on the screen each time. His hands itched to answer it, but he knew that would be rude.

It eventually stopped and he was opening another email on his computer when a message flashed up on the screen of her phone. This time he couldn't resist looking at it.

> *"Hi. Please call me as soon as you can. Have you spoken with Jacques Voester yet? I am still searching records and will widen the search nationally. Regards. Allan."*

Ryan's interest was now well and truly piqued. Who were Allan Prescott and Jacques Voester? And what records was he talking about? Were they the journalist colleagues in Johannesburg she'd mentioned?

It was a South African cell-phone number. He took another quick glance out of the window and typed 'Allan Prescott' and 'South Africa' into the search engine. If she came back in, he would have to close it down quickly. Several lines appeared, but, near the top, listed under LinkedIn was the name Allan Prescott, Private Investigator, Albion Investigations.

A shiver ran down Ryan's back despite the humidity in the room. Why on earth would she need a private investigator? What *was* she up to? Was this why she needed to go to Johannesburg? He'd been right all along not to trust Kate and now he had proof.

Chapter Twenty-Three

"I need to go to Johannesburg for a couple of days," Kate said as she climbed out of the swimming pool and dried herself on a towel.

Sara glanced up from her book in surprise. "Why?"

Kate busied herself with drying her legs. She'd been thinking about how she was going to phrase this whilst swimming lengths in the lodge's beautiful infinity pool. Built against the backdrop of large granite rocks, the pool was perched above the river, giving an unbroken view of the valley below.

"I need to meet Eliot Vince, a wildlife photographer who we are hoping will take the images for the article. He's got an incredible reputation. He's been published in *National Geographic* and all over but he can't commit at the moment. I was hoping to connect with him and pin him down."

"Okay—" Sara leant back, absorbing the late afternoon sun "—if you're sure that's what you need to do."

"It's best to do it whilst Eliot is in Johannesburg," Kate continued, "that way I can grab him before his next assignment."

She lay down on the sunbed next to Sara, squinting at

the low-lying sun. "I'll go early tomorrow morning and be back the next day by lunch time, I promise. I really want to interview Rio and Clemmie, for the article. I'm hoping Greg, my editor, will let me write a series about wildlife warriors."

Sara sat up and pushed her sunglasses onto her head. "I've got a great idea. Why don't I come with you? To Johannesburg. We can do some shopping and sink a few cocktails. I am sure I can shift the roster around."

Kate's mind raced furiously. Much as she would love to have a night out with Sara, it would be hard to conceal her plans. Aware she was juggling her personal life alongside her work, Kate knew it wouldn't be long before the two worlds collided.

"That would be lovely, Sara, but I really need to focus on work stuff whilst I'm there. Greg, my editor, has suggested I take Eliot out for dinner, you know, wine and dine him and all that."

Sara clicked her fingers. "I can help you do that. I can tell him all about the game reserve and the animals. Between us we can pretty much bowl him over."

Kate had forgotten that Sara was as stubborn as a mule at times. She leant across and gently touched Sara's arm. "Thanks, sweetie, but I think it should just be me. I promise I won't be gone long."

Sara sniffed. "I think you're up to something." Her eyes lit up. "Is he a love interest? Your boyfriend?" She pouted. "Although if he is, I will be cross you haven't told me about him."

Kate laughed. "You are incorrigible, Sara. He isn't my boyfriend. He's married. To a television producer called Hannah."

"Why the secrecy?"

Kate stamped down her impatience. "I'm not being secretive. It's how I work on assignments sometimes."

An idea hit her, one she'd been toying with since they'd found out more information about the registered owner of the gun involved with the rhino poaching. With a bit of luck it might get Sara off her back.

She bit her lip. "I thought I might also try and interview the owner of a hunting safari company Ryan told me about this afternoon. He's a person of interest with regard to the rhino poaching as the gun that was used was registered to him. His business is based in Johannesburg. I could scout around and see what I find."

Sara peered over her sunglasses. "Are you and Ryan getting on better now?"

Kate waved her hand dismissively. "Sort of…"

Although Kate wasn't so sure. That afternoon, he'd gone from being pleasantly polite to abrupt in the space of half an hour. At first, he'd allowed her to be party to information about the owner of the gun and his hunting business. But when she returned from the kitchen, she'd found Ryan slumped over the desk, his head in his hands.

"Everything okay?" she'd asked as she placed some of Prudence's chocolate brownies on the table. "I am going to head off and join Sara for a swim if that's okay with you."

Ryan hadn't replied so she'd carried on. "But if you want me to stay, or you need some help, I am happy to do so." She'd laughed, hoping to engage his attention. "I like playing detective."

But he'd continued to ignore her, pushing the seat away from his desk, his jaw tight. She'd tensed, her antenna raised. "Has something happened? Is it to do with your friend's death?"

Ryan's lips had curled into a snarl. "Nothing is wrong. I need to go out. We'll talk tomorrow."

Kate had been rooted to the spot as she'd watched him go, once again aware of the contrary nature of this man. It was only when she'd walked back to the lodge to meet Sara that she'd thought to check her phone, which she'd retrieved from Ryan's desk. A message from Allan had arrived whilst she was returning the plates to the kitchen. It hadn't been opened, but the message was still fully visible on the screen. Had Ryan seen it? Was that why he had acted so strangely with her, and if so why? It was none of his business, after all.

She repeated her suggestion about interviewing Quinton Cronje to Sara. "What do you think?"

Sara tipped her head to one side. "That might work. But are you sure that it will be safe?"

Kate laughed. "You do realise that I have travelled to some pretty dodgy parts of the world to research my articles? That I've met warlords in the Democratic Republic of Congo?"

Sara blushed. "I know, but to me you're still my best freckled-faced buddy from school."

"I'm a thirty-six-year-old woman, Sara, not an eleven-year-old running around with a hockey stick."

"Who's running around with a hockey stick?" Gavin appeared at the top of the path leading down to the pool, carrying a tray of cold beers.

He bent down and gave Sara a long kiss. Kate felt a twinge of envy. Gavin was a lovely man. Tall and blonde with a body that reflected his life as a soldier and working in the bush. They made a great couple.

"Kate is off to Johannesburg tomorrow morning." Sara pouted. "She's only just got here and now she's going again. I think we must be too boring for her. She's missing the bright lights."

"That's not true, Sara, and you know it," Kate said, grabbing one of the beers and flipping off the top with the opener Gavin had brought.

She filled Gavin in. "I have to hook up with the photographer we are hoping to use whilst he is in Jo'burg."

Gavin removed the top of his beer bottle and clinked it with Kate's. "Cheers," he said, taking a long sip of his beer. "Sounds reasonable to me. Have you booked your flight?"

"Yes, I am booked on the eight o'clock tomorrow morning from Kruger Mpumalanga Airport."

"We'll sort out a transfer to the airport for you," Gavin suggested. "It's about half an hour. Where are you going to stay? We have a couple of hotels near Sandton that we have discounts with. I'll ring one of them and book you a room."

"That would be great, thank you, Gavin. You've been so helpful." She glared at Sara, who appeared to be sulking. "At least one of the managers of this lodge is amenable."

Sara gave a mock smile and sat up, opening her beer, her voice businesslike. "Kate, about the interview with the hunting safari guy. I think that's a good idea. You could really use the interview for your article, one side of the story so to speak. But…" she held up her hand in case Kate was going to interrupt "…I think you should take someone with you. Ryan, for example. You don't know what this person might be like and Ryan has good instincts."

Kate was about to comment when Gavin cut in. "That's not a bad idea, Kate. I've been speaking to Ryan and he needs to head off to Jo'burg anyway to talk to Leonard's previous employers and catch up with Ed Webster from the illegal wildlife section of Hawks. That could all work well."

Kate's heart sank. The last thing she needed was Ryan tagging along. "I doubt Ryan will want to come with me." She pulled a face. "Is it just me or is he quite moody? One minute he's happy to discuss the case and contribute to the article and then the next he's dismissing me. I really can't read him and I'm not sure he likes me."

Sara winked. "Oh, he likes you. I've seen the way he looks at you." She made to stand up. "But if he's still being rude to you, I'll have a word with him."

Gavin gently pushed his wife back down. "No you don't. I know what you're like." He gave Kate a thoughtful look. "I don't know what's going on with Ryan at the moment, but he's a good man. A bloody good soldier and anti-poaching ranger. I think the rhino poaching has spooked him. You become complacent and think you've won the battle and then when something like this happens, you're left reeling."

"He doesn't blame himself for it surely," Kate said.

"Not exactly. Ryan's a complicated guy. He is practical and honest, but he's also introverted and sensitive, a loner. It takes him a while to trust people, but when he does he's a true friend." He lowered his voice. "Between you and me, I think he suffers a little from PTSD. When I met him in Iraq we were both out of the army and working as private security consultants. He'd been through some serious action in Afghanistan, and whilst he hadn't been medically discharged, I got the feeling there was more to his leaving the army than meets the eye."

Kate sat back in her seat and drank her beer. The sun was spreading out across the horizon in a hazy lemon glow and the bush surrounding the pool buzzed with insects. She thought about Ryan, about the way he smiled and joked with his colleagues, how he lifted his head up to the sky in the early morning air and breathed in the sweet, soft scent.

"What happened to him in Afghanistan?"

Gavin drained his beer. "All I know is that he went on an unplanned mine sweep and the team were ambushed. The info from the officers was incorrect or something. Two of his men died and three were badly injured. Ryan wasn't hurt, but I think it triggered something in him."

He touched Kate's arm. "Let me talk to Ryan about going with you. I think he'll come around to it. After all, he did say he wanted to meet with the Hawks people. You can see your photographer guy and, if Ryan's okay with it, you could talk to the hunting guy. It's worth a try."

Kate gave in. "Okay. Thanks, Gavin." It wasn't ideal; she didn't really want Ryan breathing down her neck. Hopefully, he wouldn't be interested in accompanying her anyway.

Chapter Twenty-Four

Ryan was enjoying a quiet beer at the bar chatting to Michael and tossing peanuts into his mouth when Gavin slapped him on the back. Ryan nearly choked.

"Watch it, mate!"

Gavin sat on one of the high stools next to Ryan and eyed up the beer. "Where the hell did you get that?" he asked, staring at the large glass full of dark, full-bodied English ale.

Ryan tapped his nose. "Michael's got contacts with a supplier in Johannesburg. He gets it in especially for me. It's from a local brewery near my hometown in Derbyshire. And don't worry, I pay for it myself, so you don't need to tell The Boss."

They smiled at each other conspiratorially. When Ryan said The Boss, he meant Sara, and they both knew it. Gavin reached across and took a sip, grimacing at the taste. "How can you drink this?" he asked, gratefully accepting the bottle of cold Castle beer Michael had quietly placed in front of him.

"It reminds me of home," Ryan said. "I don't mind lager but occasionally it's nice to sip an ale and imagine I am back home, sitting in the corner by the fire in The Dog and Duck, watching a bunch of old men play darts."

Gavin snorted. "I thought Africa was your home."

Ryan laughed. "It is. But we all come from somewhere."

He stared down into his glass. Drinking the local ale from his hometown brought back both happy and bad memories. Like the time he went home after receiving his final discharge papers from the army. He'd come home to see his parents and tell them of his plans to take up a job in security consulting in Iraq. It was good pay and best of all, there'd be no active service.

His mother had cried with relief. "I've been so worried about you. I know I should be used to it, what with your father being in the army – it's the only life we've ever known – but the whole situation in Afghanistan is a different kettle of fish."

She'd wiped her eyes and hugged him again, bustling around the kitchen, making tea. His father, however, had stared at him thoughtfully, his eyes a study of disapproval. Later, when he was in the local pub with his father, he'd braced himself for the tirade that would come.

"What the hell are you going to do with your life now?" his father had railed. "That security training lark is not a career. You'll be bored by the end of the first week, desperate for some action. You mark my words."

Ryan had been expecting that. As a career soldier, his father would never understand the restlessness that lived within Ryan. When Ryan joined the army, he thought he had it made. It was the sort of life he hankered for: fast-paced, on-the-edge-of-your-seat excitement. At times it was exhilarating, and other times, when they were involved with peacekeeping, it was a different pace, and he'd enjoyed the people side, helping war-torn countries rebuild their lives.

After the landmine incident and the many other situations, including the killing of civilians by British soldiers, albeit accidentally, the cause became hard to believe in. For him, at least. Lack of faith in the army had crept up on him, slowly at first and then quickly, seeping into his psyche like a virus, taking hold and forcing him to face the truth. Leaving the army was the only option. He'd tried hard to explain all of this to his father. He'd thought that as a soldier himself, his father would get it. But he was from the old-school army and to him PTSD was a dirty word.

Drinking the beer shipped from England also made him think of Jim, a true northerner and a lover of fine ales. He gulped on a mouthful and pushed away the image of Jim's body on the ground, torn apart by the explosion, his screams piercing the air.

"Mate—" Gavin brought Ryan back to the present "—I have a proposition for you."

"What is it?"

Gavin rubbed his neck and Ryan's antenna pulsed. He didn't think he was going to like what Gavin had to say.

"You know how you wanted to hook up with the guy from Hawks and talk to Leonard's previous employer?"

Ryan nodded and sipped his ale, waiting for Gavin to get to the point.

"Well, apparently Kate needs to go to Johannesburg to meet with some photographer guy, and Sara and I thought maybe you could accompany her." He raised his hand quickly to fend off any comment Ryan might make. "I know you're not keen, but she's suggested that she interview that hunting safari guy whilst she's there as a way of trying to find out more about how legitimate his business it. Sara and I feel she shouldn't go on her own and thought maybe you could go with her, in case there's a problem. What do you think?"

Ryan snorted. "I think I have been stitched up."

"Come on. It will be fine. She's booked onto the eight o'clock flight from Mpumalanga tomorrow morning. There's still seats available. You can both stay at the Jacaranda Lodge." He gave a wicked grin. "Separate rooms, of course."

Ryan folded his arms. "I have stuff to do tomorrow."

Gavin patted him on the shoulder. "I checked the schedule and you're not on duty until two days' time. If you get the early flight back on Thursday, you can be back in plenty of time for the evening patrol."

Ryan scratched his head. It wasn't a bad idea. Whilst he could talk to Leonard's ex-employer on the phone and catch up with Ed on Skype, it might be good to tie it all up face to face.

Ryan flipped the beer mat over. "Okay, fair enough. But I'm not babysitting her. It would be odd if I went with her to interview Cronje. I can base myself nearby and make sure she doesn't come to any harm."

Besides, it might be a good idea for him to keep an eye on her. She was definitely up to something, especially after that text she'd received earlier that day from the private investigator. And she'd lied to Gavin and Sara, telling them she was going to see a photographer. She'd told Ryan she would be meeting with her newspaper colleagues. Ryan had googled the *Daily Tribune*, and their bureau in South Africa was based in Cape Town not Johannesburg.

"I'll book my flight, if you can sort the hotel." He drained his beer and stood up. "I'll try to catch Ed now and set up a time to meet him."

"And I," said Gavin, "will tell the ladies, although if I know my wife, she's probably already made the bookings." He pivoted back to Ryan. "Have you got plans for tonight?"

Ryan gazed outside towards the now darkened sky, the bush closing in on the boundaries of the lodge. "Yeah, I'm heading to a Michelin-starred restaurant and then on to a club."

"Very funny. We've got Kate joining us at the house for a braai. Why don't you come?"

Ryan shook his head. "Nah. I'll grab a plate of something from the kitchen and head home. Thanks anyway. Can you tell Kate I'll meet her out the front at quarter to six tomorrow morning and I'll drive us to the airport?"

Gavin tipped his head to one side. "Are you sure? I'm doing my famous chilli sauce."

Ryan often joined Gavin and Sara for dinner in their little cottage. Even though Prudence was one of the best chefs in the whole of the Southern Kruger – in his opinion anyway – it was nice to have a home-cooked meal from time to time. He was tempted though; it would be nice to sit outside by the glowing embers of the braai and watch insects dip and dive over the citronella candles. Gavin had an extensive collection of great South African wines, one of the perks of being the lodge manager.

But Ryan was exhausted and not really in the mood for acting polite and making small talk. He patted Gavin on the shoulder. "Tempting as your chilli sauce is, I'm going to take a rain check."

"Your loss, mate," Gavin said as he walked away, a bounce in his step.

Chapter Twenty-Five

Johannesburg

Goosebumps prickled on Kate's arms as she settled on a high stool. The café had just opened for the day and the air conditioning was ramped up high, the clean smell of disinfectant and polish resonating throughout. In the corner, a young waitress was folding napkins and occasionally stealing a glance at her phone.

Kate had arrived early, managing to give Ryan the slip once they'd arrived at their hotel in Johannesburg. The flight from the Kruger was a short hop and she'd fallen asleep within minutes of takeoff, the stress of the last few days catching up with her. She and Ryan had barely spoken to each other between leaving the lodge and arriving in Johannesburg, tension still simmering between them. But the silence suited Kate, as she was feeling extremely nervous about meeting her uncle.

She was checking emails on her phone when a shadow fell across her. A tall man with a full beard and auburn hair peppered with silver was standing beside her. He was broad- shouldered with a deep tan, his face etched with wrinkles and he wore casual trousers and collared shirt, a mobile phone in a holder on his belt.

He hesitated. "Kate?"

She slid off the bar stool and held out her hand, which was shaking a little. "Yes. Jacques?"

He took her hand in his, hazel eyes examining her. "My God, it's like seeing a ghost. You are so much like Alison."

"I am?" she said, trying to appear confident. Beneath the surface she was only just holding it together, her heart beating madly in her chest.

"Yes." Jacques's face paled under his tan as he took in Kate's features. "Your chin and your nose, your hair, so like Ali when she was younger."

"Sorry, sorry." A woman bustled into the bar. "I was caught on a phone call."

Like Jacques she was tall, her hair short and curly. Her face was friendly as she took Kate's hand. "I'm Jacques's wife, Anneka."

The three of them continued to stare at each other until Anneka broke the spell. "Well, this is such a surprise." Her blue eyes assessed Kate's features shrewdly. "I knew he had a sister, of course, but I never got to meet her. Jacques had told me about her baby." She shook her head. "We had no idea what had happened to you. He did try to find you both many times, but you'd completely disappeared."

Jacques was visibly upset, his hands gripping the table in front of him. Kate swallowed the lump in her throat and gestured to the chairs. "Shall we sit down?"

They ordered coffee and Kate searched for a neutral subject to break the ice. She remembered Jacques telling her about their family on the phone.

"How old are your sons?"

Anneka beamed. "Mark's our eldest; he's thirty-six now." She pulled out her phone and showed Kate a wedding photo of a tall dark-haired man and a pretty brunette woman on the beach, smiling happily into the sun. "He's married to Effie and they have two-year-old Theo."

Jacques gave a broad smile and cut in. "Our noisy grandson."

Kate swallowed thickly. "And you have another son?"

Anneka beamed again. "Yes, Alistair. He's thirty-three and lives in New York. He's a theatre producer on Broadway. He lived in London before that. It's where he met his girlfriend, Jo. They are talking about getting married soon."

Kate examined the photos. A whole new family projecting out at her. One she knew nothing about. To think she could have been walking around London and strolled right past Alistair, not knowing he was her cousin.

Six months earlier, she'd buried her parents, thinking she was the only person left in her family. And now she had an uncle and two cousins. A new extended family.

Tears sprang in her eyes. "Sorry," she said, dashing them away. "It's a lot to take in."

The waitress brought the coffee and Anneka patted Kate's arm softly. "I'm sure it is, my dear. Jacques has been thinking non-stop about you since you called."

She handed Kate a photograph. "I found this. It was at the back of an old family album. I remember seeing it years ago, and luckily, it was still tucked away where I last saw it."

The picture showed a much younger Jacques, beardless with his hair short and a deep chestnut brown. Next to him was a woman, tall and slim, with the same colour hair and an angular face with high cheekbones and pink smiling lips. It was Alison; there was too much of a likeness for it not to be her. Kate's pulse thudded in her ears.

Jacques's face softened as he stared at the photo. "It was taken at our parents' house on the day of my twenty-first birthday. We were both heading off to new adventures, me to an engineering job in Pretoria and Alison to university. She had turned eighteen two weeks before; both our birthdays are in January." He stared fondly at the photo. "We were so eager to get away, especially Alison. Unusually, Ma and Pa were happy that day too; the mood was jolly."

Kate examined the photo, noting for the first time the wide green lawn the pair of them were standing on, and the sweep of a blue sky behind. Siblings smiling in the sunshine. Alison was staring straight at the camera, her eyes crinkled at the sides as if she were squinting into full sunlight. It was a photo full of hope.

"Can I keep this for now?" she asked. "I promise to look after it and I will make sure you get it back." She found herself babbling, a little nervous but so desperately wanting to cling on to this image of her mother. Apart from the copy of Alison's university student photo, she had nothing else to go on.

"Of course, my dear," Anneka said.

Jacques's face was grave again. "I feel awful that I never tried to find her properly all these years. It was tough for her. She didn't get on well with our pa and he was not happy with her living in the city and studying." He shook his head. "He was very traditional and believed a woman's place was in the home."

Anneka rolled her eyes. "I can vouch for that. Your

maternal grandfather was a classic chauvinist pig."

Jacques pulled a face. "It was his generation. It wasn't only women either; he wasn't happy with me clearing off to work somewhere different. Like Alison, I hardly went back once I left. Our two older brothers, Anton and Karl, were happy enough to take up the farming mantle."

Kate's throat was dry and scratchy. "Are your brothers still alive?"

"Yes, although I rarely see them. They were both young when they married." He gave a dry laugh. "They have big families – four kids each plus grandchildren."

"I think Anton has a great-grandchild," Anneka said.

Kate cupped the mug of steaming coffee. "I don't even know my grandparents' names."

Jacques reached out his hand towards hers but retracted it. Like her, he was clearly still processing their connection. "Our father was called Johannes and our mother was Katherine. I think Alison named you after her."

Kate's phone beeped on the table and she scanned the message quickly. It was from Ryan.

Where are you?

She shoved the phone into her handbag and took a sip of coffee. "Tell me more about Alison."

Jacques leant back in his chair. "She loved animals and was nuts about saving the planet. She was a badge-wearing member of Greenpeace and eager to join rallies against whale hunting and the like. This, of course, made her unpopular with Pa. He hated her joining protest marches. She was clever too; she studied ecology at Cape Town university and then went on to do a Masters in Land Conservation. She was doing all right until…"

"She met my father," Kate guessed.

"Yes," Jacques said. "Who knows how things might have panned out had she not become involved with him."

Kate gave a harsh laugh. "Well, one thing's for sure, I wouldn't be here now if they hadn't met." She met his eyes directly. "Do you really have no idea where she might be now?"

"As I told you on the phone, the last time I saw her was at our mother's funeral, but she didn't speak to anyone. She arrived as the service began and left soon after. Then about two years later I got a postcard from her from Zimbabwe. We'd moved house, so it went to our old address but was forwarded on. It was months old by the time we got it. God knows what she was doing up there. The country was in the middle of a civil war. Anyway, it didn't say much, only that she was travelling. I didn't hear from her again for many years, and then out of the blue, I got an email from her. It must be about twenty years ago now. She sent it to my work email address. I have no idea how she found me, but I suppose she'd called the company to get my details or maybe did an online search."

Kate leant forward. "What did she say?"

"She wanted money again. Only a lot more than the last time. It was for some kind of business venture she was in. I was quite taken back, angry really, so I didn't reply. I mean, I'd heard nothing for years and the only time she made contact was to ask for money."

Kate was surprised at his sudden irritation. It must have been a shock and a disappointment for Jacques having his sister pop up out of the blue asking for money. Kate would be annoyed too if someone did that to her after such a long time apart, but Alison was his sister, his flesh and blood. Did that count for nothing?

Jacques spoke softly as if reading her mind. "I regret not following it up. Alison was vulnerable and troubled. We'd probably say she had mental health issues if it were today. She was always different, even as a child. She was bright but untamed."

Kate's head throbbed. Was that why she gave her up? Because she was unhinged? Unfit to be a mother? Had her parents noticed this and offered to adopt her, to take her with them back to England? It must have been a cause for concern.

Anneka interrupted her thoughts. "Tell her, Jacques."

Husband and wife exchanged glances. A vein throbbed on Jacques's forehead, his eyes drawn into a frown.

"Go on," Anneka encouraged. "She needs to know."

A shiver ran down Kate's back. "Need to know what?"

Jacques frowned. "A few weeks after I received the email, our father died and I decided I would try to speak to her after all. Despite his disdain of her, he'd left her some money and I wanted to give it to her. I replied to the email address she'd sent the original message from but got no reply. Social media wasn't around then and I even tried contacting her old friends, but no one had heard from her in ages."

"You're right about that," Kate said. "The private investigator has found no digital trail of her at all."

"A few weeks later I got an email out of the blue from some anonymous guy using her email address and claiming to be her husband. I assumed it was a scam and ignored him, but he was persistent, emailing a couple of times and asking for money. A 'loan' he called it. He didn't give a name, and simply signed it 'your brother-in-law'. Of course I didn't send him any money and told him

I would report him. And then he sent me an attachment to the next email."

Apprehension trickled down Kate's spine. "What was it?"

Jacques's face sagged. "It was some kind of police report dating back to the early 2000s. It listed a group of people wanted in connection with an armed robbery and murder. Alison's name was on the list."

Kate was horrified. "Do you think she went to prison?"

"I have no idea. I got a lawyer to investigate it. He traced her to Johannesburg where she was listed as a suspected agitator for an animal rights group, but there was no evidence of her ever being arrested or doing time. I can only assume that this so-called husband was a fraud and it was a false document. He was clearly using her name and details to try to extract money from me."

Kate's mind rushed furiously. "I'll ask the private investigator I have been using to look into it. I don't suppose you kept the email?"

"No. It was a long time ago, I'm afraid."

"Where was the police report from?"

Jacques thought for a moment. "Pietermaritzburg."

Kate had no idea where that was. "Okay, I'll see what Allan can dig up. It might lead us to her, or at least give us some idea of what happened after that. Unless..." Kate's eyes flicked between her uncle and aunt "...you think she's dead?"

Jacques paled under his tan. "I honestly don't know, but I fear she might be. She was a natural adrenaline junkie, drawn to the wrong sorts of things and to undesirable people. The man who claimed to be her husband didn't seem like a nice person to me, trying to extort money like that."

"Maybe she didn't know about it," Kate suggested. "He might have been using her to get money."

Anneka grimaced. "Or Alison might just be plain bad. I'm sorry, my dear, I know you don't want to hear this, but if that document was correct, she did have a criminal record."

Jacques's face was furrowed in frustration. "I honestly don't believe she had it in her to kill someone. She was such a kind child. She hated it when the lambs from the farm were sent off to slaughter. She was a vegetarian long before it was in vogue." His hazel eyes were sheened with sorrow. "I should have done more to find her, but at the end of the day, she chose to disappear, not to keep in touch, and what else was I supposed to do?"

Kate touched his arm gently. "I'm sorry, I didn't mean to dig it all up. I don't even know why I am doing this. All I know is that from the moment I found out the truth, I haven't stopped thinking about her and where she might be."

Jacques gripped her hands. "I'm sorry I haven't been able to answer all your questions. I still can't believe it's you, my long-lost niece, after all these years." He reached for his coffee, his hands shaking as he lifted the cup to his lips.

Anneka fussed around him. "Do you need a pill?" she asked, filling a glass of water from the jug on the table.

"I'm all right," Jacques said. But he didn't look it and Kate eyed him worriedly.

Anneka gave her husband a pill and he popped it under his tongue and swallowed some water. "I think that's enough for now," she fussed. "He needs time to process everything."

Jacques pushed himself up. "Don't fret, Anneka." He appraised Kate, his voice steadier. "I loved my sister and I would like to know anything you find out, whatever the circumstances."

Guilt flickered through Kate. "Of course, and sorry for upsetting you."

He headed for the rest rooms and Anneka watched him go.

Anneka's voice was soft. "I know you meant well, my dear, but he had a heart attack a couple of years ago and it's best if he's not stressed about things. This has dredged up too many old memories."

Kate lowered her head. "I understand. It's been quite traumatic for me too. One day I am perfectly happy living my life in England with two loving parents and the next I find myself at a double funeral with my whole family gone and then my godfather turns up with a birth certificate indicating that Ginny wasn't my real mother."

Anneka's eyes softened. "My dear, perhaps you should honour Ginny's memory by continuing to see her as your real mother. She brought you up all these years. Doesn't that count for something?"

"Of course it does, but I do need to know what happened to Alison."

Anneka's eyes creased in concern. "Why?"

Why indeed? Why had Kate set herself on this fool's errand? What exactly was she expecting to find? By the sounds of it, it was unlikely to be the rose-tinted reunion she'd imagined, and yet she couldn't stop thinking about what it would be like to stare into the eyes of the woman who had given birth to her.

Jacques returned from the rest room and the three of

them stood awkwardly by the door. Kate gave her uncle a gentle hug.

Anneka embraced her. "Whatever you find out, please keep in touch."

Tears filled Kate's eyes. "I will. And I would very much like to get to know you both if that's all right?"

Anneka's face creased into a jovial smile. "You'll always be welcome, my dear. But make sure you don't get your hopes up too high about finding Alison. We'd hate for you to be hurt."

Those words resonated through Kate's mind as she left the bar and walked down the wide city pavement. She found a bench in a small square nearby and sent a text to Allan, who promised to do some digging into the police report Jacques had mentioned.

As the hot sun beat down on her head, she pulled out the photo Anneka had given her and examined it closely. Alison's hair was the same colour as Kate's, long with tendrils curling around her face as she smiled shyly at the camera.

The face was so familiar, as if she'd met her before. Was this because Kate was now subconsciously projecting this image into her memory bank, or was it a real memory of the woman she'd spent the first three years of her life with? Or, to put it simply, was it because the face staring back at her was so much like her own? What was it Anneka had said before they parted? "Two peas in a pod."

She checked the time. She ought to get back to the hotel to meet Ryan. He'd texted again since she'd left the bar. She clambered to her feet and then a sudden surge of dizziness hit her. She sat back down, finding the heat oppressive, and closed her eyes, taking deep breaths to control the pulse of blood in her temples.

A woman walked past with a child in a stroller, the toddler screaming as they went. Kate's head spun and an image flickered across her mind – a face sneering under a leather hat, big workmen's boots kicking a dog, a woman shouting and a child screaming, the sound of breaking glass and the sweet, sickly smell of alcohol. Where had that come from? Nausea rose in her mouth and she fell to her knees on the grass and vomited.

Chapter Twenty-Six

Ryan sat in the hotel lobby and checked his phone for the fourth time. Kate was late. They'd agreed to meet at two o'clock and travel together to Quinton's office near Mandela Square in Sandton. It was only a short walk from the hotel, but the day was so humid that Ryan had already decided they would take a taxi.

That morning he'd visited the mining company that had employed Leonard as a security guard. The personnel officer hadn't been particularly helpful. She hadn't been working there at the time Leonard was employed, and the thin file she removed from the filing cabinet didn't show anything to be concerned about. It was only when Ryan was making his way out of the building that one of the security guards on duty stopped him.

"I hear you were asking about Leonard," he'd said as Ryan walked across the lobby.

Ryan eyed the nametag on the man's shirt. "Did you work with him, Vincent?"

"Yes, for a few months. He did quite a few shifts with me."

"What was he like?"

Vincent tsked. "He was no good, always late for work

and more often than not I would find him on his phone instead of watching the security screens."

"You didn't trust him?"

"Not really, but it wasn't as if he did anything wrong. He was just not interested in the job. If you ask me, I think he was dealing on the side, or something like that."

Ryan raised an eyebrow. "Dealing?"

"Yes, or up to no good anyway. He'd sneak off for a break and come back late. Or he'd ask to leave early. Plus, I once saw him in a notorious drug bar downtown. I was walking past after my shift, I change buses near there, and he was inside with some unsavoury people. He'd called in sick that day too." Vincent pulled a face. "I might be wrong, but I can honestly say I was glad to be shot of him. Also, he told me he would never work in security in a game reserve. That's why I was surprised he'd applied for a job with you."

Ryan's brow furrowed. "Did he say why?"

"Something to do with a cousin who'd been sacked. I can't remember exactly."

Ryan was glad Vincent had sought him out; his comments echoed those of Albert back at the reserve checkpoint. Ryan was finally beginning to put together a picture of Leonard, and it wasn't good news.

His phone buzzed and a message from Kate appeared on the screen.

> *Running late. I have gone straight to Quinton Cronje's office. Will see you later at hotel for debrief. Kate.*

Ryan reread the text in disbelief. They had specifically agreed to go together. It had been Sara's request that Ryan tag along to make sure Kate was all right. He would have been more than happy to stay at the game reserve getting on with his work.

He checked his watch again; it was nearly ten past two. He swore under his breath and hauled himself up from the leather sofa in the lobby. He'd already worked out there was a small shopping precinct with a café opposite the office block. He'd grab a sandwich and a coffee and watch for her. At least he would have fulfilled his end of the bargain. As he sat in the back of the taxi, he angrily tapped out a reply to Kate, hoping she'd get it before she went into the meeting.

> *I wish you had waited to speak to me first. I wanted to brief you after my meeting with Ed Webster from Hawks. I have my concerns about Quinton Cronje. It is likely he has links with a poaching syndicate in Dar Es Salaam. Ed is investigating a shell company linked to Q. Please be careful. Don't ask too probing questions. You are there as a travel journalist not as an investigative one. Don't antagonise the man. I will be across the road in a café in the Sunshine shopping centre. R*

He pressed send and took a deep breath, slowly exhaling to calm his anger. It was on her head if anything happened, although the threat was low; it was the middle of the day in an office, after all, but he wished she'd waited for him to brief her first.

To be honest, he was more concerned about the damage she might do to the investigation. Ed and his team were pretty sure Quinton was the middleman who could lead them all the way to the top of the syndicate. But they needed to find the evidence. Not that it was Ryan's job to do that. In theory, his role, as anti-poaching control, was finished, but for some reason he couldn't let this one go. It was on his patch and it was personal.

Chapter Twenty-Seven

Quinton Cronje's office was exactly as Kate had imagined it to be. A cream leather sofa and chrome and glass coffee table adorned the reception area, and on the wall above the sofa, stretched out over a canvas, was the skin of a zebra. Kate gulped. She was surprised there wasn't a trophy head on display. Perhaps he had one in his office.

Whilst she sat on the low sofa, she perused the selection of hunting, shooting and fishing magazines on display. She knew shooting game was popular in parts of England, but she'd never really found the idea of wandering around fields on a damp autumn day, shooting pheasants, as something exciting or fun to do, even if it was an ancient activity.

Killing a pheasant was one thing, but the image of a man squatting in pride beside a dead elephant, gun in one hand, was pretty grotesque. She would have to work hard to hide her feelings during this interview, even if it *was* just a cover story. In her research about trophy hunting, she'd been sickened by the images of hunters standing next to their prey, their faces glowing with excitement. She'd read the arguments and the counter-arguments and found it hard not to take a side. In her opinion, trophy hunting was vile and narcissistic, an example of humans at their worst.

She probably shouldn't have come here without Ryan, but she couldn't face him at the moment. After being sick in the park, she'd gone to a café and bought water and mint tea to try to calm her churning stomach, but she was still reeling from her discoveries about Alison's wayward past, and from the memory flashback.

She had no idea what these images meant and why she was suddenly having them. Was it her mind playing tricks on her? After all, the human brain was capable of all sorts of things, and perhaps hers was simply planting ideas based on her subconscious.

"Miss Harper?" Quinton Cronje's deep voice startled her.

Glancing up into dazzling blue eyes, she scrambled to her feet and he engulfed her hand in a firm grip. Dressed casually in jeans and a white linen shirt with a dark tan and blonde hair, he reminded her of Robert Redford. She was mesmerised by his bright eyes, momentarily unaware he was still holding her hand.

She extracted her hand from his. "Thank you for seeing me."

"The pleasure is all mine," he replied, his eyes not even trying to hide their appraisal of her. He gestured towards his office. "Shall we go in?"

She followed him into a large office decorated in much the same way as the reception area, the pièce de résistance being the head of a huge antelope placed above the desk, with two guns hanging on the wall either side. She gaped up at it.

Quinton sat down in a black leather chair beneath the

trophy head. "Magnificent, isn't it?"

Kate's eyes darted away from the trophy head. "Um…" It wasn't magnificent. It was horrible, a stark reminder of something primitive and brutal, with its glass eyes staring creepily down at her, lifeless and eerie.

"It's a Cape eland," he informed her. "I caught it myself. It was my first proper shoot. I'll never forget the thrill of it." He puffed out his chest like a proud parent. "He's called Bertie. He's been with me for a long time, my good-luck charm."

Kate eyed the guns on either side. "And the guns?"

"They belonged to my great-grandfather. He was a farmer in what was once called Northern Transvaal; it's now Limpopo Province. The one on the right is a Westley Richards .425 calibre rifle and the other is a .450. They were used for hunting as well as farm work. In the early days, my great-grandfather would have used them to protect the land against predators like leopards and the like. They're collectors' items now."

Quinton leant forward on his desk and steepled his fingers. "Remind me again what this article is about and where it is being published."

"It's for a travel supplement in a major newspaper. I'm writing a series of articles about South Africa. We're covering all sorts of things including safari, hunting, vineyards, beaches, history – all of it."

"And the publication?" he asked. "We like to make sure we have details of all our press mentions." He gave her a huge grin, his teeth gleaming white under the dazzle of his blue eyes.

"It will be in the *Daily Tribune*, but I am not sure when it will be published," she said. "Obviously, I will let you know."

She hoped Quinton wouldn't contact the paper before she'd had a chance to prime Greg. Searching for a quick change of topic, she spotted a photo of a teenage boy on the desk, a rifle slung over his shoulder and his foot on the neck of a small antelope. "Is that your son?"

"Ya, that's Sammy." He picked up the photo frame. "That was taken on his first shoot. He's a bit older now, he's twenty, but he was around thirteen then."

"Does your whole family shoot?"

"I only have one child, and his mother, my wife, isn't that keen on shooting. She tolerates it. My business partner, Amy, however, is a keen markswoman. She has a lot of experience in the travel industry, so it made sense for us to set up the business together."

He pointed to a framed photo behind Kate of a pretty blonde woman squatting beside a large antelope in the classic proud hunter pose.

"This is Amy with a red hartebeest she killed with one shot. Aren't the horns amazing? They're like Harley Davidson motorbike handles."

Kate scrutinised the attractive woman in the photo. The reality of trophy hunting once again was staring out at her in larger-than-life images. A so-called glamorous Instagram post. She appeared to be several years younger than Quinton, and Kate had a sneaking suspicion she was more than just a business partner.

She blinked the images away. "Tell me about your business." She settled back in the chair, wanting to give him the confidence to talk freely. "Were you always into hunting?"

Quinton leant back in his chair and crossed his legs. "I

was in the army for a few years, and after I left, I travelled extensively throughout Africa, eventually settling in Mozambique and setting up a couple of businesses, one running fishing trips. The shores off Mozambique are incredible for fishing. And then I set up a cloth manufacturing business. The colourful Mozambique designs were quite popular in Europe at the time. My wife was involved with running the businesses in Maputo and I travelled extensively, building up networks. Then one day, a friend who was a professional hunter approached me. He knew I had guns and hunted as an amateur and suggested I join him as a freelancer. Most hunting safari companies hire professionals to go with the guests on their trips." He beamed across the desk at her. "After that, I didn't look back."

"What kind of trips do you offer?"

"Have a flick through this." Quinton handed her a glossy brochure. "We do offer first-time beginner trips as well as the full Big-Five luxury bonanza."

Kate shuddered at his marketing jargon. She was continually drawn to the strange eyes of the trophy overhead, wondering what the animal must have thought at that last fleeting moment before it met its death.

She forced herself back to the questioning. "How many people work for your organisation?"

Quinton settled into his chair. "I employ at any one time up to twenty people depending on the number of trips we have booked. I hire sought-after private hunters with great reputations for being good hunters and for helping the client obtain their trophy safely and in a way which ensures the animal doesn't suffer."

Kate's mouth fell open. "I would have thought it is

impossible to avoid hurting an animal if you shoot them. The aim is to kill them, after all."

Quinton rolled an expensive fountain pen around in his hands. "Fair point, but what I meant was that if someone shoots an animal in the wrong part of their body and doesn't kill them with that one shot, the animal might run off or get lost in thick bush and would take longer to die, especially if we can't find it."

"So you're saying that a clean one-off shot is kinder?"

"Yes." He tipped his head to one side. "Have you ever used a gun or gone shooting? I know the Brits love their hunting."

Kate bit the inside of her cheek. "No, I haven't, and only a small number of people hunt in Britain. It's not exactly a highly desirable hobby."

"They have been shooting and culling in England and Scotland for centuries. It's a way of keeping the natural balance of things. Much the same reason as we do it here in South Africa."

"Do you think killing endangered animals, like a..." Kate picked up the brochure "...black rhino for a hundred and fifty thousand dollars, is keeping the natural balance, given the black rhino population is now below six thousand?"

Quinton's eyes narrowed. "It's harsh, I know, but bear in mind money goes back into the pot for the conservation of wildlife, including rhinos. We are committed to ethical practices and hunting that promotes conservation of most species."

Kate wondered how much money from trophy hunting really did go into conservation.

"And what will you do when there are no big trophy

animals left? Because it's likely that will be the case in twenty or thirty years' time."

A trickle of irritation crept into his voice. "Not if we balance how many we hunt, like only killing rogue elephant bulls, for example."

Biting down a further retort, Kate carried on. "What sort of guns do you use?"

Quinton relaxed back into his chair. "Most hunters use a bolt-action rifle, like a .375. They are brilliant for accuracy and can deliver a single lethal shot from a safe distance."

Kate shuddered at the word 'lethal'. "Do you provide them to the guests or do they bring their own?"

"Hunters usually bring their own guns, unless they are novices, of course."

Kate was persistent. "But you do provide guns for some people?"

"We run three or four novice hunting trips a year and will generally provide guns and shooting instruction for the customers."

"Do the guns ever get stolen?"

Quinton frowned. "Of course not. We're extremely careful with our guns. All gun owners are."

Kate was about to ask her next question when Quinton's phone buzzed on his desk. He spoke quietly to his secretary and gave Kate an apologetic grimace.

"It appears I am double-booked. A gun salesman is here to see me. Let me pop out and speak to him for a few minutes. I can set him up in the conference room and then come back to finish the interview. Do you mind waiting?"

"No, of course not. I appreciate your time."

He pushed back his chair. "Have a flick through our

brochure whilst you wait. Can I get you anything to drink? A coffee?"

"No, thank you," Kate replied. She was glad of the reprieve; she'd heard her phone beep earlier and wanted to check it. Also, with him out of the office, it gave her time to have a quick snoop around. She wouldn't touch or open drawers, and if anyone asked, she'd say she was stretching her legs.

She waited until he was gone and pulled out her phone, reading Ryan's text and grimacing at the tone. She took in the words about not asking probing questions. Did he think she was stupid? It would be good to find something to prove to him she knew what she was doing.

Chapter Twenty-Eight

Kate scanned the room, looking for any paperwork or files lying around. But the room was sparse. To the right of the desk was a row of black filing cabinets with a few box files on the top. Quinton's desk was tidy with only a notepad by the phone and a large black leather diary. Quickly checking the office door, she made her way to the filing cabinets, but as she suspected, they were locked.

On Quinton's side of the desk, she reached for the computer mouse and moved it to wake up the console. The wallpaper image of his screen flickered into life, revealing a gruesome photo of a large lion slumped on the ground, its beautiful black mane matted with blood. Standing beside it with one foot on the lion's shoulder was Quinton, his eyes smiling under a brown leather hat.

A cold dart of apprehension hit Kate. The image was no more horrible than any of the others she'd viewed in the last few hours, but there was something about it that shocked her more than she'd expected.

The ping of an email distracted her and a message floated across the screen. Kate swallowed heavily and checked the door again. She heard the mumbled sound of Quinton speaking but otherwise all was quiet. She

flicked her eyes back to the screen and quickly scanned
the message.

> *It was good to catch up last week. Your braai*
> *was great – love that peppered steak. Have*
> *you paid off the team? We need to make sure*
> *our contact in Kruger stays quiet. Can we*
> *trust him? When can I expect the shipment*
> *from Maputo? I can get my courier to Palma*
> *by the end of the weekend. Can you get the*
> *stuff there?*

Kate couldn't read the rest of the message, and when
she moved the mouse again, a password request opened
up on the screen. Damn, she hadn't managed to read who
the message was from. But it was interesting, nonetheless,
especially the phrases 'contact in Kruger' and 'expect the
shipment'.

She opened the diary and flicked through the pages.
The pages were mainly blank but she spotted a diary note
with the letters H.B. scheduled many times throughout the
last few weeks. Whoever H.B. was, Quinton had met with
them regularly. She was still flicking through the diary for
more information when she heard someone clearing their
throat.

"Can I help you?"

It was Quinton's secretary eyeing her suspiciously
through a pair of tortoiseshell glasses.

A flush crept across Kate's cheeks. "Sorry…" She
searched her mind for a plausible excuse for snooping
at Quinton's desk. "My pen has run out and I thought I
might find one on the desk."

The secretary pulled open the top drawer and handed
Kate a biro. She straightened the diary and glared at

Kate. "Quinton should be with you in five minutes. He's finishing with the rep now."

Kate scuttled back to her seat, her face flaming as she watched the secretary leave. That was close. She wasn't sure whether the woman believed the story about the pen. She was taking a few deep breaths to calm her racing heart when Quinton breezed back into the room.

"Sorry about that. I hope Jacqui has been taking care of you." His face was unreadable as he took his seat opposite. "Where were we?"

Kate checked her notes. She had hoped to continue questioning him about the use of guns, but after reading Ryan's text she wasn't sure she should be too direct. Even so, one more probing question wouldn't hurt.

"We were talking about hunting guns. Is it true that some guns used for hunting have been linked to poaching incidents in this country?"

A slash of red appeared across Quinton's cheeks. "I don't know anything about that. I can *assure* you that all our own guns are always accounted for and the customers we deal with are upstanding people, some of them quite high up in the business and professional world: lawyers, dentists, judges, etc." His voice grew louder. "Hunting is a hobby to them, and they would certainly never do anything illegal."

Her questions had obviously spooked him, so she gave him a relaxed smile, hoping to appease him. "Sorry, I didn't mean to imply anything. I am sure you are all above board. One hears so many different reports about trophy hunting."

"Yes," Quinton agreed, "there is a great deal of false information and misconceptions about the hunting industry and its environmental effects. People do need to get their facts straight."

Kate felt the sting of rebuke and stuck to asking a few more general questions, jotting down his answers in her notepad but not really listening, her mind constantly wandering back to the email message she'd read.

When they finished the interview, Quinton accompanied her to the lift lobby. "Now, I do hope you will present hunting in a fair and honest way. After all, it is legal in this country, and there has been some form of trophy hunting in many parts of the world for a long time now."

Kate stretched her hand out to shake his. "Of course, and thank you for seeing me. It's been very interesting."

He took her hand, making sure hers was enclosed between both of his. A little power play.

She politely extracted her hand from his firm grip. "I will let you know when the article is published."

His face slid into an insincere smile. "I'll look forward to reading it."

She was about to call for the lift when he grabbed her arm. "Oh, I nearly forgot. My secretary told me you were short of a pen." He handed her a leather pouch inside which was a designer roller pen with the name of his hunting business emblazoned on the side. "Please take this. We can't have a journalist wandering around without a pen." His eyes held hers for a moment, a glimmer of a sneer touching his lips.

She took the pen and spluttered out her thanks before stepping into the lift, desperate to rush back to the hotel and take a long hot shower to remove all trace of sleaze.

Chapter Twenty-Nine

Outside the building, the late afternoon was sticky, sapping all energy from her body. Kate was scouring the street for a taxi when she spotted Ryan crossing the road towards her, his face like thunder. She'd forgotten he would be waiting in a café opposite. She was relieved to see him, and despite the grim line of his lips, his broad shoulders gave off a sense of strength and safety. Not that she needed a bodyguard, but after the last hour with Quinton Cronje, she was a little spooked, although she wouldn't mention it to Ryan, because then he would think he'd been right about suggesting she didn't meet with Quinton alone.

She gave him a sheepish smile. "I guess I am in the bad books."

Ryan's voice was tart. "I thought the idea was that I was to accompany you at least to the building."

Kate gestured to herself. "I'm alive! Nothing terrible happened to me. Except for having to listen to a man sing the virtues of hunting for forty minutes—" she gave a dry laugh "—but I survived."

"What did you expect?" Ryan snorted. "The guy was probably born with a gun in his hand."

"He's quite a man," Kate admitted.

Ryan hailed a taxi and they slid into the back seat. He swivelled around to face her. "So what was he like?"

"Slick and debonair, a classic salesman. He's absolutely convinced that hunting helps conservation."

"Did you find out anything interesting?"

Kate hesitated. "He became annoyed when I asked him if any hunting guns ended up in the wrong hands. He wasn't exactly going to tell me if they'd been used in poaching incidents."

"That's true. Anything else?"

Kate bit her lip. She had to tell Ryan about the email but she knew he'd be angry with her for taking risks. "Well, there was one thing. He had to leave the room to talk to another visitor for a while so I kind of…"

His cheek twitched. "You kind of what?"

"I snooped around a bit. The filing cabinets were locked and there was nothing of interest on his desk. Whilst I was by his computer, an email flashed up on the screen. I couldn't read all of it, obviously, nor whom it was from, but it did mention…" she fumbled for her notepad where she'd jotted down the gist of the email before Quinton came back into the room "…something about a shipment from Maputo next weekend and a courier meeting at somewhere called Palma. The sender is someone he knows well. He thanked Quinton for inviting him to a braai and suggested they move quickly. And he also mentioned 'paying off the team' and something about 'not trusting' the contact in the Kruger. Surely that points to the security guard you are investigating. What was his name?"

"Leonard," Ryan replied, "and we don't have any hard evidence yet, but I spoke to one of the security guards who used to work with Leonard, today, and he was pretty convinced Leonard had previously been involved with drug dealing here in Johannesburg, so not exactly a good past record." He tapped his thigh. "That email you spotted suggests Quinton's definitely up to something. Palma is right on the Mozambique border with Tanzania, so the fact they are sending a shipment there will be of interest to border control. Hawks are keeping an eye on him and are currently searching through his company accounts. They'll find something. If there's no link to this current poaching, they might come across a different link."

Kate suddenly remembered the diary entry. She grabbed Ryan's arm. "I also took a peek in his diary, which was on his desk. It was one of those fancy leather ones, and I found the date that the email sender mentioned, when he went to Quinton's for a braai, and the initials H.B. were entered on that date at 7 p.m. In fact, when I flicked through, H.B. was mentioned a few times, but I couldn't check any further because his secretary came in. Do you know who H.B. might be?"

Ryan scowled. "It's all useful, Kate, but you still shouldn't have gone off without me briefing you first. It's not a game we are playing."

Annoyance buzzed through her. "I know it's not a game and I said I was sorry for not waiting for you. It was easier at the time for me to go straight there from my other meeting. I can look after myself—" she glared at him "—and besides, I managed to find out some useful information."

"Even so, let's hope he believed your cover story."

Kate didn't reply. She stared out of the window, feeling like a schoolgirl reprimanded by a teacher. The taxi took the bend of the freeway slip road too fast, and Ryan's thigh bumped against Kate's. A jolt of electricity buzzed through her leg and she moved away quickly.

Ryan's leg jiggled up and down on the seat next to her and she placed a hand on his knee to stop it. "Ryan," she whispered, "I really am sorry about not waiting for you."

The tension between them was palpable. They gazed at each other, his eyes searching her face and settling on her lips. She leant towards him, hoping he would soften his stance and maybe kiss her again. But he moved away, his shoulders rigid as he stared out of his window.

She folded her arms and sighed heavily. It was clear that despite attempts by both of them to forget what happened the other day at sunset, neither of them could. The chemistry between them sizzled like a steak on a braai.

When the taxi pulled into the arrival zone at the hotel, Ryan hurried out, throwing money at the driver and striding into the lobby.

She grabbed his arm as he made his way to the lift bank. "Are you going to sulk about this all day? You're being childish. If you must know, I thought it would be a waste of your time coming with me to his office. I know you had other things to do."

Ryan stared down at her hand, which was still resting on his forearm. She snatched it back, her fingers tingling from the touch. When she met his eyes the familiar bolt of arousal hit her. He still hadn't spoken, even to accept her apology, and that riled her. She threw her hands up in surrender. "I give up. I'll meet you in the lobby in the morning to travel to the airport. Have a good evening."

A light brush of red formed on his cheeks and instead of apologising, he simply jabbed at the call button of the lift.

Kate was fuming. If he wanted any more help with his investigation, he'd have to find someone else. She had other things to think about anyway. Like finding her real mother. She certainly didn't have to hang out with an obstinate, grouchy ex-soldier.

The lift doors opened and Ryan stepped in, his brown eyes unreadable. He ran an agitated hand through his hair, clearly more affected by their chemistry than he was letting on. The doors closed and her breath caught in her throat as she realised she *did* have a vested interest in how the poaching investigation panned out. She wanted to help him catch the suspects.

And then it dawned on her. Despite all her good intentions, she was attracted to him, and she had absolutely no idea what to do about it.

Chapter Thirty

The bar was busy with early evening drinkers and hotel guests. Ryan spotted Kate almost immediately. She was perched on a stool talking animatedly to a man next to her. He assumed it was the photographer she was due to meet.

He leant against the wall near the entrance and watched her for a while. She looked relaxed and happy. The man was dark-haired and handsome, and there was a confident air in the way he presented himself, from his linen jacket to the leather satchel draped over the stool. Ryan watched as the man laughed, his voice deep and melodic. Kate responded with a girlish giggle Ryan hadn't heard from her before. He supposed that was because he'd never given her reason to feel relaxed enough with him.

He'd behaved badly this afternoon, stomping up to his room in a sulk. Before the lift doors had shut he'd glimpsed hurt and disappointment in her eyes. He'd upset her, but at that stage he was so annoyed and so aroused by her that he didn't want to be near her in case he said or did something he'd later regret.

Back in his room, he'd had a cool shower to calm down and spent an hour or so catching up on things on his laptop. But all the time, his mind kept wandering to

Kate, to what she was thinking. Her room was four doors down the corridor from his and he'd imagined her under the shower, the water cascading down her long hair and onto her body. It had been difficult to get himself back to the email he was composing.

But he couldn't hide in his room all evening. Besides, he was hungry, and so he'd come down to seek a beer and some food. He wished he hadn't been so rude to Kate now; they could have at least had a civilised dinner together.

Why was he so judgemental and prickly? He often pushed people away. He hadn't always been like that. He wasn't a natural party animal, but he had been able to hold his own socially, always happy to enjoy a beer or two with friends. But all that changed after Afghanistan, and now he found it hard to trust people he didn't know. He chose his friends carefully, constructing deep friendships only when he knew he could completely trust people. Like Gavin and Sara or Rio. All his army friends were dispersed, and whilst their friendship would never fade, it was different now. They would always be connected by what they'd gone through, what they'd lost, but they were no longer in touch, most of them settled and married, some still in the army. For the first time since he'd chosen to take on this life, this role in the bush, Ryan was lonely.

A woman walking into the bar brushed Ryan's arm and brought his attention back to the present. Her perfume was strong and musky and her eyes widened as she caught his. She was tall and leggy, like a model, her short hair crinkled against her scalp, high cheekbones slanted above full lips. She was a beauty and Ryan should have been flattered by her interest in him, but what he really wanted to do was walk over to Kate and run his hands through the lengths of her hair and kiss her senseless.

He remembered the heat of their kiss back in the bush, of how her pupils had dilated as he'd bent to kiss her. Despite him telling her the kiss was unprofessional, he'd been lying; he'd been struck by lightning the minute their lips met.

She was single, intelligent and beautiful and it had been a long time since he'd dated. But there was more to it than that. He'd glimpsed sadness and vulnerability in her; she was troubled by something. And from somewhere deep within him he'd empathised. He'd wanted to take her in his arms and comfort her and drive away the sadness.

She would definitely be a complication to his orderly life, which was why he was so prickly. He didn't want to let her in. He'd tried hard not to think about what might have happened had Gavin and Sara not interrupted their kiss. But the wonder of it was still there in the back of his mind, a glimpse of what could be, of passion as glorious as the setting sun.

The attractive woman gave him a disappointed shrug and walked off. He took a hesitant step towards the bar and his eyes met Kate's. The laughter on her lips froze and she gazed warily at him. He should leave the bar now, go and seek out a beer somewhere else and leave her in peace. But as if she were a magnet, he found himself drawn towards her.

His eyes caught hers. "Hi."

"Ryan," she replied stiffly.

He touched her arm and lowered his voice. "Sorry I was such a grump this afternoon." He gave a wry smile. "I'm always apologising to you."

She held up her hands. "It's okay. I shouldn't have gone

off like that. I guess I am so used to working on my own and being my own boss. Let's forget about it." She raised her hand towards his. "Shake on it?"

He took her hand in his, a noticeable electric tingle emanating from their palms.

She turned towards her companion. "Eliot, this is Ryan Brown, the head of the anti-poaching unit at Elephant Sands Concession. Ryan, this is Eliot Vince."

Ryan shook the man's hand. "Nice to meet you, I've seen some of your work in the *National Geographic*, the sand dunes in Namibia, I think."

Eliot greeted him warmly. "Thank you. Have you been to Namibia? It's an amazing country."

Ryan nodded. "I travelled around most of Southern Africa five years ago. Namibia was great. I'd like to get back sometime."

Eliot ordered a beer for Ryan and they chatted for a while about the wonders of the African bush and its animals and Ryan relaxed. He had to admit, the man was charming, and Kate was clearly taken with him, her hands occasionally flitting out to touch Eliot. Ryan hadn't thought of her as a demonstrative person, but she was certainly being so this evening.

Under the soft lights of the bar Kate was beautiful. She was wearing a dress, the soft green colour reminding Ryan of the ferns that grew in the wooded valleys of the Dales. Her hair was tied back in a low chignon, stray ends curling around her face. Ryan noticed a shimmer of pink on her lips and he longed to reach out and touch her.

He turned his attention to Eliot, trying to steady his skittering pulse. "Are you in South Africa for long? I think Kate mentioned she was hoping you would be able to take some photos for the article."

Eliot shook his head. "I'm heading off to Zambia tomorrow where I am doing an assignment and then hoping to have a few days R and R. I have given Kate a couple of contacts here in Johannesburg. They're both experienced wildlife and landscape photographers." He drained his drink and smiled apologetically. "I'm really sorry, I need to head off. I'm up early tomorrow for a flight up to Lusaka." He reached out to shake Ryan's hand. "Good luck with the investigation."

Ryan watched Kate accompany Eliot to the exit, a flicker of jealousy hitting him as she reached up to hug Eliot. He ordered himself another beer, scanning his phone for messages. He wasn't sure if she would come back now that Eliot had left and was pleasantly surprised when she sat back on the stool next to him, her light fragrance filling his senses.

He gazed at her and found himself melting. Her hazel eyes were wary still, but there was something else on the edges. Recognition? Desire?

His voice was husky. "Would you like another drink?" *Please say yes.*

Kate's tongue darted out to moisten her lips. "Yes, please, another glass of white wine."

Ryan ordered her drink and when it came, clinked his glass against it. "Cheers. Here's to better working relationships."

Kate clinked her glass back. "I'll drink to that. At least it would make Sara happy."

Ryan laughed. "True."

They took a long sip of their respective drinks, their eyes meeting over the rims. It appeared they were both tongue-tied and Ryan was searching for a conversation topic when Kate's stomach growled rather loudly.

She placed a hand on her stomach. "Sorry about that. I haven't eaten since that thing they called a sandwich on the plane." She placed the unfinished wine glass on the bar. "I'd better stop drinking otherwise I'll be falling off this bar stool."

"How about we head somewhere and get some food?" Ryan suggested. "I'm starving too. I did eat lunch, but then I'm always hungry. I know a great steak place that's only a short taxi ride away. What do you think?"

Kate's stomach responded with another growl. "I think my stomach answered for me."

"Great." Ryan drained his beer and hopped down from the stool. He held out his hand for Kate and she took it, their eyes meeting, heat searing through their palms.

Outside, the doorman hailed a taxi and they slid into the back seat. Ryan relaxed as the car moved out into the night, the neon lights of the city flashing past as they drove, Kate's floral perfume filling his senses.

The screen of Kate's phone lit up through the half-open zip of her bag and Ryan was momentarily taken back to the present, irritation knocking on the door. He gestured towards her phone, trying to keep the criticism out of his voice. "You're like a teenager, always on your phone. Who are all these people who keep messaging you?"

"No one exciting," she replied. "Mainly work calls."

He longed to ask about the PI guy. What was his name? Allan Prescott. But he held his tongue. They were getting on better and he didn't want to break the spell. There had been a shift in their relationship, and despite what had happened in Dubai with Gwen, he was going to take a leap of faith and trust her. He just hoped he wouldn't come to regret it.

Chapter Thirty-One

Kate was conscious of Ryan next to her as they waited for the lift to come. Like her he was watching the lights above the door as they indicated its journey to the ground floor. The air was thick between them, all the words that had flowed during their dinner now dried up.

Her heart was beating so loudly in her ears that she was certain he would hear it. He glanced at her, the dimple in his cheek twitching. His eyes held hers and she almost melted into the floor, the dark brown of his irises drawing her in.

The ping of the elevator jolted them both out of their trance and Ryan gestured for her to go in before him. She stepped in, feeling the warmth of him as he followed her in. She'd been conscious of him all evening, unable to think about anything else except what it might be like to kiss him again, to feel the breadth of his shoulders under her hands.

The dinner had been a revelation. There had been a frisson of something in the air from the moment they entered the restaurant, and Ryan had pulled out her chair for her and sat opposite, handsome and sexy under the overhead lights. It was like they were on a date, a couple out on the town for a meal. Not two colleagues working on a case. They didn't speak about the poaching incident all evening or about her decision to go rogue on the meeting with Quinton Cronje.

On the way to the restaurant, there had been one awkward moment in the taxi when her phone pinged with messages. Out of force of habit, she'd pulled it out and checked it quickly. It was a message from Allan Prescott but she'd left it unopened. There were also a couple of missed calls from a number she didn't recognise but with a South African country code. Her fingers itched to open the messages, but she'd shut the screen down and pushed the phone back into the depths of her bag, and when they'd arrived at the restaurant, all thoughts of her personal life had fled as she became absorbed in Ryan.

The restaurant was modern, all glass and chrome. The food was delicious and they'd shared a bottle of delicious Pinotage, a grape blend specific to South Africa. She'd savoured the wine and concentrated on trying to find out what made Ryan tick. He was a complicated man and she sensed a deep sadness within him. It was there in the way he sometimes removed himself, or rather his feelings, from the situation.

"Tell me more about how you met Gavin," she'd said.

He told her about how he met Gavin in Iraq. "We hit it off, partly because of our backgrounds, but also because we both loved the outdoors, hiking and stuff. Gavin invited me to his family home in the Drakensberg Mountains, and that's how I came to fall in love with South Africa."

He'd asked her about her childhood and she'd filled him in on her life, leaving out the bombshell that had dropped on her after her parents died. When she became sad talking about her parents, Ryan had reached across to take her hand in his, his eyes sympathetic.

He was a good listener, never butting in and never trying to bring the conversation back to him. She'd found herself almost wanting to tell him about the search for her real mother, the weight of the secrecy pushing down on her, but she'd stopped herself at the last minute. She still hadn't told Sara and knew that if there was anyone she was going to open up to, she should be the first.

There was a small stage in the restaurant with a four-piece band set up. Later in the meal, they'd played slow, sultry jazz tunes. Ryan had surprised her by asking her to dance and she'd sat staring at his outstretched hand like an idiot. On the dance floor there were a few couples slowly dancing around, their bodies entwined as they moved to the music. He took her in his arms and she was impressed at how well he danced, much better than her with her awkward stumbles. He held her slightly away from him and she focused on his right shoulder, trying hard to control her heart, which was beating more like the rhythm of a quickstep than a waltz.

She grinned at him. "Where did you learn to dance like this?"

He'd pulled a face. "My mum and dad were amateur ballroom fanatics and they made all of us learn. It was awful. I rebelled when I got to sixteen."

"Well, I'm impressed." She'd laughed. "I learnt at school, which was hilarious, as it was an all-girls school, so we had to practise with each other."

Ryan had smiled. "I bet I can guess who your dance partner was."

"Yep, it was Sara. I always led because I was taller."

A pair of dancers bumped into them and Ryan had pulled her closer, their bodies nestling together. The scent of him intoxicated her, sending her pulse into overdrive.

Now as they stood side by side in the lift, their fingers only inches away from each other, an air of anticipation hung between them. They exited the lift and walked slowly down the heavily carpeted hallway towards their rooms. When they reached her room, her hands trembled as she pulled the key card out of her handbag.

She gazed coyly at him, trying to form words, to say goodnight, but the flush of red across his cheeks and the dark fathomless pools of his eyes pulled her forward like a magnetic force. He reached out and placed a hand on her arm, heat burning through the soft cotton of her dress, his eyes on her lips. As if on cue, her tongue darted out to moisten her lips.

She touched his shoulder, feeling the bunch of muscles beneath his shirt and the warmth of him. "Ryan…"

He leant forward to take her lips in a tender kiss, and she knew that this time there would be no stopping them.

"More," she whispered, and he hauled her in, kissing her firmly this time.

Kate moaned softly as Ryan rained kisses down the side of her face, his masculine scent filling her senses and sending her pulse skipping wildly. His hands found her hair and he cupped the back of her neck, angling his mouth against hers for a deeper kiss. Laughter from further up the corridor drew them quickly apart, their chests panting, eyes widening as they took each other in.

She fumbled with the key card. "Shall we go in?" she asked, praying he would not walk away this time.

He took the key card from her, scanning it against the

lock. Inside, he pushed her gently up against the closed door and continued to kiss her. Her hands snaked up around his neck, pulling him closer towards her to deepen the embrace, losing herself in him. He tugged down the zip of her dress, stroking the bare skin on her back. His hands, calloused and rough from his outdoor life, were surprisingly soft and she let out a gasp as he undid her bra strap and shifted one of his hands around to cup her breast. She let her pelvis rest against his jean-clad hips, feeling his hardness against her belly.

"I want you, Ryan." She undid the top buttons of his polo shirt and pulled it over his head, revealing a well-defined chest with a scattering of light brown hair. She ran her hands over it and he shivered beneath her touch.

He held her back, questioning with his eyes one more time. She nodded her assent and he reached up to push an errant curl from her face before taking her mouth in a long, passionate kiss. Time stood still as they embraced, their hearts thudding furiously in their chests.

He lifted his mouth from her lips. "Shall we get more comfortable?"

She managed a breathless, "Yes," and he led her towards the bed where they gazed at each other in the soft light of the room.

Her hands explored his chest, moving down towards the buckle of his belt. He groaned and kissed her, pulling the zip all the way down. The dress fell to the floor and she stepped into his arms and they were skin to skin, their mouths finding each other, all sound drowned out by the thud of their hearts and the pulsing in her ears.

Chapter Thirty-Two

Ryan sat by the window in the early morning sun, watching the comings and goings in the street below. It was strange to wake up in the city, the sound of cars and rubbish trucks permeating the thick glass of the hotel window.

He'd been grinning since the moment he woke up, gazing in amazement at the sleeping woman lying next to him. He felt like a teenage boy love-struck with his first romance. It was early, so he'd let her sleep, stealing from the bed to watch the morning begin. But she'd have to wake soon; they were due to leave for the airport in an hour.

Kate muttered in her sleep. She lay on her side, her hand flung across the bed to the empty space where he'd been lying. Her face was relaxed and almost childlike, and he walked over to her, brushing the hair from her brow. He marvelled at the cute freckles that spread across her nose. Her skin was pale and smooth and he longed to run his hands down her spine again and bury himself in her. But they would be late for their flight, and besides, there would be time later, when the investigation was over and she'd finished her article. He'd take her up to Botswana, or Victoria Falls. Or maybe have a few days at the beach. She'd mentioned last night about her planned trip to Maputo with Sara. Perhaps he and Gavin could join the girls. It would be fun. It had been ages since he'd done something like that.

He was about to kiss her gently to wake her when her phone vibrated on the table beside her. He reached out to grab it but stopped. He shouldn't snoop. Especially after the night they'd just spent together. But more messages flooded onto the screen and he couldn't help himself. He glanced across at her again, her brow smooth and unbothered, and picked up the phone.

There were several messages and missed calls and one of them stood out to Ryan: Allan Prescott, the private investigator. He'd called her twice during the evening and again this morning. He'd sent a text too, and Ryan read it now as it floated across the screen.

> *Kate. Good news. I have some information back from the police. How did you get on with Jacques Voester? Did he know anything? I have been trying to get hold of you. Allan.*

Ryan's brow furrowed in confusion. Last night when he'd asked Kate about her meeting that morning, she'd told him she'd met with someone in the newspaper office the *Daily Tribune* was affiliated with. But now Ryan doubted she was telling the truth. What did the PI mean in his comment about 'information back from the police'?

He scrolled down the other messages she hadn't read, unable to open them fully. One of them, sent late last night, was from an unknown number, but Ryan knew it was a South African mobile. His heart thumped loudly in his chest when he read the words visible on the screen:

> *Miss Harper, it was nice to meet you yesterday.*

I tried to call several times last night. Would love to take you out for a drink. How long are you in Johannesburg for? Regards, Quinton Cronje.

Why on earth was Quinton Cronje messaging her? Who was Jacques Voester and why did Kate meet him yesterday? And why did Cronje want to meet her for a drink? Alarm bells sounded in his head. Could he really trust her?

The back of his neck itched. This always happened when he was bothered by something. It was like a warning sign and it had never failed him. Except for with Gwen. He hadn't got it during his time with her, not even once. He'd fallen fast, unable to believe that a beautiful, intelligent woman would want to spend time with someone like him. Why was he always so gullible? He should know better. Anger rose to the surface. Had he been duped again?

Kate rolled over, opening her eyes. He quickly put the phone back on the nightstand and walked over to his clothes, pulling on his jeans and beginning to dress.

She sat up, pushing the curtain of hair out of her eyes, her face glowing. "Hi. What time is it?" Her voice was husky, and desire rushed through him despite everything.

He kept his voice calm despite the simmering anger. "Just after seven."

She swung her legs over the side of the bed and reached for her phone. It annoyed him that she automatically did that, without even glancing in his direction.

"You've been popular this morning," he said, not even bothering to keep the irritation out of his voice.

Her face reddened at his harshness. "What's wrong?" she asked, standing up and walking over to him, the phone discarded on the bed. She stretched up and kissed him full on the lips. "Good morning."

Ryan felt his body react and pushed her away gently.

She frowned. "Why are you so grumpy?" Stepping towards him, she wound her fingers into his hair muttering, "I know just how to cheer you up," and pulled him down for another kiss.

His lips automatically responded and he let her lead him over to the bed. But when he saw her phone, lying in the middle of the cover where she'd thrown it, he pulled away.

He found his shoes and pulled them on. "Care to tell me who Allan Prescott is? Or Jacques Voester?" he snapped.

She gazed at him in disbelief. "You've been reading my messages?"

"Not exactly. They came up on the screen when I was about to wake you. The senders were quite insistent." He folded his arms and glared at her. "I think you're hiding something. Also, why is Cronje trying to get hold of you? You said he was creepy, so why is he asking you out for a drink?"

He'd spat the words out in anger and Kate took a step back as if she thought he might strike her. He ran his fingers through his hair. "Sorry, I didn't mean to shout. I don't understand what's going on with you, Kate. One minute you are involved in the case and in writing your article, and the next you keep getting mysterious calls and going off to secret meetings."

Kate snorted. "Secret meetings? This isn't some spy mission, Ryan. I do have a right to privacy." Her lips coiled in disgust. "Believe me, I have no desire to see Quinton Cronje again, and I certainly never gave him the impression I would go for a drink with him. He's a sleaze; he pretty much came on to me at the interview. It happens sometimes, and I usually ignore it, which, if you'd bothered to check, you would see I have done in this case." She snatched up her phone and held it out to him. "Would you like to check?"

She was furious and Ryan felt a trickle of remorse. She was beautiful when she was angry, with her hair flying around her face and her eyes flashing in the morning sun.

He moved away from her. "I don't need to check. If you say you didn't encourage Cronje, then I believe you."

'How kind of you," she retorted. "I am *so* grateful you believe me."

Ryan put his hands on his hips. "So who's Allan Prescott? He seems to contact you all the time." He grimaced inwardly, realising he'd just revealed to her that he'd seen her messages before.

Kate's face was puce. "I can't believe you've been reading my messages. Who the hell do you think you are? I am not one of your suspects. You had no right!"

Ryan lifted his chin. "I think I did, actually. One—" he counted off on his fingers "— you keep taking calls all the time, creeping out of earshot to speak to Allan Prescott – who by the way I know is a private investigator. Two, why is he reporting back to you about police investigations? And three, who is Jacques Voester? I am not buying your story about visiting the newspaper office."

Kate had been staring at him incredulously throughout his entire tirade. But when she spoke, her voice was quiet, a tremble beneath the surface. "It's absolutely none of your business who I meet. I fulfilled my part of the arrangement by going to see Quinton Cronje, who, by the way, might be creepy but at least he has better manners than you. What I do outside my time on this case is nothing to do with you."

Ryan bristled; this was going nowhere. "Okay, if that's the way you want to play it. I don't need your help any more anyway. But if I find you are in cahoots with that Quinton guy or anyone linked to a poaching syndicate, I will bring you down."

Kate paled under his tirade and guilt sliced through him. He was overreacting; there was bound to be a reasonable explanation for it, but right now all he could think about was that he'd been played by a beautiful journalist, again. Friend of Sara's or not, he couldn't trust Kate. There were too many unanswered questions.

He paced the room. "I don't trust you."

She lifted her chin. "I don't need you anyway. I'll finish the article with Rio and Clemmie's help. I'm going to write something about the orphanage as well, so I guess I am pretty much done with *your* input."

Ryan's nostrils flared and he tamped down his anger. "I'll still need to see the final copy."

Kate's eyes were so glacial he shivered despite the tension in the air. Gone was the beautiful, vivacious woman he'd made love with last night. "Of course. I will make sure all the boxes are ticked. But remember, it's not a glossy brochure piece; it's a feature article about poaching and as such, I show it as it is, flaws and all."

She dipped her head to tap a message on her phone, completely ignoring Ryan as he stood there. Flaws and all? What the hell did she mean by that?

After a moment, she flicked flinty eyes at him. "Still here, Ryan? I thought we had to leave for the airport soon. I guess you ought to head back to your room to get dressed. I'll see you in the lobby in twenty minutes. That should give you enough time to wash away any regrets."

He watched her tap away on her phone for a few more seconds before grabbing his belongings and heading out of the room. He felt blindsided, unable to comprehend how it had gone from being one of the best mornings of his life to a complete disaster.

His hands shook as he opened his door. He leant on it as it closed and stared across at the unused bed. Images of last night filled his mind: of Kate astride him, her long, wild hair trailing down her breasts, her eyes flashing like amber stones in full sunlight.

He showered and dressed, shoving his belongings into an overnight bag. In the lift he stared at his reflection in the mirror, thinking of last night when they'd headed up to the room, fingers touching softly by their sides, a frisson of excitement in the air as they ascended.

His limbs felt heavy and his head ached. Despite everything, he would never regret their night together, only that he'd read her messages. If only he'd ignored the ping of the mobile and taken her in his arms the moment she opened her beautiful eyes, her voice husky in the early morning light. Then they might have had a chance. But he'd killed that now, tossed it out, and now all that was left was sorrow and guilt.

Chapter Thirty-Three

The minute the door slammed behind Ryan, Kate burst into tears, anger and sorrow mixing together like a pathetic cocktail. Last night had been incredible, and when she'd woken, her eyes focusing on Ryan standing by the window with the sun streaming behind him, happiness had flooded through her. A glimpse of something good to come. A new beginning.

Then he'd shattered it by accusing her of being up to something suspicious. The way he'd sneered at her as he threw across the allegations was so different from the way he'd behaved last night. He was like a dry pile of kindling that someone had suddenly thrown a match over.

She sat on the bed and tried to make sense of what had just happened. One minute they were making love all night, dropping off to sleep in each other's arms in the early hours, and the next he was glaring at her with disdain. Why was he so suspicious? Why didn't he believe her?

She sighed. Probably because she hadn't really answered his question about Allan Prescott. She didn't want to tell him the real reason she was using a private investigator, not until she'd told Sara anyway. If today had begun differently, if he'd trusted her, she might have shared the truth. When she was ready. But it was too late now. They didn't have a future together. He didn't trust her, and she couldn't be with someone who behaved like that.

She showered and dressed in record time and walked the four flights of stairs down to reception. She didn't want to risk bumping into Ryan in the lift. Too many memories lingered there.

He was waiting by reception, his fingers tapping impatiently on the desk. They glowered at each other and she was glad that his eyes flitted away first. *Good.* He needed to feel embarrassed. He'd behaved atrociously, and she wouldn't give him the opportunity to see how much it hurt. She would get through today if it killed her.

"The taxi is waiting outside," he said as she paid her bill. "I'll meet you out there."

He strode off towards the exit and she watched him go, trying hard not to admire how handsome he was in his jeans and polo shirt. It was annoying how much her body betrayed her when it came to him. She needed to have a stern word with her hormones. After his behaviour, she shouldn't be ogling him like a teenage girl.

In the taxi they sat apart, the cracked leather of the back seat stretching wide between them. The silence was palpable with only the background music playing on the radio, which the driver would occasionally whistle along to. How different from their trip back to the hotel the night before where they'd laughed and flirted with each other as the cab drove through the neon-lit streets. Kate had teased Ryan incessantly about his secret ballroom dancing habit and he'd ragged her about how she kept standing on his foot. He'd been charming and fun and she'd taken the plunge. What a big mistake that had turned out to be.

When they arrived at the airport, Ryan took himself off somewhere and Kate sat in a café with a coffee and a pastry, the food like sawdust in her mouth. She checked her messages again and sent a reply to Allan, stating she was free to speak now before she boarded the plane. He phoned her back as the departure gate was called and she answered, aware that Ryan was nearby watching her talk as they stood in line to board.

"I've found an old charge sheet," Allan informed her, "but nothing else. Alison was one of three suspects on the list. It appears that nothing came of the charges in the end. There's certainly no evidence of a court case."

"What were the charges?" Kate asked.

"Arson and manslaughter. A security guard was killed."

Kate's legs wobbled beneath her at Allan's words. Arson and manslaughter sounded pretty serious to her. "I don't understand. If they were charged, why were they not convicted?"

"Two of them were from well-known families who paid for good lawyers; they got off." He cleared his throat. "Your mother, however, skipped bail. She's never been heard of since."

A large lump formed in Kate's throat as she struggled to keep it together. "So Alison Voester was, or still is, a wanted criminal?"

"I suppose so. I'm trying to find out if the case is still open." Allan's voice was kind as he tried to pacify her. "It's always difficult receiving this kind of news. But remember, you are only hearing one side of the story. Things are not always that black and white."

Kate finished the call and boarded the plane, only just managing to hold back the wall of tears threatening to break. After takeoff, she stared out of the window at the white clouds that formed a carpet beneath the plane. Was her real mother down there somewhere? Was she happy and settled? Perhaps married again with a life? Or was she dead, her reckless life catching up with her?

She had a sudden longing for Ginny, to have her hold her and tell her it would all be okay. Like the time she failed an exam or broke up with her first boyfriend. A mother's comfort was what she needed. Ginny might not have been the one who had given birth to her, but she'd always been there right from the moment Kate had arrived in her life. She missed her now with a sensation so visceral her chest ached.

She wished she remembered those early days in South Africa, but then how many people remembered their early life? These flashes of memory she'd been getting since she arrived here were probably only manifestations of her desire to find her real mother. She needed to accept that she might never find her, that her mother gave her up in order to pursue a different life. It was Ginny who had really cared about her and had done so right up to the last moment before she died.

Tears burnt her eyes as she remembered the last time she spoke to her mother. Ginny had called her shortly before the crash, wanting to chat and to plan a trip to the theatre in London.

"We need a girls' night out, darling," she'd trilled down the phone line. "A proper catch-up. I miss you!"

Kate had been busy when her mother called, rushing to meet an interviewee, jostling with walkers on the pavement. But they'd fixed a date via text later and Kate had booked tickets for a new production at the National Theatre the following week. They'd never made it. Her mother had been killed two days later.

Kate sniffed and brushed her tears away, shifting her thoughts to Ryan. He was sitting a few rows ahead, his right shoulder and arm hanging over the side of the seat. Why did he mistrust her so much? It was wrong of him to read her messages even if they were cryptic; it was a shame he hadn't tried to talk to her about it calmly. She might have been more willing to share with him, to tell him the truth. But he'd jumped to the wrong conclusions and his accusations stung.

Last night had been wonderful, the first time in ages she'd felt so attracted to someone. Richard, her ex-boyfriend, had been a wonderful man, fun and interesting, but they'd run out of steam, neither of them ready to settle down nor take the next step. They'd parted as friends and there'd been no one in the intervening years who'd interested her as much as Ryan.

She had to talk to him, to try to explain. They needed to sort it out before they got back to the lodge. There was the article to finish for one thing. Despite the fact she'd told him she didn't need him, he was pivotal to the story. And Sara would notice the minute they arrived that something was wrong. It was time to tell her the truth too. It would be good, she thought, to unburden herself at last.

Chapter Thirty-Four

Elephant Sands Concession,
Southern Kruger National Park

Ryan stalked ahead of Kate at the airport, heading towards the car park, the sun ferocious overhead. He hadn't spoken to her since they'd left Johannesburg but had been aware of her at the airport before takeoff, talking on her phone, her face pensive, her shoulders hunched. He pushed away the pang of remorse, for there she was once again on her phone.

He knew he should trust Sara's opinion of her best friend, but she hadn't seen Kate for many years. How did she even know what her friend was up to? So many questions whirled around in his head. He'd fallen for her and was angry that he'd allowed himself to be taken in by her.

It had taken him a long time to get over Gwen, and Kate was the first woman he'd wanted to spend time with since then. There'd been plenty of opportunities over the last four years or so – fellow rangers, scientists, charity and NGO workers not to mention guests at the lodge. But he'd busied himself with work and had not allowed anyone to break down his protective barriers. Until now.

As he walked, there was a sudden chuff chuff chuff of a helicopter landing at the nearby helipad. He instinctively ducked, his body taut. A prickle of apprehension ran down his spine. Would he ever lose this physical reaction to the blades of a helicopter? It was the one thing from his days in Afghanistan he hadn't been able to rid himself of – which was tricky. Being an anti-poaching ranger meant he often had to come in contact with helicopters, even having to travel in them from time to time. He'd tried to avoid it as much as possible, sending other members of the unit up whilst he travelled on land. But it wasn't always possible. There was something about the sound of an arriving helicopter that still made him break out in a cold sweat.

"Are you okay?" Kate's face swam into view.

She touched his arm, her face screwed up with concern. "Ryan, are you okay?" she repeated.

He swallowed down the panic and pushed her hand off. "I'm fine," he snapped. He tried to ignore the flash of hurt in her eyes and, with shaking hands, clicked the door to his car open and got in, firing up the air conditioning.

Kate stored her bag in the boot, climbing into the passenger seat, her face half hidden by a curtain of hair. He thought about the feel of her soft curls beneath his hands and cursed inwardly, reversing the car out quickly and heading out onto the highway.

They'd been driving in silence for around ten minutes when Kate spoke up, a sense of determination in her voice. "Ryan, we need to talk before we get back to the lodge."

"Sure thing," he said, "although there's not much to say. I shouldn't have read your messages, I'll admit that, but you must understand that I am right to be suspicious of you."

He felt Kate bristle beside him but kept his eyes on the road.

Kate kept her voice even. "It might seem suspicious to you, but there's a perfectly reasonable explanation. I can't tell you about it right now. Please trust me, it's nothing for you to worry about, and it's certainly nothing to do with the article or the poaching."

"And Quinton Cronje?" Ryan asked, taking a moment to glance at her. "What about him? Why was he calling you and asking you out for a drink?"

"I honestly have no idea, and I have no intention of ever seeing the man again," she snapped. "What *is* your problem, Ryan? Last night was…" Her voice dropped to a whisper.

"Last night was a mistake," Ryan continued. "I blame myself. I took advantage of the situation. We both had too much to drink and it shouldn't have happened. It was…"

"Don't you dare say unprofessional!"

Ryan winced, his stomach churning at the words. He'd said it all wrong, but the words were out there now. He didn't believe he could trust Kate. Even after last night.

For so long now he'd held regret and bitterness about his affair with Gwen deep in his chest like a tumour. Their fling had triggered a chain of events that culminated in Jim's suicide. Ryan was absolutely certain of that. Gwen's exposé had blown the lid off the whole mission. As Ryan's second in command, Jim had felt the weight of responsibility heavily, and when he survived where others were smashed to pieces on the rocky outcrops, he'd struggled thereafter to accept his right to carry on living.

Neil had more or less hinted that Jim had been struggling for years. Ryan had known it too but had chosen to bury it along with his own feelings.

It wasn't Jim's fault though; that lay with Ryan. The intel had been wrong for sure, but instead of following his gut instinct and ignoring the instructions, he'd followed them to the letter and two men had been killed as a result. Gwen had chosen to take his guilt and twist it into an emotionally charged article for the sake of a scoop.

His knuckles were white on the steering wheel as he tried to calm his racing thoughts. Kate had pushed herself up against the window of the passenger seat, obviously trying to get as far away from him as possible. He swallowed the thickness in his throat and concentrated on the road ahead of him.

When they pulled into the lodge, he went to stop her before she got out, his hand reaching across to take hers.

"Kate, I'm sorry…"

Before he could finish, she pulled her hand away and raced out of the car, a sheen of tears in her eyes. All that was left was the burning sensation of her touch on his skin.

Chapter Thirty-Five

Sara was greeting guests by reception, and she gave Kate a quizzical look as she stalked past. She called out to her, but Kate ignored her, desperate to get to her room and have some privacy. She wasn't quite ready to talk to her yet.

In her room she stripped off her travel clothes and took a long cool shower, trying hard to fight the tears that threatened to fall. She wouldn't let Ryan's cruel words hurt her. She would hold it together. She repeated it over and over like a mantra.

The phone buzzed on the nightstand as she was towelling her hair.

"Hi, honey, how are you? How was Johannesburg?" Sara's voice was cheery and upbeat.

Kate took a deep breath. "Okay. But I need to speak to you."

"Sounds serious…are you okay?"

Kate gulped. "Not really, I…"

"What's wrong? Has something happened? I've just seen Ryan and he's not in a good mood either. What happened?"

Kate sensed panic in Sara's voice and sought to calm

her. "It's all right. Nothing happened, well, not exactly. I need to talk to you though. When are you free?"

"Now," Sara replied. "The guests are checked in, and I am not required until after dinner. Come over to the house and we'll have lunch."

"Okay, let me finish changing and I'll be over in ten minutes. Not sure I can eat anything though."

On the way over to Sara's cottage, she wondered what Ryan was up to, whether he was in the office catching up on work, or in his room sulking. Her earlier hurt had morphed into anger and she was glad she didn't run into him. When he'd proclaimed that he regretted last night, that it was a drunken mistake, it was as if he'd stabbed her in the heart.

Sara greeted her at the door with a hug, silently leading her through to the cool, shaded living room. Kate sank into the soft cushions on the sofa and met Sara's soft brown eyes. Fat, uncontrollable tears fell down her face as she recounted what had happened with Ryan. Sara listened patiently, occasionally passing over a tissue or rubbing her shoulder.

"I'll bloody kill him," she muttered, clucking around Kate. "I can't believe he'd be such a bastard. I thought I knew him better. I should never have suggested you going with him."

Kate flashed a tight smile. "It's not your fault, Sara. He's right; it was a stupid drunken fling that should never have happened. I'd really rather you didn't say anything to him. I have plenty of content for the article. I can probably finish in a day or two."

Sara frowned. "He's not going to get away with it. That's no way to behave to any woman, especially my best friend."

Kate took Sara's hand in hers. "Please don't make a fuss. Let me deal with it in my own way, okay? I think he has issues with trust. I can sense something, but if he doesn't want to talk about it, there's nothing you or I can do about it. I'll chalk it up to experience. Besides—" she locked eyes with Sara "—I have something else to tell you."

"What is it?" Sara's soft voice pushed at Kate's resolve, threatening to bring back the tears.

Kate spoke quietly, almost afraid to say the words out loud. "I'm not only here to write the article; I'm here to find my mother."

Sara blinked. "Your mother? What are you talking about?"

Kate paced the room, eager to get her secret off her chest. "When my parents died I discovered a hidden birth certificate, one that they'd given my godfather Patrick to keep when we came back from South Africa." She forced down a sob. "It turns out they've been lying to me all this time and that Ginny is not my biological mother. I think my dad must have had an affair with a postgraduate student when he was in Cape Town and I was the result."

Sara's eyes widened. "Wow, what a bombshell."

"I know. My biological mother's name is Alison Voester and she gave me to my parents when I was three. The birth certificate I've used all my life was a certified copy with Ginny's name on it as my mother, dated three years after my actual birth. I had no idea it wasn't my original one." She gave a quick laugh. "I guess we don't think to check; we just take things at face value."

"Oh my God, and they never mentioned it?"

"No. I don't think they would have told me the truth ever. And they're not here now to answer my questions. I feel so…" She burst into tears and Sara took her in her arms, holding her close.

When Kate's sobs subsided, Sara paced the room. "Why didn't you tell me when you arrived? Is that why you've been distracted, running off to meet people and taking calls and stuff?"

"I wasn't ready to share it with you until I'd found out more information. I hired a private investigator called Allan Prescott before I arrived. He unearthed an uncle, one of my mother's brothers, and I met with him yesterday in Johannesburg. That's why I wanted to go so urgently."

Sara's lip wobbled. "I would have helped you."

Kate hung her head. "I know, I know…I just needed time."

Sara whistled through her teeth. "Tell me about your uncle. Does he know where your mother is?"

"No, he lost contact years ago. He's called Jacques and he's married with two grown-up sons. He tried to do his best for his sister. It seems Alison was in a bad way; she was broke and struggling to care for me." She gulped down tears. "Oh, Sara, I've found out some pretty awful things about her. She's bad, she's done stuff, and I am still no closer to finding out if she is alive or not."

Sara frowned. "Has the PI been able to find anything else?"

"Not really, just an old charge sheet for an arson and manslaughter offence. Apparently, it never came to court. She skipped bail and has never been seen since."

"Oh, Kate." Sara walked over to the small drinks cabinet in the corner. "I don't know about you, but I think

I need a drink."

That made Kate laugh, and she was grateful for her friend's kindness. They sat in the coolness of the air conditioning until the sun tipped over to late afternoon.

Sara eyed Kate over her wine glass. "Does Ryan know about any of this?"

"No, I wanted to share it with you first. I had thought about telling him last night, but after what happened this morning…"

Sara sniffed. "I think you should tell him. He needs to know the truth, about those messages and about why you are really here. It might make him understand a bit more."

"I don't know, Sara. I think he has his own issues to deal with. Have you seen the way he reacts when he's near helicopters? And do you have any idea why he would be so mistrustful of someone? I mean, one minute he's cross with me about meeting with Quinton Cronje on my own, and the next he's asking me to dance in a bar and we end up in bed together, and trust me, we weren't that drunk. And then I wake up after a truly wonderful night in his arms and he's accusing me of all sorts of things. Someone must have done a number on him."

Sara was quiet, and Kate sensed she was debating what to say. "I don't know all the details, but I do know he was caught up in a landmine explosion where members of his team were killed. He blamed himself for sending one of his team members in the front sweeping vehicle. He thinks he should have been the one to die."

Kate winced. "Yes, he told me about it. It must have been awful. I guess he's got PTSD."

"Kind of," Sara agreed. "Gavin says there aren't many soldiers who have been left unscathed."

"But what about the trust element? I can't see a connection between what happened last night and his past as a soldier."

Sara groaned. "It's really not my story to tell."

"So there *is* something?"

Sara sighed. "All I know is he was involved with a woman before he joined the security group in Iraq. She was an American journalist, Gwen somebody, and they met in Dubai and had a fling. He thought it was the real deal, but she sold his story to the tabloids. He was never named in public, but it was pretty obvious exactly who it was. He lost some good friends in the army over it, not to mention his reputation."

Kate felt a tug of sympathy. "And the woman?"

"I don't think he heard from her again. Gavin knows the whole story. Ryan was a wreck when he met him, drinking loads when off duty and getting into fights. Gavin did his best to help him. Coming to work here was the best thing for Ryan."

A rustle at the door stopped their conversation further, and Gavin arrived hot and sweaty from his day on patrol.

"Hi, Red. How was Johannesburg?" he asked as he opened a bottle of beer and collapsed onto the sofa. "God, it was a hot one today. Summer has come early."

Kate gave him a faint smile. "It was okay. I'm going to leave you two alone and head back to my room. I know you've got guest duty later, Sara, so I think I'll have an early night."

"Don't leave on my account," Gavin said. "Stay and eat with us. Sara's not on duty until after dinner."

Kate bent down to kiss Sara on the head. "No thanks, I'm bushed. I had a late night and early morning."

Gavin waggled his eyebrows. "It wasn't Ranger Ryan that kept you busy, was it?"

Sara groaned and thumped her husband on the shoulder. "Shut up, Gavin."

"What?" Gavin held up his hands. "It was a joke. Although I already sensed something must have happened. Ryan is like a bear with a sore head. He's been shouting at everyone and has switched shifts around so he can work through until tomorrow afternoon."

Sara walked Kate to the door and gave her another hug. "Try and get a good night's sleep and we'll talk tomorrow. I still think you should tell Ryan what's going on."

Kate clasped Sara's hands. "Promise me you won't say anything to him?"

Sara exhaled sharply. "I promise. But I'm not happy about it."

Sara's words echoed in Kate's mind as she walked back to her room, the ever-present chirp of crickets resonating in the air. Near the main lodge, she caught a glimpse of Ryan in the distance, climbing out of the patrol jeep, his clothes covered in dust. He stood in the compound, backlit by the afternoon sun. He'd seen her too and took a step forward, and for a moment she thought he was going to come towards her. But his head dipped and he walked in the opposite direction without looking back. Kate's heart throbbed so hard in her chest, she thought it would burst.

Chapter Thirty-Six

Kate took a deep breath and knocked on the door of the ops room. She'd woken that morning in a better frame of mind and decided that she would give Ryan a brief outline about the search for her real mother. He didn't really deserve to know, but she had to try to explain why she was in contact with a PI. After that, she'd finish the article and have no need to see him again.

She'd also decided during the early hours of the morning to stop the search for Alison Voester. Looking for someone in such a big country was like trying to find a needle in a haystack. And she clearly didn't want to be found. Alison would simply stay a mystery to Kate, no matter how painful that might be. The search had knocked Kate off course, made her forget the wonderful upbringing she'd had with her parents. She would have a few days on the beach with Sara as promised and visit Themba again before heading home to England.

After waiting until it was a reasonable time in England, she'd called Uncle Patrick, his cheerful voice automatically calming her. He hadn't asked about how things were going with her search, but Kate found herself telling him anyway – that Alison had all but disappeared over the years and that, by all accounts, she'd been a troubled woman, perhaps even a criminal.

Uncle Patrick's voice was soft down the line. "Are you sure you're all right? I agonised so much about sharing the contents of that envelope with you. You've been through so much, but I thought you deserved to know."

Kate was glad he couldn't see the tears that filled her eyes. "I probably shouldn't have come, but when I found out the truth, that they'd lied to me about my real mother all this time, I was so angry and I wanted answers. If I'm completely honest, I'm not sure I can ever really forgive them."

"I understand," Uncle Patrick had replied. "I'm not defending them, but they must have had their reasons for concealing the truth. You do believe that, don't you?"

Kate hadn't known how to answer that. Maybe with time she would understand, but without a definitive answer, she would always wonder why they'd kept such an important thing from her. The minute she'd disconnected the call, she'd curled up on her bed and thought of Ginny and Geoffrey, the people who'd always had the most impact on her life. It broke her heart when they died, but she was angry, particularly with her father, for the fact that he'd betrayed his wife by having an affair.

She was about to knock on the ops room door again when it sprang open, revealing Clemmie, her usually cheerful face sombre. "Hi, Kate," she said, standing aside for Kate to enter. The tension in the room was palpable. Ryan was sitting in front of a computer with Gavin and Rio on either side and Sara in the desk adjacent, their faces grim.

"What's wrong?" Kate asked.

"There was another incursion last night," Sara informed her. "Two men crossed the corner of our eastern boundary and entered Marula Heights next door."

Kate's heart pounded in her chest. "Oh no! Did they get another rhino?"

Ryan stared at her intently, his face pale under the tan. "Luckily, no. The two units got to them in time. We have evidence of intended poaching though – axes, pangas and a rifle."

"Thank goodness. Did your team attend?"

Sara nodded. "Rio and Ryan were called out at around three o'clock this morning. They assisted the Marula team in apprehending the poachers. Leonard is definitely the informer. He was on duty again yesterday, and one of the poachers we caught last night is singing like a canary."

Kate arched an eyebrow. "That's a breakthrough."

"It is," Gavin agreed. "We've also now confirmed that his cousin who worked for us a while back has been linked to another syndicate further north. He's currently awaiting trial."

Kate whistled through her teeth. "So what happens now?"

"We've called the police in to arrest Leonard," Gavin said. "He's still on duty, and we're keeping an eye on him to make sure he doesn't do a runner. They should be here in an hour or so. But in the meantime, the same poacher who told us about Leonard has also indicated he will give us a name in exchange for clemency."

Kate was surprised. "A name?"

"Yeah, a potential member of the syndicate," Gavin said.

Kate's eyes flicked to Ryan. "Wow, that's good news, isn't it?"

Ryan's gaze didn't quite meet hers. "I don't think it's appropriate to talk about it until we know more." He pushed the chair away from the desk. "I'm going to have a shower and try to sleep for a bit. You should rest too, Rio. It's been a long night." He ran agitated fingers through his hair. "We'll know more when the interrogation is finished later today."

He strode towards the door, his shoulder brushing Kate's. She cursed inwardly. It was the briefest of touches but her senses went into overdrive. At the door, Sara grabbed his arm and Kate heard her whisper, "Ryan, don't forget you need to apologise to Kate today."

Ryan flicked his eyes towards Kate before heading out across the compound, his shoulders rigid. Kate hid a smile, pretending she hadn't heard. Sara had obviously bent Ryan's ear last night after they'd spoken. She was terrible at keeping promises.

Kate walked back to the lodge with Sara and Gavin. "So what happens now?"

"Leonard will be questioned, and hopefully we might find out more about who is paying him," Gavin said. "Ryan told me about the information you found in Quinton's office, Kate, about a suspected smuggling trip to Tanzania. If we can connect Leonard to Quinton, then we might have the lead we are looking for. It should then take us closer to the poachers and the head of the syndicate."

"And this other poacher, the one who was caught last night, is he linked to your poaching?" Kate asked.

"Not directly," Gavin replied, "but, apparently, a friend of his knows someone who was involved with it, a woman living over the border who's been sheltering poachers in her home as they make their way in and out of the park.

The guy who was caught last night has offered to get her name from his friend in return for some kind of deal on the charges. I think he's basically trying to talk his way out of an arrest, so we may have to take it with a pinch of salt."

"Still, it might be a good lead," Kate said.

Gavin gave a tired smile. "Here's hoping."

Over coffee, Kate filled Sara in on her plans to finish the article in the next day or so. "To be honest, I just want to get it done now and head home." She saw Sara's face fall and added quickly, "After we've had our trip to the beach, of course."

Sara's face relaxed. "I can't wait, although I do wish you would stay longer. I thought you were going to have a sabbatical."

"I need to go home for a bit, Sara. I've not really stopped since Mum and Dad died, driving myself to pack up all their things and to come here and find Alison. I am so exhausted by it all. But I'll come back, I promise. I really want to help at the orphanage—" she laughed "—maybe work there, as a volunteer. I fell in love with them all."

"You'd definitely be welcome. They need all the help they can get." Sara frowned. "So you've really given up trying to find your mother?"

Kate threw up her hands. "Pretty much. I mean, what's the point? She disappeared a long time ago and clearly doesn't want to be found, and even if she does, what kind of person is she?" She shook her head. "No, it's best I leave it. If Allan Prescott unearths anything else, he can contact me by email and I'll decide whether to take it further."

"Fair enough. But I still think you should tell Ryan

about it. It might help him understand what you've been going through."

"I know you're right, Sara. I had thought I might give him a brief outline today, but with this new poaching arrest, he'll be distracted, and perhaps it's just as well I'm leaving soon. If we can be civil to each other over the next few days, it might pass, and when I come back again, it will have blown over."

Sara snorted. "Really? You're so dense at times, Kate. Anyone can see the chemistry between you two. The look he gave you this morning was pretty intense. Promise me you won't leave without speaking to him?"

Kate rubbed her brow. "I don't know, Sara. Maybe."

But she did want to speak to him, to put things right. When she'd been unable to sleep last night, she'd searched online for any information about the journalist in Dubai and the story she'd written about Ryan. It took a while, she didn't have any details to go on other than she was an American reporter called Gwen somebody, but she was never one to give up on a search and she eventually dug it up.

It was clear, after she'd read it, why Ryan would have been upset and angry about it. Gwen Hayden had led him like an innocent lamb to the slaughter of whistleblowing. No wonder he mistrusted journalists and female ones in particular. But that wasn't Kate's fault, and Ryan had still behaved badly yesterday. However, at least there was a partial explanation for it.

"Okay, Sara. If it gets you off my back, I'll speak to him. But this is his last chance."

Chapter Thirty-Seven

Ryan sipped a strong coffee, scanning through emails on his phone, feeling a little refreshed after his short nap earlier. He'd returned to his room convinced that he wouldn't sleep. After the last few days in Johannesburg with Kate and last night with the poachers, adrenaline was surging through his veins. But surprisingly, as soon as he hit the pillow, he'd drifted off into a dreamless sleep, waking early afternoon, hot and sticky on top of the covers.

In the bathroom, he grimaced at himself in the mirror. He was like the wild man of the bush. A shower and shave would soon refresh him and he'd head over to the lodge and sweet -talk Prudence into giving him a late lunch.

Prudence, as usual, pretended to be cross with him for asking for food outside meal times, but she soon reappeared from the kitchen with a bowl of steaming spaghetti carbonara. He was about to tuck in when his phone rang. It was Ed, and Ryan answered quickly. "Hi, mate, any news?"

"Yeah, the guy from last night is squealing like a pig. He's given us the name of the contact in Mozambique who 'hosted' the poachers. He didn't know her second name but we don't need that."

Ryan frowned. "How do you mean?"

"Her name is Miranda and she lives in a small town near the border with the Southern Kruger."

Ryan was still not following Ed. "You've lost me."

"You really need to read your emails." Ed chuckled. "When we were digging into Quinton Cronje's businesses, we came across a shell company, all pretty standard and above board. The name listed as the contact is Miranda Cronje, his wife. The address is in Maputo and we ran a check on it. She no longer lives there, but we did a further search with our Mozambique colleagues and have traced her to a settlement near Magude, which is a town over the border."

Ryan whistled. "So it's the same Miranda?"

"Yep."

"Cronje's wife is involved, which can only mean one thing..." Ryan speculated.

"That he's involved too," Ed finished. "The way I see it, he has his legitimate business in Johannesburg, the hunting safari company. She works for an NGO called Safe Water, which gives her a good cover and helps poachers on the sly. We sent some local police to her house this morning, but no one was at the property. The officers checked the yard and outhouses and noticed through the window of a locked room at the back of the garage several boxes piled high. They couldn't get into the room; the door was bolted with two large and shiny padlocks."

"So now what?" Ryan asked, twirling spaghetti around his fork.

"The thing is," Ed said, "we don't want to spook her. The guy in custody claims the poachers stay with her on the way back from crossing the border. She then takes them to a drop-off point, usually somewhere on the way to Maputo, and they leave the guns and the rhino horn with her. She keeps them hidden somewhere on her property before moving them on."

"So you need to get a warrant to search her house?"

Ed paused. "That's the plan, but we've also heard from another source that Cronje is up to something big. He's got a large amount of horn he needs to shift, which will probably include the horn from your recent incursion. We think he might be planning to do that soon. Once he discovers these guys have been arrested, he'll want to move quickly."

"All the more reason to nab her," Ryan said.

"Yes, but she might not have the horn any more. What we want is to get not just her but Quinton Cronje *and* the goods as well. In one big, neat package."

"I think she still has it." Ryan explained about the message Kate had seen in Cronje's office.

"Well spotted," Ed said. "So it could all go down next week?"

"It's possible," Ryan said. "Okay, so what do you suggest?"

Ed laughed down the line. "Fancy some more undercover work?"

After finishing his call to Ed, Ryan walked across the deck and leant on the railing, staring down at the waterhole. Sunbeams reflected off the water and large circular bubbles rippled on the surface, courtesy of Ziggy, the resident hippo.

He really did hope this was the breakthrough they needed. Ever since he and Rio had come across the slain rhino, his mind had been searching for answers. He wanted to get the people who did this – every single one of them. It was the same in Afghanistan. Whenever they had to deal with insurgents detonating bombs and killing innocent civilians, he'd found it difficult to quell his frustration and anger, especially when it was his own side involved.

Never show your true feelings was something you learnt in the army, otherwise *you're a dead man walking*. But this had become personal, only he didn't know why. Gavin was so good at separating personal stuff from work. He was a great diplomat and a great ranger. The best of both worlds.

A warmth spread through the back of Ryan's neck, and when he looked over his shoulder, Kate was standing nearby watching him. They eyed each other cautiously until Kate broke the spell and stepped towards him. Now was his chance. He would apologise to her as he'd promised Sara. Besides, even though he wasn't keen on the idea, he needed Kate's help again.

"Hi," she said softly, stopping in front of him. She was very pale with dark circles under her eyes and his heart fluttered in his chest as it always did when he was near her. He picked up her scent, light and floral and so alluring. He forced his eyes to move away in case he did something stupid, like kiss her.

His voice came out as a croak. "I was going to come and find you."

Her eyes were wary. "You were? Did you catch up on some sleep?"

He shrugged. "A little."

"I need to…"

"I wanted to…"

They both spoke at the same time. Kate laughed. "You go first."

He rubbed his neck. "Listen, I was out of order yesterday. I shouldn't have read your texts and I am really sorry."

Kate's face flushed and her eyes dropped away from his. "Right, well, thank you for that…"

Ryan was confused. She didn't seem happy with his apology. "What were you going to say?"

"Nothing. Let's put it all behind us. I need to get the article finished and I don't want to make it difficult for everyone else. I don't want a bad atmosphere."

"Okay." He had to admit he didn't like his colleagues knowing his personal business either. "I agree. We should try to forget about it."

Kate folded her arms. "As long as you can trust me. You made some unfair accusations."

He ran his fingers through his hair. "I know, I know. But you gave me reason."

She held up her hand. "Let's not go there again. Please believe me when I tell you I am not up to anything suspicious. It's a personal matter and besides—" she bit her lip "—it's over now, so there will be no more mysterious phone calls for you to worry about."

Ryan noted the tears forming in her eyes. "Is everything okay?"

She dashed away the tears and Ryan longed to pull her into his arms and comfort her.

"I'm fine," she said, lifting her chin and trying to form a smile with her soft, luscious lips.

Ryan remembered his phone call with Ed. "Okay. Well, I have a favour to ask you."

She raised an eyebrow. "You do?"

He gestured towards the leather sofa in the bar. "Let's get a cold drink and I'll tell you about it."

She gazed at him, her beautiful eyes sending shivers down his spine, stopping him in his tracks. He felt a fluttering from deep inside his stomach and then he realised that despite all his best intentions to push her away, he was falling in love with her. How the hell had that happened?

Chapter Thirty-Eight

South Africa–Mozambique border

The sun was gaining height in the horizon, sending bright shards of morning heat towards them as they drove directly east towards the border town of Lebombo. Ryan slowed the car down as they neared the border gate patrol.

"You will need to get your passport out and ready," he said. "There are two checkpoints, one where you need to complete a form and a second one where they stamp your passport."

Kate pulled her passport out of her bag and waved it at him. "All set."

A small line of cars was visible in front of them as they approached. Ryan pulled his passport out of the glove box and tapped impatiently on the steering wheel.

Kate took a sip of water and tried hard not to stare at him again. She'd been taking sneaky glances at him ever since they left the lodge. Things were on more of an even keel between them now. He'd apologised to her yesterday, although in her opinion, that only for snooping on her phone. What happened between them that night in Johannesburg and the consequent argument the next morning had not really been resolved. It hung in the air like an invisible cloak. But she was glad he'd reached out to her and asked to help check out the contact in Mozambique.

"All I want you to do is more or less the same sort of thing you did with Quinton," he'd said to her yesterday afternoon. "Quinton's wife, Miranda, has been named by a contact of the poacher we apprehended yesterday. She's the coordinator and education officer for the western Maputo region of Safe Water. The area is fairly remote and she wouldn't have much supervision. Couple that with its proximity to the border with the Kruger and you've got a perfect place to hide poachers."

"And you want me to interview her?" Kate had confirmed.

"Yes, your story would be that you are writing an article about various NGOs operating across Southern Africa. It may lead to nothing, but it's worth a try. I'll go as your driver, using my own car so there's nothing to link me to the game reserve. Whilst you are with her, I'll snoop around the yard. We need to find something before we send the big guns in. So we don't spook her."

Kate had had her doubts. "But surely she'll want to check my credentials?"

"It's possible. But we'll have to take a chance. I'll call the Safe Water head office in Maputo tonight and leave a message. At least that way you can tell her you tried to make contact."

After she'd left Ryan in the bar, Kate did some research on Safe Water. It was run by a Scottish guy called Cameron McVie. There wasn't much information on Miranda Cronje on the website, other than mentioning her name and role in the western region. Nor did Miranda have any kind of social media presence. Quinton, on the other hand, was all over social media, toting a gun and posing with dead animals as well as sitting in yacht clubs with attractive women or foreign dignitaries. One woman in particular was in a lot of his photos, his so-called business partner, Amy Burton. Kate briefly wondered why his wife, Miranda, was living in the middle of nowhere whilst he enjoyed the comforts of urban life in Johannesburg and what she must think of him working so closely with a woman like Amy Burton.

"Did the local police visit Miranda?" she said as they waited for their passport and visa checks.

"Yes, but they didn't find anything suspicious. She wasn't there at the time. There was a room off the garage, which was locked with a fairly new padlock. A neighbour they spoke to said she definitely had people coming and going at all hours of the night but—" he shrugged his broad shoulders "—without proof…"

They completed their border checks and drove through into Mozambique.

"Did you contact Miranda's boss?" Kate asked. She was getting nervous about meeting this woman and the pretence of the interview.

"No," Ryan said. "The office number didn't seem to work but I found a cell-phone number for him, so I left a message on his cell phone, telling him I was an editor from a British paper and was hoping to send a freelancer in to talk about the NGO, preferably with a field worker. I told him I'd found Miranda on the website and suggested we talk to her as she was the nearest to where our correspondent was currently based."

"And he hasn't called back?" Kate asked.

"Not yet. But that's okay, I'm pretty certain she'll be in. Apparently, the plates of her vehicle were picked up late yesterday coming off the highway. Wherever she was yesterday morning, she's come back."

"What if she doesn't let us in?"

"Hopefully she will. She would have no reason to be suspicious of us."

"I didn't find much information about her when I searched yesterday," Kate said.

"I know. She's certainly kept a low profile, unlike her husband."

"I couldn't agree more," Kate said. "He's a philanderer if ever I saw one. Hence his phone call to me." She shuddered.

Ryan glanced at her, his cheeks stained red. "Sorry again about jumping to conclusions on that one."

Kate chose to stay silent and Ryan switched on the GPS. "The town she lives in is off the main road to Maputo. It should only take half an hour or so from here."

They drove in silence, Kate staring out of the window at the landscape, which had changed from bush to town to farmland. The roads were lined with potholes and Ryan drove carefully to avoid them. Kate watched his hands on the steering wheel and allowed herself to drift back to that night in Johannesburg when he'd run his fingers down her spine, caressing her and making her skin come alive. She closed her eyes, willing the images away.

Outside Magude, they located Miranda's house at the end of a long rutted track that led out towards the bush. A house was a grand name for what stood in front of them. It was more like a large shack, its corrugated tin roof rusted, the paint chipped. A long wooden veranda, or stoop as it was called in Africa, ran across the front. Alongside the house was an overgrown driveway and a large garage.

"Whatever she's being paid by the NGO," Kate muttered, "it's obviously not enough. This place is a dump."

"It's no worse than a lot of people have to live in," Ryan pointed out, "but you're right, it is rather neglected, which begs the question, why is she living like this when her husband is living in a gated community in Johannesburg?"

Kate stared up at the house. "Why indeed."

In front of the garage was a utility truck, its white paint covered in red dust, a tarpaulin half draped over boxes on the back. A woman appeared from the side of the house carrying a small cardboard box with 'Safe Water' written on it. She was tall and lean, with grey hair, which hung in a thick bunch down her back.

Her gaze was not welcoming as Ryan and Kate climbed out of their car. "Who are you?"

Kate stepped forward, her hand outstretched to shake Miranda's, but the greeting was not reciprocated. "Hello. Are you Miranda Cronje? I'm Kate Harper from the *Daily Tribune* in England. My editor spoke to your boss Cameron McVie, yesterday. I'm writing an article about the work that is being done in different NGOs across Southern Africa. Did he get in touch with you about it?" Kate crossed her fingers behind her back, hoping Miranda's boss hadn't contacted her after Ryan left the message yesterday.

Miranda rolled her eyes. "No. But then that's no surprise. He never tells me anything." She hoisted the box further onto her hip and headed towards the truck. "I can't help you, I'm afraid."

Kate's mind furiously sought for a solution. "That's a shame. I've only got another day before I head back to the UK. Could you please spare me a few moments? I have mainly spoken to education and conservation NGOs and it would be great to cover the type of work your organisation is doing."

Miranda put down the box and stared thoughtfully at Kate. "I suppose I could…"

"That would be so great," Kate enthused. "I promise I won't stay longer than fifteen minutes or so." She noticed an old brown leather suitcase on the veranda next to the door. "Are you going somewhere?"

Miranda's face reddened and her eyes immediately flitted to the truck. "I'm off to Maputo early tomorrow morning to take some hygiene kits back. They're out of date."

As she spoke, several silver bangles jangled on her arms. Entwined within them were several thin beaded bracelets. Kate noticed a nose ring and on the woman's slender ankle, a silver anklet with a St Christopher charm and two silver bells. A sudden shiver ran down Kate's back, like someone had stepped on her grave. She closed her eyes for a moment and an image settled behind her eyelids, of a foot adorned with a dangling anklet pirouetting on a colourful rug. She opened her eyes and stared straight into the face of Miranda Cronje, who was looking at her as if she'd gone mad.

She shook off the strange thoughts and stepped towards Miranda. "I'll try not to take up too much of your time so you can get sorted for your trip."

Miranda eyed them both and placed the box on the

truck. "Let's go inside."

Kate shot her a grateful smile. "Thank you. I really appreciate it."

She took a quick glance at Ryan, who was leaning silently against his car, arms folded, and followed Miranda up the rickety steps.

Chapter Thirty-Nine

Kate followed Miranda through the front door and down a stuffy corridor to the kitchen at the back of the house. It was a square room overloaded with clutter. Every available surface was covered with dirty glasses and crockery. An old wooden dresser sat against one wall, piled high with leaflets and paper. "Take a seat." Miranda pointed to a chair at the kitchen table. "Would you like some tea?"

"Yes, please." Kate took the only available seat at the table, the other three being covered in magazines and clothes. The room smelt of burnt cooking and rotting rubbish from an overflowing bin.

Miranda lit a gas ring and popped the kettle on to boil. "Is your companion not coming in?"

"No," Kate replied, "he's happy sitting in the car. He'll probably crank the air conditioning up and he's got a cool box with water, so I am sure he'll be fine."

Kate watched as Miranda flitted around the kitchen, washing mugs for the tea and hastily clearing a space on the table, clearly embarrassed by the state of the room. She placed a steaming cup of tea in front of Kate, its strong fruity aroma providing relief from the other odours in the room. She sat opposite Kate and glared pointedly at the kitchen clock on the wall. "Shall we get started?"

A sunbeam streaming through the dirty kitchen window bounced off Miranda, sending a halo of bright light over her grey hair. Kate squinted in the light and examined the woman's face more closely. She was thin with pale, leathery skin hanging off her arms and a scraggy neck like loose crepe. Her eyes, however, were the colour of amber, with flecks of green running through them, shining like jewels in the gauntness of her face. Once again, a jolt of recognition flickered in Kate's belly.

She took a sip of her tea. "Is this rooibos? My parents used to drink it all the time."

"Yes, it's my favourite brew."

Kate continued to ask general questions, wanting to ease Miranda into the interview. She was prickly, her eyes sliding from side to side nervously, her hands flitting around the table.

Kate ran a hand over the pretty patterned tablecloth. "I love this material."

Miranda stared down at it, a grim line across her face. "It's rather faded now, but it was once colourful. It's a *capulana*, made specially in Mozambique. I used to run a business in Maputo manufacturing tablecloths and linen. They were once quite popular."

Gazing around at the kitchen, with its yellow walls and faded batik blinds, Kate saw the remnants of a home despite its dishevelment. "How long have you lived here?"

"Around ten years now," Miranda replied. "I moved here to run the western region field office. Before that I worked in the office in Maputo."

Kate saw her glance at the clock again. It was time to move the conversation on. "Tell me about Safe Water.

How did you come to work for them, and what sorts of projects do you work on?"

Miranda's voice was flat as she filled Kate in on her work, speaking almost as if she were reading from a manual. There were certainly no inspirational stories of her work, which Kate would have expected from someone working in a community setting. Whilst Miranda droned on about hygiene kits and building wells, Kate made quick notes, all the while conscious that she needed to keep Miranda talking to enable Ryan to have time to scope out the yard and outbuildings.

Miranda reached across to the dresser and plucked a booklet from the top of a dusty pile of magazines. "Would you like one of these brochures about the charity? Unless you already have one?"

Kate took the brochure, its cover greasy and smudged. "No, I don't have one. Thank you."

Miranda gave a dry laugh. "I still don't believe anyone would want to read an article about a water NGO; it's not exactly riveting stuff."

Kate gave her a confident smile. "You'd be surprised what people like to read."

Miranda snorted and turned her back on Kate, clattering plates into the sink and rinsing them. She obviously thought they were finished.

Kate spotted Ryan's head duck beneath the side window. She checked to see if Miranda had seen him, but luckily she was still facing away, the points of her shoulders tense in her freckled back.

Kate searched her mind for another question, anything to keep Miranda busy. There were five framed photographs on the wall either side of the window. The images charted a life, a newly married Miranda and Quinton smiling into the camera; Miranda with a newborn baby; Miranda with a laughing toddler, playing with a puppy; Miranda and a young child building a sandcastle, squinting into the sun; Miranda lying on a patchwork blanket, holding a smiling baby aloft.

Kate's spine tingled again. There was something so familiar about that last photo, from the colourful blanket to the dappled sunshine on Miranda's face. She glanced down at Miranda's anklet again. What *was* it about these images of feet dancing in the sunshine?

In one of the photos, she spotted a blonde boy grinning widely, holding up an enormous fish. It was the same photo as the one on Quinton's desk, the one Quinton had said was of his son. She examined it closely and saw the boy's resemblance to Miranda. Despite being fair, like his father, a tinge of gold and red ran through his hair. Miranda, it occurred to her then, had once been a redhead, her hair now a salt and pepper grey, bleached almost white from the sun.

"Someone likes fishing," she remarked, nodding towards the photo.

Miranda gave a tight smile. "That's my son, Sammy. He caught a lot of fish on that trip."

"Where were you?" Kate asked.

"Off the coast at Vilanculos. On an island called Bazaruto."

"Is that near Maputo?" Kate asked.

"No, it's about five hundred kilometres further up the coast. We used to go on holiday there, camping and fishing, and further north towards Beira." Her face brightened. "It was Sammy's favourite place."

"Sounds lovely," Kate said, noting the way Miranda stared at the photo, her mouth suddenly drooping. "Where's your son now?"

Miranda's shoulders sagged. "He lives in Johannesburg. With his father. He's twenty, and there's more opportunities for him there." Her face lit up. "I am going to see him in a couple of days though. We're going fishing up at Bazaruto as a matter of fact. I can't wait."

She was suddenly animated, talking about seeing her son, and Kate wondered if she was lonely living out here in the sticks, away from him and civilisation.

"Why don't you live in Johannesburg," she asked, "with your husband and son?"

Miranda's eyes narrowed. "I don't think that's any of your business."

Kate blushed. "Sorry, you're right. It must be tough, though, not seeing them all the time. But at least you've got the fishing trip coming up. When are you going?" Kate thought it might be helpful to get a timeline of Miranda's plans, in case they needed to follow things up.

"I'm leaving for Maputo at first light. I will take the boxes to head office and then my son and husband will arrive later in the afternoon from Johannesburg. We will take the boat out as soon as we can after that."

Thoughts raced through Kate's mind. If Miranda was travelling up the coast to Bazaruto tomorrow, she must be taking the horn with her. It all made sense – the delivery of boxes to Safe Water in Maputo, the fishing trip up the Mozambique coast, and the date in Quinton's diary for the planned shipment across the border to Tanzania.

Whilst Miranda was still facing away from her, she took a quick peek out of the back window and caught a glimpse of Ryan disappearing behind the garage. Her pulse skipped. Luckily, Miranda hadn't seen him, but he needed to be careful. She had to find an excuse to distract Miranda.

"Can I please use your bathroom?"

Miranda whirled around suddenly, dishcloth in hand and confusion on her face. It was as if she'd forgotten Kate was there. "Yes, it's right at the end of the corridor, on the right. The hot water tap is stiff, so you'll need to give it a good twist."

Kate headed out into the corridor, her legs a little shaky. She found the bathroom and quickly ran the cold tap, splashing water on her face and checking to see if she could spot Ryan out of the small window to warn him. But he was nowhere to be found.

Chapter Forty

Ryan waited a few minutes after Kate and Miranda entered the house. When he was certain they were settled, he grabbed his phone from the car and made his way over to the truck. If Miranda spotted him, he would simply say he was stretching his legs.

He hoped Kate was all right. When he'd asked her to help last night, she'd initially been unhappy to take part, questioning him as to whether what they were doing was legal.

"It's not illegal as such," he'd answered. "Ed suggested we simply try to get a feeling for how involved she is. She might be high up in the chain, receiving the goods from the poachers and passing it on under the guise of her NGO to the port at Maputo. All it will take is a couple of bribes here and there to custom officials and the goods will be gone. Or it may be that she takes the poachers in, helps them get away and that's it. But we need evidence either way, and if she is only a small cog in the wheel, the police may be able to get more names from her as part of a plea bargain."

"But I can't do that, Ryan," Kate had protested. "I'm a journalist, not a police officer."

"I know," Ryan had placated her. "You only need to distract her with this pretend magazine interview, and I'll do some checking around the property. It will be perfectly safe, and if I find anything, I can hand it over to the police."

Kate had grudgingly agreed, and he hoped she was managing to cope. Miranda didn't appear to be the most willing of people.

At Miranda's truck, he lifted up the tarpaulin and saw five large wooden crates with Safe Water emblazoned across them. Checking over his shoulder, he climbed up onto the truck and flicked one of the metal clips on the lid. It came undone easily and after opening the other three clips, he peered into the crate. It was full of pipes and wires and meter boxes. Nothing suspicious at all, the sort of paraphernalia you'd expect for water engineering.

He checked the other four boxes on the back of the truck. Only one other had clips on, like the one he'd just opened, but the lids on the other three crates were nailed down firmly, and when he tried to lift one of them, it felt much heavier than the unlatched one. Did it contain a different type of cargo?

He replaced the tarpaulin and climbed down, dusting a red sheen of sand off his shorts. He walked slowly towards the garage and the back of the house, careful to duck down near the side windows. He heard voices through the open window. A blind was midway down and he hoped they hadn't seen him.

The back yard was big and unkempt. There was an old whirligig-style washing line sitting in the middle of a dry, dusty lawn and an untended vegetable garden. A veranda ran across the back of the house, its wooden railings chipped and with a few broken planks on the floor. The sun was bright and strong on the faded rattan sofa. It really was a ramshackle house, sad and neglected.

The door at the side of the garage was not bolted, with two shiny padlocks hanging open on the latches. The police had mentioned that the room was locked when they visited the day before. He checked over his shoulder and carefully pushed the door open. It caught on the door jamb, and he shoved it with his shoulder. Inside, the room was empty apart from a few shelves holding paint pots and a discarded broom lying in one corner. The boxes the police had reported were gone. They had to be the ones on the truck ready to be taken to Maputo. The question was, what was in those he couldn't open?

He left the room and surveyed the other side of the garage, further away from the house. Unlike the rest of the yard, this area was tidy, the ground freshly dug, or at least, it had been turned over in the last few days. He kicked at it with his boot, sending small stones and red dirt flying. Two old tyres leant upright against the wooden wall of the garage, the grass beneath them a different shade, as if something had been resting there recently and then been moved somewhere else.

With no spade to hand, he kicked the loose soil with his boot again. When the top soil was removed, he squatted down and pulled the dirt out with his hands, making good progress. There was definitely something underneath, and he finally hit the hard surface of an object. Scraping away the last bit of loose dirt, he made out the rusty top of a piece of metal. Something was definitely buried here.

"What are you doing?" An indignant voice brought Ryan whirling around. Miranda was standing over him. He jumped up and quickly brushed the dirt off his hands, sending clumps of earth and dust everywhere.

He swallowed heavily, noting a gun poised in her arms and her hand flexed over the trigger.

She gave a dry laugh. "Don't worry. I'm not going to shoot you. But I would like to know what the hell you are doing."

He gave a sheepish grin and gestured to the back of the garage. "Sorry, I really need to pee…"

Miranda gave him a look of disgust. "Didn't look like that to me." She jerked her head to the house. "You will have to come inside and use the bathroom. We are finishing up anyway."

He followed her onto the veranda and into the depths of the house, sweat trickling down his back. In the kitchen, Kate was nowhere to be seen and his neck pulsed with worry. Had he misjudged Miranda's risk level? She had a gun, after all, one she'd just pointed at him, and he'd let Kate go into the house with her alone, like a lamb to the slaughter.

Chapter Forty-One

Kate crept out of the bathroom and instead of heading back to the kitchen, found herself drawn to the other rooms off the corridor. A quick check wouldn't hurt. In the main bedroom, a mosquito net hung above a large wooden bedstead, gaping holes in its grey gauzy material rendering it virtually useless. An empty vodka bottle lay on the floor next to the bed and a fly buzzed around the window.

She found another bedroom, with a single bed and a faded map of the world on the wall. The lamp hanging from the ceiling showed images of characters from the children's film *Toy Story*. On the door jamb, she spotted a child's name, Sammy, written at different heights and dates. A child's growth chart, like the one Geoffrey and Ginny had done for her. A lump caught in Kate's throat. Potential criminal or not, Miranda had clearly tried to make this a home for her son.

The final room off the corridor was the living room, surprisingly large given the size of the house. Despite the furniture, it emanated an emptiness, unlived-in and unloved. The light was dim in the room, the air stuffy. A painting hung above the fireplace. It was of a monkey in a tree, its face half hidden by a large tropical flower, and in the distance a splash of blue from the sea beyond. She read the artist's name, surprised to find it was Sammy Cronje. He was a talented artist and she wondered how old he had been when he painted it. In this sad and neglected room, it shone out, a beautiful beacon of light.

She heard voices outside and made to leave, but a photo on the mantle beneath the painting caught her eye. It was of two people standing on a wide green lawn, a man and a woman. She squinted at it in the gloom of the room, the familiarity drawing her in. Heart thudding, she picked it up, moving towards a window for better light, and ran her hand over the glass, brushing away the dust and revealing the exact same photo her Uncle Jacques had given her, of him with her mother Alison. Two red-headed siblings smiling in the sunshine.

She stifled a gasp, reeling with dizziness. This wasn't possible. Her mind must be playing tricks on her. Why would Miranda have this photo? She clutched at the back of the sofa, to steady herself, trying to make sense of it all. The voices became louder; it was Ryan and Miranda. She replaced the photo on the mantle and rushed towards the door, banging heavily into a coffee table. She cried out at the sudden pain and her leg knocked a glass bowl onto the wooden floor beneath. It shattered, echoing loudly in the silent room.

Footsteps clattered down the corridor, and Ryan called out to her. She took one more glance at the photo and fled the room, all the while knowing that no matter how hard she tried, she couldn't deny what she'd just discovered.

Chapter Forty-Two

Miranda looked at Ryan's dirty hands and pointed to the sink. "You can wash here. Miss Harper is using the toilet at the moment."

He scrubbed his hands with a hard cake of soap, all the while aware of Miranda's gaze on the back of his head. The clock ticked loudly in the room. There were two mugs on the table and Kate's notebook lay open, her pen resting in the centre. Two mobile phones sat on the dresser next to the table. Miranda's eyes slid sideways to them and she reached across and flipped them both upside down.

"So," he said, trying to be conversational, "you're off to Maputo?"

"Yes, I have to take some out-of-date boxes back to the warehouse."

"Do you stay over when you go there?"

"Sometimes. It's not far to drive in a day."

"Do you have a dog? I saw a kennel out the back."

Her lips drooped into a sad line. "I did. He died a couple of days ago. Got bitten by a mamba."

"Oh shit, I'm sorry. How old was he?"

"He was nearly thirteen and arthritic, so he couldn't get away quickly when the snake struck."

"Did you bury him in the yard?" Ryan asked innocently. "Only I noticed some freshly dug earth by the garage. Must have been a tough job to do on your own. You'd have to dig quite a deep trench."

She gave him an icy stare. "Yes, it was hard going but I had no choice. I was on my own and he'd have rotted in this heat."

Ryan decided to change the subject. "Will you have some time to enjoy the beach when you are in Maputo?"

A smile flitted across her face. "I'm heading up the coast for a few days. Going to do some fishing, with my son, Sammy."

"Nice," Ryan said. "I've gone fishing there a few times. Do you have a boat? Or do you go on one of those organised charters?"

"We'll use my husband's cruiser. It's kitted out for fishing."

Ryan feigned innocence. "Does your husband work locally too, or in Maputo?"

She gave him a hard stare. "No, he lives in Johannesburg but tries to get back as much as he can."

Ryan kept his voice light. "Is it a big boat?"

But before Miranda could answer, there was a loud crash and a shout from somewhere inside the house. Something had happened to Kate and he rushed out of the kitchen, his pulse thumping in his ears. In the corridor, he hesitated, not knowing which room to go into. Kate appeared by a door, shaking and pale, like she'd seen a ghost.

Relief flooded through him. He reached gently for her arm. "Are you all right?"

She stared at him blankly as if she didn't know where she was before blinking. "I'm okay. I went into the wrong room and banged my leg on a coffee table. I knocked a glass bowl onto the floor."

"Did you cut yourself?" Ryan asked, trying to pry her clenched fingers apart.

Kate shook her head and wrapped her arms around her body, her shoulders tense and shaking.

Miranda stalked up to them. "What the hell is going on?"

Kate was trembling beside him.

"Kate, I mean Miss Harper, accidentally knocked a glass bowl off your coffee table," he said politely. "Do you have a dustpan and brush? I can sweep it up."

Miranda pushed the living room door firmly shut. She glared at Kate. "What were you doing in there? I thought you needed to use the bathroom."

Kate's voice was soft. "I did. I got lost on the way back and went in there by mistake. I am so sorry about the bowl. I can give you some money for a replacement."

Miranda flicked her hand. "Don't bother. I'll sort it later." She put her hands on her hips. "I'd like you both to leave now. I've got lots to do before I go."

Ryan checked on Kate again. She was staring towards the closed living room door as if her life depended on it. *What's wrong with her?*

Miranda glared at Ryan. "Didn't you need to use the bathroom?" She pointed towards the end of the corridor. "It's down there, nowhere near the living room."

He saw Kate blanch at Miranda's sarcasm and forced a smile onto his lips. "Thanks. In all the excitement I almost forgot. I'd hate to be stuck with a full bladder on the drive back."

He placed a hand gently on Kate's back and pushed her

towards the kitchen, his voice soft. "Why don't you pack up your things and we'll get out of here?"

She stared at him, her eyes cloudy with confusion, but finally moved away, following Miranda back to the kitchen.

In the bathroom, he thought about his discovery in the yard. That mound of earth was not covering a dog's body, not unless she'd buried it in a metal chest, which was feasible, but it would take some digging to bury a chest, and he doubted she could have done that by herself. The ground was dry and dusty. And besides, if it was only her dog's body under the dirt, why did she threaten him with a gun?

In the kitchen, he found Kate shoving her things into her bag, her face still as white as chalk. He gave Miranda a polite smile. "Sorry again for disturbing you."

Miranda busied herself with wiping down the kitchen bench. She was clearly eager to be rid of them.

"All done?" he asked Kate.

Her voice came out in a croak. "Yes."

"Right. We'd better hit the road." He gave an imperceptible nod towards Miranda, hoping Kate would pick up on his meaning and thank her.

Kate blinked. "Thank you, Miranda, for talking to me. I'm really sorry about the bowl."

Miranda gestured towards the front door, her tone stilted. "Forget about it. It was nothing of value."

They took their leave, Kate almost running down the front steps. The car was fiercely hot and Ryan ramped up the air conditioning. Miranda stood on the front stoop and watched them leave, an ugly twist to her mouth.

They drove in silence through the small settlement and

onto the main road.

When he couldn't stand it any longer, he blurted out. "So what on earth is wrong, Kate? You were upset about the bowl, but Miranda wasn't that bothered about it. Did something else happen, before I came inside?"

Kate's eyes were large in her pale face, her voice flat. "Nothing happened. It shocked me, that's all. I didn't notice it in the dim light of the room."

Ryan was confused. "Okay, but something seems to be bothering you."

"I *said* I am fine," she snapped at him. "Can we please drop it?"

Ryan tamped down his impatience. "Sure. Why don't you tell me how the interview went? Did she say anything interesting?"

Kate played with the little rhino pendant around her neck. "Not really. It was quite boring. She talked about what she does for the charity, how they put together the infrastructure and skills to build wells and toilets in remote areas, how they go into schools and communities and make sure they understand basic hygiene."

She pulled out her water bottle and took a long drag, her hands still trembling.

"So, nothing of any interest at all?"

She shook her head and leant forward in her seat, her face ashen.

Ryan frowned and continued to drive towards the highway. "I think she's going to shift the horn on Cronje's boat. She told me she was heading up the coast to go fishing with him, on his boat. I think that's odd, don't you? I mean, her and Cronje clearly don't have much time for each other, what with her living on her own in the bush in another country."

Kate didn't reply, her face pensive. He was about to tell her about his discoveries in the yard when she called out suddenly. "Can you stop the car? I think I'm going to be sick!"

Ryan reacted quickly, pulling over on the side of the road, sending a couple of stray goats running. Kate opened the car door and almost fell in her haste to rush to the side to vomit.

Ryan climbed out and hovered nearby, wanting to help but not knowing what to do. He grabbed her water from the car and squatted down beside her. She was still kneeling on the dusty ground, strings of saliva hanging from her mouth.

He handed her the water. "Are you okay?"

"I think so."

She drank from the bottle and wiped her face with the back of her hand. Ryan rubbed her back gently and helped her to stand. She wobbled a little and he steadied her, his heart banging in his chest. "What caused that?"

"I don't know. Nothing…"

He handed her some tissues from the car, and she wiped her hands and face and got back in the car. "Are you sure you're okay to carry on? We can wait a bit longer."

"No, it's hot sitting here. I'm all right now. Let's head off."

"If you're sure," Ryan said, switching the air conditioning to high. "I'll stop at the service station near the border gate and you can freshen up there, maybe have a cola or something."

Kate's face was still pallid, her hands fidgeting on her lap, pulling the tissue she held to pieces. "Sure, thanks."

Ryan restarted the car and pulled out onto the road. What on earth had really taken place in Miranda's house? This couldn't possibly be just because of a broken glass bowl.

"I found something interesting outside whilst you were with Miranda," he said, thinking he would try to distract her.

She glanced at him, her face still pale. "Oh?"

"There's a mound of freshly dug earth near the garage. Someone has definitely been digging there recently and tried to cover it with old tyres. The grass is brown in some parts, where the tyres were lying before they were moved. I managed to scrape the top surface of the dirt away and my hands hit something hard a few inches down. Something hard, like metal or tin."

"What do you think it was?"

"I don't know, a chest maybe."

"Why would she have a chest buried in her back garden? It doesn't make any sense."

"You're right," Ryan mused, "but still...there was definitely something buried there. It could be where she hides the poachers' guns? She has a gun herself, a bolt-action rifle, a hunting gun. She threatened me with it when she found me outside digging."

Kate's voice was shrill. "Well, she is married to Quinton Cronje; she's bound to own one. That doesn't make her guilty of anything. And you were snooping around."

Ryan gave a dry laugh. That was true. He was glad to see some of the old Kate returning, even if she was being argumentative.

He tapped his fingers on the steering wheel. "There was something odd about the boxes on her truck though. Two of the boxes were attached by clips, easy to open. They held pipes and water meters and stuff. The other three, however, were nailed down and were much heavier to lift. Plus, when I was in the kitchen, I noticed she had two phones. She wasn't happy when I noticed them; she turned them over so I couldn't see the screen. She's definitely up to something."

"Lots of people have two phones, and perhaps she hadn't got around to securing those two boxes properly. We did arrive out of the blue right as she was loading them all. None of those things make her guilty, Ryan."

Ryan frowned. "What's got into you, Kate? You've been acting strangely ever since you went into her house."

"Nothing," Kate spat out. "I think you're looking for trouble that doesn't exist. She's nothing but a hard-done-by wife of a dodgy businessman, living in the middle of nowhere in a dead-end job. None of that points to suspicious behaviour."

"Well, that's where you're wrong, Kate," Ryan rasped. "You know as well as I do that she's taking the rhino horn in those crates to Maputo to hand them over to Cronje. She is definitely involved in the syndicate." He thumped the steering wheel impatiently. "I hope we hear back from the fraud team soon. I *know* there's a link between the Cronjes and this poaching incident."

Silence dropped in the car, tension dripping from both of them. They'd been driving for quite some time when Kate spoke up, her voice quiet and small.

"Would she go to prison if she was found guilty?"

Ryan frowned. "What do you mean?"

Kate's beautiful, tired eyes caught his. "Would she be sent to jail, for helping the poachers?"

Ryan's nod was emphatic. "Almost certainly. It's a crime, Kate. Whether you do the killing or house the poachers or smuggle out the horn, it's a criminal activity, which deserves to be punished by imprisonment at the very least."

Chapter Forty-Three

Kate lay in the cool of her room and tried to quell her manic thoughts. When they'd got back to the lodge, she'd headed straight to the solace of her room. It was quiet when they arrived, the late afternoon lull before dinner, and she was glad Sara was not around. She needed to be alone, to think through what had happened in Miranda's house. What she'd discovered.

The phone on the nightstand rang and she ignored it. It had rung a couple of times earlier, probably Sara checking up on her. The sun was setting, and she expected her to knock on her door at any minute. She must get her act together, process what she'd discovered and put on a brave face.

She closed her eyes and went back to the photograph, the one of her mother Alison and her Uncle Jacques. She still couldn't make any sense of it. Why would Miranda have the same photo? She kept telling herself it was coincidence, or that she'd imagined it. After all, she'd only glimpsed it for a minute, in a dim room. Who was to say the woman in the photo was Alison, or the man Jacques?

But in her heart, she knew it was true. The photos in the kitchen of Miranda when she was a younger woman didn't lie. In every single one of them, her hair was a riot of uncontrolled red curls, long and thick down her back. Just like Alison in the photo.

Kate was once more assailed with the image of a woman dancing to George Michael, laughing and lifting her arms up high towards a blue sky, eyes squinting in the sun. She now knew that the woman was Miranda. And the little girl sitting on a blanket under the tree clapping her hands was her.

She now knew that Miranda Cronje was her real mother, that she was once known as Alison Voester. It all added up when she thought about it. Alison had disappeared over thirty years ago and Miranda Cronje was clearly living the life of a hermit in Mozambique, separate from her husband and son. The scant information Kate had gathered about her, mainly from Safe Water's website, was that she was born in Mozambique and had lived in South Africa for a while before returning to Maputo, her supposed hometown. Kate suspected that was made up, all part of a second identity, which then led Kate to the horrific thought that everything she'd learnt so far about Alison, about the charges of arson and manslaughter, was probably true. Her mother was an escaped criminal, living in another country, under another name.

She rolled off the bed and put her head in her hands. Never in her wildest dreams did she ever think her biological mother would end up being someone like this. When she'd embarked on this journey to find her mother, she'd honestly thought she'd find someone normal, that she'd track her down, knock on her door and her mother would answer, surprised but pleased. She would invite Kate in and they would talk. Her mother would show her photos of her life, her family and tell Kate she'd regretted giving her up, that she'd never stopped thinking about her.

But Alison was not like that. Alison had possibly killed a man and had gone on the run, changed her identity and moved to Mozambique. She'd obviously tried to live a normal life with Quinton and Sammy, but even that had gone wrong, and now she spent her days exiled in the bush, helping poachers smuggle out their goods. What had happened to the young woman Jacques had described to her? The woman who wanted to save the whales and stop animal testing? How had she ended up so far away from where she'd begun?

A rap on the screen door startled Kate, and she took a deep breath, trying hard to calm her beating heart. Kate made out the shape of Sara standing under the outside light. "Kate. Are you all right? Ryan told me you'd been ill this afternoon."

Kate had no idea what to say to Sara. She couldn't make sense of anything. She had to buy time, figure out what she was going to do next.

"I'm fine," she called out. "I think I had a bit of heatstroke. I'm just out the shower and I'll be over for dinner soon."

Sara was silent, and Kate waited for her to protest. But she didn't, offering only a quiet "okay" before heading away. Through the small side window of the room, Kate watched her go and felt a pang of regret. Should she tell her about Miranda? That she suspected her of being her real mother? It was all so surreal that Kate wasn't sure where to begin.

Think, Kate. Be logical.

She grabbed a notepad and jotted down bullet points. The process soothed her. She was an investigative journalist; she was good at getting to the bottom of things, to solving problems. And that's what she would do now.

She snatched up her phone and dialled Allan Prescott, praying that the cell-phone signal would work. When his voicemail kicked in, she told him in a shaking voice about what she'd found in Miranda's house. It was only when she hung up, as she was scrolling down her missed calls, that she came across Quinton Cronje's number, remembering that he'd called her the other night in Johannesburg. An idea hit her. She could call him and pretend it was a follow-up to her interview and somehow casually ask about his wife. Surely he wouldn't be clever enough to connect the dots. His phone went straight to voicemail. This time she made sure her voice was calm and business-like.

> *"Hi, Quinton, it's Kate Harper here. I am so sorry I missed your call the other night. I was out with one of the paper's photographers. Anyway, I wondered if we could have a quick chat. Nothing to worry about. I'll tell you when you call me back."*

She hung up quickly, her hands shaking. It was only when she was on her computer doing yet another search on Miranda Cronje/Alison Voester, that it dawned on her: Miranda was a suspect in a rhino-poaching syndicate and a wanted criminal in South Africa. Quinton was quite possibly the kingpin of that syndicate. And there was no doubt in her mind that he was the man in her flashback, the one wearing the leather hat and kicking a dog with his workman's boot. They were dangerous people. What the hell was she doing trying to play happy families with people like that?

Chapter Forty-Four

Ryan was surprised when Sara returned without Kate; she rarely failed on her missions. "Is Kate okay?"

Sara's face creased with worry. "She says she's coming over for dinner, but I don't know... How sick was she? Maybe she's got a stomach bug."

"She was only sick once and we stopped a couple of times on the way back," Ryan said. "I assumed she'd got car sick or something, or perhaps was dehydrated, but..."

Sara noticed him frowning. "But now?"

"Things have been a bit up and down with Kate and me over the last day or so."

"That's because you've been a complete idiot, Ryan," Sara said frankly.

He ran his hand through his hair. "I know."

He was worried about Kate though. On the way to Miranda Cronje's house, she had been curt with him, but she had engaged in conversation, nonetheless. On the way back, however, she'd said virtually nothing. When he thought about it, she'd been strange from the moment she'd broken that damn bowl. Something had definitely happened with Miranda. Concern flooded through him. Had Miranda threatened Kate? But if so, why hadn't she told him about it?

A group of guests came bounding into the bar, their faces flushed and happy from a day out in the bush. The sky was awash with yellows and oranges, and Sara immediately switched into host mode, calling out over her shoulder to Ryan before she left.

"Maybe it's time the two of you sat down and talked things through, about the other night and stuff. Perhaps that's what's bothering her. You promised me you would talk to her."

Ryan had to admit she was right. If Kate was still upset about the other day, he ought to make amends. She'd helped him out today, after all.

"Don't worry, Sara. I'll sort it out."

Besides, he wanted to update her on the latest news from the police. They'd interviewed Leonard, and he'd confessed to passing on locations and information to the poachers. He didn't know who was paying him; it had all been done through an intermediary down in Malelane. Ryan shook with anger at Leonard's indifference. It might have meant a few hundred rand here and there for him, but it had led to the death of an innocent rhino.

The net was closing in, and with a bit of luck, they would have enough evidence to charge Quinton. Ryan had contacted the police in Maputo, telling them Miranda and Quinton were heading there in the next twenty-four hours and planning a so-called fishing trip up the coast.

A thought struck him. He'd ask Kate to come to Maputo with him in the morning. It would be great for her article, and when it was all over, when the arrests had been made, he would take her to a swanky restaurant by the beach and tell her how he felt about her.

The air was warm and a golden glow shone over the riverbed as he bounded up the steps to Kate's room. He spotted two elephants on the other side of the riverbed, their ears flapping in the early evening heat. He smiled, eager to get Kate out of her room to look at them.

He was about to knock when he heard her voice through the sliding mesh door. She was on her phone, and when he heard her mention Miranda Cronje, he jolted, wondering who she could possibly be talking to. He stepped closer to hear more.

"Thanks for calling me back. Can you find out more information about her?" Kate was saying. "She's the wife of Quinton Cronje, owner of Sterling Hunting Safari in Johannesburg. I think she might be…"

Two baboons chasing each other scampered onto the deck, sending a wooden chair flying.

Ryan froze as he heard Kate calling out. "Who's there?"

She slid open the door and blinked at Ryan, her phone still in her hands. "How long have you been standing there?"

"I just got here. I was about to knock when the baboons turned up." He pointed to the guilty animals as they sat on the railings grooming themselves.

Her eyes flitted away from his. "Can I call you back?" she said to the person on the other end of the phone. Ryan watched as she hung up and came to join him on the veranda. "What did you want?" she asked.

Her abruptness annoyed him. "I actually came to check on you." He glared at her. "Sara is worried sick about you, but you appear to have made a remarkable recovery. You are, as usual, busy on your phone. Who is it this time?"

She flinched but didn't answer. He folded his arms. "Is

it Allan Prescott by any chance?"

Kate's eyes flashed angrily at him and colour crept into her face. "It's none of your business. I told you in Johannesburg, it has nothing to do with the poaching incident. It's private." She spat out the last word, and Ryan backed away, shaking his head.

Frustration bubbled inside him. She was still lying to him. "I don't know what you're up to, and if you say it's nothing to do with the poaching, I have no choice but to believe you, but that doesn't mean I can trust you." He stalked down the steps, the lightness he'd felt earlier about taking her to Maputo now gone.

"Ryan, wait!" he heard her calling after him. "I'm sorry, I…"

She was standing on the path outside her room, her face brushed gold by the setting sun. With five long strides, he could be standing in front of her and he could take back his words and lose himself in her. But he continued walking, not wanting to hear any of her excuses, or be taken in by her soft lips. His feet were as heavy as his heart felt, and when he looked back over his shoulder, she was gone.

Chapter Forty-Five

The rain surprised Kate when she slid open the door. She hadn't heard it during the night. It was early, the dawn still an hour or so away. The air was cooler but held the threat of heat. She inhaled the scent of rain on earth, something that had always calmed her but today yielded no comfort.

She was about to do something awful and she hated herself for it. She had pondered for hours, thinking through plausible reasons as to why Miranda would have that photo. But it always came back to one thing. Miranda was her real mother, a coincidence she could never have expected when she embarked on this search. Or was it fate? Kate was not a fatalist, but perhaps her becoming involved in the poaching investigation was the catalyst to lead her to her mother.

The PI had promised to get onto Miranda Cronje's background search first thing today, but she couldn't wait. Goodness knew how long that would take. After all, Miranda hadn't been found all these years, so the chances of him finding anything new were slim. Besides, Kate knew where to find her now, so why waste time? She'd called Sara as soon as Ryan had left and pleaded sickness again. Sara had been insistent they call a doctor, but Kate had lied, making up a story about migraines.

"I've been getting them recently," she'd told Sara. "I think it was triggered when we were in Mozambique and I didn't have my tablets with me. But I've taken two now, plus the anti-nausea one, so I should be fine after a good night's sleep."

Sara had finally accepted Kate's decision to have an early night, but Kate sensed her reluctance. She hated lying to Sara, which was why she'd made the decision to leave the lodge early that morning. To get to Maputo and find Miranda. To confront the truth.

The plan had come to her late evening as she sat on the veranda, the stars twinkling endlessly above her. Miranda had told them that she was on her way to Maputo, to deliver some boxes and to meet her son and husband. They were going on a fishing holiday, to Bazaruto, by boat later in the day. All Kate needed to do was to get to Maputo before Miranda set sail.

The police were closing in on Miranda and Quinton, and it would only be a matter of time before they found the evidence they needed. Miranda's real identity would be revealed and she would be arrested, not just for being part of a poaching syndicate, but also for killing a security guard all those years ago. Kate did not want her to be caught until she'd had time to talk to her. Alone.

She'd found an early flight from Nelspruit to Maputo for the following morning and booked herself on it. She'd sneaked down to reception, careful to check that Sara was nowhere around. Otto, a friendly porter, was on duty and she asked him to take her to the airport, telling him she needed to go back to Johannesburg to meet another photographer. He'd eyed her warily, but said nothing. She was a guest after all. It had been easy to convince him.

But now as she walked quietly towards reception, she worried about who she would run into. It was earlier than the scheduled game-drive time and so should mean there would be no one around, but apprehension still crept up her spine.

Otto was waiting for her by the jeep, bundled up in a fleece jacket and wiping sleep from his eyes, and she felt guilty she'd got him up so early.

"Thank you so much for taking me," she told him as she got in the car. "I know you were working late last night, and I really appreciate it."

Otto gave her a wide grin. "It's no problem. I was on early duty anyway. And I've got some days off coming up. I can catch up on my sleep then."

Kate held her breath until they crossed the cattle grid and made their way along the road leading away from the lodge. She felt nauseous. What was wrong with her? Stealing out in the middle of the night on some wild goose chase. She should at least tell someone where she was going. What if something happened to her?

Otto noticed her discomfort, his friendly face concerned. "Are you feeling all right?" he asked as they drove towards the main road.

Guilt flickered again at his kind words. "Yes, thank you. I'm a bit tired. I'm not used to these early mornings like you."

She made a mental promise to message Sara the minute she landed in Maputo. It was cowardly not to ring her, but at least if she gave Sara a brief outline of her plans, it would buy her some time. She had no doubt that once Sara knew where she was, she'd be on the next plane to join her.

Chapter Forty-Six

It was raining heavily when Ryan made his way to reception. It was the first rain for many weeks, summer now showing itself. The air was close and the sky the colour of gunmetal. He'd booked himself onto the mid-morning flight to Maputo where one of the police officers he'd been speaking to would pick him up. The case had been handed over to the police now, but he still wanted to see it through.

"We've not spotted her truck yet," the investigating officer, Sergeant Perez, had told him on the phone the night before. "We sent a team over to the Safe Water depot, but the compound and buildings were all locked up. We visited the manager, Cameron McVie, but he knew nothing about Miranda Cronje delivering any boxes. In fact, he told us he'd had her in for a disciplinary a couple of days earlier. She'd been neglecting her duties over the last few weeks; not taking the kits out to the outlying villages, that kind of stuff. She had been suspended from her job pending an inquiry."

Ryan had whistled through his teeth. "Then that begs the question, where was she taking those boxes, and what was in them?"

He'd spent the rest of the evening thinking about the case and about Kate. Were they linked? He sensed a connection between Kate's behaviour, her calls to a private investigator and to Quinton Cronje, and that phone conversation he'd overheard last night. What was it she'd said? *Something about finding out anything about a Miranda Cronje?* He'd presumed she'd been speaking to Allan Prescott, and if so, why? But no matter how hard he tried, it all went around and around in his head.

Sara had told him that Kate was in bed with a migraine, yet when he'd seen her she'd been perfectly all right. She was lying to her best friend and that bothered Ryan. Sara was the sweetest, most trusting person he knew. Why was Kate treating her like this?

At reception he spotted Otto parking the airport jeep. "Have you been to the airstrip?" he asked. "I didn't think anyone was due in today."

Otto shook his head. "No. We've got some guests due in this afternoon. I've just taken Miss Harper to Nelspruit."

Ryan did a double-take. "What? When?"

"First thing." Otto bit his lip. "She's going to Johannesburg, I think. Something about meeting a photographer."

Anger resonated through Ryan. She'd used that excuse before.

"Did I do something wrong?" Otto asked.

Ryan made to placate him quickly. "No, not at all."

He strode out of the reception, heading for Sara and Gavin's quarters. It was time to find out what the hell was going on.

Gavin opened the door to him, his face fresh and cleanly shaven. "You look like hell, mate," Gavin said as he led

Ryan to the kitchen.

"Thanks," Ryan snorted. "You'd be like this if you'd had a sleepless night."

Gavin put his hands on his hips. "Rhino poaching or Kate?"

"Both. Although mainly Kate. I know she's Sara's best friend, but she is the biggest pain in the arse I have ever met. Did you know anything about her going back to Johannesburg today? Otto took her to the airport early this morning."

Gavin's brows furrowed. "No. Sara didn't mention it."

"Mention what?" Sara appeared in the kitchen, pouring herself a coffee from the pot.

Ryan tsked. "Apparently, Kate's done a runner to Johannesburg. Otto took her first thing."

Sara's mouth fell open. "That's ridiculous. I spoke to her at ten o'clock last night. She had a migraine; that's why she threw up yesterday. I told her to get a good night's sleep and rest today. She used to get them at school; they were really bad sometimes."

"Well, she's made a miraculous recovery," Ryan said dryly. He ran his fingers through his already untidy hair. "Sara, I know she's your best friend and you trust her, but I think she's an informer or something."

Sara snorted. "An informer? Honestly, Ryan, you've got completely the wrong end of the stick. It's not something I should tell you but…"

Ryan interrupted. "Can you tell me why she is so secretive? Last night I went to speak to her, and as I arrived at her room, I heard her speaking through the open window. She was talking to someone about Miranda Cronje, the woman we spoke to yesterday. I think she was on the phone to a private investigator, Allan Prescott. Anyway, she was asking him to find out more about Miranda."

Sara poured him a coffee and pushed the mug towards him. "Take a seat, Ryan, and I'll tell you what I know. It's not what you think, believe me." She took a sip of her coffee, her eyes sad. "Kate's not involved with anything illegal or sinister. Yes, she's here to write the article. But—" she bit her lip "—she's also come to South Africa to find her real mother."

Ryan blinked. "Her real mother?"

"Yes. She discovered after her parents died that Ginny wasn't her real mother. Apparently, her father had an affair with a postgraduate student at Cape Town university when he was working there and Kate was the result. Geoffrey and Ginny adopted Kate when she was three and took her back to England. She never knew anything about it until her godfather gave her the original birth certificate after her parents' death."

Ryan mulled the story over. "So this Allan Prescott is searching for her real mother?"

"Yes," Sara confirmed, "and when she was in Johannesburg, she met her uncle, who the private investigator had unearthed. But she drew a blank, her uncle not having seen his sister for over thirty years. In fact—" Sara's brow furrowed "—she told me she was going to give up her investigations, which is why I don't understand why she's gone back to Johannesburg."

Ryan's brow creased. "What was her real mother's name?"

"I can't remember, Alison something. Why?"

Ryan remembered the name of the other man Kate had

mentioned in a text to the PI. "Is it Alison Voester?"

"Yes, that's it. How did you know?"

Ryan shrugged. "No reason. But that still doesn't answer the question of why she's gone to Johannesburg at the crack of dawn, and why she's asking Allan Prescott about Miranda Cronje. None of it makes any sense."

Sara's phone pinged with a message. She picked it up and read the message.

"It's from Kate." Her face paled. "She's not in Johannesburg." A look of panic crossed her face. "She's landed in Maputo—" she scanned the text further "—and she's gone to find Miranda Cronje."

Gavin was confused. "I thought you spoke with Miranda Cronje yesterday, Ryan? Why would Kate want to see her again?"

The answer suddenly dawned on Ryan. "Because Miranda is her real mother or is connected to her."

It all made sense to him now. The phone calls and messages to the private investigator. Kate's strange behaviour after she'd met Miranda and the question she'd asked him in the car on the way back, about what would happen to Miranda if she was convicted.

Sara paced the room. "She told me the other day that she was looking for her real mother. I suggested she should tell you, that it might make things better between you, that if you had known what she was really up to, you might not have been so angry with her. I had no idea she even suspected this Miranda woman."

It was all beginning to click into place for Ryan. "That's because she didn't know, until we visited Miranda yesterday, at her home. Kate was behaving really oddly after our visit. I've no idea what happened, but something spooked her."

Sara picked up on his train of thought. "She must have discovered something, when she was at Miranda's house."

"Exactly," Ryan said.

His face was serious. "We need to get to Maputo and find Kate. Quinton Cronje is about to smuggle rhino horn out of Mozambique. The police suspect Miranda has been storing it, disguised in the Safe Water boxes, and that now they're about to shift it on his boat. Miranda told us yesterday that she was taking the boxes to the Safe Water depot, only her boss told the police last night that he knew nothing about it."

"Oh God," Sara cried. "Is Kate in danger?"

Ryan's face creased in worry. "It's possible. Quinton Cronje is involved with some unsavoury people. We have to find Kate before she finds them."

Gavin jumped into action. "You contact the police in Maputo, Ryan, and I'll get onto the private charter company and try to get us a flight over to Maputo from the airstrip. It will be quicker than Airlink."

Sara grabbed her phone. "I'll try calling Kate. Hopefully, I can catch her before she gets to Miranda. She had just landed at Maputo when she texted me." Her chin trembled. "It's all my fault. I should have made her tell you what was going on, Ryan, instead of letting her keep quiet about it."

Ryan touched her gently on the shoulder. "You weren't to know. You were protecting her secret. You are a great friend to her."

Gavin embraced Sara tenderly. "We'll find her, don't worry."

Ryan hoped Gavin was right. He raced to his office,

his heart thumping in his chest. He would never forgive himself if something happened to Kate. He thought of her lying in bed with him that night in Johannesburg, of her long red hair trailing across his chest as they talked. She'd made him laugh that night, made him feel alive for the first time in years. He had to find her before it was too late. He wasn't going to let another person die under his watch.

Chapter Forty-Seven

Maputo, Mozambique

Kate's taxi pulled up alongside the marina, her heart pounding from both apprehension and exertion. She hoped she'd made it in time. She'd come so far now; she had to find Miranda.

It was noon and the sun roasted overhead, leaving her hot and sweaty in her T-shirt and long trousers. She sprinted through the large entrance gates towards the boats. Above, the sky was a perfect azure and the sun glinted off the white hulls of the sailboats and cruisers. She placed a hand over her forehead to shade her eyes, casting about for Quinton Cronje's boat.

"Can I help you?"

She spun around to see a security guard emerge from a small kiosk by the gates. He moved towards her and she took a deep breath, hoping he couldn't hear the furious beating of her heart. *Act normal.*

"Yes, thank you. I'm looking for a boat called *The Hunter.*" It had been easy to find details of Quinton Cronje's boat on the yacht register online.

The guard consulted the clipboard in his kiosk, running

his hand down the list of boats. "It's docked over in Bay C, number twenty-three."

Kate's pulse raced. "Is it still here?"

The man tapped the clipboard. "According to the paperwork, but you'll need to check in the office." He pointed towards a small cabin tucked to the side of the marina's indoor docking sheds. "Nico will be able to help you."

Kate gave him a coy smile. "Can I find the boat myself? Perhaps you could point me in the general direction and then I won't need to bother Nico."

He hesitated. "You're really meant to check in with the office. We can't just let anyone in. These boats are worth a lot of money."

Kate pushed up her sunglasses onto her head to make full eye contact with the guard. If the boat hadn't left, she still had a chance. She scanned the name on his badge. "Peter, I've come all the way from England to track down an old family friend. I've heard she is at the marina and I really want to catch up with her before she embarks on her trip."

She crossed her fingers and hoped he'd agree to bend the rules. She hated lying to him but she had no choice.

He frowned. "Okay, you can check to see if it's there, but if you decide to board the boat or go anywhere on it, you must report in first."

She gave him a wide smile. "Of course and thank you. Can you show me which way to go, please?"

He shuffled the paper on his clipboard and pulled out a map of the marina. "You can keep the map," he said, pointing at Bay C.

Kate saw the docking numbers clearly marked in each

section. Number twenty-three was halfway down one of the four long lines that made up Bay C. She hurried towards the boat's location, all the while hoping she hadn't missed them. Her mouth was dry and her nerves were frayed. It was all very well tracking Miranda down, but she hadn't thought about what she was actually going to say to her.

At Bay C, the boats changed from catamarans and sailing boats to leisure cruisers, some of them fitted with large fishing poles at the back. Maputo was a popular destination for fishing trips, the waters around the numerous archipelagos teeming with fish and marine life.

She'd neared number twenty-three when she spotted Miranda on the jetty. She was sitting on a box-shaped concrete plinth, a bag at her side and a mobile phone in her hand. Now that she was about to be face to face with her, Kate couldn't move, her feet heavy on the wooden planks beneath, her pulse skittering.

Miranda saw her approach and rose to her feet, moving quickly towards Kate, confusion on her face. "What are you doing here?" She frowned. "Are you following me?"

Kate held her breath as Miranda drew close, her long skirt fluttering in the breeze. The two women stared at each other, Kate taking in the suspicious glare of Miranda's green-flecked hazel eyes.

Kate finally found her voice. "I'm not here about the article."

Miranda's voice was harsh. "Why are you here then?"

Words dried in Kate's mouth like sawdust. Two gulls on the top of a boat shrieked and swooped up towards the sky. Beyond the marina's waters, the sea was a deeper blue. It stretched endlessly towards the horizon, as did the cloudless sky above.

She took a deep breath. "I'm looking for my mother."

Miranda frowned. "What's that got to do with me?"

Kate thought of the photo of Jacques and Miranda burning a hole in her handbag and she fished it out.

"What the hell is going on?"

Kate whirled around. Quinton was standing directly behind her on the dock, his hands on his hips. He walked the short distance to them, his feet pounding the wooden planks, and gazed at Kate in surprise. "What are you doing here?"

"You know her?" Miranda asked Quinton, surprise registering on her face.

Quinton's nostrils flared. "Yes, she interviewed me in Johannesburg the other day, about hunting safaris. It was for a travel magazine." He cocked his head towards Miranda. "How do you know her?"

Miranda's cheeks flushed. "I don't really. She came to the house yesterday telling me some story about writing an article on water NGOs. I caught her driver snooping out the back. And now she's followed me here."

Quinton glared at Kate. "Who exactly are you?"

"It's the truth; I *am* a journalist," Kate said, backing away, aware that Quinton had come closer, a menacing snarl on his lips, "from England, like I told you. I wanted to…"

But she didn't have time to finish as Quinton grabbed her arm, twisting it behind her back.

"You're lying. I think you're an undercover cop. Jacqui, my secretary, told me she'd caught you nosing around my office. I knew something wasn't right about you. That's why I rang you that night, to ask you out for a drink. I wanted to suss you out"—his voice was silky, but simmering beneath the surface was something much more sinister—"and then I got your voicemail last night, asking about Miranda, which I also thought was rather strange."

Kate had forgotten about her late-night call to Quinton.

"She's from the police?" Miranda exclaimed. "That must be why her driver was checking out the yard. He was a cop too."

Quinton snarled at Miranda. "You bloody fool. How much did you tell her?"

'Nothing," Miranda shrieked. "I answered her stupid questions about Safe Water, that's all."

The anger coming off Quinton as he gripped Kate's arm was palpable. He sneered at Miranda. "I told you to never talk to anyone without running it by me first. You stupid woman."

Kate's eyes slid to her bag discarded on the jetty. She hoped they hadn't noticed it, that it would remain hidden behind the concrete plinth. If it was discovered by one of the security guards, they would at least work out who she was, and once the police had it, hopefully a connection to her and Miranda and Quinton would be made.

But Miranda had noticed the bag too and picked it up, showing it triumphantly to Quinton. "It's her bag. This should tell us if she is a cop or not. There might be ID in there."

Quinton snorted. "An undercover cop doesn't go around with identification. Bring the bag. We can throw it all into the sea. We don't want anyone tracking us."

Kate struggled against his strength. "No, please let me go. I'm not a cop; I promise you. Let me explain…"

"Shut up!" Quinton tightened his grip and Kate watched

with dismay as Miranda scooped up her bag and searched it.

"There's no time for that now," Quinton growled.

Kate's eyes flicked towards the marina office in the distance, hoping to see Peter or his colleague Nico. If she screamed loudly enough, they might hear her.

As if sensing what she was about to do, Quinton placed his other hand over her mouth and hissed at Miranda. "Let's get her on board before she attracts attention. Is everything loaded onto the boat?"

"No!" Kate screamed, kicking out at him as he got her in a headlock.

Miranda's eyes widened with panic as she watched Quinton drag Kate up the gangplank and onto the boat.

"It's all sorted, Quinton," she said, following them on board, "but what the hell are we going to do with her? If she is police, there might be others on the way."

"All the more reason to get the hell out of here. Quick, open the cabin door. Let's get her out of sight," Quinton grunted.

Kate struggled against him with all the strength she could muster. He was strong, and she gagged on the hand clamped across her mouth, suddenly losing all the strength the earlier adrenaline had given her. Miranda opened the hatch to the cabin and Quinton hauled Kate down the steps. It was stuffy inside, and the boat rocked from side to side with their movements.

"Let me go. I won't talk, I promise," she panted as she tried to extract herself from his grip.

Quinton pushed Kate onto the bunk, holding her hands firmly.

"Pass me the rope," he ordered Miranda.

Miranda was still staring in shock and disbelief at Quinton. Kate took the opportunity to kick out again, but her foot hit the edge of the bunk, a sharp pain searing down her leg.

"Quickly!" Quinton barked at Miranda.

Miranda sprang into action, grabbing the coil of rope and helping Quinton to tie Kate's hands and feet.

A wave of panic engulfed Kate. "You can't do this to me," she exclaimed. "The police are on their way, they know where I am, and I told the security guard which boat I was looking for. You haven't got a chance; they'll find me before you've left the harbour."

"Shut up, bitch," Quinton snarled, knocking Kate hard on the cheek with his fist and sending her flying across the bunk where she hit the side of her head on a metal handrail.

She gazed up in astonishment, Miranda and Quinton's faces swimming in her eyes before darkness engulfed her.

Chapter Forty-Eight

Kate's eyes fluttered open, needle-sharp bolts of pain shooting through her head. Her body trembled and sweat dripped down her forehead. At first she thought she was back in her bed at the lodge. Then she remembered: she was on Quinton's boat, tied up in the cabin. She wondered how long she'd been unconscious and whether they'd left the marina. The boat was gently rocking beneath her, which made her wonder if they were moving.

The air in the cabin was stifling, and sun streamed through the tiny portholes. She sat up slowly, wincing, and swung her legs over the side. Her feet and arms were still tightly bound together and there were red marks where the rope cut into her skin.

Above, she heard Quinton and Miranda, their voices rising to full pitch in a shouting match. She flinched at a thump and bang from the deck, wondering what was going on. She tried to stand and fell on her side, hitting her hip on the wooden frame of the bunk. She must have emitted a sound for within seconds there was a clatter of feet above and the door to the cabin sprang open. Miranda stared down at her, her eyes fraught with panic.

Suddenly, Quinton shoved her down the steps and she

groaned as she fell. "You can stay down there with her. I'll throw you both off the minute I get into open water; you're no good to me now."

Miranda landed heavily on her knees, her face creased up in agony. "No, Quinton," she screamed, "don't do this, I didn't mean it! I had nothing to do with her being here, I swear. All I want to know is where Sammy is. You promised me he would be coming on this trip. I need to see my son!"

She collapsed on the cabin floor, panting and sobbing, her chest heaving in distress.

"Are you okay?" Kate asked, wriggling off the bed, trying to reach Miranda on the floor.

Miranda kicked out at her. "Stay away from me! It's all your fault. You shouldn't have come snooping around. If you'd just stayed away, I would be with my Sammy now." She pulled her knees up to her chest and sobbed into her skirt.

Kate's mouth was dry and she croaked out the words. "Please, Miranda, help me. You can't let him do this. Whatever he's told you, it's a lie." She eyed the radio console on the bench opposite and whispered to Miranda. "You could call for help."

Miranda's head popped up and she hissed at Kate. "Be quiet; he'll hear you. We're only an hour up the coast and the engine's stalled. He's trying to sort it. The last thing you need is another backhand from him."

Miranda's face was red, her hands trembling. Kate had to convince her to help them get away. "I am not a police officer, I promise you; I am a journalist like I told you, but that's not why I wanted to speak to you."

Miranda's lips curled. "I don't believe you. If you're

not police, why do you have a photo of me and a file with my name on it – my real name?"

She reached into a storage box and pulled out Kate's leather tote bag. She tipped out its contents onto the bunk. Kate scanned the items for her phone, her heart sinking when she couldn't see it.

Miranda found the photo of her and Jacques and shoved it in Kate's face. "Why do you have this? I know you saw the same one in my house. I went into the living room to clean up the broken glass and I noticed you'd moved the photo." She shook her head in dismay. "All I wanted was to finish this goddam job and see Sammy. Quinton promised me…"

Kate saw red. All Miranda could talk about was Sammy. She had absolutely no idea that her daughter was sitting in this cabin with her.

"Yes, I did see the photo," she snapped, "the one of you with your brother Jacques."

Miranda grabbed Kate's arm, making her wince. "What the hell do you know about Jacques?"

"I know that he's your brother and you used to be called Alison Voester. I know you're still on the run from the police after setting fire to a drug-testing warehouse in 1988, that you changed your name to Miranda Cronje, that you have lived a lie for over thirty years. I know that you killed a man!"

Miranda slumped against the wall. "What? How do you know all of this? You have to be a police officer. How else would you know?" She scrambled up. "I'm going to get Quinton in here now and tell him to finish the job. He wanted to throw you overboard when he knocked you out, but I talked him out of it. I suggested we leave you on one of the islands further up the coast. We'd be long gone by the time you were found. I should have let him kill you."

Kate watched with dismay as Miranda headed towards the hatch. "Wait! You can't kill me, please! I am not the police. Please, you have to believe me." She was screeching now, desperate and fearful. "Please, Miranda. Stop! Listen to me!"

Miranda's eyes were hard and flinty, her hand poised to bang on the cabin door. "Why should I?"

"Because I'm your daughter," Kate said softly. "I'm Katie."

Chapter Forty-Nine

Kate watched Miranda slump against the door, eyes wide in her ashen face. "Katie?" she whispered, slipping onto her knees and vigorously shaking her head. "No, no, it can't be you."

Kate's stomach tightened. "It is me. I'm the daughter you gave up. It's all there, in the file in my bag, an adoption certificate signed and dated by you. I don't really remember anything about it. I was young and I must have blocked it, but since I've been in South Africa, I've had a few flashbacks. Of a woman with red hair wearing a long skirt and dancing in the sunshine. You gave me up, to Geoffrey and Ginny Harper."

"No, no, no…" Miranda moaned "…you're not her, you're a policewoman, undercover…"

Kate's face crumpled. "Can't you see?" She pointed to the photo of Miranda and Jacques that had fallen on the floor. "I am your daughter…look at it, see how much I look like you?" She gave a bitter laugh. "We could be sisters."

Miranda stared down at the photo and back up at Kate. "How can this be?"

The cabin was silent apart from the soft thumps above,

where Quinton was trying to fix the engine. Kate held her breath, and Miranda collapsed onto the bunk next to her, realisation dawning on her face.

She angled her body towards Miranda. "My parents never told me the truth, and I didn't have any reason to believe otherwise. Then—" she took a deep breath "—they were both killed in a car accident six months ago and I discovered my original birth certificate, the one they'd kept hidden from me, alongside the adoption papers." She pulled a wry smile. "I was pretty floored, and angry."

Miranda gazed at her, confusion clouding the green flecks in her hazel eyes. A shiver ran down Kate's spine. The similarity between her eyes and Miranda's was uncanny. People had always commented on how unusual and beautiful Kate's eyes were. Both her parents had blue eyes, and she'd always wondered where the colour came from, had always assumed it was a genetic throwback. Now she knew.

Miranda's voice was raised. "I never expected to see you again; that was the deal. Once I signed the papers and they took you, I was to never get in touch, ever—" she lifted her chin "—and I kept my end of the bargain. Why didn't you let sleeping dogs lie?"

She was breathing heavily, her hands resting on her knees. Kate was silent, waiting for her to calm down. Miranda was thin, with leathery skin hanging in clumps off her arms. There was a faded tattoo of a dolphin on her upper left arm, and her fingers were adorned in chunky silver rings.

Kate softened her voice. "I am sorry if I've shocked you. I was pretty surprised myself."

Miranda stiffened. "What is it you want from me?" She

gave a bitter laugh. "Because if it's money, I don't have any."

Kate bristled. "Is that what you think? That I've come to claim an inheritance of some sort?" She tried to stand but sank back down, her legs still bound in the rope. "I'm here because I want answers. I want to know what happened with my father and why you gave me up, why you let them take me away."

Miranda eyed her. "Were you not happy with them? They were rich and respected, everything I wasn't."

Hot tears filled Kate's eyes. "I was happy, of course I was. I was devastated when they died. But from the moment I found that birth certificate, everything changed. I need to know, to understand. You have to tell me."

Miranda stood, stumbling a little on the rope by Kate's feet. "I don't need to tell you anything. You're nothing to me but a mistake."

Kate flinched. "You can't mean that."

Miranda threw up her hands. "I can't give you what you want. I made my decision all those years ago. I didn't want to be tethered to a child. There was no great love affair with your father; it was a stupid fling. We met at a seminar. He was giving a lecture and I asked him lots of questions, and then after, at the drinks reception, he came over to speak to me. A few days later, he tracked me down and we began to meet regularly. I hadn't planned on sleeping with him, but he was an attractive man and I was bored with the younger men I hung out with." She paused, her eyes distant in memory. "Geoffrey was sexy and interesting and worldly. There was a moment I thought he might leave his wife for me, but of course, that was never going to happen."

Kate listened intently, fury bubbling at the thought of her father's behaviour. "Did you ever meet my mother?"

Miranda shook her head. "I saw her from a distance a few times on campus, once or twice with Geoffrey."

"What happened when you discovered you were pregnant? Did you tell him then?"

"No, I'd broken up with him by then. I was fed up with being the other woman, the clandestine meetings and his overpowering control. He wanted me but only on his terms, and I was restless; I wasn't even sure I wanted to finish my degree. A group of my friends were heading up to the Northern Cape to live in a commune for a while and I wanted to go along."

"When did you tell him about me?" Kate repeated. "Or didn't that matter to you?"

Miranda rolled her eyes. "By the time I found out I was pregnant, I was nearly three months along. I was up north and happy, free from the constraints of conventional life and heavily involved with Greenpeace." She twisted the large silver ring around her index finger. "I had you and for the first year you were brought up collectively. That was the whole purpose of communes."

Kate mulled over Miranda's words, trying to imagine herself living in a community, being passed from person to person. "Did you love me at all?"

Miranda raised her eyebrows. "Does it matter now?"

A lump formed in Kate's throat. "Of course it matters. You need to tell me the whole story; you *owe* it to me."

Miranda's eyes flared. "I don't owe you anything. If it wasn't for you, I wouldn't be here, stuck in this boat with that jerk up there." She pointed her hand towards the deck. "I would have finished my degree and got a career and made a difference to the world, helped people, animals…"

Kate pushed away the pain that flowed through her veins. "Instead you ended up killing an innocent security guard, marrying someone who makes money out of trophy hunting and poaching and for what?" Her throat was constricted, tight, but she carried on. "If you were such an eco-warrior, why did you allow yourself to go along with it?"

Miranda stared at her, a mixture of defiance and sorrow reflected in her face. "It was a simple matter of economics." Her eyes flitted away. "I needed money and it was the easiest way to do it. To be honest, the number of animals involved over the years was miniscule."

Kate slumped forward, unable to comprehend the coolness that surrounded this woman. "Then I'm glad you gave me up. My mother, Ginny, was a hundred times the person you are."

Miranda snorted. "But it didn't stop her buying you though, did it?"

Kate jolted. "What do you mean buy me?"

Miranda smirked. "Do you seriously think I would have given you up without striking some kind of deal?"

Bile rose in Kate's mouth. "I don't believe you."

Miranda gave Kate a look of pure malice. "Sorry to disappoint you, Katie, but it's the truth."

Kate tried to process what Miranda had told her, unable to believe her parents had paid to adopt her. She stared down at her bound hands, the rope chafing her wrists. It was stuffy in the cabin and her stomach churned.

The engine of the boat roared to life briefly and then stalled. It sounded like Quinton was close to fixing the motor. If they didn't hurry, the boat would be hurtling its way up the coast, further away from safety. She had to enlist Miranda's help. Even if she didn't care about the daughter she gave up, Kate needed to convince her to do something. She eyed the radio console again.

"Miranda," she hissed across the small cabin, "how far from Maputo are we? We've got to call for help. The coastguard could be here quickly."

Miranda's face was blank. Despite her earlier bravado, she was now in a trance.

"Come on, Miranda, untie me and we'll get some help."

Miranda's eyes were wild. "He's got a gun; it's no use. I am as disposable to him as you are. He'll shoot us both."

"We'll have to find a way," Kate implored. "We can't give up."

Occasionally the engine coughed as Quinton turned the key, cursing loudly when it didn't start.

"Miranda," Kate whispered, "we can use the radio to call for help. I can do it, but you'll need to untie me and distract him."

Miranda jumped up suddenly, fists clenched. "No!"

Panic rose in Kate. "Why not? It's the only chance we've got. What if he ties you up too? We have to act now or it will be too late."

"What does it matter anyway?" Miranda wailed. "My life is more or less over. I've lost Sammy because Quinton's poisoned him against me. I won't be able to go back to my house or my job and Quinton has already found a replacement for me," she grunted. "His so- called business partner, Amy. There's nothing for me now."

Kate was furious. "My life matters to me. I know you don't care about me; you gave me away after all, but I have a life, a job, people who love me. I have everything to live for."

Miranda let out a sob, shaking her head back and forth. "I can't take any more, no more, no more."

Kate began to shake. She'd wanted to cajole Miranda, shame her into doing something, but she'd gone too far. "I'm sorry," she said softly. "I didn't mean to upset you. I have no idea what you went through all those years ago. I was just a baby. I came to South Africa to find you, to discover what happened to you. Please don't do this. It's me, Katie."

Miranda's chest was heaving. "I don't know what to do," she whispered. "It's too late now. He'll kill us both. He doesn't care about anyone, never has. He's had so much power over me all these years; I'm caught in his web."

Tears glistened in Kate's eyes. "What power?"

Miranda stared in the distance. "I loved Quinton from the moment I met him. He strolled into my life like a summer breeze." She eyed Kate. "You were two when I met him. I'd left the commune and moved back to Cape Town. I was working in a pub and he walked in, placed his leather hat on the bar and that was that. I was smitten."

"What happened then?" Kate asked.

Miranda gave the ghost of a smile. "At first he accepted you. I was living in the grotty flat above the bar and he moved us to his mother's house out of town. He supported us, visiting most weekends. He'd bring beer and dope for us and toys for you, and we'd get stoned and hang out. Then he'd go back to the city and I'd be alone again. It was good for a while, but then one day you were ill, a sore throat or something, and you grizzled all weekend. Quinton blew his top and I shouted back at him, so he hit me, sending me flying."

Kate gasped. "Did he hit you a lot?"

Miranda shrugged. "I learnt how to make him happy, to please him. He asked me to do jobs for him, sell drugs in the local town, and life marched on. Then one day, he asked me to go on a fishing holiday to Mozambique with a few of his ex-army buddies and their wives and girlfriends. I told him I couldn't go; it was not a holiday to take a boisterous toddler on and there was no one to look after you. I was completely estranged from my family and friends." She shuddered. "Quinton was so angry he shoved me to the ground and punched me. He took off in his truck and I didn't see him again for four months." She sniffed. "Then about six months before your third birthday, he returned, contrite and seductive. He told me he wanted to set up a fishing cruise business in Maputo, with me, that it would be a fresh start. I was too weak to fight him and desperate for his affection, so I agreed. He said he was selling his mother's house to use the money for the business but needed more and he'd found a way to get it. He wanted me to offer you to your father, for money."

Kate's heart jolted. "I think I can guess the rest," she said. "Quinton found my father and Ginny and they agreed to adopt me."

Miranda gave a slow nod. "Quinton tracked them down easily. I'd put Geoffrey's name on your birth certificate and Quinton threatened to blackmail him if he didn't pay to adopt you. Geoffrey's career as a senior lecturer in London would be in tatters if Quinton sold the story to the tabloids. They travelled back to South Africa to get you." She gave a wry laugh. "They were so desperate to have a child they would have paid for you without being blackmailed."

"And you handed me over," Kate stated, "just like that."

Miranda gulped. "I had no choice."

Kate was livid. "You *did* have a choice. What I don't understand is how you ended up being on the run, changing your name, if you were meant to be sailing off into the sunset with Quinton."

Miranda's voice was monosyllabic. "It was one last job. To get the money for Mozambique. He told me the raid on the cosmetics factory was to stop their use of animals for testing. We could kill two birds with one stone: take the goods to sell on and then burn the factory. There were no animals there, so it would be safe. I believed him, of course. I still dream about that night; I swear I didn't know there was a security guard on duty."

"And you were arrested?"

"Yes. There was video footage of me lighting the fuse."

"How did you manage to skip bail?"

"One of the group had a good lawyer; he got us all off on bail. But I couldn't see how I would not be found guilty. They had proof, after all. Quinton suggested skipping bail, changing my name and fleeing to Mozambique, and that was that. We settled there and were happy for a time."

"And Sammy, when was he born?"

Miranda's face lit up. "I was nearly forty when he was born. He wasn't planned, but I was over the moon."

Jealousy flickered low in Kate's belly. Miranda was clearly devoted to Sammy, had brought him up, cherished and loved him. It was irrational to envy the young man who was her half-brother. After all, it wasn't his fault Miranda chose Quinton over her. She was about to ask about Sammy when Quinton opened the cabin door and peered down.

"Miranda," he snarled, "quit your talking and come up and help me. I need another pair of hands to get the belt off the alternator."

Miranda froze on the spot and Kate seized her chance.

"Miranda," she whispered, "we need to use the radio and call the coastguard. Now is your chance to pay him back for everything he's done, to make sure he gets what he deserves. We have to act now. Don't you want to see Sammy?"

Miranda was dazed, hesitant, but when Quinton began to climb down the ladder, she sprang into action, stretching a leg onto the bottom rung. "I'm coming and don't worry, she's told me about the investigation and what the police suspect. We can use her to bargain with. Like a hostage." She flashed Kate a brief look before disappearing through the hatch.

Doubts clouded Kate's thoughts. Was Miranda really going to help them escape or had she once more fallen under Quinton's spell? It was hard for Kate to read her. The sad truth of the matter was that Miranda, the woman who'd carried her for nine months and given birth to her, was, in all respects, a complete stranger.

Chapter Fifty

Below deck, Kate tried to digest everything Miranda had told her, her justifications for the decisions she'd made over the past thirty years, giving up Kate, committing a criminal act and going on the run. Miranda was an outcast, a person who lived on the fringes of society. There was something to be said for nurture versus nature. What would Kate's life have been like had she stayed with Miranda all these years?

Her heart ached when she thought about her parents, Ginny in particular. What would they have thought of her looking for her real mother? Would they have been hurt? She felt so hopeless. Ever since the day Patrick had given her the envelope, she'd been chasing rose-tinted dreams of a caring mother who had never forgotten her little girl. Who'd given her up for all the right reasons. Who had loved her enough to do so.

Quinton's raised voice jolted her from her thoughts and she leant forward, trying to stretch across the room, the rope around her feet biting into her ankles. But the rope was fixed tight and she was stuck.

A clattering and banging came from above and Miranda let out a high-pitched squeal. The thump and drag of footsteps continued. A struggle was taking place. Their voices became louder as they came to a stop directly above the hatch.

"Give me the gun," Quinton roared.

Miranda has the gun? Kate's pulse jumped.

Miranda sounded surprisingly calm. "Don't come any closer."

Quinton gave a derisive laugh. "You don't really want to shoot me, Miranda. This is silly. Put the gun down and let's talk."

Kate held her breath as she listened to them from below.

Miranda's voice was shrill. "I *said*, don't come any closer. I mean it – I'll shoot."

"Come on, baby," Quinton taunted. "You know you love me; you wouldn't hurt me. We can be together again, like the old days."

The boat rocked with the roll of a sudden wave, sending Kate onto her side. Above, the sound of scuffling continued and then with a huge bang, the gun went off and Kate's already erratic pulse went through the roof.

Quinton shrieked. "You bitch!"

Fear pulsed through Kate as the hatch opened and Miranda slid down the ladder, the rifle still firmly clutched in her hand. She threw it on the floor and tried to latch the door, her hands shaking. Quinton was screaming and swearing, his fists banging on the door with threats to kill them both.

"Quick, untie me and I'll call for help," Kate shouted.

Miranda fumbled with the rope around Kate's feet, finally releasing them, and was working on removing the ties around her wrists when Quinton's fist crashed through the wood. With one final pull, Kate's hands were free and she raced across the cabin, switching on the two-way radio with shaking hands. Miranda froze, her eyes darting back and forth as Quinton fought his way in.

"Get the gun," Kate shouted. "We have to stop him."

Miranda picked up the gun and pointed it at the door just as it splintered and Quinton's mottled face appeared, blood dripping down his shoulder.

Kate twisted the dials of the radio, frantically searching for the correct channel.

"Mayday, Mayday, this is *The Hunter*. We need help. We've been abducted and held at gunpoint. Over."

The radio crackled and hissed and she repeated her appeal, almost screaming as Quinton slid down the ladder towards them, his anger palpable.

Hot tears coursed down her cheeks. "Mayday, Mayday, please help…"

The radio spluttered into life. "Receiving," a disembodied voice echoed through the speaker. "Hunter, what is your location? Over."

Relief flooded through Kate. She snatched up the receiver, but before she could reply, Quinton grabbed it and ripped the cord out of the machine. The cabin fell silent except for their panting and the squawk of a seagull above.

Quinton's shirt was blood-soaked, his eyes wild. He raised his foot and kicked out at Kate, sending her flying onto the floor. She tried to get up, but pain in her left shoulder coursed through her.

Miranda launched herself onto Quinton's back, her hair wild around her face as she wrestled Quinton to the ground. Kate eyed the rifle lying on the floor. If she could reach it…

But Quinton had clocked what she was doing, and with a roar, he flung Miranda on the floor next to her and snatched up the rifle.

He faced them both, gun poised. "It's time to finish the job once and for all." He sneered at Miranda. "I knew you would miss that shot, Miranda. You don't have the skill."

Miranda found her tongue. "You think so? You're wrong. For years I've put up with your bullying and aggression. I've had enough of your treatment of me. I think it's time you discovered what it's like to be on the receiving end."

She leapt up with an energy Kate wouldn't have expected, grabbed the gun off Quinton and in a split second she raised it and fired, the force of the recoil sending her sliding back onto the cabin floor. Quinton's eyes rolled back in shock and he staggered forward, clutching his chest and moaning. He took a few more steps then slid down the wall, groaning, blood spreading everywhere. He slumped forward onto the floor and lay silent.

Kate watched in a daze, panting rapidly. A dark pool of blood crept out from beneath him and she crawled across the floor and checked for a pulse. He was dead. Vomit rose up into her throat and she retched onto the cabin floor, a string of saliva hanging from her mouth.

Miranda wailed and hauled him over, shaking his floppy, lifeless body.

"Quinton," she whispered. "Oh God, what have I done?"

Chapter Fifty-One

Ryan's pulse was galloping as the police car raced away from the airfield towards the marina in Maputo. He was sweating heavily, a mixture of fear and the intense heat of the small plane they'd flown over in. It had all happened quickly. Once Gavin got mobilised, he'd organised the flight with a friend who owned a Cessna Caravan. Sara had insisted on going, and Gavin and Ryan were unable to persuade her to stay.

"I'll never forgive myself if something happens to her," she'd cried.

Gavin had stayed behind to cover the lodge, with Ryan promising him he'd take care of Sara. Ryan had contacted Allan Prescott before they left. The PI was unwilling to discuss Kate's details with him, citing client confidentiality, but Ryan had been insistent, telling him the police wouldn't take kindly to his unwillingness to cooperate.

"She called me late last night," Allan finally admitted. "She'd found a photo when she was in Miranda's house, of Miranda as a young woman with her brother Jacques. It was exactly the same as the one Kate's uncle gave her. I think it spooked her. I've been trying to find out more about Miranda Cronje, and as you said, there is virtually no information out there. I did, however, get some mug shots scanned through to me first thing this morning, from the police in Pietermaritzburg. Kate's mother, Alison Voester, was charged in 1989 with arson and manslaughter. She escaped bail and has been on the run ever since. The photo of Alison, aged twenty-eight, does look like Miranda, albeit with the obvious time lapse. I hadn't even had a chance to even tell Kate about it." His voice notched higher. "She didn't tell me she was planning to go off and find Miranda. I would have tried to convince her to wait if I'd known."

"So Alison Voester must have changed her name?" Ryan said.

"Yes," confirmed Allan. "She somehow managed to completely disappear and establish herself as Miranda Cronje in Mozambique. She's been there ever since."

Ryan had hung up, asking Allan to call him immediately if Kate made contact with him. "Tell her to stay put and not do anything dangerous," he warned him.

But Ryan suspected she was already with Miranda. Kate was not an excellent investigative journalist for nothing. He looked at Sara, who was staring pensively out of the window of the police car.

"She'll be all right, Sara. She's a tough cookie and she has a sensible head on her." The stories Kate had told him about her investigative work made him think she was level-headed. He hoped he was right.

Sara twisted on her seat to face him. "I wish she'd answer her phone. I've called so many times and left messages and texted, but nothing…"

The police officer's two-way radio spluttered into life

and he snatched it up. Ryan could just about make out the words of the person on the other end. The boat sailed about two hours ago with three people on board. A man and two women.

"The officers at the marina have contacted the coastguard," the officer told him when he finished the call. "They'll send a launch out shortly. We'll know more when we get there."

"How much longer?" Ryan asked as they raced down the pot-holed streets towards the sea.

"Five minutes," the officer replied.

At the marina, there was a flurry of activity, with several police cars and customs officials milling around the jetty. Ryan's contact, Sergeant Perez, was waiting to update them. "According to the security guard, she arrived about three hours ago. She told him she was meeting a friend who was on a boat called *The Hunter*."

"Cronje's boat," Ryan clarified.

"Exactly. About half an hour later, he was by the main office when he heard an altercation by Bay C. By the time he checked over there again, it was quiet. Then he saw *The Hunter* leaving the marina, so he didn't think anything of it. We've heard from coastal rescue that *The Hunter* sent a Mayday about an hour ago but then stopped all communications. We have a rough location for the boat. It's about sixty kilometres up the coast and we're about to launch a police boat. We've managed to get both Quinton and Miranda Cronje's cell-phone numbers and we're tracing their GPS location. Do you have the number of the other person on board?"

Ryan gave Perez Kate's number. He grabbed the police officer by the arm, eyeing Sara, who was out of earshot.

"I'd like to come with you if I may."

Sergeant Perez shook his head. "I don't think that will be possible. Let us handle it."

Ryan leant forward on his seat. "I have to come with you; I insist. I need to make sure Kate is all right. I'm ex British army; I know how it goes and I won't get in the way, but I must be there when you find the boat."

Perez eyed him through the rearview mirror. "Okay, but you don't even move an eyebrow unless I say so."

Ryan nodded. "Understood."

Sara, who'd been on her phone to Gavin, glanced up at him, her brown eyes full of anguish. "What's going on?"

"They've found the boat out at sea," he said. "It sent a distress message about an hour ago. It's emitting a partial signal, but no one is answering. They're trying to locate the boat using their cell-phone locations, but they only have a rough idea of where it is. I am going to go with them." He touched Sara's arm. "We'll find her."

Chapter Fifty-Two

Kate knelt beside Miranda and tried to pull her away from Quinton. She was lying on top of him, his blood seeping into her clothes.

Kate brushed a long strand of Miranda's hair out of the way and tenderly touched her face. "Miranda, it's over. He's dead. We're safe now."

Miranda continued to shake her head, her hands frantically feeling Quinton's chest for signs of life. "No, no, he can't be dead!"

Kate tried again to pull her away. "He's gone, Miranda. Let's go up on deck to see if there is a boat coming."

Nausea rose in Kate's mouth. She had to get out of the cabin into the fresh air. She tried not to panic at the thought of being out at sea in a broken-down boat, with a dead man below deck. She prayed the Mayday call had connected before he ripped the cord out.

Miranda groaned and rolled onto her back next to Quinton, her arms covering her face as she wept. Kate was at a loss; she didn't know what to say to Miranda. How did you comfort someone who'd spent their whole life pretending you never existed? Someone who was so enthralled with one man that they allowed it to ruin their life? Miranda had once been a young woman embarking on a quest to save the things she cared about the most – animals and nature – and she'd somehow ended up on the other side of the equation, at war with herself.

Kate left Miranda and pushed away what was left of the cabin door, her legs like jelly as she stood on the deck. She scanned the horizon, not really knowing which way to look. A long thin line of land stretched out in the distance and she wondered if it was the mainland or an island. She knew that hundreds of islands ran up the coast from Maputo all the way to the border with Tanzania.

She checked her watch. It was three o'clock. She had lost all sense of time. She raised a hand and touched her cheek where Quinton had hit her. It felt puffy, but otherwise the pain had subsided a little. On the back of her head was a large egg-shaped lump where she'd banged it on the metal rail.

She shivered despite the hot sun overhead. A gull shrieked above and she watched it land on the prow. The boat was tilting gently in the waves, its anchor chains down. At least they wouldn't drift too far.

Perhaps with Miranda's help they could try the engine again, but even if they got the motor to work, she didn't think they would have any idea which way to go. She sat down on a bench and put her head in her hands, trying to think what to do.

A loud crackle emanated from below deck and she darted back down into the cabin. The radio was spluttering to life. She could hear the whistling and beeping of the frequencies, and voices fading in and out. But she couldn't speak to them. The communication cord lay abandoned on the floor.

She called out, nonetheless. "Hello! Can anyone hear me? Can you help? Hello?"

The radio hissed as it moved from frequency to frequency and she frantically turned the dials, scanning the instruction poster on the wall, crying out for help as she went. Miranda lay on the floor behind her, her eyes glazed and her body still listless. Kate blew out a puff of frustration. There had to be a way. A thought struck her. Why hadn't she thought of it before? She was such an idiot.

"Miranda—" she knelt on the floor beside her "—where's your cell phone? We could try emergency services."

It was possible. There were islands not far away from them; even one bar of coverage would do it. Enough to make an emergency call anyway.

She shook Miranda again. "Where's your phone?"

Miranda rolled away, drawing her knees up into a foetal position and muttering to herself. Kate cursed and cast around the cabin for any sign of the shoulder bag she'd seen Miranda with. Then she noticed the belt around Quinton's waist, a mobile phone stashed neatly in a pouch. She reached across to get it, averting her eyes from the mass of blood that pooled on his face and chest.

Outside on the deck, she spat out a mouthful of bile and took a few deep breaths. With shaking hands she pressed the buttons on the phone. The screen sprang to life, a photo of him and an attractive blonde woman in the background. Kate recognised her as Amy, the English woman he'd told her about. There were many messages and missed calls from her too. She'd been trying to call Quinton all day. Kate squinted at the last message, sent only forty minutes ago. It must have been ringing silently on his belt the whole time.

But then, maybe that would be a way out. She could call Amy back from his phone and beg her to get help. She tapped again and a password request popped up on the screen. She cursed, scrolling up and down, hoping an emergency icon would appear. Some phones had them. But each time she tried, a password request jumped out at her. Close to tears, she discarded the phone and slumped onto the floor, hanging her head in her hands.

Dizziness hit her in the heat of the late afternoon and as the waves gently rocked the boat her eyes drooped. She was so tired; all she wanted to do was to lie down and sleep for days. She'd been on an emotional rollercoaster, from her parents' deaths to the truth behind her maternity. Her last thoughts as she lay on the deck, the boat creaking around her, were of Ryan's chocolate brown eyes creasing up at the sides as they danced together in the restaurant in Johannesburg. And of his honesty and strength, a compass which she prayed would guide him to her now.

Chapter Fifty-Three

Ryan saw the boat before anyone else. He'd been sitting at the front with binoculars since they'd left the marina over two hours ago. He hadn't budged even though his shoulders and upper back were uncomfortable. He had to find her.

They'd still not heard any more from the boat's communication system and any cell- phone signals they had picked up kept dropping off. The breakthrough had come about half an hour earlier when the radar suddenly picked up Quinton Cronje's phone signal.

"It's coming from directly north-west of here," Perez had told him as the launch picked up speed. "They must have been heading for the island of Bazaruto. I suspect he was planning on stopping there to refuel. There are a few quiet coves and sleepy villages where a fishing charter like his wouldn't be unusual. He's probably even got contacts up and down the coast ready to help him."

Ryan had continued to scan the horizon. There was an officer up in the lookout doing the same thing, but it made Ryan feel useful. He was angry with himself. When he'd heard her talking on the phone the night before, he should have demanded that she tell him everything. Even if it meant she hated him for it. It might have kept her safe. He'd failed her just like he'd failed his team that day in Afghanistan.

He'd closed his eyes for a bit, taking a rest from the relentless blue water and sky, and when he'd opened them again, he'd seen it – a sliver of white on the horizon.

"It's over there," he called out, pointing directly to his right. The police watchman had spotted it too, and the boat slowed down to change course.

Ryan's heart beat furiously as he watched *The Hunter* come closer. There was no sign of anyone on deck and he gripped the side of the boat, anxious to get there and find Kate. He didn't care about the Cronjes or even about the rhino horn. He just wanted to hold Kate in his arms, for her to be safe.

Perez touched his shoulder. "I want you to go into the control room when we draw up alongside. You're a civilian and you can't be involved. I've gone out on a limb to let you on the boat in the first place."

Ryan reluctantly headed to the control room, apprehension prickling down his spine. He watched impatiently as Perez and two of his men donned life jackets and protective gear ready to board *The Hunter*. They drew up alongside the boat and Perez called out their approach through his megaphone.

No one appeared, save for a seagull, which ran along the side of the boat and flew off squawking. Ryan swallowed, perspiration trickling down between his shoulder blades. He wanted to jump the short distance between their boat and *The Hunter* and find Kate. The waiting was killing him.

Perez repeated his request through the megaphone, and

when still no one appeared, he gestured to one of his men to board. The man jumped on, his gun poised, and waved back to Perez, pointing to the back of the boat to inform him of his direction.

Perez followed him on board, moving to the front and towards the cabin below. Ryan waited, his heart in his mouth, his knuckles white as he gripped the table. He was one minute away from ignoring Perez's command not to join him on the boat when the man himself popped back around the side of *The Hunter* and waved to him.

Ryan was by the side of the boat in a second. "What is it?"

"We've found Miss Harper; she's alive. She was at the back of the boat lying on the deck. I think she's got a head injury and is probably dehydrated. She's sitting up now and we'll get her on board in a minute."

Ryan's voice was terse. "And the other two?"

"Quinton Cronje is dead, gunshots to the shoulder and chest."

"And Miranda Cronje?" Ryan wondered if Kate had managed to tell Miranda she was her daughter.

"She's alive, but distressed and in shock. She's covered in blood. I'd say she killed Quinton. She was lying next to him in the cabin."

Ryan placed a foot forward, craning his neck to see over Perez's shoulder to the boat. "Can I come on board?"

Perez frowned. "It's a crime scene. I shouldn't really let you…"

But Ryan ignored him and leapt over the side and onto the other boat. An officer was tending to Kate, giving her water he'd found in a cool box, when Ryan raced up to her.

Her bowed head lifted up as he approached, her face small and pinched. His heart galloped in his chest and he took a deep breath to calm it. He knelt down and touched her softly on the face, noting the bruised and swollen cheek. She was so beautiful and he longed to kiss her.

He took one of her hands and lifted it up to his lips to kiss. "You're safe now," he told her. "I won't let anyone hurt you any more, I promise."

She gazed at him with those beautiful amber eyes. "What took you so long?"

Chapter Fifty-Four

Maputo, Mozambique

Kate leant back on the soft pillows of the hotel room and watched the man beside her sleep. It was late, the red numbers on the clock showing it to be nearly two in the morning. She stroked his hair, still damp from his shower, and ran her hand over his stubbled cheek. He was wearing the white fluffy robe he'd taken from the bathroom, having no clothes with him to change into. In their haste to get to Maputo, neither Sara nor Ryan had thought to bring a change of clothes. Even Kate had only the bare minimum she'd thrown in her large tote bag. Gavin was coming in the morning with supplies for them all.

She couldn't believe it was only eighteen hours or so since she'd stolen away from the lodge on her mission to find Miranda. So much had happened since then. She lay back on the pillow gingerly, her head still hurting from the bump she had taken.

When they arrived back in Maputo, an ambulance had been waiting. The paramedic greeted her warmly, trying hard to convince her to get checked out properly in hospital.

"You've got a massive bump on your head," he'd said. "How long did you say you were knocked out for?"

"I don't exactly know. Maybe an hour? All I remember is being hit hard on my face and I fell onto the bed. I must have hit the back of my head on the metal rail."

Whilst she was being examined inside the ambulance, she watched through the open back doors as Quinton was taken off on a stretcher, his body shrouded in a white sheet. Miranda followed shortly after, staggering on her feet between two police officers, her hands cuffed. Kate had tried to climb off the bed in the ambulance and get to her, but the paramedic and Sara had held her back.

"Let them check you out first, Kate," Sara had said softly. "You can see her later. When the dust has settled."

Kate was worried about Miranda's mental state. She had hardly spoken from the moment Quinton drew his last breath. She was in shock, Kate supposed, and she hoped she was doing all right in the local police lock-up they'd taken her to. There was still so much to unpick in Miranda's life, so much to learn and understand. And now she had a half-brother too. Her heart went out to this unknown young man on the death of his father and his mother's impending prison sentence.

She lay down and faced Ryan. He had been so incredible after she was rescued, attentive and caring. She'd managed to convince the paramedic and Sara that she didn't need to go to a hospital. Ryan had checked them all into a hotel near the beach. He'd booked two rooms, assuming Sara would share with Kate. She needed someone to keep an eye on her every hour or so in case she had concussion.

But Sara had other ideas. She'd cited extreme exhaustion, telling Kate in an excited whisper that despite not trying for a baby at the moment, she'd fallen pregnant. She'd taken Ryan's room key and headed off, refusing to budge. She was not very subtle.

In their room, they'd both showered and tried to eat food from the room-service menu. Ryan kept checking her pupils every half an hour or so, lifting up her eyelids and peering in until Kate had swatted him away. They'd put on the television and watched an old episode of *Friends*, the volume on low. Kate saw his eyelids droop and switched off the television. He'd been asleep for a while now, his brow relaxed in slumber.

She tried to sleep, but the memories of the day filled her mind. Ryan mumbled in his sleep and rolled over, his eyes flitting open. She could drown in those brown irises, and he had the longest eyelashes she'd ever seen. He reached up to brush her hair out of her face and she moved closer, enjoying the feel of his body close to hers. She traced a hand down his chest where the dressing gown gaped open.

"Kate," he warned.

Ignoring him, she dropped her hand lower, loosening the belt and tugging it out of the way. He grabbed her hand gently and tried to pull it away. "No, you have to rest," he said, his lower body betraying him. "You've got concussion."

She gave him a feline smile, placing her lips near his. "Shut up and kiss me, Ryan."

Chapter Fifty-Five

Kate held her hand over her eyes to shade them from the dazzling sun and spotted Ryan further up the beach. He was walking in her direction, his feet bare and trousers rolled up. He was talking on his phone, his face serious.

She flopped down onto the soft white sand and inhaled the sea air, stretching her arms above her and slowly unfurling her spine. Her entire body ached from the exertions of yesterday, but otherwise she felt okay, refreshed even. She had woken up late, the sun streaming through the half-open French door of the hotel room. She was alone, but she could tell by the still damp towel that Ryan had not long woken.

She'd come from having breakfast with Sara on the hotel's large wooden deck facing the seafront. Sara was on good form, bright-eyed and raring to go. She'd asked Kate to tell her about what had happened on the boat and about Miranda.

"I can't believe Miranda Cronje is your real mother," she'd said, stuffing yet another pastry into her mouth. "Talk about a coincidence."

Kate grimaced. "I know. It was quite a shock when I discovered it. That's why I didn't want to tell you until I knew more."

"Did she tell you why she gave you up?"

"More or less," Kate confirmed. "It was Quinton pulling the strings right from the beginning. She met him when I was around two years old and he took it upon himself to track down Geoffrey and Ginny and convince them to adopt me." She pulled a face. "When I say convince, I mean blackmail. He told Dad that he would tell the university about his affair, that he would ruin him if he didn't agree to pay to adopt me."

"God…how awful," Sara muttered.

"I know. I might have felt differently if I'd known my own mother effectively agreed to accept money in exchange for me."

"But from what you told me it sounds like she was coerced," Sara reminded Kate. "She did it to protect you, from Quinton."

Kate's voice trembled. "I've been so angry with Dad for having the affair, for cheating on Ginny. I couldn't get past the lies."

Sara laid a hand on Kate's. "None of this is your fault. Secrets and lies have a way of twisting themselves around people and ruining their lives. Geoffrey and Ginny did the right thing by getting you away; they didn't think about the consequences for Miranda or Alison as she was then. They were desperate for a child—" she touched her stomach gently "—and I for one understand that."

Kate had been amazed at the wisdom of her best friend. "You're right." She wiped a tear away from her cheek. "Miranda's life was controlled by that man from the moment she met him. She started out with such good intentions, wanting to stop testing on animals. Yes, she was a hard-core vivisectionist, but there are worse things you could be. Quinton was all about control and power and money. He never really cared about any of the causes Miranda did. It was all a show."

"Well, he's dead now and he can't hurt anyone any more."

"He's still pulling the strings even in death," Kate said. "Miranda's waking up in a prison cell and will be the only one punished."

Sara's face was serious. "She has been involved with criminal activity for the last few years, Kate, and she escaped bail all those years ago. There has to be some kind of justice."

Sara was right, of course. Miranda had to face the consequences of her actions.

The police had been unable to locate Kate's phone on the boat, so Kate had borrowed Sara's and called the police station to enquire after Miranda, where they informed her that pending a medical assessment she would appear in front of a local magistrate to be charged. She'd called Jacques too, shocking him with the news. He'd offered to come to Maputo, to help where he could and they discussed what to do about Sammy and whether anyone had been in touch with him. Kate had no idea where to locate her half-brother.

"Let me see what I can find out," Jacques had promised before he rang off. "The poor lad needs to know what's going on with his parents."

Kate now watched Ryan approach and marvelled at the way his shoulders filled out his shirt. He had been so supportive yesterday and last night, keeping an eye on her after her head injury. He hadn't asked any questions or even tried to talk about what happened on the boat. Today she would go to the police station to make a statement and she wanted him with her.

He reached her side, sitting next to her on the sand, kissing her lightly on the cheek. "Morning, sleepyhead." He reached up and tenderly touched her cheek, grimacing at the black and yellow bruises across it. "You look like you've done ten rounds in a boxing match."

Kate laughed. "You should see the other guy," she quipped. And then she remembered that Quinton was dead and that Miranda was sitting in a prison cell and her smile faded.

"Hey." Ryan tipped her chin up, his brow wrinkled in worry. "Are you really okay? You're not feeling dizzy or nauseous? I wouldn't have left you sleeping, but I had to make some calls and I didn't want to disturb you. I gave Sara the room key and asked her to keep an eye on you."

"I'm fine," Kate replied, touching his shoulder gently. "A little shaky when I first woke up and the whole of my body aches, but I'll survive."

Ryan pointed at the cell phone in her hand. "You've managed to get yourself a phone. God forbid Kate Harper should ever be without one. It wouldn't be right."

She punched his arm. "This is Sara's phone. I needed to make a few calls this morning. She spoke to Gavin earlier and he's on his way here."

Ryan's voice was tentative. "And Miranda?"

"She's undergoing a medical examination and will possibly appear in court later." She pointed at the phone on his lap. "You've been busy on the phone too.'

"I was getting an update from the police here and in Johannesburg. They found nearly half a million dollars of rhino horn in the hull. As we suspected, they were hidden in the Safe Water boxes. They also found four guns, probably the ones used in recent poaching attacks. The good news is that now we have the rhino horn, we can check its DNA and hopefully link it to the rhino poached on the reserve. It will make it easier to get a conviction."

Kate's blood pounded in her ears. "What will happen to Miranda?"

Ryan stared at her, his eyes hidden behind his sunglasses. "What do you think, Kate? She'll be charged, of course. She's a pivotal member of a poaching syndicate, not to mention she has a record for arson and manslaughter." He ran his fingers through his hair. "You can't seriously expect her to get away with it?"

Kate got to her feet and glared at him. "Do you have any sympathy at all? The poor woman has been through hell all these years, I haven't had the chance to tell you but she…"

Ryan jumped up, his voice raised. "I don't want to hear it, Kate. She's known what she's been doing for a long time now. Whichever way you see it, she's guilty."

Kate's stomach plummeted. "She's my mother, Ryan. Can't you see how torn I am? I have to help her no matter what."

"Biology aside, Kate, Ginny was your mother, not that woman. Miranda gave you up and never once thought about you. And she's spent the last few years being part of a syndicate that killed innocent animals. You say she was badly treated by her husband? I think she used it as an excuse. She was too lazy to earn a proper crust. They all are. Anything for a quick buck, and never mind the outcome."

Kate's eyes narrowed. "I can't believe you're saying this to me, Ryan. How can you be so callous?"

Ryan's face was like stone. "That's easy. You saw the rhino with her face hacked off. You've bottle-fed the calf left behind. All I have to do is remember those images and any sliver of sympathy I might have had for the poacher disappears."

Kate was gobsmacked. "Then I guess we have nothing to say to each other."

She grabbed her bag and turned away, desperate to hide the angry tears in her eyes.

Ryan grabbed her arm. "Wait. What the hell are you talking about?"

She swallowed down her sorrow. "I need to support Miranda, Ryan, no matter what. She's been through a lot and she has nobody. I'm not saying she's not guilty, but there are reasons why she did what she did, and I think we should at least give her a chance to explain, to make her case. And besides, I have Sammy to think of. He's my half-brother, after all."

Ryan shook his head. "You're kidding yourself, Kate. By all means, give her the support you think she needs, but remember one thing – she is guilty and the past has finally caught up with her."

"You're asking me to choose between Miranda and you," she cried, anger bubbling to the surface.

Ryan's voice was hoarse. "I'm not doing that, Kate. I'm telling you how I feel about it all. I have to stand up for what I believe in, otherwise what's the point?"

Kate lifted her chin. "Fair enough, but you can't go through your life without trust. Life is full of risks, and I don't just mean the physical ones. Sometimes you have to take a leap of faith."

Ryan's eyes narrowed. "I'll be sure to remember that."

He walked back up the beach and Kate watched him go, her heart feeling like it might break into a hundred pieces.

Chapter Fifty-Six

Kate was uncomfortable and restless as she sat on the green plastic chair in the waiting room of the police station. It was stifling, the old wooden fan above rotating slowly, its blades sticking each time it moved past the two o'clock mark. The sky, visible through the small window at the end of the airless corridor, was cloudy, the morning sun trying to break through. Nerves pulsed in her stomach as she waited to see Miranda. She was due in court soon and Kate really wanted to speak to her beforehand.

When she'd come to the police station the day before, Miranda had refused to see her. A duty lawyer was in with her at the time. He'd come out of the meeting flustered, his head low as he told Kate that Miranda was determined to plead guilty to all charges including Quinton's death.

"I am pretty certain I can get her off on the charge of the manslaughter of Quinton Cronje," he'd said, wiping beads of perspiration off his face. "It was self-defence, after all, and you were witness to this, I believe?"

Kate told him exactly what happened on the boat. That they'd both been in a dangerous situation with a man who was unstable and a crack shot. Miranda had no choice. She was protecting Kate as much as herself.

According to the lawyer, Miranda would appear in the magistrates' court the following morning and would be charged with possession and attempted smuggling of rhino horn, but on the outstanding South African charges of arson and manslaughter, they would have to wait to find out if she would be extradited. The lawyer confirmed it would be unlikely, the case file long since closed. Apparently, there was no direct proof that Miranda was the one who had lit the fire. The CCTV cameras had melted before any conclusive evidence could be revealed.

Kate had shaken her head, remembering Miranda's words on the boat when she'd told her that Quinton had held the security guard's death over her head as a way of coercing her into working for the syndicate. In the end, Miranda had spent more than half her life in hiding for what turned out to be an empty threat.

She scrolled down her phone to read a new message from Sara, who was checking on her. Sara had stayed until yesterday afternoon, wanting to support her, but Kate had sent her back to the lodge.

"I've totally disrupted your life with all my personal problems," she'd told her. "You need to get back and put your feet up."

Sara's pregnancy was a source of great excitement and trepidation to both Gavin and Sara, and after Sara having two miscarriages, Kate wanted to make sure she took it easy.

After Ryan had left her on the beach yesterday, she'd been shattered, struck down by the impossibility of their situation. She wanted a future with him, but not if he wouldn't even try to understand the predicament she was in. She was using every ounce of strength she had to let him walk away and not give in to him. She had to forgive the past in order to move forward. She had to see this through no matter what.

Her phone buzzed. It was Jacques.

We've landed. Should be with you in an hour. J

Kate's heart lifted at the thought of seeing her uncle again. His kind and gentle demeanour was just the support she needed. And he had Sammy with him. She still couldn't believe she had a half-brother. When she was a child, she'd so longed for a sibling. Being an only child had its advantages – you always had your parents' attention, you didn't have to share your toys or the chocolate biscuits – but there were times when it really bothered her, like on holiday where she would have to play in the sand on the beach by herself or trail around art galleries without someone of a similar age to poke fun at the paintings with.

Sergeant Perez opened the interview room door and beckoned them towards him.

"You can come in," he said. "She's agreed to see you."

Kate entered the interview room, her legs as heavy as her heart, and took a seat at the small trestle table. The interview room was even more oppressive than the waiting area, its windowless space like a sauna. She was so busy looking down at the scuffed table she didn't notice Miranda enter the room until she was sitting in the seat opposite. She met Miranda's lifeless amber eyes and her chest tightened. They stared at each other, the clock above the door filling the silence with its incessant ticks. Miranda's face was grey and Kate noticed that all her rings and bracelets were gone, her knuckle joints chafed and red.

She was the first to speak. "How are you feeling?"

Miranda gave a half-hearted shrug. "I'm okay."

Kate held Miranda's gaze. Only three days before, she'd believed Miranda had ruthlessly given her up for money, a chance to live the good life without the shackles of a child. But she'd been wrong, Miranda had tried so hard to care for her for the first three years of her life and had then given her away to protect her. She had sacrificed her own happiness to give Kate a good life.

As if reading her mind, Miranda leant forward. "I want to tell you the truth, about why I gave you away," she said. "It was never about money, not for me anyway. That was all Quinton's plan. He found your birth certificate and, without telling me, tracked your father down in London. I never knew all the details, but your father reacted quickly, travelling back to South Africa and meeting with Quinton." She gave the ghost of a smile. "Geoffrey didn't even question it; he merely glanced at the birth certificate and agreed to adopt you. It was your mother, Ginny, who suggested a paternity test." She laughed. "I remember Quinton being annoyed about that. In those days, the test results took a long time. But at least it was proof for your parents, especially as they were paying so much money to adopt you."

Kate's voice was croaky. "How much did they pay for me?"

Miranda named a large sum in US dollars. It was a great deal of money for the time. Kate was shocked.

She glared at Miranda. "You've told me how I came to be adopted but not why you agreed to it. Why you gave me away."

Sorrow filtered across Miranda's face and she reached out a papery thin hand to hold Kate's. "I tried so hard to be a good mother. I wanted the best for you. I was finally turning my life around. I loved living in Quinton's mother's house in the outskirts of Johannesburg. I had even got a part-time job in a local gas station and I was making a home for us. Quinton flitted in and out of our lives, full of promises and new ideas. He'd promised to marry me and make you his daughter—" she gulped "—but then one day he arrived with some drugs for me to sell in town, told me I had to earn my keep. I complied, of course, and the whole thing spiralled from there. I did try to escape a few times, well, at least to get away from his control. I even emailed Jacques from an internet café in town, but he refused to help me—" a large tear splashed down her cheek "—but that was no surprise. After all, I'd long rejected my family."

Her eyes brimmed with tears, and sorrow pulsed in Kate's stomach. She searched for the right words, for something to say to comfort this woman who had fought and lost so valiantly. In the end, she chose the only thing she could remember from those three years she'd spent with her.

"It's okay, Mama."

Miranda let the tears fall then. "My Katie, my lovely, sweet little girl."

Sergeant Perez popped his head around the door to tell Kate the lawyer had arrived and needed to talk to Miranda before she appeared before the magistrates. Kate dashed away her tears. She wasn't going to waste the last few minutes crying.

"I am going to come and visit you in the detention centre once I am able to," she promised.

Miranda's jaw clenched. "You don't have to. I don't

want to see you. I don't want to see anyone."

But Kate was vehement. "No, that's ridiculous. I came all this way to find you. You've shut people out for a long time now. Jacques is on his way here now, with Sammy. We are *not* going anywhere. I will keep coming to see you until you give in. I can be persistent when I want to be."

A whisper of a smile had flitted across Miranda's lips. "I think you must have got that from your father. Geoffrey could be very persuasive."

"At least let us try to be a family in whatever shape it takes. I've got no one now." Kate gulped. "Six months ago I thought I was an orphan, but now I have you and Sammy and Jacques and his family."

"Is my Sammy really coming?"

"Yes, Mama," she said. "Sammy is really coming."

Miranda had slumped forward, tears falling down her cheeks. "Giving you up hurt so much, but it was the best thing for you."

"Perhaps," Kate said. "But it wasn't the best thing for you, was it? You loved me; I know that – it's there in my dreams. You used to dance with me under the shade of a tree, twirling me round and round until I got dizzy. I haven't forgotten."

Miranda reached out to touch Kate's hands. "Neither have I, Katie."

The door opened again and the lawyer appeared, a tentative smile on his face as he placed files on the table. "I'm sorry to interrupt," he said. "We need to go through the details for the hearing." He tipped his head towards Kate. "I take it you'll be there."

Kate gave her mother a determined look. "Yes. I will."

Back in the waiting area, Kate filled a plastic cup with

water from the cooler. She took a sip, grimacing at the lukewarm temperature. The door to the police station opened suddenly, bringing in with it a blast of hot air and Jacques and Sammy. Kate jumped to her feet, staring at her half-brother, suddenly shy, still trying to believe she had a blood sibling, a person who shared the same genes. She gazed at him in wonder. He was tall and lean, with a freckled complexion much like hers. His hair was strawberry blonde, with a few red tinges in the long streaks that fell over his forehead. He had Quinton's piercing blue eyes and strong chin.

She took a step forward. "Hello, Sammy. I'm Kate."

Sammy glanced back at Jacques, who smiled widely at them both from beneath his bushy moustache and then stepped towards her just as a ray of sunlight broke through the clouds and streamed into the corridor.

Sammy's voice was croaky as he took her hand. "Hello."

Chapter Fifty-Seven

Kate sat on the sand by the hotel bar and watched the tide roll in and out. The beach was deserted except for two fishermen bringing in the catch. She dug her toes deep into the sand and watched the men pull and jostle with the nets in the tide. She inhaled deeply, the salty air filling her lungs and invigorating her. She'd come to love this place and could see why Miranda had once called it home.

Miranda had told her all about her early years in Maputo when Sammy was little and how they would chase baboons away from their beach braai and dig deep trenches in the sand. In the days before she was transferred to the detention centre, she'd sat with Sammy and Kate, filling them in on her life, her dreams, telling them the truth. Once she opened up, it was astonishing to see her finally come alive, to see the person she really was.

Behind Kate, towards the hills, the sun was slowly setting. The birds, noisy now the heat had gone, were calling to each other amongst the palm trees that fringed the beach. In the distance, the low beat of music vibrated as the bars along the beachfront threw off their daytime slumber and prepared for the evening ahead. Hordes of backpackers and travellers arrived, their skins pink and flushed from a day on the beach or out fishing.

Kate stood and stretched, brushing sand off a new pair of harem trousers. She'd soon run out of clothes, having hastily packed the bare minimum in the mad rush to find Miranda. The street that ran behind the beachfront hotels had many boutiques and shops and Jacques's wife, Anneka, who'd arrived the day before, had accompanied her on the shopping spree, a joyful morning after all the pain of the last few weeks.

She scrambled over the thick sand, climbing the steps to the deck that overlooked the beach. Jacques and Anneka were waiting for her at a table, two glasses of beer topped with white froth sitting in front of them.

She plonked herself beside them, fanning her face with the cardboard menu on the table. "Where's Sammy?"

"He's gone to his room for a shower," Jacques said. "Let me get you a drink and I'll order a beer for Sammy. I think he needs it."

Jacques strolled over to the waitress, and Kate watched the door, waiting for Sammy. Sammy and Jacques had come back from a meeting with the undertaker. Jacques was helping Sammy put together a small funeral service. Quinton was to be cremated and his ashes scattered out to sea. Kate wondered how many people would be at the crematorium the next morning.

She thought back to the day Sammy had arrived in Maputo, the day they first met. He'd been shy to begin with, but they'd slowly begun to speak to each other. With sixteen years between them and two completely different upbringings, it was tricky at first, but gradually she'd drawn him out. He was obviously grieving for his father. No matter what anyone thought of Quinton, he was

Sammy's dad. She longed to hug him and tell him she understood. She'd lost her parents recently, after all.

She remembered the sad look in his eyes the first time he came back from visiting his mother. He'd come out of the room, his eyes wet with tears. Jacques had embraced him in a big bear hug, slapping his back and soothing him.

"How was it?" she'd asked.

Sammy's eyes had met hers. He'd been so defeated. "All right, I guess. She didn't say much. Just stuff, about how she felt. I didn't know what to say to her." He flicked strands of hair off his forehead. "She looks terrible. I haven't seen her for a couple of years. I had no idea."

He'd gone on to tell Kate and Jacques how Quinton had kept him and Miranda apart. He'd moved Sammy to a boarding school in Johannesburg when he was thirteen and whilst Sammy had gone home to Miranda for holidays, Quinton had filled his head with stories about Miranda's previous life, her criminal activities and her madness.

He'd bought Sammy all the latest gadgets and let him have parties with his school friends in his huge Johannesburg house. Sammy had soon begun to believe the tales Quinton fed him, had even questioned Miranda about them.

"I wish I'd given her a chance to explain," he'd said. "I was so horrible to her."

"Don't beat yourself up," Kate had said. "She's been through a terrible ordeal. She'll need time to recover. She loves you so much; she told me on the boat how much you mean to her. I know you are hurting about your father, but she needs you right now."

Jacques returned with their drinks and took a long sip of beer, the froth coating his moustache. Anneka scolded him and Kate laughed. She enjoyed their company. In a way, it was a bit like being with Geoffrey and Ginny. Jacques tapped his fingers on the table and jiggled his legs.

"Sit still, for goodness' sake," Anneka said.

Kate grinned. "He's like Sammy. When we were waiting to see Miranda yesterday he was fidgeting in exactly the same way."

Jacques chortled. "When I saw him in Johannesburg, I couldn't believe how much he's like my two boys —" he looked at Kate "—and you, you're the spitting image of Alison, especially your eyes. Hers are pretty unique. No one else in the family had them. We've all got brown eyes."

Kate had a sudden vision of Ryan, his brown eyes crinkling up when he smiled, or darkening with passion when they'd made love. She tried not to think of Ryan, had been pushing him to the back of her mind since they'd argued on the beach. He hadn't contacted her since that day, making his feelings clear.

She took a mouthful of wine and watched Sammy bound down the steps to join them. His hair was still damp, curling around the collar of his shirt, and he grabbed up the glass of beer and drank quickly, almost draining the whole thing before placing the glass down and belching loudly.

Everyone laughed and the evening moved on, to the clink of glasses and the low murmur of conversation. The sky darkened, with only the bright stars above and the soft beams of light from a half-moon. Kate took a deep breath and gazed up to the sky, imagining Ginny and Geoffrey dancing amongst the stars, watching over her. Tears filled her eyes, the grief still raw. She missed them so much, had been so angry with them for lying to her, for concealing the truth. But she had to let go, accept what had happened in the past. It was the future that mattered now.

She had been busy making plans. Miranda was now in a detention centre awaiting sentencing. The police had dropped the charge of manslaughter for Quinton's death. It would be a few weeks before anyone would be allowed to visit her, so Kate had decided it was time to get back to the article. She'd been in touch regularly with Sara and was due to fly back to South Africa the next day. Sara had questioned her about what happened with Ryan, but Kate had merely told her it hadn't worked out between them.

"Will you be okay when you see him?" Sara had asked when they'd spoken on the phone the day before.

"I'm not coming back to the lodge yet," Kate had replied. "I have what I need for the article, but I do want to write a follow-up piece about the rhino calf. I'm not trying to avoid Ryan, honestly," she'd stressed. "I wanted to do some voluntary work anyway, and so I called Marta the other day and it's all set up. I will help them out for a few weeks and continue to write a series of articles about wildlife conservation at the same time."

Sara had been a little frosty after that conversation, but when Kate had promised to meet Sara in Johannesburg for a weekend away, she had softened a little.

Kate had emailed Greg and asked for an extension, promising a longer and more detailed report, and luckily he'd granted it. She was a free agent for a few months, giving her a chance to work, visit Miranda and get to know her South African family.

Later that evening, as she lay in her hotel bedroom listening to the waves roll onto the sand, she'd been unable to get Ryan out of her head. She longed for him, for his strong, quiet presence. Despite everything, he'd got under her skin, just like the beautiful African bush he called home.

Chapter Fifty-Eight

Ryan glared at the full moon and switched off the engine. He'd been on duty all day and was now covering Gavin's night shift. But he didn't mind. Gavin had gone to Johannesburg with Sara for the first baby scan. He was thrilled for them both, keeping all his fingers and toes crossed that this baby would arrive as planned in six months' time.

And it stopped him from thinking about Kate, about how he'd let her walk away and had lost what was probably the best thing to ever happen to him. He'd been a fool. What was it Sara said when she came back to the Kruger after the events in Maputo? He was "an obstinate, stupid ass", or words to that effect.

It had been two months since he'd met Kate, and two full moons had passed. After Maputo, he'd come back to the game reserve determined to put it all behind him, to forget about her. But she was everywhere around him – in the bar at the lodge, by the deck at sunset, in the brilliant glow of stars above. When he drove the jeep out on the savannah he felt her presence, the wind whipping her unruly curls up in the air, her pink lips drawn into a wide smile as she watched the animals around her.

Kate was now at the rhino orphanage; she'd gone there six weeks ago. Sara had wasted no time in telling him all about it.

"She's actually sleeping in the night boma with Themba." Sara had laughed. "I would love to see that. Kate Harper was never one for roughing it when we were at school, but I suppose she's changed over the years."

Sara had carried on talking, but Ryan hadn't really listened. He'd been too busy imagining Kate lying on a blanket of hay with a rhino calf, straw sticking in her hair.

Ryan knew that Miranda had pleaded guilty to various charges and was awaiting sentencing. Ed had told him that Quinton's partner, Amy Burton, had been arrested at Johannesburg airport. She'd been trying to flee the country to join Quinton in Dar Es Salaam, unaware that he had been killed. For all his bravado and swagger, Quinton Cronje was only the middleman of the syndicate, merely a fixer, an intermediary who used his connections to get to the animals.

Amy's father, Hugh Burton, the H.B. in Quinton's diary, was the kingpin of a syndicate that stretched from Europe to Africa to Asia. It was small compared with some of the syndicates, but Ryan was glad they'd managed to catch them. A few less poachers in the world was better than nothing. But now that it was all over, instead of feeling the elation he should, there was only a void, an empty space in his life where Kate belonged.

He finished his patrol, parking the jeep up as the dawn began to appear dusty pink to the east. He sat in the vehicle listening to the engine tick over as it cooled down. He watched Johannes, one of the guides, help three elderly German tourists into a jeep and bump their way out of the compound, their faces lit with excitement as they entered the bush. It made him think of Kate the day they'd seen the pride of lions, of the sheer joy in her beautiful face.

As promised, she'd sent him the article copy to approve. It was extremely well written, a truthful portrayal of the world of wildlife protection. She had shone a light on his world, the life he cared so much about and the work they all did to protect animals. She had intuitively known, right from the outset, that he wanted to be the protector, the one who slayed dragons to protect the innocent. But she'd also known the reality, that sometimes even he couldn't protect things from causing hurt.

A sharp pang of longing hit him, visceral and real, and he rubbed his chest. He had to put things right with Kate, to see if there was a chance for them. The thought she might reject him again scared him, but he needed to take the plunge, to put all those self-destructive, negative thoughts behind him.

The chain of events that killed Jamie and Matt, and eventually Jim, was not caused by a bad decision on his part. At the time, it had been easier for him to believe he was responsible for their deaths. The pain of his guilt helped hide the true pain of what he'd witnessed. No one, a civilian or a soldier, should ever have to witness the devastating horror of a bomb exploding in front of them.

When the rhino had been poached under the full moon two months before, the gore and horror had come back and his natural response had once again been to blame himself, to believe he had failed. But he hadn't really;

he'd done his best. Life was, after all, far from perfect. He climbed out of the jeep and headed to his room, eager to shower and change and get himself right back into the jeep. He was going to find Kate and take a leap of faith.

Chapter Fifty-Nine

Kate was taking a long drink of cold water from her water bottle when Marta strode across the outside boma towards her. It was midday and she and Themba had taken refuge in the shade of a large marula tree.

She held her hand over her eyes to blot out the bright sun. "Hi, what's up?"

Marta didn't usually venture out in the midday heat, choosing to stay in the cool of her air-conditioned office. Such as it was. Since arriving at the orphanage, Kate had come to realise how basic their facilities were. But she was working on that and, using media contacts, had begun to set up a series of fund-raising campaigns back in England.

"You have a visitor." Marta's voice brought her out of her daydream.

"I do?" She wondered if it was Sara, but then remembered she was in Johannesburg having a scan. She'd promised to send a digital copy of the ultrasound image later.

"Who is it?"

Marta winked. "Better you come and see for yourself."

Kate followed her out of the boma and through one of the large sheds towards the main house. Her T-shirt was damp with sweat and her knees dusty from kneeling beside Themba, and she wished she'd had time to freshen up. She was running her fingers through her hair, pulling out leaves and pieces of straw when she came face to face with Ryan.

He was waiting on the veranda, leaning against the railing. When he saw her, he straightened, his eyes seeking hers. Her pulse skipped madly. She'd longed for this so much over the last few weeks, imagining the moment, wishing it to come true. And now he was really here, staring at her with those warm chocolate eyes.

She smiled at Marta, who scurried past them, taking Nero the dog with her as she went inside. Kate gestured across the compound to a small hut set up high, a tiny stoop out the front. They walked silently across the soft sand until they reached a set of wooden steps. Kate held onto the wooden balustrade and drank in Ryan. His face was unshaven as usual and there were new specks of grey in his dark brown hair. He needed a haircut, she mused; strands curled over the collar of his shirt.

"Hello," she finally said. "I've been hoping you'd come. What took you so long?"

A dimple appeared in his face and he gently kicked the dusty ground. "I've been busy."

"So I hear."

He raised an eyebrow. "Let me guess. Sara has been talking about me."

"A little," she admitted. "She told me you'd been punishing yourself with extra shifts and that you were like a bear with a sore head most of the time."

He looked sheepish. "I may have gone a little bit crazy." He gave a grin. "On the plus side, I have earned brownie points with the team. They owe me lots of extra hours now."

They carried on staring at each other, the heat pressing down on them. Ryan took a step towards her, his eyes earnest. "I wanted to thank you for the article. It was…" he searched for a word "…truthful and accurate."

Kate went to speak. "Ryan, I…"

But he held up his hand for her to stop. "I am so sorry for the things I said to you on the beach. I had no right to judge you or your decisions about your mother. It must have been a huge shock for you to discover the truth, and the horrible coincidence of who she turned out to be." He shook his head. "I couldn't get past the criminal parts, the bad things that she'd done, and I didn't give you a chance to explain." He ran his fingers through his hair. "I have been a complete fool. An obstinate ass, as Sara called me. I can't expect you to choose between your mother and me. I know you care what happens to her and that you understand what she's done. Blood is blood and I should have been more supportive."

Kate's heart soared. She had longed for this moment since the day he walked away from her on the beach.

She touched his arm. "We've both been obstinate. I keep thinking about you and I don't want things to be over between us. I know you had a terrible experience in Afghanistan and when you met Gwen, you trusted her to help you, but she took advantage of you and let you down. I would never do that to you."

Ryan reached out and pulled her into his arms, staring down with his soulful brown eyes. "I know you wouldn't." He kissed her softly on the lips then, and she melted against him, feeling the solid beat of her heart.

When they came up for air, Kate lifted her chin. "For the record, you were right."

He lifted an eyebrow. "About what?"

"Ginny is my real mother, or was. She loved me from the moment I arrived, she cared for me, tucked me in every night and brought me up." Tears glistened in her eyes. "Miranda may have given birth to me, but Ginny was the one who helped me bloom."

Ryan wiped a tear off her cheek. "How is Miranda?"

Kate gave a sad smile. "Still not wanting to see me, or Sammy, or anyone, but we'll keep trying."

Ryan kissed her forehead. "I love you, Kate," he said, his eyes crinkling at the corners.

"I love you too," she said softly.

They kissed some more, the afternoon sun warm on their heads.

"So what now?" Ryan asked, gently lifting her chin with his hand.

She placed a hand over his chest to feel his heart. "I thought I might hang around with you for a bit. Get to know this beautiful country you call home."

His chocolate eyes held hers. "I'd like that very much."

She stretched up on her tiptoes and kissed him full on the mouth, pressing her chest against his. He tightened his arms around her, deepening the kiss, his desire obvious. But she pushed him away, laughing.

"Not yet, my love," she taunted as she headed back across the compound. "There's a hungry three-month-old rhino orphan to feed."

THE END

Acknowledgements

To my husband, Andrew, for his patient and constant support. It's never an easy road living with a writer.

To my daughter Chloe for her thorough reading and editing in the early days of this story.

To my sons Alex and Harry for always asking me how my writing is going.

And to my two four-legged muses: Archie, who is now in doggy heaven but sat by my feet during the first draft and to Benji, the miniature poodle who now keeps me company.

To my writing friends, Fiona, Sue and Zofia. Our lunches and conference outings are always such fun in the lonely world of being a writer. And thank you for all the WhatsApp editing and suggestions.

To children's author and close friend, Kate Peridot, thank you being such a great sounding board.

To my close friends who have 'lived' through this story with me, endlessly giving me encouragement. You may know the story back to front but I still expect you to buy a copy!

To Susan Buchanan, for your thorough editing and encouragement. Thank you for championing my story.

To the Romantic Novelists' Association and their incredible New Writers' Scheme. And to my New Writers' Scheme reader who gave me such encouragement and confidence.

To the wonderful team at Helping Rhinos and all the incredible conservationists who work in the field in South Africa. The work that they do to protect and help rhinos and other wildlife is truly inspirational. If you would like to know more about rhino conservation or make a donation, please do take a look at www.helpingrhinos.org

I read many books and articles about rhino conservation and poaching for my book, including, 'Poached: Inside the Dark World of Wildlife Trafficking' by Rachel Love Nuwer;

"Saving the Last Rhinos: The Life of a Frontline Conservationist" by Grant Fowlds and Graham Spence and "The Wildlife of Southern Africa" Ed. Vincent Carruthers. I also found a plethora of articles and videos from conservationists, national parks, wildlife protection agencies and charities, all of which were incredibly informative and useful.

And to my readers. I do hope you enjoy this story. It's very close to my heart and I am so glad to finally see it out there in the world.

About The Author

Vanessa previously worked in healthcare management. She studied English Literature at the University of Queensland and completed a Write Better course at the Faber Academy in London. She has been writing a regular column for a local newspaper for over seventeen years.

Vanessa is passionate about conservation and is a proud supporter of UK charity, Helping Rhinos, contributing wherever she can to raise awareness of the threat to this iconic animal.

As a storyteller from an early age she enjoys writing character-driven women's fiction with love at the very heart of the story.

Vanessa lives in Berkshire with her husband and miniature poodle Benji. 'Secrets at Sunset' is her debut novel.

Connect with Vanessa on social media.
Instagram: @vanessawoolleywriter
Threads: vanessawoolleywriter
Facebook: Vanessa Woolley Writer
X: @VanWooll
Blue Sky: @vanwooll.bsky.social

Or you can find out more from her website:
https://vanessawoolley.wordpress.com

Printed in Dunstable, United Kingdom